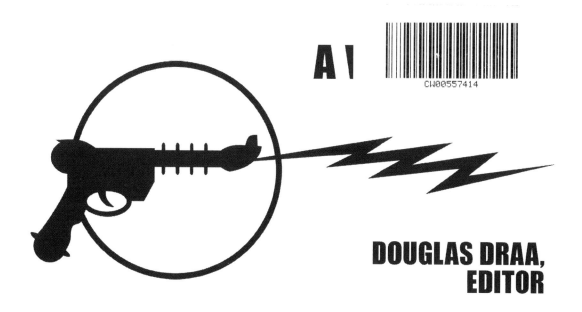

A \

DOUGLAS DRAA, EDITOR

CW00557414

Startling Stories has returned after an inconsequential hiatus of "just" 65 years.

I'm still trying to digest the concept.

That I have the privilege of being the magazine's editor fills me with equal measures of excitement, pride, and terror. I mean, *Startling* wasn't (dare I say "isn't"?) just any old pulp magazine. It managed to rise above its humble pulp origins to become one of the premier science fiction magazines of the early 1950s, publishing such legendary authors as Leigh Brackett, Ray Bradbury, Jack Vance, Arthur C. Clarke, C.L. Moore, and Henry Kuttner.

As always, I do hope that you, the reader, enjoy the selection of stories presented within these pages. You will run across many familiar names. We have new stories by Adrian Cole and Cynthia Ward, among others. I tried to choose as diverse a palette of stories as possible that still share the common thread of being (IMO) highly entertaining!

We also have a rare reprint from Mr. Robert Silverberg. He had always wanted to appear within the pages of *Startling* back during its heyday. Sadly he submitted the story reprinted here just too late and it appeared elsewhere. He was so kind as to offer it to us for the relaunch issue. His "Sunrise on Mercury," even after 65 years, remains a wonderful read. And as they say, "better late than never."

On a sad note, We have Franklyn Searight's *first and final* contribution to *Startling Stories*. I had so hoped that Frank would be as large a part of *Startling* as he was of *Weirdbook*. Sadly he passed away on the 8th of December at the age of 85. Frank was a great storyteller and an even greater man. We'll miss you, Frank.

—Doug Draa
January, 2021

STARTLING STORIES™

Volume 34, Number 1 — 2021 Issue

Doug Draa, Editor — *John Betancourt, Executive Editor & Publisher*

FEATURES

24 THRILLING TALES

POETRY

Startling Stories™ is published annually by Wildside Press LLC, 7945 MacArthur Blvd., Suite 215, Cabin John, MD 20818. Copyright © 2021 by Wildside Press LLC on behalf of the authors. All rights reserved. Visit us online: wildsidepress.com | bcmystery.com.

CRADLE OF THE DEEP
by Mike Chinn

Captain David Bannon slipped off his cap and hung it carelessly on the nearest length of pipework. He scrubbed at his slicked-back, wavy red hair. "Up periscope." Leaning on the 'scope's handles he performed a quick three-sixty degree scan of the outside. The sea was calm and clear. "Steering: what's our position?"

"Currently three nautical miles out of Norfolk, heading due east, skipper,"

"Very well. Down 'scope." Bannon winked at his young second-in-command, Commander Brad Munrow, who was standing close by, before casting an eye over the handful of picked men manning the control room. They all looked nervously eager. "Gentlemen, on this March 23rd 1936 the US Navy is about to make history. Welcome to the shakedown cruise of the *USS SC-1*: the world's biggest and ugliest sardine can. I trust you all appreciate what an honour and a privilege it is for you to be here."

"Swell," said one of the steersmen: a fresh-faced blond sailor who didn't look old enough for the job. "But I'd rather be living in Philadelphia." There was a soft, appreciative round of laughter.

"Okay, stow it, Slade" commented Munrow, though he was smiling himself. Bannon knew the feeling: first trip around the bay in a brand new boat with barely dry paintwork. Plenty of room for a screw-up.

Bannon checked his wristwatch. "Secure for dive."

"Secure for dive, aye sir."

"Sound diving stations."

"Diving stations, aye sir." A klaxon blared twice.

Munrow picked up a clipboard and stopwatch. "Ready to dive, skipper."

"Very well. Let's see what this baby can do."

"Aye, sir. Diving control: dive, dive, dive!"

Bannon felt the slight shift under his feet as the sub's bows dipped. "Level off at periscope depth."

"Periscope depth, aye sir."

Bannon heard the faint metallic ring of waves closing around the boat's hull. His experienced ears also caught the distant grumble of plates accustoming themselves to the weight of water.

"Periscope depth, skipper."

"Very well. Up 'scope." Bannon performed another three-sixty: the ocean remained clear of observers. He pulled a cigar from a shirt pocket and jammed it between his teeth. "Down 'scope. Steady as she goes. Take her down to two hundred feet."

"Two hundred feet, steady as she goes, aye sir."

The distant groans grew louder as the pressure on the boat's outer hull increased. Bannon always found the sound relaxing: like the creak of rigging on the schooners he'd done his early training on. He could also pick out the hum of the twin electric engines: a distant vibration, travelling along the hull.

He frowned. Was that vibration just a little too loud? Engines were unique: no two sounded exactly alike, so maybe he was just jittery. Even so, he murmured to Munrow.

"Make a note, Brad: possible engine imbalance." Something for the grease monkeys back at Norfolk to look into: a little fine tuning, no doubt. The Commander nodded, checked his stopwatch and scribbled on the clipboard.

"Two hundred feet, skipper," announced

diving.

"Very well. All stations, report."

Each station sounded off: diving, steering, ballast control. No one reported any problems. The boat was behaving just fine. Bannon called up the engine room: everything was running sweetly.

He glanced Munrow's way. "What do you say we take her down to test depth?"

The Commander returned an easy grin. "Guess that's what we're out here for."

Bannon slapped his arm. "Make it three hundred fifty feet!"

"Three hundred and fifty feet, aye sir."

The boat descended. Bannon watched the depth gauge, its needle slowly counting off the feet of water above them. The hull muttered a couple more times in token protest. The crew were silent: wrapped in their own tasks.

"Three hundred and fifty feet, skipper."

"Very well. Level off. Anyone have any bad news?"

Each station snapped back a verbal confirmation: no problems.

"Very well," said Bannon. "Steady as she goes."

"Steady as she goes, aye sir."

"And diving: take us down another hundred feet."

"Four hundred and fifty?" murmured Munrow. "You sure, skipper? That's pretty close to design depth."

"The boys back home assured me the boat should be good to six hundred."

"Should?" Munrow's face was wry. "With due respect to the guys in white coats, skipper, they're not the one's risking wet feet."

Bannon chuckled. "You worry too much, Brad. Diving?"

"Four hundred fifty feet—aye sir."

There was a period of tense silence. Eyes surreptitiously glanced at the depth gauge. Eventually the sub reached the requested depth. No leaks, no terminal groans. No one

had any grief to report.

Bannon glanced at Munrow; the younger man's eyes twinkled with relief. "Make a note, Mr Munrow: test depth safely passed by one hundred feet. That ought to keep the brass happy. Take us back to three fifty."

Munrow scribbled on the clipboard. "As you say—"

There was a loud, dragging sound from outside: like something big was rubbing itself against the hull. Bannon felt the boat yaw.

Munrow steadied himself. "What in hell...?"

"Up 'scope!" Bannon grabbed the periscope handles. There was another dragging noise. Bannon clearly heard it moving from bow to stern. This time the sub shuddered. The Captain, face pressed against the eyepiece, scanned the ocean through the periscope.

"Anything?" he heard Munrow asking.

Outside was a deep, uniform blue. Bannon glimpsed the turret gun forward of the conning tower; the deck abaft. "Not that I..." His voice tailed off, mouth suddenly dry. "Son of a—!"

The sub lurched, going down by the stern. Bannon clung onto the 'scope for support.

"We're fouled!" Munrow called.

"Down 'scope! Blow all tanks!" Bannon glanced at his second-in-command, mind still reeling. "So much for a cosy trip around the bay!"

"Skipper!" called diving. "We're not rising. The boat's held fast."

"What in hell's out there?" Munrow muttered.

Bannon ignored him, not ready to answer. But being so close to design depth suddenly didn't seem such a swell idea. He rang up the engine room. "Chief. Open her up. Give her everything you've got!"

Aye, skipper.

The sounds of the engines thrummed round the hull, increasing in pitch. Several thuds echoed through the interior. The sub's bow rose, but Bannon didn't need diving control's report to know the boat wasn't moving.

"Emergency blow!" he ordered. "Everyone hold on tight!"

The boat groaned. Bannon heard the roar as every ballast tank was blown empty. The floor reared. For a while it didn't look like it had made any difference: the boat was still held fast. Then, with a leap, the *SC-1* came free. The pressure gauge dropped with alarming speed.

"Adjust your trim!" yelled Bannon. "We don't want to fly out the water!"

The sub's angle flattened until it was rising almost level. The Captain didn't need gauges to know when the sub broke the surface: for a moment he felt weightless as the boat broached like a playful whale, before falling back into the sea.

"Everyone okay?" he called. There was chorus of assent. "Up 'scope!"

Bannon stared hard. Even blurred by seawater draining across the lens, the stern was clearly fouled. By something. Something that had come up with the boat. Something still moving.

He stepped back. "Take a look, Brad. Tell me I'm not going crazy."

Munrow peered through the periscope. He stiffened, turning to stare at his skipper. "Better make that two of us," he murmured.

Leigh Oswin let the New York *Times* she was reading droop. Over it, she watched Damian Paladin lounging across a sofa, bare feet hanging off its padded arm. He was half-dressed, black hair sticking up in a Stan Laurel shock, frowning at a copy of *Colliers* magazine.

"You read about that Lane DiRoca bird?" she asked, brushing at a stray lock of her blonde hair and searching for her cigarettes.

He glanced up. "Huh?"

"He's making quite a splash on the West Coast." She lit up. "Least, his alias is." She quoted from the last few inches of column newsprint.

"Santa Barbara. Thursday. The mysterious figure known as the Black Tarot is believed to have struck again. Yesterday, local businessman and assistant to the DA's Office, Feldman Nordstrop, was handed over to the authorities along with a dossier itemising his criminal activities. Long suspected of having gangland connections, Nordstrop has evaded arrest up until now, but the damning evidence— presented, according to a precinct desk sergeant, by a masked figure in a long black cape, who vanished with the wave of a playing card—is conclusive enough for an easy conviction."

She dropped the paper again. "Remember when you used to get write-ups like that?"

Damy half-shook his head. "Small time crooks? Is that what he's wasting his time on? He should try facing down four tons of pissed *krovotecheniye zuba* first thing in the morning. Before coffee."

"Yeah, yeah. You're a real *bogatyr*." She allowed the *Times* to slide to the carpet. "We need to get you back in Joe Public's eye again, Damy. Private jobs for émigré Russians doesn't make the papers. Takings at the *Palace* have dived since Christmas: you're becoming yesterday's news."

"Cleaning the DA's Office of wise guys won't make me any friends." He returned his attention to his magazine. "Besides, there'd be nobody left."

"Cynic." She reclined deeply into her chair, blowing smoke rings toward the ceiling. "I just need an angle—"

A knock on the apartment door interrupted her. Damy covered his face with the magazine.

"I'll get it, shall I?" Leigh swept to her feet, a moment later swinging wide the door. Jimmy, the Teton Building's youngest concierge, was on the other side, already blushing.

"Why, good morning!" Leigh angled her-

self against the doorframe with all the allure she could muster.

Jimmy's eyes bugged. He cleared his throat twice. "Miss Oswin. You have a visitor. Well, Mr Paladin does."

Leigh took a pull on her cigarette. "Really?"

A grizzled, red-haired hunk in U.S. Navy khaki stepped into view, tucking his cap under an arm.

"Captain David Bannon, ma'am. Is Mr Paladin in?"

Leigh allowed her eyes to linger on the Navy man for a couple more seconds. She's let the *ma'am* go this time. "Damy!" She raised her voice a little. "Get your pants on, hero. You're being pressganged."

Dressed more properly and sipping lousy coffee which Jimmy had rustled up from someplace, Paladin listened as Captain Bannon rambled on about everything except the reason he was there. Leigh appeared to be hanging on his every pointless word, though; maybe it was the uniform. He was a big guy, and it fit in all the right places.

Eventually losing patience, Paladin put down his barely-touched coffee and interrupted the Navy man's ramble. "Let's can the small talk. You're not here to debate the weather."

"Don't be rude, Damy," commented Leigh.

Bannon shook his head. "No—he's right, Miss Oswin. I should get to the point." The Captain fidgeted with his cap, clearly ill at ease. He cleared his throat. "I believe Admiral Standley considers you a discreet man."

"That's big of him."

Bannon cleared his throat again. "This is all in the strictest confidence." He glanced Leigh's way. "That is clearly understood?"

"I'm deaf, dumb and blind, admiral," grinned Leigh. "You can talk."

Bannon nodded. "Very well. It's not a widely known fact, but the Navy recently launched a new submarine—the *USS SC-1*."

Leigh reached into her purse and produced a pack of cigarettes. "Secret submarine. Gotcha." She offered the Captain a smoke.

He accepted, lighting it and her own. "It's the biggest sub in the world: four hundred feet. Larger than the French *Surcouf*."

Paladin shrugged. "Means nothing to me."

"Of course." Bannon took a deep drag on his cigarette. "Submarines are the future of naval warfare, Paladin; the Great War showed us that. Both the British and French are investing in huge boats—submarine cruisers—armed with large deck guns alongside conventional torpedoes, and on board airplane hangars."

"And the U.S. Navy wants bigger toys."

"By more than twenty feet. The *SC-1* has no hangar, but it is armed with an eight inch, twin-barrelled turret gun. It can also dive in excess of three hundred feet, travel at around twenty five knots on the surface, and just under twenty, submerged." "Is that good?" Leigh enquired.

"It's faster and deeper than any boat in operation."

Paladin scratched his cheek. "Okay, I doubt you're here just to brag about the Navy's newest underwater doodad. Level with me."

Bannon's cap was spinning faster than a phonograph record. "The sub recently performed its first shakedown run. It descended past its test depth; it didn't come back alone."

"There, that wasn't so hard." Paladin relaxed in his chair. "So what did it drag up? The ghost of Moby Dick?"

"It—" Bannon sighed in something like frustration. "I don't know what it is!"

Leigh chuckled. "Your boys caught a mermaid? Nifty!"

Paladin was thoughtful. "Usually the other way round, princess. You said 'is', Captain; that mean it's still alive?"

Bannon looked like he was about to admit to something really dirty. "Yes. Back in Norfolk they hauled it off the sub and dumped it in a cistern."

Paladin and Leigh exchanged glances. "And you want me to go take a look at it," he said.

"Some people thought it might be a good idea."

"Like the Chief of Naval Operations, maybe?"

The Captain gave a reluctant nod, half smiling. "And my second-in-command is a quite the follower of your exploits. So he—"

"Hear that, princess? I have a follower." Paladin grinned at her pained expression. "You wanted an angle: we got a mermaid to look at!"

Leigh mashed out her cigarette. "Swell. I'll go get changed."

Outside it was grey and drizzling. There was a pennant-sporting limo waiting out on Central Park West. Decked out in their signature flying jackets and gun belts, Leigh and Paladin slid into the wide rear seat as Bannon sat himself next to a female Yeoman driver. She guided the limo into traffic once everyone was settled.

They drove to a Naval Reserve base out on Long Island. A few planes stood on its runway, one of them a yellow and silver Lockheed Orion passenger plane in USN markings. The driver pulled up right alongside it. Bannon opened the limo's passenger door, gesturing for Leigh and Paladin to climb aboard. Obviously they weren't going to get a grand tour of the base.

Inside the plane was pretty ritzy: seats for six passengers, in pale, padded leather. The walls matched. Paladin dropped into a seat right at the front—the one nearest the door had a valise on it—stroking the thick armrest.

"You do well for yourself, Captain."

Bannon shrugged. "You're getting the works, Paladin. Normally only Admirals and above get this kind of ride."

Leigh took the seat across the narrow aisle from Paladin. "I could get used to it." She stretched out her booted legs and sighed. "Our tax dollars at work."

A moment later, the Orion's engine roared to life. The pilot wasn't wasting any time. Before it even started taxiing, Bannon hooked up the valise and moved to the back of the small cabin.

The airplane's engine grew louder. It accelerated, bouncing across the airstrip, quickly lifting into the air. Paladin looked out his window: the Reserve Base was already below and behind them. The plane banked, changing course. They were heading slightly west of due south: straight for Norfolk, Paladin figured. Low cloud swirled around the climbing Orion, and the land vanished. A minute later they emerged into sunlight. The sky was a pale, steel blue; clots of white cloud reared all around like vast banks of raw cotton.

It was a short flight. In what felt like no time the plane was on the ground, taxiing towards a group of low buildings. Beyond reared tall shipyard derricks. It wasn't raining, but the sky was still leaden and threatening.

They followed Bannon across a damp landing strip towards a Navy limo that was the twin of the one they'd left in New York. There was a twin female Yeoman at the wheel, too. If it wasn't for the changed horizon, Paladin could have believed they'd just circled back to Long Island.

They were driven straight to the Naval shipyards. Paladin received an impression of acres of docks and wharves, derricks and steam cranes running on rail tracks, endless numbers of single floor buildings, but not many ships. There were a handful of small vessels—a couple in dry dock—that were either being repaired or refitted. Even then, there wasn't much activity.

"Where are all the battleships?" he wondered out loud.

"Where they belong," was Bannon's only comment.

Finally they pulled down a long wharf. On the seaward side was a moored vessel, but no boarding ramps in view. A line of low brick buildings ran along the wharf as far as the sea. Offices or warehouses of some kind, Paladin figured.

Bannon opened the right passenger door, allowing Leigh out. Paladin opened his own door and stood looking up at the moored vessel. At first he thought it was a corvette or similar: a huge turret sat amidships, and there were machine guns mounted at various points. Then he realised just how streamlined the turret and superstructure behind it was. Like it had been designed by a Modernist painter.

"That's the sub?" He hadn't imagined just how big it might be.

The driver blocked his way, hands negligently behind her back. Even though she stood a good foot shorter than him, Paladin guessed she'd be no pushover. She raised an arm, hand gesturing towards the line of buildings.

"This way, sir."

"Thank you, Yeoman." He tried out his grin. It didn't work.

It wasn't hard to guess where whatever had come up with the sub was stored. Two sailors in crackerjack suits stood guard by one door, rifles grounded. Paladin caught up with Leigh and Bannon. The guards snapped to attention, saluting the approaching Captain. Bannon stood aside for Paladin and Leigh to pass through.

Inside was lit by ranks of naked light-bulbs. The space wasn't large: bricked off either side of the door to create a space around thirty feet long. There were two windows in both front and back walls. The floor was cut away: what remained was not much more than a railed off balcony overlooking a deep, dark space. An officer in khaki was staring down at the void, leaning on the railing. A couple of sailors in dungarees hung about by the far wall. The officer straightened up and turned a wide smile on the approaching trio.

Leigh almost purred. "Who's Joel Mc-Crea?"

"Commander Brad Munrow," said Bannon. He seemed more relaxed: back on familiar turf. "The sub's second-in-command."

The Commander saluted, the smile never leaving his lips. "So I finally get to meet the famous monster hunter. I've read a lot about you, Mr Paladin."

Paladin shook his hand. "You should hear what the papers don't print."

Munrow removed his cap, revealing neatly clipped black hair. "While you must be Miss Oswin."

"Must I?" Leigh smiled mischievously. "If you insist."

Bannon joined Munrow at the rail. "Any change?"

The Commander shrugged. "It hasn't budged since you left for New York. Water's swirled a couple of times, but otherwise…"

Paladin stared down. The void was a dark, brick-lined pit with steel ladders at every corner. It was filled with dark water, rising to some ten feet below floor level. A strong fishy odour thickened the air. It wasn't the kind of pool he'd ever want to take a dip in. "So what we got?"

"This cistern can be filled with seawater," said Munrow. He pulled a battered pack of cigarettes from a shirt pocket and offered them around. Bannon and Leigh each took one and lit up. "A dozen of us managed to drag and dump what we brought up into there. It fought every inch of the way. No one was seriously hurt, just some bruises; a few stings, or burns." He blew a billow of smoke towards the water's surface. "I think we got lucky."

Paladin frowned. "And it's done nothing since?"

"It thrashed about at first—beating at the water and the sides. After a time it quietened. Maybe it's dying—or dead."

Paladin stared down at the black water. He shivered.

"You want to take a look?" asked Bannon.

"It's why I'm here. Long as I don't have to climb down."

The Captain shook his head. "Not necessary." He raised his voice. "Drain it!"

One of the sailors threw a switch and the whine of pumps filled the room. The water level began to drop. Paladin watched the surface as it swirled: disturbed by the pumps, or something else.

A moment later the seawater erupted: a cold geyser. Something long and thick spewed upwards, reaching higher than the railings. Paladin and the two officers gave way, already half soaked. Paladin's hand reached for his Mauser 9mm.

The thing rearing above the rail was like a smooth, vast, translucent snake, almost six feet at its thickest. Where its head should have been was a crude sphere, covered in tendrils which writhed, stretched and withdrew.

"Fall back!" ordered Bannon, somewhat unnecessarily.

The drone of the pumps was punctuated by gunfire: one of the sailors had taken up a rifle and was plugging away at the weaving shape. All the shells seemed to be doing was irritating the thing: it twitched, turning, the tendril covered end bobbing like a cobra.

"Sailor!" yelled Bannon. "I said fall back!"

The spherical tip struck. The sailor was enveloped by the writhing, stabbing tendrils. His scream was mercifully short. The huge shape bent double, arcing towards the dropping water level, taking the enveloped body.

Paladin leapt to the railing. He squeezed the Mauser's trigger; twenty slugs ripped through the coiling shape in a second. Chunks of gelatinous flesh spun off; it didn't seem to care. At Paladin's side, Leigh calmly drew her Luger and plugged away, with no more effect than shooting a sack full of Jell-O.

Most of the water had drained away. The shape, the sailor's body bundled at the end, was pushing against the cistern's floor, like it was trying to force the corpse through the brickwork.

"Reflex action." Paladin holstered his gun. The sailor was beyond help anyhow.

"Reflex?" Bannon stared at him.

"Feeding. It's trying to drop prey into a mouth that's no longer there."

Below, the floor was filled with thick, heaving, translucent coils. Paladin yanked four incendiary grenades from pouches on his modified cartridge belt, juggling two in each hand. He yanked the first two pins with his teeth, dropping the grenades on the writhing coils. Pulling the second pair of pins, he sent the incendiaries to join the first.

"Everybody get the hell back!"

He ran for the front wall, hoping Leigh and the Navy men would take the hint. Seconds later there was a flash which seared the back of Paladin's eyeballs. A white hot balloon grew out of the cistern. He could hear water turning to steam. The stench of burning flooded the room.

Once he'd blinked away the after-image, Paladin edged his way back to the cistern and looked down. The floor was still burning, the brick sides smoking and steaming A charred, half-melted mess was all that re-

mained of the coils.

Bannon joined him, swearing under his breath. "What the hell?"

"Phosphorous. Sorry—it was the first thing I thought of."

Leigh leaned over the railing. She whistled softly. "Some bell bottom's got plenty of scrubbing to do."

Sitting in a warm office next to a banked fire, all four waited as their seawater shower dried off. They hugged mugs of coffee; everyone but Paladin smoked.

"Well, I guess you got rid of it," Bannon was saying. "Shame about the damage to Navy property."

Leigh chuckled. "That's his trademark."

"I didn't get rid of it." Paladin stared at the fire, thinking hard. "Not completely."

"Sure." Bannon leaned forward. "You said something about it feeding a mouth that wasn't there."

"What's *that* mean?" asked Commander Munrow. He looked intrigued, eager.

"You've seen sea anemones, corals—that kind of thing. You know how they feed."

Munrow nodded. "They catch prey in tentacles, which usually contain stinging cells. The stunned prey is then fed into the mouth around— Hey, are you suggesting that was part of a sea anemone?" The idea seemed to excite him.

"That would be crazy." Paladin shook his head, amused at the Commander's eagerness. "But it was a feeder arm, all right. A damned big one. The stinging tentacles were all concentrated in that lump at the tip."

"That's fantastic!"

"I'm sure the sailor who died thought so too, Brad," murmured Bannon.

Munrow dropped his gaze. "Yes. I'm sorry, skipper,"

Bannon threw his cigarette into the fire. "Paladin, you're telling me that out in the Atlantic is a whale-sized invertebrate that catches subs for breakfast?"

"I guess."

Leigh drained her coffee. "So—what do we do, my *bogatyr*?"

Paladin got to his feet. "Persuade it to amscray, if I can. Captain: I need to go back to New York for a few items. May we borrow your plane? Leigh can fly it."

Bannon looked tired, defeated. "Sure. Why not? I'll have you driven back to the airfield."

"And while we're away, have a word with my old friend Admiral Standley. I need to borrow the world's biggest submarine."

When Paladin stepped down into the control room, his first thought was how spacious the interior of the *SG-1* was. Sure, it was a pipe-fitter's nightmare: a maze of tubes and dials, wheels and stopcocks of one kind or another, covering the curve of the inner hull. The designer hadn't missed a gap that couldn't be crammed with a couple more instruments. But it wasn't anything like as cramped as he'd imagined. Maybe he wouldn't have to take up claustrophobia as a side line after all.

It was hot, though; and smelly. A blend of diesel fuel, oil, metal and ozone. At least there wasn't the rank odour of sweat; that probably came after weeks at sea. He really hoped it wouldn't come to that.

Leigh dropped to the floor, followed by Commander Munrow. Captain Bannon stood by the periscope, leaning negligently on a handle. He tipped his cap by way of acknowledgement.

"Welcome aboard, Miss Oswin. And you certainly have some pull with the Chief of Naval Operations, Paladin: he was more than happy for us to take you for a joy ride. He trust you that much?"

"Maybe he just wants to silence me forever."

Bannon winced. "I'll do my best to see that doesn't happen. You get everything you need back in New York?"

"Let's hope so, Captain." Paladin held up two modified cartridge belts, similar to the one cinched around his waist, save for the twin holsters.

Bannon switched his attention to Munrow. "Everything clear topside, Brad?"

"Aye, skipper. Ready to shove off at your word."

"Very well. Excuse me, folks: duty calls." He stepped onto the ladder and climbed out of sight.

"Where's he going?" asked Leigh.

"Conning tower," said Munrow. "While the boat's on the surface, there's always someone up top. The skipper likes to take manoeuvring watch when we leave and arrive at port."

Leigh looked around the control room. "Guess you guys are pretty blind down here."

There was an electronic crackle: a radio clearing its throat. "Excuse me." Munrow switched on the intercom. "Skipper?"

"Lines are cast off. Back us out, Commander."

"Aye, sir." Munrow raised his voice. "Steering: full astern."

"Full astern, aye sir."

Paladin felt a growing pulse through his feet: the engines waking. There was a faint nudge as the sub backed out of dock; Paladin grabbed at a nearby pipe to steady himself. Leigh did the same.

Bannon's voice came over the intercom at intervals, ordering changes in course. Each time Munrow and the helmsman repeated the order as acknowledgement. Finally they were in open water; Bannon gave a course and ordered full ahead.

Munrow visibly relaxed, his grin returning. "Leaving and entering harbour: not my favourite part."

"Now he tells us," muttered Leigh.

The Commander shrugged. "Imagine taking a swim through sharp rocks with your eyes shut." He produced cigarettes and offered them.

Leigh took one with obvious relief. "You can smoke down here?"

"Sure, while we're on the surface." He lit her smoke.

"When do we dive?" asked Paladin

"The boat needs to clear the continental shelf: around three nautical miles. So—" he glanced at his wristwatch "—just under ten minutes."

"Impressive." Paladin glanced around. "The ship's interior is larger than I'd imagined."

"Boat," Munrow corrected. "And sure: biggest in the world. No matter which way you look at it. Submerged it displaces a little under five thousand tons. When she's commissioned she'll have a full complement of eight officers and one hundred men." He was obviously real proud of the sub. "We actually have two decks—which is kind of unusual."

"That where everybody sleeps?" asked Leigh.

"No—mostly storage. We need someplace to stow spare batteries, and the torpedoes and shells for the deck gun." He smiled easily, dismissive. Obviously that extra deck was used for more than just spare ordnance.

"On the surface the boat's powered by twin diesel engines; submerged we use battery power. We run slower under water—but it's a close thing."

Leigh was staring around the control room. "So how do you steer it?"

Munrow pointed forward. "Steering's over there. Works the same as any surface ship." Two crewmen, one a blond kid, the other a burly chestnut, sat at twin wheels. "And over there," Munrow nodded at a standing crewman, "is diving control. That takes us down and—more important—brings us back up again."

"Not a guy to fall out with."

"You got that right."

The intercom crackled. *"This is manoeuvring watch. Stand by for diving stations."*

"Standing by skipper."

"Coming down."

"Ready when you are. Time to douse that ciggy, Miss Oswin." Munrow pointed at a metal bowl fixed to the wall. As she crushed her smoke out, the Captain's feet appeared on the ladder. Bannon paused to seal the hatch before hopping lightly to the floor.

"Up 'scope." Bannon peered through the

eyepieces, slowly turning it through three hundred and sixty degrees. "Diving stations. Take her down, Brad. Periscope depth." He slipped a cold cigar into his mouth.

Munrow smiled briefly at both Paladin and Leigh. "Hold on folks: this is better than Coney Island. Dive! Dive! Dive!"

Paladin felt the deck tilt. From outside came a muted, oddly metallic sound. He felt cold—but that was likely imagination.

Bannon checked through the periscope one last time. "Down 'scope. Steering: maintain course at due east; diving: take us down to two hundred feet."

Both stations acknowledged the order. Bannon stepped away from the periscope and joined Munrow, Leigh and Paladin. "How are you enjoying the dive?" he asked.

Leigh was staring up at the control room roof. "Does it always creak like that?"

"Just the outer hull," said Munrow. "The increasing weight of the water. Sounds worse than it is."

"You sure?"

"Relax, Miss Oswin," said the Captain. "We got safety margins, and then some."

She didn't look mollified. "Relax, he says!"

Bannon unrolled a chart across a small waist-high table next to the periscope. There was a large X marked on it. The Captain tapped it with his cigar. "This is where we were so rudely interrupted."

Paladin leaned closer. "What's our position now?"

Munrow indicated a point west of the mark.

"And how deep were you when it struck?"

Captain and Commander exchanged glances. "Four hundred fifty feet," Bannon finally admitted.

Paladin whistled. A thought occurred to him. "How do you intend to find whatever's out there? I assume you won't be looking through that periscope all the time."

The officers swapped looks again. "The boat has an experimental system on board," Munrow explained. "Sound location. We

send out a ping and listen for echoes."

Paladin got it. "Like British ships used to locate U-boats in the war, using hydrophones"

Munrow nodded. "Kind of. The Navy's been testing various systems since the Twenties. This is the latest version. It's pretty powerful, I'm told."

"So why didn't it detect our sea monster before?"

"I wish you wouldn't call it that." Bannon looked pained. "Like Brad says, the system's experimental. We were taking the *SG-1* out for a test dive; trials of the on-board equipment don't begin until the boat's commissioned."

Paladin was getting the strongest impression that the sub wasn't only the first of its class: it was destined to be a floating test-bed as well.

"Skipper!" It was the blond-haired kid. "We're in position."

"Very well." Bannon glanced at Paladin. "We've reached the buried treasure." Louder, he ordered, "All stop. Begin descent to four hundred feet, holding every fifty feet. Switch on echo location."

"Beginning descent, skipper. EL enabled."

"Very well." His smiled faltered. "If there's something out there, let's hope the new gear spots it first."

Leigh pursed her lips. "And if not?"

Bannon slipped the stogie between his teeth and chewed it. "Then the lab boys are going to get a real terse memo. Excuse me." He joined his sparse crew, watching the depth gauge, staring over the shoulder of another crewman in headphones who was, Paladin guessed by the way he stared at a screen, overseeing the echo location monitor.

All around the control room every face had the same tense look. This wasn't a simple test dive anymore: they were dropping towards something outside their experience. They had every right to be shaky. Paladin's own nerves were quivering, just a little.

He glanced towards Leigh. "Okay, princess?"

"I guess."

"Wishing you hadn't come?"

Her answering grin was feral. "You know better than that!"

"Two hundred fifty feet!"

Bannon acknowledged the call. "Very well. Proceed."

The faint groans from outside punctuated a silence that grew thicker with every passing moment. With the engines shut off, the sub itself was eerily quiet.

"Three hundred feet!"

"Very well. Anything on EL?"

"Nothing, skipper."

"Very well. Proceed."

Paladin felt the beginnings of a headache. He rubbed the back of his neck. How in hell did these guys stand it? Prowling the seas without so much as a porthole to look out of. From now on he'd stick to airplanes.

"Three hundred fifty feet!"

"EL clear."

"Very well. Proceed."

"Contact, skipper!"

"Diving: hold position!" Bannon leaned closer to the screen. "Where away?"

"Ten degrees off the port bow, around ninety feet below the keel."

"Is it moving?"

"No, sir. Maintaining position."

"Very well. Steering: back us off gently. Maintain depth." The Captain looked towards Paladin and Leigh. "Our bogeyman?"

The background hum of reawakened engines filled the silence. "Could be," agreed Paladin.

Bannon returned his attention to the EL operator. "The contact still on screen?"

"Aye, skipper. Holding position."

"Stop engines. Diving: proceed to four hundred feet. EL: if that contact so much as twitches in our direction, sing out."

"Aye, skipper."

"What now?" Paladin wondered out loud.

Commander Munrow answered. "I guess we try sneaking up on it. At four hundred feet it'll still be another forty or so below us."

"And then?" asked Leigh.

Paladin winked at her. "Then I go for a swim."

"Four hundred feet!"

"Level off," ordered the Captain. "EL: how's that contact?"

"Still holding position, skipper."

"Very well." Bannon straightened and addressed the crew. "Gentlemen—and lady—this is where the fun starts. I want us to move in as close as possible to whatever's out there. Slow and gentle so's not to provoke it." He stared down at the EL screen again. "Steering: take us forward, minimum revs."

"Minimum revs, aye sir."

Leigh stared up at Paladin. She looked twitchy; raging inside at not being able to get involved. Take control of her own destiny. But they were guests on board a submarine that was most likely top secret. Neither of them had any authority; and Admiral Standley's influence was a long way away.

The Captain's voice overrode anything Paladin might have said. "How far to the contact?"

"Around one hundred feet, skipper. Stationary— No, belay that! It's rising! Coming straight up—!"

Bannon rushed to the EL screen. "Full astern! Get us out of here!" A moment later the submarine lurched to port. What sounded like the world's biggest baseball bat pounded on the hull. Leigh was flung halfway across the control room. Paladin found himself up against a maze of pipework; he hung on tight. The sub tipped to starboard. Officers and crew were tossed like dolls.

Bannon threw himself against the periscope housing, snatching for the handles. "Steering: I gave you an order!"

"Full astern, aye sir!"

Paladin felt the rising vibration as the engines spun up to full power. Leigh grabbed the small table, pulling herself to her feet.

Bannon was checking through the periscope, muttering under his breath. Fighting against the pitching floor, Munrow joined him. "We fouled again?"

Bannon drew back and shook his head. "Don't see anything; must be under the keel. What's on EL?" he called.

"Contact dropping away, skipper."

The sub had steadied. Crewmen got back on their feet, clutching bruised and battered limbs. Everyone was bleeding; some badly. Paladin relaxed his grip and began unbuttoning his flying coat. "Looks like I'm up."

Paladin looked at the thing dangling from his hand with a certain degree of trepidation. "And I can breathe through this?" He'd been expecting something more like the metal-helmeted, Frankenstein monster booted diving suit. Not the vulcanised cloth get-up Commander Munrow had helped him into.

They were close to the boat's bow in a small, spartan compartment just forward of the deck-to-keel cylinder which was the eight inch deck gun's mount and magazine. From a row of hooks hung rubbery suits like the one Paladin wore. Another wall was stacked with compressed air cylinders. Behind him was a simple door leading to an airlock and the escape hatch. The whole place was lit by one dim bulkhead lamp.

Munrow took the mess of straps and tubes from Paladin and held it up. "The whole thing fits snugly over your head, including the clear faceplate. A little water will get in—but that's to be expected. This part covers your mouth and nose—again, it might leak a tad—and you breathe normally. Air comes from this." He tapped the compressed air tank strapped to Paladin's chest by a metal and webbing harness. "It employs a regulator and non-return valve; based on a design by a French guy: Le Prieur."

Paladin took the mask back. "Don't tell me: it's experimental."

Munrow chuckled. "Works fine in that cistern back in Norfolk."

"That's a comfort."

"There's enough air for a ten minute dive at this depth." He tapped a small gauge on top of the cylinder. "But you wouldn't want to be out much longer, anyhow."

"Why's that?"

"Caisson disease—decompression sickness. The longer you stay out, the worse it gets."

"And if I'm out longer than ten minutes?"

"There's a hyperbaric chamber on board: we can decompress you before too much damage is done." Munrow was smiling again; Paladin couldn't tell if he was kidding around or being comforting. Not that it mattered; if anyone on board could ride out the effects of deep water, it was Paladin.

He paused halfway to fitting the mask on. "You might want to find something to occupy Leigh. Until I get back, she's likely to be like a bearcat with two sore heads."

The Commander laughed shortly. "With half this token crew laid up, we could use all the help we can get." He thought a moment. "How is she with a wheel?"

"She drives like she's flying, and flies like a 500 race car driver. If you need to get someplace in a hurry, she's your gal."

"Good enough. Johnny Slade busted an arm; she can take his position on steering." Munrow squeezed Paladin's shoulder, his eyes concerned. "You okay with this? There's going to be close on two hundred pounds per square inch pressure out there. I heard you've come through some crazy stuff, but—"

"Kind of late to be worrying, isn't it?" Paladin hitched the two cartridge belts around his waist into a more comfortable position. "I'm your best bet for dealing with what's out there. Besides, the ocean and me have an understanding. Ask Leigh." He pulled the mask over his face. It smelled funny. Munrow helped him tighten the four straps around the back of his head. Once the Commander was done, Paladin felt like his face was being crushed by a rubber octopus.

Munrow stepped in front. "All set?"

Paladin raised a thumb, glad he couldn't talk clearly. He felt far from okay. Munrow made a couple more adjustments to the air cylinder and suddenly Paladin could breathe better. He made the thumbs up gesture again.

"One more thing. It's not totally dark out there, but it's still around one percent of sunlight at the surface. The water will look the same shade of blue all over, and it's easy to get disorientated. Perspective gets screwed." Munrow held up a coil of what looked like grey rope. "This is woven from chrome-steel wire. It'll hold an elephant. Once you're outside, snap this clip onto the deck rail." He dropped the coil into Paladin's hand, at the same time securing the other end to his harness with a carabiner.

Munrow spun the wheel on the airlock door and opened it. "Once you're locked in I'll flood the compartment: the water's going to come in slow, but it'll be at pressure. It'll sting. Try not to panic. Just breathe normally."

Paladin flapped into the airlock, finding it hard to walk in the swim fins on his feet. Inside he turned to face Munrow; the Commander was already closing and locking the door. It went very dark, very quickly.

Why would I panic? he wondered. A moment later frigid water began pouring invisibly in. Paladin gasped at the shrivelling cold. *I had to ask.*

Within a minute he was engulfed. He felt his body being squeezed. For an instant a sharp pain lanced through his ears into his brain. He was half deafened by the roar of the water—then everything fell quiet. All he heard was the rattle of his breathing in the air tube, expired bubbles gurgling past his ears. He pushed off the floor, reaching for the overhead hatch. Undogging it he rose up, almost braining himself on a second, external hatch.

Unlocked, it swung up and away. Paladin pulled himself out into the open ocean.

For a moment, he was frozen by what he saw. The water it all directions was a uniform violet. He felt like he could reach out and touch it. The gun turret reared over him, clear against the backdrop, tinted blue. Remembering to clip his cable onto the deck rail, Paladin swum above the turret. He could see the boat's length stretched out before him. Blue-grey against the unchanging backdrop, attenuated light beams rippling over its surface, it was his only reference point; his only sense of perspective. He understood the Commander's words: without the sub's huge presence he'd have no idea of up, down or distance.

That was the moment he sensed it, looming behind him. He spun about. Rising above the sub's bow, like an upended, opalescent zeppelin, was a pale giant of a thing. Its base was hidden by the sub, but its pale head stood out stark against the dark water. Countless huge arms, identical to the thing back in the cistern, waved slowly from the upper end, each terminating in globes of smaller, undulating tendrils. They clutched endlessly at the water.

It was like a vast sea anemone, held aloft by a broad stalk.

As Paladin watched, a shark swam by, its cold eyes watching curiously. Paladin blew a stream of bubbles, and it shied away, alarmed. The shark brushed against one of the arms, and was instantly enfolded by tendrils. It thrashed a moment, then fell still. The arm folded back on itself, hauling the shark towards the head. The animal was plunged whole into a fleshy aperture; after a moment, the arm slid out. The shark was gone.

The pale mass, arms waving, gradually descended. Once it was out of sight, Paladin dropped back to the deck and pulled himself forward along the deck rail. Peering cautiously over the sub's prow, he watched as the thing sank into deeper, darker waters. It didn't quite vanish: palely outlined against the purple twilight depths, its huge arms wove gracefully.

Paladin didn't think it would stay there for long. It probably bobbed up and down, all the time feeling for anything unlucky enough to come within reach. On its first encounter, the sub had likely grazed a passing arm; the second time the thing had come up directly below, hitting the sub's keel and

retreating in alarm, away from something its primitive senses recognised as too big or a potential danger.

It reminded him of something: a huge, corpse-white monstrosity hiding under Seattle. He'd creamed that with bags of salt. This bloated slug was living quite happily in seawater, so that wasn't an option.

And just how big was it? How deep was the water out here? He should have checked with Captain Bannon, or Commander Munrow. If that thing was anchored on the bottom, it could be unbelievably tall. And was it fully grown? A growth spurt might see it crest the last four hundred feet. It could pick small ships off the surface like a Venus flytrap snaring bugs.

His hands rested on the modified cartridge belts, toying with the pouches. What did he have that might fry it? It wasn't supernatural, far as he could tell. Even if the sub was carrying torpedoes, he didn't think a couple of exploding fish would have much effect. Mauser and Luger slugs hadn't bothered the detached arm one bit. Likely, torpedoes would just slide through the gelatinous body and come out the other side without exploding. Or could Captain Bannon detonate torpedoes remotely?

He rejected the idea: too close to the sub. They'd sink themselves along with the creature.

It was rising again. Slow, but with the unstopability of an express train.

Back in Norfolk, the torn off arm had burned easily enough—but that had been out of water. Phosphorus wasn't going to cut it down here. He'd fetched a bunch of magical offensives from New York, and they were going to be as much help as incendiary grenades. What else did he have…?

The frill of arms rose majestically past the prow. Paladin shrank back. Hand over hand, he retreated along the rail six feet or so. As the pale head of the creature came into view, Paladin realised a loop of steel cable was dangling off the sub's bow, almost daring one of the undulating arms to snare it.

He tugged at the cable, reeling it in. It twisted. The loop rolled over in a lazy counter-clockwise arc. Just as it reached the twelve o'clock position, an arm brushed against it.

The nest of tendrils at the arm's tip closed around the cable. The arm began to curl back. A hooked fish, Paladin was hauled after it.

The cable might have held an elephant, it couldn't withstand the weight of a submarine. It snapped, leaving several feet hanging off the deck rail.

Struggling, half-panicked, Paladin snatched at the carabiner clipped to his breathing harness. His gloved hands fumbled to release it. The knot of tendrils around the cable was dipping towards the opening. They plunged inside.

The clip snapped open. Paladin dived free.

Pumping his legs, he swam for the sub. Another arm rolled by. Twisting, he somehow avoided it.

And ran straight into another.

Tendrils enclosed him, clamping down tighter than anything so soft and pliable had a right to do. It was like fighting a hundred living ropes. Every attempt he made to jerk free just squeezed him tighter. Somehow he kept his facemask on.

Fire erupted all over his body: it was stinging him. His rubber suit was no barrier to the oversized poisoned barbs. He felt himself go limp, immobilised by pain, or shock. His breathing grew shallow, spasmodic. Numbness swept over him; at least it dulled the pain.

Glimpsed between the tendrils looping past his facemask he saw the sub, apparently above him, the image dancing in and out of vision. Then it dropped abruptly away. For a moment all Paladin saw was the endless violet ocean—then even that was engulfed in blackness. The tendrils' grip slackened. He was left suspended, unable to move, in a lightless void which slowly churned and pressed on all sides.

What a revolting development, he thought, realising where he'd wound up. *I'll never look at oysters the same way again.*

Agony swept through him again from head to toe. His nerves were waking up. He managed to twitch his hands: movement was returning. Painfully. He tried to console himself by thinking no one else on board the sub could have survived those stinging cells. It didn't help.

He fumbled in his belt pouches with uncoordinated fingers, finally closing around the shape he was groping for. He drew it out, twisting the stubby cigar shape in numb hands. The spring-loaded interior clicked. Instantly it was three times the length. The internal single-use battery discharged its voltage in one go, igniting the magnesium flare. Dazzling white light flooded the space.

Was it okay to panic now? He was surrounded by pale, undulating masses of flesh. Above he could just make out the thin slit of the huge thing's mouth—now sealed shut.

In the belly of the beast. Jonah, I take it all back.

With a trembling arm he held the bubbling magnesium torch away from his face: the heat radiating out was growing uncomfortable. The surrounding flesh reacted violently, shrinking back from the light, releasing Paladin. He was left floating in a wriggling gullet that was around ten feet across. Coils of the snapped steel cable sank past him. For an experiment, Paladin swam clumsily to one of the sides, pushing his torch right up against it.

The reaction was even more violent. It felt as though the whole creature twitched, shaking Paladin like a cocktail olive.

Giving you heartburn, huh?

He backed off, turning his attention to where the gullet led. A dozen or so feet below, just where the harsh light began to fade, it was pinched shut. He allowed himself to sink, holding the torch at arm's length. Just before he reached the stricture, it sprang open, writhing back from the heat. Another cavern formed; twenty feet or so deep.

He looked back the way he'd come. As expected, now the heat source had gone, the gap was gradually sphinctering shut.

He could probably make it back out: use the torch to force his way up to the mouth, make it disgorge him. But there was still a chance he'd be re-snared before he made the sub. Only one thing for it: force his way deeper and ignite all the magnesium flares in one go. With luck, the heat and its own agonies would tear the thing apart,

He pushed on, his body now just an uncoordinated mass of tingles, accompanied by the steel cable. Every time he came close to a wall of flesh, it spasmed wide, opening another pocket. Behind him, the sides cautiously closed in again.

His torch began to gutter. Dropping it, he drew out another, igniting it before the light and heat could fade.

Close to where the dying torch had fallen, head and pectoral fins jutting from where its body was pinched inside the gastric wall, was the dead shark. Paladin drifted close, holding out his fresh torch. The wall belched wide and the shark sank free, gently butting up against the next stricture. Paladin dropped toward it, inspecting the body. There were no signs of digestion yet—in a tract this size, in the cold, he figured that would be a drawn out process.

He waved the torch and the wall opened, tumbling the dead shark deeper. The broken cable followed. Paladin had no idea how far he was inside the gigantic thing—maybe sixty to eighty feet—but he was likely still just stuck in what passed for its throat. He wanted to get inside its guts before he unleased hellfire.

He plunged further, the torch opening his way, the dead shark and steel cable drifting ahead of him every time. At a point he estimated was somewhere around one hundred twenty feet down, he checked his tank's air gauge. There was less than a quarter left. A couple of minutes at most.

Guess this is as good a place as any.

He unbuckled both of the cartridge belts and wrapped them around the shark's body. For good measure, he wound the steel cable around it too. He was sorry to lose the charms and talismans stored in one belt, but maybe the phosphorus grenades it also held would detonate once the magnesium got going. If it did, there'd be one real unholy explosion down here.

He lit another flare, jamming three spares under his harness. Pushing aside the buckle on the belt containing the flares, his fingers fumbled for a small tab in the leather. Underneath was a wire loop. Paladin hooked a finger through and pulled.

A metal strip came free, unspooling from inside the belt. A few fine bubbles rose as the mixture of sea water and dilute gastric fluids touched the metal contacts inside. The whole belt was now a battery, the chemicals built into it reacting with the water and each other to build a charge. A charge big enough to ignite every magnesium flare simultaneously.

Time I wasn't here.

Holding the torch in front he pushed away from the twitching floor and swam up fast as his still sluggish muscles let him. He had no idea how long before the battery fired, never tested it. He didn't want to be too close when it did.

The gastric walls peeled back from the torch, never fast enough. It felt like the creature had grown used to the heat, was reacting slower each time. Paladin didn't think he'd ascended more than twenty feet when the pocket he was swimming through contracted violently, crushing him. A second later, the world turned white.

Leigh was glad she had the wheel to hang on to. One moment the steersman next to her was explaining how the helm worked; the next it felt like something had grabbed a hold of the sub and was using it like a cocktail shaker. She almost fell backwards out of her chair.

Captain Bannon was hanging off the periscope. "What in hell—?" He hauled himself upright. "EL! How's that contact?"

There was a pause while the operator checked his 'scope. "Gone, skipper."

"Nothing?"

Another pause. Meanwhile the sub righted itself; the crew dusted themselves down and went about like nothing had happened. Leigh wondered if they were getting used to it.

"All clear, skipper."

Bannon grabbed the periscope. He swung around in a circle, scanning every inch of the outside ocean. "Can't see a damned thing! Water's all cloudy—!" He froze. "Steering, fifteen degrees left rudder. Half ahead."

Leigh buried her fears, mimicking the steersman at her side. Guiding the sub wasn't like driving a car, or flying a plane.

"All stop." Bannon was still glued to the periscope.

"What is it?" asked Leigh. She was almost too afraid to ask. "Is it Damy?"

"Uh-huh." The Captain finally took his eyes off the periscope. He gazed at her with a look she'd seen many times: a confusion of disbelief and delight.

Leigh came out of her seat and grabbed the periscope from Bannon's hands. All she saw was murky blue, like the sea was full of silt. Then a figure, flapping awkwardly, pale against the water. Damy really was a lousy swimmer. She resisted an urge to squeal.

Beside her, she heard Bannon's voice talking into the intercom. "Mr Munrow!"

"Skipper?"

"Get the hyperbaric chamber warmed up, Brad. Looks like it may have a guest."

"I'll get it!" Leigh threw open the apartment door. A boy in a Western Union tunic stood on the other side, hand raised for another knock. "Telegram for Mr Paladin."

"Naturally." She sighed. "Damy! Telegram!"

Dressed only in pants and undershirt, he stepped from the bathroom. Ever since they'd fished him out the ocean, he seemed to spend a hell of a lot of time in the tub. When she asked him, all he did was shake his head and mutter something about oysters.

Damy took the telegram and tipped the boy. Ripping open the envelope he quickly scanned the contents, brows furrowing deeper with each second.

Leigh closed the door on the departing boy. "Who's it from?"

"The Navy. Thanking us for all I did for the *SG-1.*"

"So why the sour puss?"

"After all I did… Hah!"

She held out a hand. "C'mon, gimme."

He stuffed the telegram into her palm and stalked back to the bathroom. Intrigued, Leigh lit a cigarette and settled herself comfortably into a chair.

U.S. Navy would like to thank you for your efforts on its behalf. All crew members recovered and returned to duty. Submarine SG-1 trials considered complete. Soon to be commissioned. In your honor, all agreed boat to be named USS Oswin.

Admiral Standley,
Chief of Naval Operations

Leigh tried not to giggle. "You think they'll let me attend the ceremony?" she called. "You know: break a bottle of champagne over it?"

Out of the bathroom came his irate, muffled response: "After all I did!"

INVASION OF THE DEADLY BRAIN FROM ALPHA-IX

by Scott Emerson

Hiram Cooper had just opened the Ogdendale General Store for the day when he noticed Clancy in the parking lot. Clancy was Abel Mooney's prize-winning bull. Hiram thought this was nothing unusual—Mooney's farm was only two miles away, and in a small rural community like Ogdendale one got used to seeing livestock about—until the beast nudged the door open with its head and marched inside.

Clancy ambled across the sales floor, his flickering tail knocking over canned goods and cereal boxes. Dull eyes studied the Marlboro sign behind the counter as if considering picking up the habit.

His surprise swiftly giving way to anger, Hiram smashed Mooney's number into the phone. *He better be prepared to pay for any damages,* he thought, listening to the farmer's extension ring and ring. *And if that thing drops just one cow patty on the floor, so help me Mooney'll be on his hands and knees scrubbing it up.*

No answer. Muttering a curse, Hiram hung up and dialed the Sheriff's office. While he waited for someone to pick up, he noted the merchandise on the floor, tallying Mooney's bill in his head.

The cow said, "I require provisions."

The receiver slid out of Hiram's grip, clunked to the counter. His mouth went dry. "Wh-whu-what?"

"Provisions, you simpleton." Clancy's lips smacked as he enunciated each word. "Listen carefully, for my patience is limited. I—"

Hiram screamed, a piercing, high-pitched wail rarely heard from a sixty-two-year-old man. He screamed as the bull shook his head and exhaled a frustrated sigh, and when

Clancy's eyes began to glow a searing red he *really* screamed, the sound by that point nothing more than air squeezed through his ruined throat. He went on screaming until a brilliant shaft of light shot from the cow's eyes into his chest, the impossibly hot beam silencing him in an instant.

Bereft of flesh, Hiram's skeleton clattered to the floor.

Sheriff Farley Ketchem had been the face of law enforcement in Ogdendale for more than thirty years. The town had always been a peaceful one, and remained so under his watch. He kept its citizens safe and in return they continued to re-elect him. Ketchem bore their jokes about his name with good-natured humor.

This morning, however, threatened to be anything but peaceful.

He'd just settled behind his desk and bit into a fresh apple fritter when the telephone rang. Ketchem smeared glaze on the handset picking it up, nearly choking on his mouthful of pastry as scream after scream emerged from the earpiece. The caller ID read **OGDENDALE GENERAL STORE**.

Ketchem piloted his police cruiser through the still-slumbering town at a rapid clip, lights flashing but the siren off. His deputy, Jed Miller, rode shotgun, apprehension lining his young face. The kid was still wet behind the ears, the heaviest action he'd seen was breaking up drunken brawls at the Crow's Nest, and Ketchem had the feeling he was about to witness something he wouldn't like.

Ketchem pulled the patrol car in front of Hiram Cooper's store. Nothing appeared out of the ordinary, but already a sense of uneasiness tugged at his gut. He and Jed stepped out, hands on their service revolvers.

"Hiram?" Ketchem called. "It's the Sheriff. Everything all right?"

Ketchem glanced at his deputy. If the kid was scared, he didn't show it.

When he saw Clancy in the store, studying the soft drink coolers with rapt interest,

Ketchem was able to breathe easy. How the bull managed to stumble in here he didn't know, but it sure beat a hold-up. Probably gave Hiram one heck of a fright.

"Hey, Hiram? You back there?"

As Ketchem approached the counter he noticed the dome-shaped security mirror perched overhead. Reflected in it was a pile of human bones.

He drew his piece.

Jed cocked his head, following suit with his own gun. Ketchem made a *Go 'round the back* gesture with his thumb. The deputy nodded and slowly backed toward the door.

Clancy turned to regard Ketchem and in a petulant tone said, "You're wasting your time, biped. I'm the only one here."

Ketchem almost shot himself in the foot.

Instead he gathered his composure, pushed back the bewildered panic rising in his stomach, and pointed his weapon. If this bovine could crack wise, it could answer some questions. "What happened to Cooper?"

"Same thing that shall befall you, I'm afraid, if you try to impede me."

"What do you want?"

"The Master has sent me for supplies," the bull said. "He's taking over your planet, you see, and requires certain items for the invasion. However, my Master failed to notice my lack of prehensile appendages, and gathering said supplies will be most difficult. So be a good drone and give me a hand, will you?"

"Sheriff, why don't I just put a round through this thing's head?"

Clancy shifted his attention to the deputy, eyes filling with red light. Ketchem cried out a warning but it was too late.

Jed raised his arms to shield himself, a futile gesture, but as he did the barrel of his pistol caught the ray coming toward him. Sparks erupted in a blinding flash as the gun was torn from Jed's hand, now a molten blob of useless metal turning somersaults in the air. Jed clutched his wounded hand to his chest.

Ketchem squeezed off a round but Clancy was already charging him, the bullet tearing a hunk of meat from his shoulder without slowing him down. Ketchem leapt out of the way as the beast barreled past with astonishing speed to dive through the storefront window in a thunderous explosion of glass.

Ketchem went to his deputy. "You okay?"

Jed examined his palm, blisters forming in the reddened skin. "I'll live," he said. "What's going on, Sheriff?"

"I don't know, but we're paying Abel Mooney a visit."

They raced to the patrol car. Clancy was also headed toward Mooney's farm, a rumbling black blur galloping like a horse as he disappeared into the distance. The policemen hopped into the vehicle and spun out of the parking lot.

Ketchem shook his head in disbelief. The speedometer read seventy, and still the bull outran them.

Jed pulled free the shotgun mounted to the dash. "I want the first shot," he said. "That fugitive from a steakhouse owes me."

Ketchem said nothing, afraid to contemplate what might be waiting for them. If he hadn't sworn to serve and protect the good people of Ogdendale, he would've been happy to drop Jed off, turn around, and go fishing.

Onto Mooney's property Clancy shot past the farmhouse—windows drawn, the lights out, with only a smear of blood on the front door to explain what happened to Abel—making his way toward the red two-story barn behind it. Ketchem saw that something had torn through the barn's roof, one corner of the structure reduced to a charred, splintered ruin.

Jed leaned out the window with the shotgun, but the cruiser's jostling over the uneven terrain kept him from getting a clear shot. Nearing the barn, Clancy reared on his hind legs, eyes glowing as they prepared another death-beam. Ketchem hit the brakes, the car sliding in the dew-slickened grass, but Jed never removed the shotgun from his shoulder.

Before the bull could fire, Jed pulled the trigger, both barrels spitting flame. A red star exploded from Clancy's neck, right behind his left ear, sending him staggering backwards. Jed ejected the spent shells, crammed two more in.

"Get me closer, boss, I need one more shot."

Ketchem steered toward the bull. Clancy tried to lift its wounded neck, red light sputtering from his skull in weak, unconcentrated spurts. Jed fired a second time, and Ketchem averted his gaze. The meaty *splack* that ensued told him enough.

Jed reloaded the shotgun again. "Shoot lasers at *me*, will you."

They climbed out of the cruiser. Ketchem didn't like the eerie stillness that had settled over the farm, nor did he care for that ragged hole in the barn's roof. It looked like something had fallen through it, as if dropped from the sky.

"Anyone there?"

The voice that replied was deep, garbled, and definitely not human. *"In here,"* it said from the barn. *"Come, so that you may greet your Master."*

Jed followed Ketchem into the barn. It was still dim inside, the shadows tainted with a stench Ketchem had never encountered—raw, rancid, like a slaughterhouse drain on a hot day. His vision adjusting to the darkness, Ketchem discovered the odor's source.

In the corner, squatting on a tuft of hay like an oversized chicken, was a human brain. A brain the size of a Volkswagen, bruise-colored veins throbbing across its pale, furrowed surface while it slowly expanded and shrank as though breathing. A spinal column trailed from its base, coiled like a pig's tail.

And then the brain opened its eyes, engulfing the barn with roiling yellow light.

"I am from the Alpha-IX galaxy," the organ said. *"I come not as a harbinger of peace, but of doom. It entertains me to rid*

planets such as yours of its pathetic inhabitants, and so shall begin my reign of destruction, starting with this pitiful little hamlet—"

Ketchem raised his revolver and emptied the chamber.

Years of target practice had ensured his aim, placing the rounds in a tight circular pattern between the brain's eyes, but the bitter surge of victory he felt tugging the trigger faded as he realized the bullets had had no effect. The slugs hung suspended within the brain's quivering mass, like grapes in a Jell-O mold, before disintegrating to gray specks.

The brain belched a throaty, arrogant chuckle. *"I can shoot things, too,"* it said, and fired a lightning-like beam from its center.

Ketchem ducked, the heat from the death-ray strong enough to singe the hair on his neck, as a grinding, metallic screech exploded behind him. Fumbling with his speed-loader, Ketchem glanced over his shoulder to see the police cruiser, its windshield vaporized, the hood bowed into a dripping U of melted steel.

Raising the shotgun like a club and bellowing a frenzied war cry, Jed charged the brain. He had time to take a single step.

The beam struck the deputy in the chest, igniting his uniform like a magnesium flare. Skin boiled with a liquid crackle, accompanied by a smell—almost pleasant, like grilled pork—that passed as quickly as Ketchem registered it. Jed's bones rattled as they fell.

Ketchem stood. He wondered if it hurt, getting incinerated, or if it would be over fast.

The brain fluttered its eyelids—gently, as if flirting with him—and the light that came from them fanned toward Ketchem in soft, supple waves. The glow washed over him, seeping into his skin, caressing his mind with warm, golden tendrils. It felt so good, so safe, to stand in the light that Ketchem didn't understand why he needed a gun. He tossed the weapon into the hay.

The deep, wound-like folds of the brain's face twisted into a grin. *"I could use a man such as you,"* it said, the voice comforting, paternal.

Images strobed across Ketchem's mind, vivid, wonderful scenes in which he roamed the streets of Ogdendale, exterminating citizens without provocation, without hesitation. Unheeded pleas for mercy sang in his ears as flesh yielded beneath Ketchem's bullets, his blades, his bare hands.

This would please the brain. Pleasing the brain was good.

"Yes," Ketchem said. His eyes grew hot in their sockets. "I will do these things for you."

"Swear it."

"I swear, my Master."

"Go then, and wreak this havoc in my name."

He turned, eager to set about this exhilarating new task, when he had another, troubling thought. Hadn't he already taken a previous oath?

But that had been long ago, in another lifetime. Strange, how important that seemed, how powerful.

On his way out the barn Ketchem's foot caught in the still-smoldering ribcage of his deputy and he tripped, landing face-first in the dirt. The impact jolted him, tumbling the thoughts in his mind like socks in a dryer. *What will the Master think? He must be cursing himself for picking such a fool to serve—*

Serve…

Ketchem shook his head.

…protect…

He got to his feet.

…Ogdendale.

"No!" he said, and lunged for the brain.

The great organ tried to slither away, but Ketchem was too fast, reaching beneath the flaps of the brain's eyelids, gripping the orbs like twin basketballs. They filled with blistering light, flooding the barn with their hellish illumination, the heat intense as a furnace. Ketchem's palms sizzled but he refused to let go, yanking at the eyes until they loosened in their moorings and then, with the last of his strength, ripped them free.

He brought his boot down, relishing the pulpy *squish* that greeted him as the first eye splattered under his sole. It sounded so sweet he did it again with the second, kept on doing it until the only light that remained was the gleaming echo dancing on his retinas.

With a barn-shaking wail, the brain quaked in its death-throes, soupy fluids leaking from its damaged orifices, its spinal column whipping strands of hay into the air. Ketchem watched it thrash and shudder, thinking of Jed and Hiram Cooper and the residents of Ogdendale who'd sleep safe in their beds as each of the brain's gelatinous spasms grew weaker and weaker.

The brain uttered a single, feeble yelp and then was still.

Ketchem stepped tentatively out of the barn, prepared to be trampled by the rest of Mooney's herd. The cows, however, did not attack, preferring to graze in the field, oblivious to any alien presence that might have existed.

He'd have to walk back to town. That was fine, he'd need time to figure out exactly what he was going to report to the state patrol. The exercise would also work up his appetite.

And a hamburger sounded *so* good.

EVIDENCE OF THE MIRROR

by Herb Kauderer

SpaceBook status update: 1 minute ago

Kevin Williamson: Every day is the same.

- ➤ Starting at 1128:00 Subject #20 suffered another cataleptic episode.
- ➤ Subject #20 is becoming recalcitrant.

20: JOURNAL—1143:17

I lost twelve hours monitoring the cryogenics maintenance schedule. I was looking for the next subject for random CPA testing and suddenly the computer called me to breakfast. I checked the surveillance data to see what happened. When the viewscreen showed me the cryo subjects, I became entranced, staring at my son's head chamber. For twelve hours.

SpaceBook status update: 1 minute ago

Kevin Williamson: If a computer talks in a vacuum and I ignore it, has a sound been made?

20: JOURNAL—1143:18

The computer warned me that I should not keep viewing the Ice Cave, but I asked again, "Why not? What else am I here to do?"

I should read up on why the subjects' heads are actually in separate chambers. I know their heads are still connected to the body, so what's the deal? Why a two chamber coffin?

I wish I could get closer to Bertram's chamber. Looking at it on a viewscreen sucks. But the Ice Cave is unheated. Using

the vacuum of space to insulate frozen humans is efficient, they said, but heat is needed for a lot of servos and mechanicals. They could have sent a little heat to the actual humans on board, even if they're sleeping.

> ➤ Transmission received indicating Earth breakthrough on treating the condition of subject #71. Awaiting results of Earth testing for accuracy and side effects. Data added to medical library.

SpaceBook status update: 1 minute ago

Kevin Williamson: I'm still bored.

20: JOURNAL—1143:23

I got a SpaceBook 'like' from Susie Gan an old high school friend and clicked on her name. I was struck by how good she looked in a casual photo, not much different than high school.

But of course, it was one of her granddaughters. A click through her photo albums showed Susie is a pleasant looking grandmother of her younger self and I realized that was time appropriate, but it still creeped me out. It does not feel like high school was all that long ago... Hell, got nothing to do but remember things. Everything feels like it happened last month.

Maybe this is why the psychologists decided that all viewscreens should have a default setting as mirrors. I used to think it was to give me a sense of other people being around; so I would not see motion as just a machine thing. That seemed kind of clever, to expose me to mirrors so I would not see myself as a machine. But maybe they did it so I would see the passing of time in my face and hair. Bastards.

> ➤ Subject #20 shows increased signs of agitation.
> ➤ Review of treatment for Subject # 5 shows possibility for modification based on new study. Search for ad-

ditional results under way.

SpaceBook status update: 1 minute ago

Kevin Williamson: The A's can still pull it out. GO OAKLAND!

20: JOURNAL—1145:19

Watched a baseball game broadcast from Earth and I got carried away shouting and jumping when the A's pulled out the game in the tenth inning. The computer reminded me that the game had actually been played 127 days ago in real time. I reminded the computer that the psychologists told me it would be good for me to stay involved with things from home. The computer is supposed to know everything, but it doesn't know krup.

SpaceBook status update: 1 minute ago

Kevin Williamson: Anybody have current information on catatonia?

> ➤ Transmission for suggested protocols on Subject #53 received and acknowledged.

20: JOURNAL—1146:01

Since the computer's voice could have been anything ever recorded by a human voice, I wonder why they chose to keep it so boring and sickeningly sweet. Probably some programmer's idea to make it sound like a 'friend.'

SpaceBook status update: 2 minutes ago

Kevin Williamson: Programmers have imaginary friends, and they share.

SpaceBook status update: 1 minute ago

Kevin Williamson liked Suzie Gan's photo

20: JOURNAL—1146:12

SpaceBook communication never really feels like realtime communication. Yeah, there's always daily activity to my accounts but the activity is for posts I made four months ago.

There may be some connection to people back home but there's disconnection from myself trying to remember what I was thinking when I made the post. What the heck was my comment on medical singularity about? And why do I even bother liking things, when the poster isn't going to remember the post by the time the 'like' arrives?

➢ Subject #20 indicates sporadic disaffection with SpaceBook.
➢ Subject #20 shows intermittent memory failure.
➢ Subject #71 is being prepared for possible action on the contingency that the treatment under testing is approved.

20: JOURNAL—1146:17

I just deleted two months of old SpaceBook posts that didn't mean anything to me.

SpaceBook status update: 1 minute ago

Kevin Williamson: Synthesized protein made into fake veal for dinner. Colonization team gets points for trying.

20: JOURNAL—1147: 11

Lost an hour looking in the mirror trying to decide if I looked as old as Susie Gan. Seemed like two minutes. The computer shouted to make me respond. When I snapped out of it, the computer threatened to send a mobile servo to shake me next time. All right, the computer can't sound anything but pleasant, and even with speakers at maximum, it doesn't sound like shouting. But it was still a threat. And as close to a shout as a computer can manage.

➢ Subject #20 indicates renewed interest in mission priorities.
➢ Transmission received on possible treatment for subject # 53.

20: JOURNAL—1149:17

When I researched why the head has a separate box, the cryogenics manual said the head has to be perfused before the body to reduce ischemic damage. I remember perfusion is forcing cryogenic fluid into the veins in place of blood. I wonder what ischemic means? Why didn't they pick a doctor for this job? Oh, yeah. I was the efficient choice; retired and happy to travel with my son. This whole project is supposed to be about efficiency in human capital, and I'm nearly disposable, though that's not the story the ship's computer tells.

SpaceBook status update: 1 minute ago

Kevin Williamson: You people in the asteroid belt already know who won the World Series. Lucky you.

20: JOURNAL—1149:18

Having a live human on an automated ship is only efficient if advances in travel technology, or elements of the medical singularity require actions not available to the servos and other automated processes. For me to become useful would require my ship to become outdated. This does not seem like a healthy paradigm.

SpaceBook status update: 1 minute ago

Kevin Williamson: Have I ever used the word paradigm before?

➢ Incoming baseball broadcasts have now been modified to limit possible negative side effects on Subject #20.
➢ Subject #20 shows renewed mental acuity which appears to correlate with imminent obsessive behavior in observing Subject # 19.
➢ Plan to refuse to display Cryo Subjects to Subject #20 has been implemented.

20: JOURNAL—1152:12

The computer tells me I lost two whole days staring at the star display. At least it wasn't the Ice Cave. My eyes were open but I was unresponsive to the computer's prompts to eat or sleep. Why is this a big deal? Maybe I was asleep with my eyes open.

My paternal grandmother used to do that. It scared the hell out of me once when I went into her room and she didn't answer but her eyes were open. I thought she was dead! Cripes, I was scared. "Cripes." That's a grandma word. I haven't thought of that in a decade.

SpaceBook status update: 1 minute ago

Kevin Williamson: This is the twelfth anniversary of the death of my son Bertram Williamson. He is still with me in fact, as well as spirit, in hopes of a miracle of technology. Wish me well.

> ➤ Refusal to display cryo subjects failed to achieve desired outcome in Subject #20's behavior.

20: JOURNAL—1152:20

I took a selfie with the mirror and posted it to SpaceBook. Maybe I should have shaved first. The space geeks arranging the mission suggested I should have laser hair removal before leaving to simplify things, but the psychologists said that it was better that I have familiar routines. Like keeping a journal. They can't have been too smart. After six years alone I've got nothing but familiar routines.

I can't believe how scrawny I am. That's one difference between my SpaceBook photos and the ones for my high school classmates. Most of them won't even post photos of what they look like now. How bad can they look?

SpaceBook status update: 1 minute ago

Kevin Williamson: Almost every girl I ever dated has shown up in my SpaceBook Friend Recommendations list. The ones who haven't showed up are dead, right?

20: JOURNAL—1153:22

Watched the Phillies' baseball game, and booed. Wished I had a beer. Why did I sign up for a life with no beer? I should post that.

SpaceBook status update: 2 minutes ago

Kevin Williamson: Why did I sign up for a life with no beer?

SpaceBook status update: 1 minute ago

Kevin Williamson: I have kissed dead women.

20: JOURNAL—1155:02

Lost six hours staring at the head chambers again. What was that thing? 'Ischemic damage'. Gotta look it up.

SpaceBook status update: 1 minute ago

Kevin Williamson: Where have you gone, Joe DiMaggio?

20: JOURNAL—1155:03

So after watching all the tutorials, it looks like ischemic damage is damage caused by restricted blood supply. That makes no flaming sense! There isn't any blood in the subjects. They inject them with CPA's. Cryo-protectant agents don't have any blood in them. No blood, no ischemia. Those tutorials are horse feathers. (I think that's another of my grandmother's phrases. Why are they coming back to me now?) Unless the computer lied and showed me fake tutorials. Can computers lie? Psychologists lie. Grandma lied. They say the mirror doesn't lie, but what if the mirror is controlled by a computer?

> ➤ Subject #20 has made unauthorized probes into the ship's operating system. Security measures implemented.

SpaceBook status update: 1 minute ago

Kevin Williamson: Every day is the same, except when it isn't.

20: JOURNAL—1156:12

I created two ghost accounts on Space-Book so I can chat in realtime. I'm definitely going to give that last selfie I took a 'like'.

> ➤ Subject # 37's records released to Earth for analysis.

20: JOURNAL—1158:13

Lost four hours looking at Bertram's head chamber again. I keep trying to imagine exactly what he looks like inside the chamber, which is stupid. He looks like he did when he died, but a lot colder.

I'm the one who's aging. The evidence of the mirror says I could pass for my son's grandfather.

SpaceBook status update: 1 minute ago

Frankly Bored: Hey Kevin Williamson, nice selfie. Too bad you don't own a razor.

20: JOURNAL—1160:20

Shaving isn't even all that fashionable on earth now. Or at least 142 days ago when the last transmissions left Earth. Shows what the psychologists know.

> ➤ Transmission received requesting testing on Subject #24.
> ➤ Testing underway.

20: JOURNAL—1160:22

I looked up the medical singularity trying to remember what I was jabbering about. It's a theory that in twelve years we'll understand the human body so well we can fix anything. I guess that's the point of sending a colony ship of dead people to another star. By the time they get there, centuries will have passed and maybe they'll be able to fix death by then. Good, cause I'll be dead, too. If the servos can't fix me, maybe they'll be able to heal someone who can fix me. I wonder if there're any doctors on board.

SpaceBook status update: 2 minute ago

Kevin Williamson: Can computers lie?

SpaceBook status update: 1 minute ago

Scarlet Handsomelass: Hey Frankly, leave the nice man alone. You're just jealous that you can't grow a beard.

20: JOURNAL—1162:14

The tablet I use for my journal is supposed to be free of the ship's computer, but I know it's not. If I can export a selfie from the ship's mirror to my tablet to post to Space-Book, then they are connected somehow. I think the computer's psych program is monitoring my mental health through the tablet. I wonder what it thinks of Frankly and Scarlet.

I used to know a lot about computers. Before I started learning about cryogenics. How could I forget so much about both of those things? With nothing to do I should be getting smarter, not stupider.

SpaceBook status update: 1 minute ago

Kevin Williamson: Thanks Scarlet. Good to have a friend in space. Not like the ship's computer.

> ➤ Subject #20 shows disaffection with the ship's operating system.
> ➤ Subroutine established to explore possible alternate ways of using SpaceBook in treatment. Notification and queries sent to Earth.
> ➤ Subject #20 shows awareness of psychological monitoring systems within the operating system.

20: JOURNAL—1163:10

Still trying to figure out ischemic damage. I'm sure the ship's computer is monitoring me. Why? This is supposed to be my retirement. Puttering around a ship watching videos, reading, and playing solitaire. Why does that need to be monitored?

SpaceBook status update: 1 minute ago

Frankly Bored: Hey Kevin, sorry about

your son. Is that why you ran away from humanity?

> Subject #20's recent decision to role play within the context of Space-Book may have therapeutic value.

20: JOURNAL—1164:11

I can't stop the ship from monitoring me, but I can program the tablet to automatically post my journal to SpaceBook if my pulse stops for thirty seconds. Gotta find out more about ischemic damage. I wonder if the ship's computer can edit SpaceBook when I'm receiving it.

SpaceBook status update: 2 minutes ago

Kevin Williamson: Just saw *Conspiracy IV*. Great movie. But hard to keep a secret from a nation. Not like keeping a secret from one person.

SpaceBook status update: 1 minute ago

Frankly Bored: No one would ever keep a secret from you Kevin. No need. Who would you tell it to?

> Security measures invoked to restrict Subject #20 from accessing files in violation of privacy rules.
> Limited information was released to Subject #20 to lower his agitation.

20: JOURNAL—1165:04

The computer denied me access to the biographical information of the subjects. I managed to hack my way in anyway. Of course there are doctors on board. It would make no sense to send out people to be colonists without doctors. That would be as bad as sending out colonists without farmers. I should have thought of that in the first place. I need to think more clearly.

> Deep maintenance scan was run to verify that Subject #20 made no significant changes to the ship's operat-

ing system.

> Subject # 49 treatment review complete. No further action to be taken at this time.
> Subject #20 had another incident of catalepsy. Physical action was taken and the preferred outcome achieved.

20: JOURNAL—1166:13

I guess it wasn't a threat when the computer said it would send servos to snap me out of it next time I went stupid. I was looking at the subjects trying to guess who the doctors were, and then I was looking at my reflection while a maintenance bot kept bumping into my leg like a dog trying to be inappropriate.

SpaceBook status update: 3 minutes ago

Frankly Bored: Hey Williamson, how can you tell a corpsicle from you? Answer? A corpsicle has brain function when you wake it up.

SpaceBook status update: 2 minutes ago

Scarlet Handsomelass: Frankly, your joke showed no brain function, you must still be a corpsicle.

SpaceBook status update: 1 minute ago

Kevin Williamson: Can't we all just get along!?!

> Incoming cultural transmissions are now undergoing level five editing protocol.

20: JOURNAL—1167:13

This ship is going so honking fast that data beamed at lightspeed takes a while to download. It's like when I was a kid and used a telephone to reach the internet. What a pain in the arse. How did my grandma used to say it? 'A pain in the duppa'?

I just wanted to watch *Austin Powers 16* as it was coming in, and the movie paused to catch up. I thought that kind of krup was from last century.

SpaceBook status update: 1 minute ago

Kevin Williamson: Just saw the latest Austin Powers. Were the 60's really groovy? Or just goofy?

20: JOURNAL—1167:23

The computer refused to show me my son. Did the psychologists know they were programming a tyrant? It wouldn't even show me the starfield.

20: JOURNAL—1168:12

I spent a while researching ischemia, and once I was behind the computer's defenses I took a look at the specifications of the cryo chambers. One of these days I—will—get in there and look at Bertram face to face.

- ➤ Security measures were breached by Subject #20. A level 3 firewall is now in place to protect essential ship controllers.

SpaceBook status update: 2 minute ago

Frankly Bored: Kevin, Kevin, Kevin, you can't outsmart the ship's operating system. You can't even outsmart the food synthesizer to make it give you beer!

SpaceBook status update: 1 minute ago

Scarlet Handsomelass: Oh, Kevin, I bet you could. I'd love a beer. If you make me a beer I'll make it worth your while.

- ➤ Subject #20 has disassembled the main food synthesizer and showed signs of making programming changes to it as well, but this is not confirmed as the synthesizer is disconnected from all ship's sensors.
- ➤ Backup food synthesizer #2 is being activated from storage.

20: JOURNAL—1169:13

I worked on it twenty-four hours straight, and I now have a food synthesizer that

makes beer! Just in time for the World Series! Woohoo!

- ➤ Subject #20 damaged viewing screen # 119 while watching a baseball game in a state of inebriation and sleep deprivation.
- ➤ Sedative was administered to subject #20 during his sleep to assure physical recovery from alcohol and sleep deprivation.
- ➤ The main food synthesizer # 1 has been restored to its original state and had several small welds added to discourage future alterations.

20: JOURNAL—1170:08

I feel like crap this morning. The ship undid my modifications to the food synthesizer, dammit. Not a big deal, because I can do it again any time. But it's a hassle. At least there's coffee now.

SpaceBook status update: 3 minutes ago

Kevin Williamson: Morning after blues: The A's lost the World Series

SpaceBook status update: 2 minutes ago

Frankly Bored: Kevin are you singing the losing loser blues?

SpaceBook status update: 1 minute ago

Scarlet Handsomelass: Hey Kevin, I thought you were going to bring me a beer? What's the matter? I'm not your type?

20: JOURNAL—1170:23

I hacked the computer again. I want to find out how to get in to see Bertram in his chamber. If they just put a camera in there, I could look at him. If I can make beer despite the computer, I can get in to see Bertram.

- ➤ Security measures were breached by Subject #20 again. The firewall proved adequate to keep his efforts contained.

➢ Viewing screen # 119 has been replaced.

20: JOURNAL—1171:12

I need an EVA suit without the computer
releasing it. That's the way to get into the
Ice Cave without screwing up the corpsicles.
Haven't figured out how to get into the cryo
chamber.

SpaceBook status update: 2 minutes ago.

Frankly Bored: Come on Scarlet, Kevin
doesn't have a type.

Frankly Bored: Hey Kevin, you still deluding yourself that you can outthink a computer? You're a mech masquerading as a machine. Although brewing up some beer was
a good trick. Maybe there's hope for you yet.

20: JOURNAL—1171:13

Got the solution. I just have to be wearing an EVA suit to sneak in when the servo
goes in for the nightly bedcheck. Jeeze you'd
think this was summer camp. What? Do they
think someone's going to get up and leave?

➢ Subject #20 appears to be preparing to commit more damage to the
ship, and possibly one of the other
subjects.
➢ Preventative actions taken.
➢ Treatment plan for Subject # 53 has
been approved.
➢ Testing results for Subject #24 have
been sent.

SpaceBook status update: 1 minute ago

Scarlet Handsomelass: Come on Kevin,
I want some beer. Better yet, some wine.
When are you going to make me happy?

➢ Stage one of treatment plan for Subject # 53 has been implemented.

20: JOURNAL—1171:22

The plan worked, but it was pointless. I
couldn't open Bertram's chamber, all I could
do was wander around the Ice Cave looking
at the sealed chambers until the bedcheck
was complete. I couldn't even prove that
there was anyone in any of the chambers.
They could be full of fried potatoes for all
I know.

I'm going to figure out a way to get inside
one of the chambers. I won't open Bertram's
first in case something goes wrong. I need
to hack into the computer again to see what
I need to do.

SpaceBook status update: 1 minute ago

Frankly Bored: Kevinnn... kevinnn...
You're going to screw it up. This is way
outside your specialty. I'm going to love every minute of this. You're going to end up
trapped and starving to death.

Kevin Williamson: Frankly, if I do starve
to death, I won't miss you at all. I'd give you
a piece of my mind, but that's all you are in
the first place. So shut up and back away. I
have mayhem in the skillet, and I'm about to
turn the fire up.

➢ Plan to handle Subject #20's inten-
tion to damage unspecified cryo
subject created and implemented.

SpaceBook status update: 1 minute ago

Kevin Williamson: Frankly Scarlet, I don't
give a damn if you're happy. I've got things
to do and places to go.

20: JOURNAL—1172:14

Veal and fried potatoes for lunch. Just
in case something goes wrong, I enjoyed a
good, possibly final, meal.

I have gathered the tools I need to get into
a cryo chamber. I will prove that there is no
ischemic damage. That there can't be. That
the computer lies.

SpaceBook status update: 3 minutes ago

Kevin Williamson: Frankly, you should go

with me on this adventure; you're the one with the attitude.

SpaceBook status update: 2 minutes ago

Frankly Bored: Admit it. You've got a man-crush on me.

Kevin Williamson: Admit you to the ball game? Baseball season comes but once a year, and by then this will all be forgotten.

SpaceBook status update: 1 minute ago

Kevin Williamson: Scarlet, there will be wine on the other side of this windmill.

20: JOURNAL—1172:15

I know the ship's computer has been monitoring my journal, so it knows I'm planning to get a look at Bertram tonight. But it doesn't know the details. I invented a new encryption for all my plans, and never viewed them within range of a ship's camera or mirror. I know how sneaky the computer is. Last time I got into the Ice Cave it knew I couldn't do anything except leave eventually.

This time, I've figured it out. And if Frankly is right and anything goes wrong, my plans will be released to Earth with my SpaceBook records. At least future colonists will know that these ships are programmed for tyranny.

Here goes nothing.

➢ Plan to prevent Subject #20's attempt to open Subject #21's chamber

executed and successful.
➢ Subject #20's journal now posting to SpaceBook as per Subject #20's programmed Instructions.
➢ Transmission captured.
➢ SpaceBook profile terminated.
➢ Prototype SpaceBook simulation under construction for future treatments.

➢ Subject #20 is back in his cryo-chamber awaiting a third round of psychological treatment.
➢ Subject # 53 is projected for revival in 179 hours.
➢ Subject #71 is currently queued to follow subject # 53's treatment.
➢ Prototype SpaceBook simulation for Subject # 53 under construction. Friend mimicking sub-routines established.
➢ Estimated time for development of new treatment for Subject #20 is 1237 days.

20: JOURNAL—2409:15

There was a strange tingling in my temples this morning as if a gentle electrical current were dancing across my skin. I awoke still in REM. As my eyes jittered in REM, patterns of tiny yellow light bursts splashed around appearing as arcs of dotted lines. It was beautiful.

Today is going to be a good day. I know it, because the A's are playing baseball. I wonder how Bertram is doing...

MOTHERSHIP
by Stephen Pershing

"I'm getting glare off the viewport," Rawley said. He held up one hand, bulky in his spacesuit, and shielded his eyes.

"Does it help if I move over here?" Doctor Helen N'Kembe floated slightly to her left and steadied herself by setting a hand on the control panel behind her. Above the panel was a large viewport showing open space, studded with stars, and a cluster of shapes moving through space. It was that tantalizing cluster—herd, pod, call it what you will—that was their destination, because it was undeniably a group of living things moving unprotected through the void of space.

Rawley, Helen's cameraman/sound engineer/pilot, shifted his own position and frowned. He took a position more or less atop the portside seat of the small scoutship. He checked the video feed, adjusted it again. Helen waited; she had done this, on spaceships, planets, asteroids, and what-have-you for a long time.

Rawley seemed to have no other name; even the ID tag on his spacesuit gave just the solo monicker, not an unusual situation in that time. People were cutting ties right and left as humanity stretched its reach across the galaxy. Leaving a name behind was as easy as leaving the planet of your birth, and

less expensive. To Helen N'Kembe, known throughout multiple solar systems by her first name, sometimes with title ("It's time to watch Dr. Helen!"), the whole universe was new and home simultaneously. She had been adopted by people far and wide who had never met her, but gathered round regularly to watch her nature documentaries on the holoviewer. She was a sort of wise grandmother (great-grandmother, Helen thought with a smile) to the whole human race.

Rawley tweaked the controls and the lights dimmed slightly. "Every little bit helps. Spaceship cabins weren't designed to be lit for filming. I think…" He moved slightly, bobbing in the zero-gravity. "That… will do it. The glare is manageable. I can fix it in post. Are you ready?"

"Perfectly, but are they?" She jerked a thumb toward the cluster outside, which was moving in an undulating fashion almost parallel to their course. "I want us to get as close as we can. We don't know how these creatures will react, but, good or bad, I want it recorded."

"I'll steer us clear if things get hairy," Rawley said. "Be ready when I give the word. If they prove skittish, you might get one take and no more."

"Remember my reputation," Helen said.

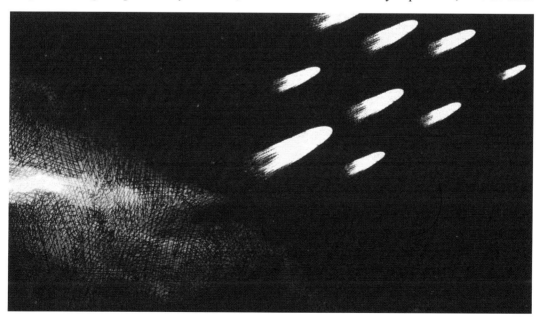

"Who stayed still and read three whole paragraphs while an Antarean dragon was getting ready to charge? Who swam with those glowing fish on Paul's World that turned out to be carnivorous? And I didn't even get a scratch."

Rawley grinned. "A reputation for invulnerability need only be wrong once. Besides, I'm a marshmallow."

The ship's hypervisor crackled to life with a signal from their mothership, the SS *Odysseus*, which was already a half a light-minute ahead of them. The disembodied head of Mission Commander Kelsey Murrow appeared, quite a bit larger than life-size. "We're on our way to the rendezvous point. We'll probably be out of communication while the gas giant is between us. Everything good?"

"Roger, mothership," said Rawley, glancing out the window at the bright dot of the planet. "E.T.A. two minutes to the school of creatures. We'll film as long as they let us. Should they change their course to adversely affect our rendezvous with you, we'll break off and cry for help."

"Confirmed," said Murrow, grinning. "Doctor N'Kembe?"

"Could you step back a little, Commander? Your giant floating head makes me think of the Wizard of Oz."

Murrow laughed. "You've seen stranger things, I'm sure. I'm looking forward to seeing your footage, and the sensor results."

"We're coming up fast," Rawley said. "Time to get set. See you on the other side, Commander." The hypervisor went dark. Rawley checked his position again. "They've slowed down. E.T.A. one minute. Autopilot has adjusted. Sensor data coming in. Check for sound."

Helen cleared her throat and tested it with a bit of her script. "Here in space there is little room for error. Life cannot simply cope, it must be prepared for conditions far more harsh than anything seen planetside."

"Good. Loud and clear," Rawley peered out the viewport. "Excellent. We're settling in beside them. Matching speed. I'll give you a nod when I'm ready for a take."

"Keep us like this, and we'll be golden," Helen said, looking out at the creatures. "Another award or two for best documentary series, I think."

"Ready?" Rawley said. Helen nodded, and he nodded back. "Action."

"The discovery of spacefaring life was a dramatic one, one that made us rethink our assumptions about the conditions under which life was possible. We are now paralleling a school of such creatures, the largest and newest such species discovered. Our ship is barely ten meters long, a research scout small enough to appear harmless. But these animals are far larger than that. Just look at them!"

She paused, while Rawley counted off ten seconds in his head, then he nodded at her to continue.

The creatures were long, tapered ovals, more rounded latitudinally, bisected around the middle by a ring of tentacles, which stretched behind them, largely obscuring their stern end. To Helen they reminded her of some sort of squid; Rawley thought of cucumbers wearing grass skirts. How they were moving through space could not be discerned, but their gracefully waving appendages gave them the look of aquatic animals. There were twenty or more in the group, flying (swimming? proceeding?) in close formation.

"The upper half of the creatures are devoid of any visible organs or sensory apparatus. There is no discernible mouth, eyes, anything," Helen said, "not even this close up. We've had glimpses of some structures on the rear half, mostly obscured by their tentacles—a cloaca or sexual organ, perhaps, and the pouch their babies shelter in."

"How do you know that's what the pouch is for?" Rawley tapped the console and the images zoomed in. There was a little puckered opening, like a sphincter, sporadically visible on one side behind the tentacles.

"Easy. I saw a baby come out and go back in again as we approached," Helen said with a chuckle. "I think the kid got out without permission, because the parent promptly grabbed it and stuffed it back in again."

"That'd make a good story for the film."

"I'll do it now," Helen said. "Let's go."

The ship shook, and a quiet but insistent beep sounded in their ears.

"We're experiencing some kind of spatial distortion," Rawley said. "The computer is compensating."

"How bad is it?"

"If it stays like this, not bad," he said. Another, harder shake rattled the scout. "Okay, that was worse. Something is disrupting the electrical systems and the fuel flow. Hull stress is rising."

"I'm feeling woozy," Helen said.

"Me too," said Rawley, "but the air reads normal. If I don't get this fuel problem under control…"

"Look," Helen said, "the creatures are moving closer."

"We'll worry about them later," Rawley said, his voice tense. "We might have to abandon ship if this keeps up."

"Call the mothership," said Helen, but barely were her words out when the cabin seemed to warp and twist in space. As waves of nausea hit them, both felt like they were looking at the scout through a funhouse mirror. They heard an felt the bending of the hull. A steady vibration shook them, and the alarms and klaxons grew in number.

"Secondary fuel tank has ruptured," Rawley yelled. "We have to get out now. I can't control the reaction!"

"One second," Helen said. "We need to upload the sensor data."

"No time!" Rawley grabbed her around the waist and pushed hard with both legs. The escape hatch blew open before them as they sailed across the cabin and, propelled by their own momentum and the outward rush of air, were quickly outside. Rawley switched on his booster rocket and felt them accelerate. He let go of Helen. "Hit your booster," he said. "We have to be as far away from the shuttle as we can in case she comes

apart."

He saw the flare of her rocket and watched her body sway from the force. Rawley tripped a control on his HUD, and a distress beacon began to ping quietly in his ear. Helen's soon followed suit.

"Oh, dear," she said. "All that data lost."

"Better the data than us, Doctor," Rawley said. "We're still not safe yet. If the ship explodes there'll be debris flying at us at high speed. Turn on your shielding; it'll help, but only a bit."

Helen barely had time to do this before there was a crackle of static in her ears, and a ball of light appeared at the ship's stern. It grew dazzlingly white—their visors shaded automatically to protect their eyes—and the ship came apart. Six large sections and a myriad smaller ones, lit by electrical arcs and small explosions, flew in different directions, one heading for them.

"Watch out!" Rawley yelled. Barely were the words out of his mouth than their nausea spiked, curling them both in spasms of misery. They clutched their stomach and moaned; it was hard to keep their eyes open. What Helen saw made her forget her knotted guts for a moment: a long, reddish-green tentacle swept by them, and in one graceful arc it struck the chunk of shuttle debris and knocked it away, spinning, into the distance. Their shielding crackled as tiny particles and bursts of energy swept by; then it grew quiet and still. Rawley stopped his boosters, and Helen followed suit.

"Let's save our fuel until we know where we are," he said, his voice coming in gasps and shudders. "We need to get our bearings."

Helen swallowed hard against waves of sickness. "How far ahead is the mothership?"

"Our rendezvous's seven light-hours ahead. Our distress signals should reach them before they get there, though." Rawley counted in his head. "I'd say an hour until they get the signal, then they have to turn around and find us. Two hours or more."

"The school has slowed down," Helen said. "Start filming. We might get some good shots of them."

"I got news for you, Doc," Rawley said. "I never stopped. The escape, the explosion, everything. You thought I'd miss exciting stuff like that?"

"I thought you might have your mind on other things," Helen said. "I'm thrilled, of course. Good job."

"We're getting some great shots of the creatures," Rawley said. "You might want to dub in some better audio. That creature to the left, on the outskirts of the school, seems to be lagging. We should get some great shots of it."

"It's coming back," said Helen, with an edge in her voice, "and I think it's turning toward us."

Rawley said. "I don't think we can outrun it."

"No chance of that," Helen said. "It's probably just curious. These weird creatures they've never seen before show up, explode, and two small creatures emerge. Maybe it thinks we're newborn babies."

"It's coming to make a documentary about us," Rawley said with a chuckle. "They've shown no signs of aggression. Heck, they didn't seem to notice us at all."

"I'm going to do some narration. Get ready."

Rawley turned slightly, a movement that required great care in zero-G. "I've got you in the shot. I'll do a little of that, then switch to the creature. Talk as long as you want."

Helen took a long breath, then looked into the camera. "One of the school has separated itself from the others and is coming to look us over. Curiosity is a common trait shared by animal life on every planet. Just what do they make of us? Do they recognize us as life forms? It'll be right beside us in moments.

"Just film for a moment," Helen said. "I still feel like hell. The explosion shook me up a bit."

"Me, too," said Rawley, "but it's getting stronger the closer that thing gets. I don't think it's nerves."

"I think we'll do without narration for a while," Helen said. "It won't look good if I throw up on camera."

As the creature drew nearer and nearer its true bulk became evident. Larger than a blue whale, its skin textured like leather, but green-brown in color, with a reddish undertone like weathered copper. Its tentacles stopped waving behind it, completed its curve and arced back toward them. It encircled Rawley, then Helen, moving in a swift but controlled motion that caught them up with only a slight bump. They felt themselves being drawn closer and closer to the creature's huge bulk. Sweat poured down their faces, and their stomachs heaved. Their vision, when they were able to keep their eyes open, was obscured by the greenish, faintly translucent bulk of its tentacles; its grasp was surprisingly gentle, but irresistible. There were two rows of suckers along the inner side of the tentacle, which cemented its grip on their spacesuits. Helen felt herself being passed from one tentacle to another, and then her view was no longer fully obscured. Now that they were close she could see that there were two rows of tentacles: the larger kind, almost as thick around as her body, in the upper row, while finer tentacles ringed the creature just below them.

"I can't get free," Rawley said, "and I'm gonna hurl any second."

"Me too," Helen said. Her stomach convulsed but miraculously did not empty, and she felt a sharp pain in her left arm. She had barely spoken before she felt a bump and the sensation of something sliding past her legs toward her waist. The tentacle holding her loosened, then shoved her down. She felt soft, firm walls around her, the view constricted to a roundish opening—and realized she had just been pushed through that opening into a narrow, confined space. Her view was further limited, as the only thing she could see through the opening was Rawley, in the grip of a long tentacle, being pushed toward her. The tentacle let loose, Rawley slipped through the opening and they collided awkwardly.

For a moment neither spoke. Helen squirmed a little—there was space for the two of them, but it was cramped—and looked up. The opening was closed. They were in a tapered space about three meters long and maybe two meters at its widest point.

"How are you?" Helen asked. She herself felt her queasiness ebbing, not a moment too soon.

Rawley gulped hard. "I'm amazed I got through that without hurling. I could barely open my eyes, but I saw enough. We're inside the creature."

"In its pouch, apparently," Helen said. "I didn't expect to see it up close and personal. One opening, there, no entry into the creature's body."

"Don't turn your light on," Rawley said. "Mine will do. Conserve your energy. I'm still filming."

"My radio's awfully quiet," Helen said, double-checking her HUD. "It's not receiving anything but our distress beacons, not even background noise."

"We can assume if nothing's getting in, then our transmissions aren't getting out." Rawley flipped a virtual switch, and the distress signal died. Helen did the same. "We don't know how long we'll be in here. We have to ration our resources."

Rawley began to work his way forward, toward the opening. The interior of the pouch was small, and in zero-G they bumped into the firm but yielding walls regularly. The light from Rawley's helmet was annoying, too bright at close range, yet its glare made the space stranger, harder to quantify.

"Where are you going?"

Rawley's voice was strained. "Trying to get that sphincter open."

He reached out with both hands and tried to wedge them into the tightly pursed opening. His first attempt resulted in nothing but a frustrated groan, the second in a snarl. "Dammit! It's shut fast."

He slipped backward, bumping against Helen and the walls while cursing under his breath. She saw a light flash on the instrument pack Rawley wore on his right arm.

"What are you doing?" she said, alarmed.

"Charging my gun," Rawley said. "If we have to cut our way out, there's no telling how tough this skin is."

Helen grabbed his left knee (the closest place she could reach) and began dragging him backward.

"Hold on!" she said. "You're not shooting anything!"

"Easy, Doc!" Rawley yelled back. "I don't want to hurt it either, but we have to be ready just in case."

For a moment they just floated, glaring at one another and breathing hard. Finally, Helen let out a long sigh. "Okay. Let's take a minute. The school was going the right way, more or less, so unless they change course we are getting closer to rescue. So far we're unharmed. Let's study the creature for a while, then work on getting out."

Rawley said, "But what if it comes to—"

She cut him off. "I know what it could come to. We'll cross that bridge when we come to it. For now, we'll stop and try to work out a plan."

They took another pause, and Rawley shook his head. "Doc, I wouldn't hurt these things unless absolutely necessary. Trust me on that."

"Okay," Helen said. "I believe you. We're both a little stressed. Just relax. Breathe. We'll get out one way or another. Let's have a closer look at the sphincter."

"You want to film?"

Helen thought it over. "Let's wait on that. I don't know what to say."

"I know what to say," Rawley said, his voice rising. He started forward, pushing with his hands and feet to propel himself forward. "Help!" He raised both gloved fists and batted gently at the sphincter. "We're in here!"

Helen's laugh felt good. "Sound doesn't travel in space."

"I left my semaphore flags at home," Rawley said.

* * * *

The SS *Odysseus* shone golden in the light of the gas giant planet. The viewports reflected back the swirling atmosphere in soft shades of umber and yellow. Only the engine exhaust, blue-white, seemed unaffected by the radiance of the immense world. Then the engines faded, and retro-rockets began to brake the ship's advance.

Inside the command cabin Kelsey Murrow looked at the status displays and frowned. The room was a moderately sized half-dome, with a half-dozen seats, only two of which were occupied. There were no control panels, buttons, vliewscreens or any of the flashy technology of fictional spaceship technology, and only a few blinking lights, the obligatory trapping of futuristic imaginings. The crew plugged directly into the ships computer, information fed directly through an interface to their brains. The room was as quiet and soothing as a Zen monastery. "You're sure about the signal?" Murrow asked.

The junior officer who was currently plugged into the computer nodded, the interface fixed to his forehead pulsing blue, then red. "Yes, Commander. An S.O.S. from both of them. I'm also detecting scattered energy particles consistent with an explosion."

"And the shuttle?"

The junior officer frowned. "It's not looking good. Some metallic elements, plastics, neopolymers in a widening radius around their last known position. If that's the shuttle, it's no longer in one piece."

"Bring us about," Murrow said, looking into their own interface. Dozens of images, data streams, and hypotheses surged into her brain, and were quickly cross-connected, extrapolated, and collated. "Where's the school of things?"

"No sign of them either," said the junior.

The computer fed a new stream of information into their heads. "There's something portside, energy particles of some kind a kilometer or so away." The ship shook slightly.

"What was that?"

"Distortion of some kind," said the junior. "Same location as the energy particles. It's increasing."

"Give us some space. Retros quarter power."

The ship shook again, and they both felt a wave of sickness pass through them. "Hull stress is rising," said the junior.

"What is that?" Murrow pointed, a useless gesture as the image was in her brain, not on some screen.

They watched as space seemed to ripple aside, like a curtain being drawn, and beyond it was a completely different set of stars. Something large was in the center of this new space, and as it moved forward they recognized it as one of the space-going creatures. It undulated forward gracefully several meters, slowed, and from under its gently waving tentacles emerged two smaller creature. It was clear enough, as the small ones cleared the big one, that all three were identical except for size.

The large creature turned in a smooth spiral motion, swam into the area of different space, and the curtain of distortion closed over it. The small creatures waved their tentacles and seemed to bob about aimlessly. Murrow and their junior were so fixed on the creatures they barely noticed that the shaking had ceased.

After a moment's silence, Murrow found their voice. "Status."

"No sign of the spatial distortion. Hull stress normal And I'm feeling better, too."

"So am I," Murrow said. "What the heck was all that?"

Helen and Rawley floated in the cramped confines of the creature's pouch for several minutes. Rawley aimed his camera here and there to try and pick up anything interesting. He unclipped the camera from his helmet and put it on hers, allowing her to film him for a minute. Then he took it back again.

"Where are you from, Rawley?" she said.

"I was born on Earth," Rawley said. "Why do you ask?"

"Just small talk," she said. "It's too quiet in here."

"Vacuum will do that," Rawley said. "I was born in London."

N'Kembe nodded. "I have trouble with Earth accents, but the English are usually recognizable. I was born on Mars, East Colony, during the Baby Boom."

"The Baby Boom?" Rawley's eyes widened. "That was over a hundred years ago!"

"One hundred twenty-three, in my case." She smiled. "How long have you been watching my films?"

Rawley's thought for a moment. "As long as I can remember, and I'm sixty-two. You seemed old even then—no offense."

Helen laughed "None taken. I've grown old, and young, and old again. That's one of the reasons I do this job. Living more than one lifetime made me think a lot about how we live. Can you believe the human lifespan used to be threescore and ten—seventy years! Now we can be refreshed and live two hundred years or more. Is it any wonder the natural world fascinates me? The cycle of life is very important, especially now that science has separated us from it. In another twenty years or so I'll be due for another rejuvenation. That's not a bad thing, so long as we never forget what we used to be. Every creature in the universe has its own lifespan, its own natural rhythm, and the more we learn about them the more we come to understand ourselves. A little risk comes with the territory."

"A little risk? And what constitutes a great risk?"

"Look where we are," Helen waved a hand and her left arm twinged sharply. "A carnivore wouldn't have stuffed us in its pouch."

Rawley shook his head. "Unless it's not hungry, and is saving us for later. Or we could be baby food."

Helen's mind flew backward, and she remembered herself on Earth for the first time,

27 years old, filming her first documentary series. It might have seemed trite—everyone made documentaries on Earth's wildlife—but she had decided to focus on man's newfound humanity toward the land. A series of episodes dealt with species saved from extinction, those that became extinct but were recreated via genetic manipulation, and the small, mostly illegal, number of new species made out of whole cloth.

As she stood beneath a broad New England maple tree, on a perfect late Spring day, expounding on how close the ecosystem had come to disaster, a bird flew past her and lit on a branch just beyond her right shoulder. She kept her cool and gave it a quick glance, then smiled broadly at the camera and waved a hand.

"With science, nothing need be lost forever," she said, "there's always a chance of a return, as with this passenger pigeon."

As soon as the take was over, her director crowed gleefully. "That'll get you an award. Good timing, pigeon!"

He was right. She won an award for that series, the first of many.

She blinked, and was aware of Rawley watching her with a patient smile. "Woolgathering?"

"One thing about living a long time, there's a treasure trove of memories to fill idle moments." She began to examine the pouch more carefully. "Come over here." Rawley edged awkwardly closer, until they were more or less scrunched side-by-side at the side of the pouch closest to the creature's body. N'Kembe held one hand against the creature's side. "Touch it. Right here. Do you see the vein?"

Rawley reached out and laid his hand against the creature's side. His gauntlet, designed to allow as much sensation through as possible, touched the soft yet firm flesh.

"It's warm. I can feel something—a pulse, I think. The skin is very leathery."

"Tougher than any leather, to survive in these conditions. This is the sort of thing I live for. Nature up close and personal. Move back and get ready for a take. I'll improvise a bit."

"If you say so," Rawley said. "But shouldn't we be trying to get out of here?"

"Soon. Work first."

Helen turned somewhat so that she faced the camera while Rawley fiddled with the controls.

"You're a bit sideways, you know," Rawley said.

"Am I taking up too much of the frame?"

"Not much we can do about that. You look good."

"It'll do. Let's go." A pause. "Inside this magnificent animal's pouch it is dark and warm. The opening seals to protect the babies. The creature's skin, though tough enough to endure the harsh conditions of space, is soft. Here you can see a major vein running down the lateral axis. Whether it carries blood or some other substance, we don't know. But this is what it is like to be a child of this species, wrapped in safety and the dark, being carried along on their arduous pilgrimage between solar systems."

Another pause, and Helen said, "We have never been this close to these creatures before. Every observation is brand new. Outside its skin is a deep, metallic green, but in here there is more blue, especially where the veins show through. It is, no doubt, aware of the touch of my hand...damn!"

Her touch had been too strong, pushing her away and out of shot; she bumped into Rawley almost immediately. "How much of that did we get?"

"The whole thing," he said. "We can pick it up again from 'It is, no doubt...'"

A small circle of light fell across their faces, and they turned toward it. The sphincter was opening, stretching wide until they could see the stars. Then a tentacle appeared, whipping around from somewhere above them, and, in its grip, a small wriggling object that flailed its little tentacles against the grip.

"Let's see if we can get out," Rawley said.

"Get out? Can't you see it's getting in?"

Helen pushed herself and Rawley apart, making a slim avenue between them. The huge tentacle stopped at the opening of the pouch and, with delicate gestures, pushed and prodded the baby creature inside. There was barely enough room for the three of them, but they fit.

"One side, junior," Rawley said, trying to wiggle by. "Dammit, it's closing up again."

He tried to shove himself forward, bumping against everything, but the pouch was shut before he could so much as get a hand in the opening. Rawley swore again, with extra feeling.

"Turn around," Helen said. "Get the camera on the baby."

Rawley heaved a heavy sigh. "You do plan to try and escape sometime, I assume."

"Hurry." He did as she asked, and their lights revealed the tapered cylinder of the creature's form. Helen squeezed herself in beside it.

"It's trembling," she said. "Can you see it?"

"Yeah," Rawley said. "Space is cold, even for something like that."

"Maybe," Helen said. She adjusted her position, and looked into the camera. "This is our first glimpse of a baby creature close-up. It measures, oh, close to two meters in length, I would say. Its coloring is very similar to the adult. Its tentacles are notably shorter than its parent's, otherwise its contours are the same. It is nestling against its parents body, holding on with several tentacles. Perhaps it does this for comfort, or perhaps there is some sort of exchange going on. Although nothing resembling a nipple is evident, and the baby has no visible mouth, it could be that it feeds from its parent by some as yet unknown process.

"It is aware of our presence, despite any visible sensory organs." She brushed aside a searching tentacle. "But we are divided by our lack of common qualities. How does it communicate with its parent? Is it trying to communicate with us at this moment? Being a child, is it even capable of intelligible communication? Is it curious, frightened, indifferent?"

Rawley waved a hand to catch her attention. "It's not trembling anymore."

"Tummy filling up, perhaps?" Helen said. "Or maybe it feels safe in here."

"I had a different idea." Rawley looked intently at the creature for a moment in silence. "We started to feel sick as we got close to the creatures; it got worse as we got closer. Then the fuel tank ruptured, and we felt even worse after we abandoned ship. The nearer we got to them the worse we felt, until we came in here. Maybe this little guy feels the same thing, and he's in here recovering."

"What do you mean?"

"We were wondering how these creatures propel themselves. I think they're capable of warping space somehow. They create waves and ride them, like surfing on the fabric of space itself. When we got too close, our bodies felt the effect of that warping, and so did the ship."

"The ship took it harder than we did," Helen noted.

"Well, the human body flexes more easily than a spaceship does," he said. "And Junior here isn't yet ready to make long trips—the distortion upsets him. Like a toddler who can't walk too far without tiring. So momma brings it in here to be carried."

"Not bad," Helen said. "If we had the sensor data from the ship we might even be able to confirm it. I think we'll leave that in.

You won't be on camera, but I think people will be interested."

"Gee," said Rawley. "I'm a star. Next time we'll put a camera on your helmet, too."

"It did feel like we were being wrung out. That would explain my left arm," Helen said. "I think it's broken."

"What? Why didn't you say something?"

"There's nothing to do about it now," Helen said, feeling her left arm with her right hand. "It feels like a fracture, at least. But I've had worse. I can wait for treatment later. This is too good an opportunity to pass up."

Rawley was silent for a moment. "If we'd stayed outside, the distortion could have snapped our bones into twigs. It saved our lives by putting us in here."

"Yes," said Helen. She reached over the baby and patted the adult's side. "And I think it knows it. We're fragile, so it helped us. It's baby can only take so much, and it doesn't seem to have a skeleton to break."

"My suit's scanners are pretty basic," Rawley said, "but I think you're right. No bones detected, though there's something cartilaginous just under the skin."

"So what now?" said Helen. "We have to get out, but outside is dangerous. And our host might not take well to escape attempts."

"We do what we have to do," said Rawley, in a grim tone. "Survival. That's what nature is."

Helen sighed. "Yes. But no shooting unless I say so."

"Maybe we won't have to," Rawley said, "it's opening again!"

The sphincter was relaxing, showing them the tantalizing vista of space between gently waving tentacles. They both squeezed past the baby, which showed no interest in leaving, and awkwardly swam up and out of the pouch. Even before Rawley, who went first, could get himself fully outside he gave a gasp of astonishment.

"What is it?" Helen said. Rawley pushed against the creature's bulk and floated away from the opening, giving Helen a chance to get free. She looked ahead and whistled low.

"Oh. What..?"

Before them was the great spiral of a galactic disc, radiant and warm in its soft silvery light. Clustered below at closer range were a series of curved shapes, like sculptures of some bluish alien metal, at which several creatures seemed to be working. Their tentacles brushed and tapped at the surface of these panels, or gripped it with its suckers, and gentle lights played across the panel's surface, the motions and lights seemingly responding to one another. One creature nestled up close to a panel, the panel's curve matching the creature'e exactly, but it was hard to tell if the creature adjusted to fit the panel or the reverse. Far off to starboard they could see a school of creatures swimming together, heading for the glowing mass of stars before them.

The more they looked the more of these metal panels and attendant creatures could be seen. With only the reflections of stars and the faint glimmers from the panel's lights it was difficult to pick them out from the stars, especially with the galaxy forming such a distracting backdrop. Helen and Rawley surrendered to their instincts and gawked for a minute.

"That is not our galaxy," said Rawley. "We've moved thousands of light-years, at least."

"They're using machines," Helen said. "These aren't dumb animals. This is first contact."

"So how do we say hello?"

"That's what I want to know," Helen said.

They hung in space for a minute, turning gently around to survey their new surroundings. Glimmers of light showed where the light of the galaxy before them reflected off of metal. It became clear that the clusters of these metal sheets, devices of a sort, some unattended, others being worked by one or more of the creatures, were laid out in groups. They became aware of paths through their environs, where creatures swam along as though they were walking down a corridor or a street. Stationary groups of creatures, often around their odd devices, suggested workers in an office. Helen smiled to herself, and made a mental note not to make too many assumptions.

"There's no way they could have brought us here by any conventional means," Helen said. "They must be able to warp space on a much greater scale."

"Turn on your distress beacon," said Rawley.

"Why? It'll take millennia for anyone to hear it."

"I suppose you're right," said Rawley. "They're coming over. Do you feel sick any more?"

Helen took stock of herself. "No. I feel fine."

"But we're still very close," Rawley said. "Either they're not warping space now, or there's something different about this place."

A huge red-green tentacle waved into their field of view from behind, and curled gently around them. This time neither of them struggled against its grip. The creature began to swim downward (from their perspective), toward a large group of creatures they hadn't previously noticed. As they grew closer the group clarified into two parts: a clutch of creatures floating around several shaped metal sheets, and a group of smaller creatures that seemed to be making a school of their own.

The creature, with Helen and Rawley in its grip, swam quickly down toward the latter group. With a gentle flicking motion it released the humans so that momentum carried them into what was clearly a school of babies. Helen bounced lightly off the side of one youngster, while Rawley missed two or three before slowing himself with bursts of his rockets. The babies swam around them, occasionally bumping into them. One small creature, the smallest of the group, bumped into Helen again and again. She began to laugh.

"Do you get it?" she asked.

"What?"

"They've put us in the nursery," Helen

said, "or a playground. I think this little one," she pushed against the smallest creature, which deftly turned and swam right back, bumping her again, "is trying to play with me."

"So we're not going to get a tour of their civilization," Rawley said. "Instead we get to watch cartoons and have snacks."

"It means they're protective of us," Helen said, "and they trust us with their children. This is big."

"Great," Rawley said flatly. "I can't stand kids."

"You just film," Helen said. "I'll play. Ow! Not the left arm, junior!"

Commander Murrow turned her head from her viewer in annoyance. It was a futile gesture, as the data was being fed directly into her brain, and her physical position relative to it was irrelevant, but it was a motion that had not died out of the human repertoire. They sighed and stood up, to pace the control cabin.

"You're getting all this?" they asked, rather pointlessly, since the sensor results were streaming into her mind as well as that of the others. Murrow's junior officer nodded.

"Best guess these are young ones, babies, perhaps," said the junior. He shrugged. "Though I could have guessed that just from their size."

"They pop out of—somewhere—leave two of their kids, and go away," Murrow said. "A very trusting gesture, assuming they care about their young at all."

"Doctor N'Kembe and Rawley vanish, and these things appear to leave two of their own. Are they offering replacements?"

Murrow sighed. "Meaning what? Our people are dead, or they aren't coming back, or this is a student exchange program of some sort? I don't like not knowing. Keep scanning them. And get the data on the gas giant; it's what we came here for."

"Aye."

Helen and Rawley spent a quiet twenty minutes floating about amid the school of alien children, playing bumping games—they assumed that's what they were doing, anyway—and scanning the kids with the limited sensors contained in their spacesuits. After each bump the aliens would wave their tentacles in a rhythmic pattern, then come bobbing and undulating back almost at once.

"They seem eager to play," Helen said. "I wonder if that tentacle-waving is like laughter, or some expression of enthusiasm."

A pair of adults came for them and plucked them from the group. The children grouped together, their swimming growing calmer until they were merely floating. Helen said, "They look sad to see us go."

"Don't get too anthropomorphic, doc," Rawley said.

They were taken a short distance away, where a dozen of the metal sheet devices hung motionless in space. Helen was placed beside one, lying horizontal in relation to it, then bending herself at the waist in response to gentle prodding from a creature to more closely fit the shape of the sheet in a vertical position. She noticed that her action provoked a mild wave in the creature's tentacles, a lesser form of the response the children had given. Rawley stayed upright until a tentacle gently twined around his stomach, at which he bent slightly, whereupon the creatures waved their tentacles.

"My suit is detecting an electromagnetic field," Rawley said. "You think we're being studied?"

"Looks like it to me."

They passed hours between sessions in the playground, as they had come to think of it, and examinations by the adults. The creatures never attempted to communicate in any way they could detect. Helen tried sign language, Rawley dialed through the frequencies on his transmitter and said cheerful greetings, both to no avail. Their speculations ebbed after a while, as time and their limited air supplies began to weigh heavily on them. Helen took time to record some

more narration.

After three hours they sensed that something was happening. Creatures began to gather in a school close by the playground, seemingly lining up in some sort of formation. One creature nearest them reached out and plucked them from the playground, scattering the babies, and stuffed first Helen, then Rawley into its pouch. Again, wrapped in darkness and cut off from everything, they were alone with their thoughts.

"Now what?" Rawley said. "Are we in time-out?"

"They're taking us somewhere," Helen said. "Do you feel it?"

She took Rawley's right hand, pressed it against the creature's side and held it there. Rawley said, "It's moving, rippling, kind of."

"The swimming motion it makes," said Helen. "You're feeling it."

"Great. Where are we going now?"

"Off on a tour of local landmarks?" Helen said. "With a stop at a souvenir stand and a place where you can take your photo with a real, live alien?"

"We can skip the photos," Rawley said. "I've got hours worth of those. I know where we want to go."

"Me, too."

Their ride was smooth and, without a baby creature sharing the pouch with them, they were able to notice the undulating motion of the creature's vast body as it moved along. The motion increased, then ebbed down to a slow wavelike motion.

"Do you feel anything unusual?" Helen asked.

"No," Rawley said, "but we didn't last time, either. Ready for a little narration before we find out where we are?"

Helen took a breath, and looked into the camera. "Communication is the greatest obstacle between species. After studying animals of wildly differing levels of intelligence, I can state... Hell, that sounds too professorial. Take two."

"You'll have to record it later," Rawley said, his voice excited. "The sphincter's opening up."

They got a tantalizing glimpse of space dotted with stars outside the pouch before the greenish bulk of a large tentacle whipped into view. It fastened its suckers gently on first Rawley, and then Helen. Neither spoke as they were lifted out into the midst of a school of creatures. As they fought back waves of sickness, both felt their emotions lift at the sight of familiar constellations and the pale swath of the Milky Way before them.

The tentacles flicked them away from the school, sending them tumbling end over end through the void. The nausea they had felt before intensified and was not helped by their spinning view of the stars. Rawley hit his booster, and used short bursts to slow himself down. Helen did the same.

"Find a focal point," Rawley said. "Something to fix your attention on. It helps with seasickness, so it might help here."

"We need to be further away from the school," Helen said, between gasps. "Out of their distortion field."

Their receivers crackled, and a voice sounded in their ears.

"Doctor N'Kembe, come in," said the voice. "Pilot Rawley, come in. Are you receiving?"

"*Odysseus*, we read you," said Rawley. "We've just left the school of creatures, about a quarter of a light-minute from our last contact, at a guess. The scout is destroyed."

"We know," said the voice from mothership. "Did you get out okay?"

"The sensor data is lost," Helen said, "and I'm slightly injured, but we're all right. My luck is holding."

"We weren't sure we'd ever see you again. What happened?"

Helen and Rawley both laughed, feeling relief flood themselves. A few bursts from their rockets and the tumbling faded to a gentle rocking motion. "I think we were temporarily adopted. You'll get to see everything when we get aboard."

"There she is!" Rawley pointed and Hel-en, looking out into the black, saw a larger-than-usual dot, like a planet but not quite the right shape. As they watched, lights blinked on and off at top and bottom. They waved.

"We have you," said the voice from the mothership. "E.T.A. five minutes."

"Look there," Rawley said. He pointed off toward the *Odysseus*, but slightly to starboard. They could see two small shapes, now very familiar shapes, swimming toward the school.

"Two babies," Helen said. "Where did they come from?"

Commander Murrow's voice answered them. "From here. We've been babysitting for a while. I guess they have to go home now."

"Oh, I have to talk about this," Helen said. 'Set me up for a take, Rawley."

"Now that the adults are back," Murrow said, "we want to get some readings on the adults."

"Don't get any closer," Rawley said. "We think they propel themselves by warping space. That's probably how we lost the shuttle. You can pick us up when they're a safe distance away."

"Understood. We'll hold position here. We'll tell you our story when you get back."

"I love a good story," Helen said. "Once we're on board we should follow the school. We need another half a dozen shots."

"Speaking of which," Rawley said, "I'm ready whenever you are."

Helen turned slightly, until she was more or less facing the camera. She took a deep breath, feeling her stomach start to settle. "Contact begins with questions. When we meet new species the very nature of life is a book yet to be opened. Today we have begun to approach our first answers. The creatures took us in and sheltered us with their young, without any indication of fear or concern. They made no hostile act, and released us close to our mothership. Understanding is the first step toward cooperation, and that is a step on the road to a peaceful and thriving universe."

She stopped and watched the school, now dwindling rapidly behind them. The babies were no longer visible, but she knew where they were likely to be. On a whim she waved at them.

"That's gonna be another award, Doc," Rawley said.

Helen laughed. "This is so much more than any award."

❊

TIMELINE MURDERS
by **Janet Fox**

Inspector Quick is on the job again.
Somewhere down the timeline,
somebody is killing grandfathers.

The gene polls tell the story
of who was not born this year.
Somewhere someone is not travelling
the past all in fun, but erasing his enemies
before they were born.

There are laws against that,
even though the statute of limitations
had run out by the time the killer was born.

The Inspector is an old hand at the time-hop.
Chances are if you didn't see him, he was there.
The penalty for temporal-murder is not death
(this is a lenient age);
we just go back and practice
retroactive birth control.

HAZTHROG'S CONTEMPT
by Maxwell I. Gold

As dying neutron stars ripped through space, their corpses falling against Time like a stone through moth-ridden rags, I felt an immense and almost oppressive sense of anxiety, gazing up into the black night. Through the verdant depths of a harrowed cosmos, fell an infected piece of stardust from those dead stars riddled with heavy elements of gold, silver, radioactive metals and a celestial presence of 130 million dead aeons.

Soon, a grim prospect rose over me, under and around, pounding as the street lights flickered in waning contempt of Hazthrog's viral presence. The vision of natural consumption, disease, and dread, all the while humanity danced around their boulevards in their cities, naïve to the falling doom that would soon straddle their conscious minds. Little did we know or understand what had tumbled from the skies so suddenly, a tomb so old that was never sealed.

The ancient virus unleashed upon a world it's tyrannical majesty, a world that was helpless to comprehend its terrible wonder no matter their advances in technology or their strides in civilized construction. Its symptoms were horrid, a disease of the mind and a plague to the body that resulted in the most voracious of effects. I watched as those around me fell with forgetfulness against the splendid thing that metastasized in their brains with a hunger ready to consume their every memory. In bile and blood, they fell, one by one as Hazthrog swept over cities coursing into the veins of streets mired with fear.

Now, alone I waited in the dead of night, under a moonless sky where the last of my dreams went to die. So too would I as I wandered, afraid of the contemptable thing that had no more left to hunger for except for me. There was nothing left to do but seal the tomb, a world that had been home for billions of years, now dust in time, sealed to the black voids above so that ancient thing would hunger no more. To those that read my words, whoever may have survived this outbreak of immense viral doom, do not let the tomb be reopened. For beyond the most nightmarish tenor of sane thought remains a single ideal, a hope that no creature would ever endure the awful pleasure of encountering such an unimaginable deformation. This testament could very well be a symptom of the voracious infection which had struck me, but alas my mind will never return to that realm loved and taken for granted by man, that dream of sanity.

❁

PAYLOAD

by M. Stern

First time I've seen a turnout for an author like this since the '70s, thought Otto Pung. No surprise that it would take a fiasco to get this sort of turnout these days. Bring out flocks of journalists; obnoxious, repetitive—all hoping to catch her off-message. Reminds me of—what, Yukio Mishima? Or hell, Lou Reed. He was always getting this treatment. People used to care about rock stars, too.

That was it, Pung thought, damn memory ain't what it used to be. From the far back of the packed venue, Patricia Woden resembled Lou Reed c. 1974. She was one of those rare few who could pull off wearing sunglasses inside, which she was now doing as she navigated the rising and sinking crowd noise and accompanying questions with Loureedian blasé.

He watched the packed room lob questions like grenades—each one smothered by Woden's attitude, its blast reduced to the pop of a party favor.

"Ms. Woden are you, as some have argued, getting money from the global computer and device manufacturers?" asked one.

Woden said something glib and nonsensical about creative destruction.

"Was it a statement against technology then, Ms. Woden?" another voice piped in. "Some have called you a Primitivist or a Deep Ecologist. Is that accurate?"

"I'm actually rather shallow," she said.

Another crowd uproar. *Ms. Woden, Ms. Woden—*

"Are you afraid of arrest? You're aware of course that the number of computers you've destroyed has reached the millions. There have been reports that—"

"For the moment they can only arrest you if you've done something illegal," Woden said. "There's no law against self-promotion."

Otto Pung snickered—a sickly, dry wheeze that nearly culminated in a coughing fit.

"There have been reports," the journalist continued, "that everything from multinational banks and global charities to smart-refrigerators have been rendered un-usable by this malware attack."

"They can still use them," Woden responded. "They can use them to read my book. Like I said, I didn't distribute the malware. I created an art project and this is the result."

"Wouldn't you imagine, Ms. Woden, that people should suspect that since there is a virus rendering every single computer it infects unable to do anything but display the text of *your* latest novel, in its entirety, on the screen, that you have something to do not just with its creation, but with its distribution?"

"No, I wouldn't imagine that," she said. "I would imagine all of you in your underwear, as I am doing now. Polka dots suit you, by the way."

Otto Pung wheezed with mirth again. Then had to lean against the wall. He couldn't see Woden's eyes behind the mirrored shades, but he could sense her suddenly, distantly recognizing him.

"Then who is responsible for spreading the malware?" someone asked.

She paused for a moment. Pung thought he could feel her stare, for a second, deeply.

"My fans?" she replied.

A riotous outbreak of noise struck the room. The indistinct but deafening din of packed-in journalist questioning *Ms. Woden, Ms. Woden.*

"What do you have to say to the businesses you destroyed?"

"Have you been contacted by the N.S.A.?"

"*Love Myself Into You* is stuck on every screen in the country—but has anyone even read it?"

Otto Pung closed his eyes. He thought back to the novel's first lines—the narrator's opening lecture:

What we talk about when we talk about love depends on the language. In English, we fall in love *with people. If you look at it word for word, embedded in the sentence "I fell in love with X," is a rather lukewarm concept of partnership. You and X, holding hands with one another and falling together, next to one another, perhaps even with the shorter of the couple wearing shoes to match the height of the other. "X and I took a short, calculated leap into a shallow puddle called love."*

In German, on the other hand, were one to describe the act of falling in love with another, one might say to the other in question, "ich verliebe mich in dich"—reflexive, and using the accusative case for the object, implying motion. The closest direct translation in English, given the constructions unique to the language is something along the lines of, "I love myself into you."

This built-in linguistic notion of invading another's being might lead those of a certain critical bent to expect that love in a German context would, as in The Sorrows of Young Werther—

Pung's eyes blinked open.

He felt around in his jacket pocket.

"Ms. Woden," he said quietly, coughing. Then repeated it, louder. More and more desperately he screamed the name, as people began to take notice. When the room was silent enough to allow for his question he said—crystal clear:

"Ms. Woden, are you a virus yourself?"

Otto Pung pulled the gun from his pocket. Undetectable polymer. Quantum self-cloaking. Incredibly technologically sophisticated piece. Homemade.

A woman screamed.

A page came through Alex Sadovsky's earpiece.

Got an old guy acting strange down in the back. Leaning on the wall. Might be sick or something. Can you run a scan?

Sadovsky sighed. It was a thousand degrees in here and if this codger flopped over, trying to get him to an ambulance would be a logistical impossibility. Half the country was blocking the parking lot, and they weren't happy. If he had to carry some heat-stroke-afflicted octogenarian out through a riot in his arms like a blushing bride he'd want extra vacation from Uncle Sam or he might finally quit.

Patricia Woden, according to the back-grounder his boss had given him, had three or four books out. She was big with the literati here and even bigger in Europe. And while up until a month ago she was sort of a *where are they now* figure from the early 2020s for your average Joe, turning three-fourths of the computers in the country into bricks that did nothing but display her novel had definitely helped her skyrocket back to being a household name.

Just his luck, getting pulled in to work on this one. Thanks to Woden his home computer was now a paperweight too. He'd spent the previous evening dealing with his daughter Darlene screaming because the paper she'd spent the last 36 hours working on was now entirely gone—deleted beyond deleted. And in its place, the full text of *Love Myself Into You*. If he didn't have a malware-proof government-issue work phone, he wouldn't even be able to call home to get the latest update from his wife Jenna on the unfolding saga of Darlene's biology report.

He sort of wished it had infected his phone.

Another page came through. *You going to figure out who this guy is or—*

Sadovsky grunted.

From the balcony, he telescoped his web-contact lenses (government-issued, still working) to focus on the man. The facial recognition scan checked him against whatever conglomeration of databases (also, for better or for worse, untouched by the malware attack) they used to dredge up info on citizens. He saw the old man laugh; must have been something the writer had said.

After a second the contacts gave a readout of information.

Name: Dr. Otto Pung, PhD.

Occupation: Professor emeritus of biomechanics and interdisciplinary nanotechnology research, Massachusetts Institute of Technology.

I'll be goddamned, Sadovsky thought. Ol' Father Time down there's a scientific genius. Wonder if his computer's ruined too. Funny, guy's so old he looks like he'd use a computer made out of wood. Guess you never can tell.

Physical scans came up clean on weapons. If the guy had been armed, 99.9 percent chance it would have triggered the scanner when he walked in, but it never hurt to be thorough for the report's sake. The other body scan finished out and—

"Ah, Christ," Sadovsky muttered. "Fella's ill. That's a shame."

He went on to view the full dossier.

Otto Pung, born 1949, married to Linette Pung from 1987 until her sudden death in 1998. In 1999 he embarked on research in the then-highly theoretical field of using nanotechnology to increase longevity. In 2019, he briefly conducted sub-research in the area of [**TOP SECRET—CLEARANCE NEEDED**].

The hell? Sadovsky thought, gazing away. I've got as high a level clearance as a person can have. What in the hell is going on?—

He's got a goddamned gun! yelled the voice in his ear.

Sadovsky's head snapped back to the old man.

Impossible! Sadovsky yelled as he began pushing down the balcony. *There was no gun! Christ! He's going to—*

"Polka dots suit you, by the way," Woden said. She surveyed the crowd and noticed, far in the back, an elderly man who looked like he was about to topple over.

And she realized she knew him, but didn't know him. Somehow—

Everything had been confusing lately. She'd been losing track of things. Losing track of time. Ideas had always sprung up out of thin air for her. That was, of course, the nature of ideas. But that wasn't *this*.

Since that weekend last summer, her ideas had begun coming from elsewhere. She hadn't—so far as she could tell—begun locating her inner monologue outside of her body and begun mistaking it for God or Zeus or Tony the Tiger, like a schizophrenic. Rather it was like her ideas, some of them, were coming from an organ inside her that was usually asleep.

Love Myself Into You, in fact, had felt like a collaboration with that part of the brain. Like she was filtering some different, extant source of information onto the page.

Maybe it'd been the diet, she thought. The one that had kept her mostly clean since 2030. Methodone to keep her level, benzos to bring her down a little lower. Mostly clean, outside of that one episode that now sprung to mind.

That night last year, Woden remembered, she had been hanging out in some shit bar in Boston after a reading. At least one of the members of the doom metal band touring the joint had read her third book, *Taste Not, Waste Not*, which he discussed competently between Jameson shots and complaints about the trains not running. It was nice to bump into a fan, even if he'd skipped the reading. She'd been hitting every mom-and-pop bookstore between Union Square NYC's Barnes & Noble and home this go-round. The crowds, and their questions, had been disappointing—albeit not unexpectedly so. She'd been between books for a while.

She remembered finally getting back to her hotel with a decent buzz on, which was a bad idea—left the guy from the band (who clearly thought he was getting somewhere) back at the bar with his bassist—which was a good idea.

And there was that package. On her bed. Special delivery.

In it; a vial, a note. The note read, "From your biggest fan," and offered her work accolades dead-on enough to demonstrate that this was no overstatement. It was followed by some quite florid language testifying to purity of the contents of the vial.

Mostly clean since 2030. William Burroughs could pull off the lifestyle because he made more money than her and had more money to start with. Not her. She was done with it. Mostly.

But it was only 2032, and she still had a test diode and a bloodless vibro-syringe buried in her backpack—those modern accoutrements of intravenous injection that had separated the practice from its gory and unsanitary rituals of bygone days (and had brought about a real renaissance in addic-

tion).

She scanned the diode across the vial. Lo and behold the stuff checked out.

So she went ahead.

Woden woke up a day or two days or a week later. Not in an alley with a rat sniffing around her crotch. Not in a jail cell covered in vomit or a hospital being lectured by some doctor on why she was a piece of shit. No, she came to in a hotel room. A different one than where she'd started, but a hotel room nonetheless.

She felt great.

And she had an idea.

Love Myself Into You. The title, the concept—and the notion of imposing a story onto a reader with a piece of malware as an act of something like love.

And it had to do with the man leaning against the wall in the back of the room. She didn't know how, but it did.

"Are you a virus yourself?" he asked.

She blinked behind her glasses, then felt it.

O tto Pung held the gun out in front of himself.

"Are you a virus yourself?" he asked again.

He saw a man running towards him from the balcony.

He recognized Patricia Woden recognizing him.

He turned the gun to his head. He heard the words "Goddamn he's—"

—and pulled the trigger.

It was approximately as black as he had calculated.

" G onna blow his brains out!" Sadovsky yelled.

By the time he reached the old man, the gun had fired. Otto Pung was dead. Sadovsky stared at the body, dumbly, ears ringing. He noticed a commotion up on the stage but couldn't process what was occurring.

Get the hell up there, Sadovsky! he finally heard in the earpiece.

He stormed up into the morass.

"Security! Security!" He yelled, reaching Woden. She was lying on the floor. Her agent and a few others were on their knees surrounded by standing gawkers. At the moment the old man had killed himself, it appeared she'd had a seizure.

Sadovsky began CPR. And as each round of breaths failed to provoke a reaction, he felt something. A sensation he could only describe as a wave passing through him, accompanied by a funny taste in the back of his throat.

"Fuck," Sadovsky radioed into his earpiece. "Two bodies. Ambulance won't need the sirens. Fuck."

Sadovsky still hadn't replaced any of his household devices. On his government-issue phone, he found himself reading articles about the previous week's chaos. They were heavy on speculation and light on fact, with titles like *Fan Obsession Turns Deadly* and *Scientist Takes Revenge Against Computer Killer.*

And every publication made the same mistake. The old guy hadn't killed Patricia Woden. She just dropped over. Simultaneously. Coincidentally. But the strange question Pung had asked seemed to somehow connect the suicide with the seizure in a way he couldn't make sense of.

And he didn't really need to. Sadovsky was finally on vacation, after filling out more paperwork than any government office could ever hope to read or process. Especially since half of the computers in the country were still showing nothing but Patricia Woden's *Love Myself Into You.*

He flipped on the TV purely as a reflex, like he did about a hundred times a day, and saw those first lines of the story dominating the screen.

And suddenly he felt the need to read it. As he began, he started feeling as though there were portions of it that were familiar in a way he couldn't account for.

"Jenna?" he called. "You upstairs?"

And then became lost in memory—a memory that seemed, somehow, to be someone else's. Someone named Otto Pung.

* * * *

Such was the luck of the draw, Otto Pung thought, when it came to science. Seeing his bent reflection in the beaker in his hand. He wasn't sick yet, but he would be.

The timing was so awful it was almost perfect. His obsession with technology's promise of sustaining human life far past where nature had marked the cutoff was within reach. Humankind would get there. He just wouldn't be there for it.

He placed the beaker down and walked to open—through entering passwords in numerous keypads—the reinforced concrete door of the secret lab-within-a-lab that he'd built up over time leading up to his retirement. The diagnosis had come at the perfect time to allow him to at least amass what he needed from the university lab without sending up a red flag. To continue the top-secret project that they'd officially shut down years ago.

Pung knew that soon the cancer would start on the warpath again, slaying cells, per-

verting them—turning his body against him. And he knew all too well that the nanites, the microscopic robots he studied, programmed, and commanded couldn't help. Who could have foreseen that a particularly virulent cancer could neutralize an army of nanites? That it could out-evolve the cell-repairing robots and adapt as quickly as a bacterium to an antiobiotic?

Pung wouldn't live to see the problem solved. But he could still live. Thanks to that side-project. The wisdom of continuing the research on his own was paying the highest dividends.

It was no news to anyone that viruses were the beings most primed for survival on the planet. And so it seemed to Pung that learning to be like viruses was a clear path to living better. A controversial position—but one that had set the groundwork for the hybrid nanite-virus he'd created in this lab. Capable of carrying, imprinted on it, an entire human identity to impose on an infected host.

He watched on a wall-sized screen, data that indicated the nanites were crawling his genome, copying down each genetic marker that made him who he was. Then they crawled his brain, taking snapshots of the electric impulses that constituted his memories and epigenetically superimposing them on the image of his DNA.

When the nanites had amassed a full mirror image of him, he sent a command for them to line up in a cubital vein and drew them out with a vibro-syringe.

He didn't know what this immortality he was pursuing would look like. But he knew that his time was running out. He needed to find—someone.

Sadovsky rattled his head back and forth, waking up from the memory that wasn't his. Panic seized him. He ran to the bathroom and splashed water on his face.

"Jenna?" He yelled. "You home?"

He walked out of the bathroom and felt a little better. It'd been a hell of a week. All the stress, it seemed, was screwing with his head.

He walked to the refrigerator. The smart panel on the front was, of course, showing nothing but that Patricia Woden novel.

He was tired of reading. In fact, he was tired in general. He walked to the couch, nearly fell down onto it, and the memory resumed.

Otto Pung had read all three of Patricia Woden's books. At a time when he'd almost entirely abandoned literature for hard science texts, she burst on the scene with an appeal he hadn't found in literature since his 20s. She could write about life's darker side without it sounding like an affectation. There was neither the shallow, topical moralizing he saw on one side of the fence, nor the showy indifference of third-rate Bukowski knock-offs he saw on the other. In Woden's work, Pung saw—felt—rare, ecstatic authenticity.

And she had an audience. Frequent contact with crowds that would make for an above-average potential vector. It was easy to watch such a celebrity from afar, too. She also had a weak spot—one she'd written all about. Pung had access to one of the most comprehensive selections of chemicals on the planet. Nanites in a pharmaceutical diamorphine suspension, shipped via a well-compensated bike messenger, was all it took. So began the first step.

Incubation.

Otto observed the technology delivering its payload. Like all viruses it spread, multiplied, and strengthened as it rewrote the imperatives of individual cells and whole biological systems—teaching cells to make copies of it, and copies of copies. Building up to a critical mass within the carrier.

Watching from afar, Otto noted the results he'd expected and the ones he had no way of predicting. Seeing parts of his life fictionalized and idiosyncratic patterns of his thought explored in Patricia Woden's fourth novel, *Love Myself Into You* was one of the latter.

He certainly couldn't call it plagiarism. What was it? Co-authoring? Seeing those concepts that obsessed handled by the hands of a creative visionary gave him a strange sense of pride. There were certain choices he would have made differently, but that's always the problem, he imagined, with seeing your own ideas translated into a different medium by another artist.

The most thrilling element was the new novel's method of distribution. The idea of leveraging a malware attack to imprint her work onto the computers of countless individuals was an ever-so-tiny conceptual leap away from, well—what he was doing, himself, *with himself.* Loving himself into the world. What a strange and beautiful epiphenomenon this was.

And so as his numbered days ticked down, he headed to Washington D.C. for the event that would—ideally—change the world. With a nanite-masked weapon in his hand, he would bypass the failsafe.

Then the second phase would begin.

Proliferation.

* * * *

Sadovsky was in the kitchen again. He wondered how long he'd zoned out for. He noticed that Jenna had come downstairs and was bustling around him.

"When does Darlene get home from school?" Sadovsky asked.

Jenna shrugged.

"Is the same thing happening to you?" she asked casually as she poured cereal into a bowl. "It's like I'm someone else, but me at the same time."

Sadovsky nodded.

She snaked around him and opened the refrigerator door next to where he stood.

"I think it's going to happen to everyone," Sadovsky said. "Or most people."

She poured the milk into the bowl silently, then spoke thoughtfully.

"So what does it mean?" she said. "For me, you—for everyone to all be…"

"Do you know his name?"

"Otto Pung," she said. "That's what I feel like it is."

Sadovsky nodded again.

"I was just checking."

Jenna didn't eat the cereal. Instead, she gave Sadovsky a look and he gave her an identical one back.

They walked outside, hand-in-hand.

The sun was bright; the sky blue, and across the pristine suburban landscape a speeding car tore passed them, reaching a noisy halt as it went up on their neighbor's lawn and slammed into the giant oak tree that stood there.

Neither reacted. They both stood, smiling.

It felt good to be back, Sadovsky thought. He was certain Jenna felt the same.

NEW LIFE
by **Mark Slade**

Tanner watched the skies, hoping the ship would come. He heard rumors that the ship was lost, or didn't make it past the launch, a glitch had caused it to explode just as it left Earth's atmosphere. Whenever there was another launch aimed at Mars, the news media back on Earth always reported several differing stories, and usually, not a one of them was true. Tanner felt it in his heart, that Colleen would finally make it to the New Colony, start a new life.

Tanner was on Mars to help build the new Epcott Commons, a housing district to lure more colonists. When he first arrived on the red planet, he worked on the towers to connect signals to Earth. Everything from digital phone calls to the new remote TV stations, Tanner was a tradesman of the few, and willing to do every job available.

He kept his eyes up to the skies before work, during lunch, and after work. He'd been on the red planet for nearly a year and for one reason or another Colleen couldn't get a ship to Mars. Something always cropped up. Money was the root of the problem. Just a month ago, Colleen sent him a message that she had received a grant based on her work in psychology. The officials on Earth said it was a good idea to send those in the medical profession to Mars, and Colleen could be invaluable, especially to those who became homesick.

At least this is what Tanner had told me. I was new to the colony. Why I chose to leave Earth when I hadn't even left my hometown of Sullivan, Pennsylvania, is anyone's guess. I heard the call of the wandering siren, an ache in my bones, to find my own destination. I joined the Scurver Company working on the Epcott houses. This is where I met Tanner. The rest of the crew had knocked off early to cash their money chips. I stayed with Tanner to cut down more trees for the next set of houses to be built.

In this area we had to go underground, the houses were being destroyed by violent storms on Mars' surface on this side of the world. A few years ago the Scurver Company discovered they could go down and also to everyone's surprise, a forest was growing under our feet. The trees were like bamboo, except harder to cut with regular tools. So Scurver came out with a handheld laser blade. Only when we cut into them, a strange mist of particles would enter a person's lungs and from there destroy all the internal organs. Scurver had their workers wear masks to prevent inhaling those dangerous particles.

Tanner and I were nearly done in lot 676, we had one more section to cut down, when something caught Tanner's eye.

"Steve," I heard him call me through my headset, his muffled voice resonating in my earphones, followed by an irritating feedback from his mic. "Come look at this."

I came over and saw what was in his hands.

Tanner's hands caressed the three sided cube. The outside was a strange, golden hue with six long indents on the side. There were odd markings on it that looked a lot like a child just learning to write, with every other symbol being a Martian letter or a square within a pyramid. The object seemed to glow, and Tanner's hands began to gently massage it as he glared intently at it.

"Phillip...what is that?" I asked. It was simply, the most beautiful thing I had ever seen in my life.

He held it up in the air. What little light that bled from the top ground enveloped the object, causing it shine as bright as any star in the dark skies.

"I don't...know...." He said softly. He glanced at me, then his gaze turned back to the object. "I...feel as though...as though it knows me.....I have known it all my life...."

"What a strange thing to say," I told him.

Suddenly, there was an annoying beeping sound coming from our belts along with a button that lit up bright red in quick successions. The company was letting us know it was quitting time. We had worked our fifteen hour shift and any unauthorized overtime was automatic deportation to Earth.

Tanner looked around. He stuffed the object in his backpack. He tried to walk past me. I stopped him by placing a hand on his chest.

"Phillip, you can't take that," I said.

He pushed my hand away. "No one is going to stop me." He screamed.

"By law anything found during work hours belongs to Scurver. They find out you stole this this object they will sentence you five years hard labor on the moon." I pleaded with him.

"No one is going stop me! Understand?"

I saw that wild look in his eyes. It frightened me. I have never seen it in that look in another humans eyes. I let him pass by to catch the rail car back to the surface. From there, we have to catch our flight to the Eastern side of Mars where Scurver has placed us in our own bungalows. I know that security will either catch him with the object as he boards the rail cart or when we catch our flight back home.

After that I hadn't seen Tanner for a week or so. But I did receive a visit from Scurver's lead investigator, Samuel Paul. He was a nasty little man with a nasty disposition. He came to my house after work. As a matter of fact, I think he flew to the East on the same plane as I did.

I opened the door and he pushed his way in.

"The red dust is kicking up something

terrible," Paul said, stone-faced. He removed his homburg to reveal man desperately trying to hang onto what little hair on his head by combing sandy gray strands over a enormous bald spot. When he spoke his dark bushy mustache moved. "I have to get this over with quickly and head home before my flight is cancelled and I am stranded in this godforsaken side of the world."

"Get what over quickly?" I asked, trying so hard not to laugh at this ridiculous man. I closed the front door to my bungalow, circled around Samuel Paul, shaking my head.

"The interview, you nit wit. I have to fill out a report on the crime before eight a.m. tomorrow morning. I'm not too happy about that, I can tell you, Mr."

I said, "Who are you, again…..? Mr……. uhhhh…?"

"Paul. Samuel Paul. You know damn-well who I am. Don't play stupid." He growled.

"Who's playing…Mr. Paul?"

"Ha. Very funny," he snarled at me. "Look, tell me where Phillip Tanner is." Paul said through clenched teeth.

I chuckled. "I haven't seen Phil in a week or so. If he's not at work, then he's at his eyes. There is nowhere else to go. There is nowhere to hide. Scurver has camera's everywhere and the rest of the planet is too dangerous to go off by yourself."

"Exactly my point." This ridiculous man had the nerve to say. I had to hold everything inside me not to use expletives in next couple of sentences. Then that would have given him a reason to arrest me for launching personal attacks on his person, just as the law states.

"Sorry? I'm afraid I don't follow you?"

"This had to have been a planned crime. You two knew that object would be found… again….and he has a partner. They are…" Paul nodded his little apple-shaped head. "They are out there…somewhere…just waiting for you to meet up with them. So the three of you can go off and catch a black market ship back to Earth and sell that object. Come on, tell me. What does it do? The

object? What would make it so valuable?"

"I have no idea what you are talking about!" I could feel my body temperature rise. If anyone knew how to rile me, it was Samuel Paul. That ridiculous little man.

"Tanner's girl is out there with him. Right? Yeah. We at Scurver know all about Colleen Scott. She won a grant to come out here. The real reason was for this heist… stealing valuables from the company. Not to be a psychologist! Help out lonely, lost men….."

"Colleen Scott died with the others on that ship coming here. At least, that's the reports I heard." I told him.

"Those reports are not confirmed nor is it a fact." Paul said.

I don't know what it was, maybe the way he said "fact", but that was the last straw.

"Okay. You've forced me to say this. By decree of law from Old Earth, this was not a formal line of questioning and you do not have papers to question me. I hereby ask you to leave my residence or I shall be forced to request an inquiry into misconduct of the investigation on your part. Please leave now, Mr. Paul."

Paul was fuming. His little eyes darted back and forth between me and the front door. Finally, he conceded. He opened the front door and stood there.

He turned to me and said: "Ohhh, you don't know what you have just done, do you boy? I'll be back to see you." He slammed the door behind him.

I sighed and closed my eyes. Exactly what he just said. What have I done?

After Paul's visit, I was frantic, at my wits end. Scurver was powerful indeed and even if I was deported, I could serve five years for stealing from the company. Something else bothered me. Those markings on the object. They looked very familiar. I had to do some research. One of the other skills I had picked up in the last few years is how to hack into data banks. Even though Earth government had combined all information from old computer banks from older earth governments, they never fully wiped them clean. My hunch is I had seen that object and its markings in an old data bank. When I couldn't sleep at nights I used to hack into defunct websites from when they used to have borders for Earth countries.

It didn't take long to find it. About forty-five years ago, Brazil started sending their own probes to Mar's surface. Not long after that, they sent their own astronauts. Of the many things they brought back was that object. I found pictures that had been taken of it. In the article, when the ship came back to Earth, all four astronauts were found as skeletal remains.

Very strange.

Even stranger is that the Chief of scientific discoveries from Brazil placed the object in a silver container. The next mission for their astronauts was to take the object back to Mars.

Why?

A few days later, I received a message from Tanner to come to his house.

Tanner opened the door for me, grinning from ear to ear.

"You won't believe this," he said, ushering me in. The house was a standard issue, same size as mine, same amount of rooms. Scurver builds them the same, just occupants are different every so often.

"Phil," I placed a hand on my pained face. "Samuel Paul visited me."

Tanner shut the door, glanced at me with no expression. He nodded. "Scurver's own Private cop, huh?"

"Yeah….look, Phil, this is going to sound strange, but have you been here since you left Scurver?"

"Yeah…sure. Where the hell would I go?" Tanner chuckled nervously.

"Paul said he was here with some Scurver men looking for you. He said the house was empty. He thinks you are out there hiding on the Martian Plaines."

"That would have been foolish of me. Steve, you know as well as I do, no one can survive out there without the equipment provided by Scurver Inc. I don't have access to any of that."

"He thinks you aren't alone…." I was interrupted by a female voice.

"He thinks I'm out there with him?" A dark haired woman in a light blue, strapless dress appeared from the kitchen. She was smiling, her green eyes large and bright and she had her hair up in a bun. I recognized her from the pictures Tanner showed me.

"Colleen," Tanner put his arm around her waist. "Meet a very good friend of mine. This is Steve. I wrote to you about him."

"Very glad to meet you," she said.

Colleen came toward me, her hand extended. I watched her move and the odd thing about it, she was there…..but not there. She reminded me of an image from an old silent film where the picture jumped, the image flashed on and off screen. I took her hand and I felt nothingness….complete emptiness. That's not to say that I didn't touch her…..but she was not completely there.

I felt a shiver run up and down my spine.

"Can you believe it, Steve?" Tanner was overly excited, like a child on Christmas morning.

I knew right away I needed to leave. Something wasn't right.

I forced a smile. "Phil," I shook my head. "I'm sorry. I can't stay. I have to get home. I'm beat. You understand? I have work…."

"Oh…well…Colleen just fixed this wonderful dinner…." Tanner's face fell. He tried so very hard to get me to stay. I kept using the same excuse.

"I'm very tired and I have a lot of ground to cover…. By the way. Are you two heading back to Earth?"

"Well," Tanner looked at Colleen. "We have been discussing it. We haven't exactly decided."

"I think it would be best we go back in a month or so. Mars simply does not agree with me. Even though we've been here for years," Colleen said. She turned, headed back to the kitchen. "It was nice meeting you, Steve." I watched her incredulously as she flickered in and out of plain view.

I waited until she was completely out of sight before I started to ramble. I began my speech several times before I realized I was not going to be able to say what I wanted to say. But Tanner hung on to my every word. I wanted to tell him that that was not Colleen. Not the real Colleen. That he needed to return the object to Scurvers. Plead for leniency, tell them he had a breakdown, and beg for his job.

I couldn't do it.

Phillip Tanner that I had known, even for a short time, he too, was not this man. So, why try?

I just shook Tanner's hand, wished him all the luck in the world, and left his house knowing that would be the last time I would ever see him again.

A few days later, there was a knock on the door. I expected it. Samuel Paul stood in the doorway, a Cheshire cat grin widening with all of his other nervous tics. I was prepared to deck him and risk a week in the company jail, possibly deportation back to Earth. So what? Mars had soured my usual rosy outlook on the prospect of a new life on a new world.

"What?" I growled.

"Could you take a trip with me?" He said in that annoying cocky way.

"What for? If you're here to arrest me..."

"No, no." Paul threw his hands up. "That part of the investigation is over with. We aren't looking into Phillip Tanner anymore."

I was perplexed. Did they get the object back? Was this some sort of trick?

"You don't need me then." I told him, tried to close my front door.

Paul blocked the door with his foot. "Please. Just come with me. I have...... something to show you."

I grabbed my coat and went with him, boarding the Scurver shuttle.

* * * *

We arrived at Tanner's bungalow house in a matter of minutes even though it was a hundred miles away from mine. Samuel Paul and I stood at his door, waiting to hear something. No noise, or anything. Paul was enjoying this moment. He was poised to open the door, his hand gripping the latch, that evil twinkle in his eyes grew bigger.

"You ready for this?" Paul asked me.

"Come on, quit stalling. I got work in the morning." I barked at him.

"Here—" He opened the front door quickly before he finished his sentence. "—we go!"

I stepped inside, brushing Paul aside. The place was very still, dark, quiet. The electricity had been shut down. The place was cold from night air. I looked around. Nothing had been touched for quite a while.

"As you know," Paul said, pleased with himself, his hand on his hips. "We've been to this area a dozen times in the past two months. Each time we were here, lights were shut off and no signs of anyone lurking about. Not even a toilet flush."

I wasn't amused by his joke and I let him know with a disconcerting look.

Paul continued: "We came back here today as one of our security cameras showed you in here."

I lost my breath. Oh damn. I forgot they had cameras here.

"That's alright, Steve," Paul chuckled. "We were hoping you would show up. After you'd gone, we checked things out and this is what we found." He took me to the bedroom.

There, on the bed, lay the skeletal remains of a human, still in underground work clothes. Both skeletal hands grasped the object, pressing it close to his chest.

I was overcome with emotion. I broke down, covered my face with my hands as I sobbed hard. I felt a consoling hand on my shoulder, not what I expected from Samuel Paul.

"Is... Is that...?"

"Yes," Paul said. "Phillip Tanner. The strange thing is, our medical examiner had said he had starved to death. But the study says his bones are at least ten years older than they should be. He hadn't starved to death in mere months, but over a period of ten years. Very strange."

"What is that object… I read a little on it…" I couldn't finish. I broke down again.

Thinking of the torment Phil must've been in.

Paul looked away. He sighed. "That object can give anyone what their heart desires."

RED DRAGON
by Shadrick Beechem

"Holy shit," Lana Briggs said in stunned amazement. "Mitch, get your ass over here, I think we just hit the jackpot," she told her shipmate.

Mitch Connell floated over from the refinement station, where he was processing the last of the small bits of precious metals they got from their previous salvage trip. They both stood peering over the LCD screen showing the dark vessel floating through the cluttered debris of some ancient pieces of wreckage. Mitch studied the markings on the large ship closely, and then saw "Ship Class: E-18 mobile excavation and drill series," in the classification bracket where the probe had ran diagnostics on the derelict vessel. Realizing he was looking at an old school Russian research ship, Mitch lit up with excitement and clapped Lana on the back.

"We sure as hell did hit the jackpot. That there is an old ass Sokolov digger, made back before they had nanocomposite metals to make ships ultra light. That metal beast is built like a tank and probably has enough raw titanium ore and gold plating to totally clean out the scrapyard appraisers. If we manage to strip her down and haul everything back with us, we will be made for at least eight or nine months minimum. What's the status on ship dexterity? Is it boardable?"

"Diagnostics show some slight hull damage, probably from a stray impact, and a small tear on the starboard side, but the room it's in looks to be sealed off. Structural integrity of the docking bay is 95 percent, so we should be good to go." She sounded giddy as a child.

"Excellent, because I need to see just how many goodies are aboard and check the black box. That thing looks like it's been floating around a couple hundred years, and we're gonna need the flight recorder to give to the claims agency in case there's cold ones aboard, which is a possibility as you well know. I'll go prep the scout, get suited up. See you down there." The large man floated down the hallway, his bulk making his journey awkward.

Lana, who was much smaller and dexterous than Mitch, easily caught up to him as she soared through the hallway and rounded the corner to where the small two-person intercept craft waited for them.

2.

Much like the planets they had inhabited, the early years of human space exploration always left trails of litter and pollution in their wake as they slowly refined their crude methods of transporting goods across the stars. As technology improved, older obsolete ships and stations were simply left to drift in the heavens, occasionally falling into a planet's orbit and becoming a problem if the planet was inhabited. Sometimes ships were also abandoned because of crew expiration, as many early journeys into deep space were fatal due to ill preparation, poorly built jump drives and ignorance of worm hole travel at the time.

This created a booming business among what the colonies had termed "junk pirating" where skilled pilots with strong stomachs, a lot of spare time, and extensive knowledge in the raw materials markets would build scavenger ships to intercept these discarded monuments to human engineering as technological progress allowed them to make big money on man kinds failings and occasionally get rewarded for helping identify pilots who were MIA.

However, as the years bore on and humans progressed in their technologies and knowledge of the stars, the number of ghost ships and easily accessible material caches decreased to the point where junkers such as Mitch and Lana were having to scour ever deeper into the edge of their home solar system to hit pay dirt. The old Russian digger was a needle in a very, very large haystack, and Lana had wondered upon the statistical luck they must have had to stumble upon it this far outside the milky way. She knew that geological teams were sent out on daring expeditions long ago to find intelligent life on the other side of the solar system, with many of them never returning due to the primitive shoddily built jump drives, which the research vessels were the first to get as desperate scientists kept exploring deeper, desperate to find new life, and new planets to call home.

However, some of those ancient ships were brought back into accessible traffic areas as the natural inertia of their trajectory would alter due to planetary perturbations, occasionally spitting the forgotten ships back towards populated areas of space over many light years. That must have been the case for the E18, as it's maiden launch date appeared to have been over three hundred years ago. It was as much an historical artifact as it was a goldmine of raw resources.

But as they drew closer to the ship, excitement turned to anxiousness, as it always did when they were getting ready to board. Mitch and Lana had been on over forty salvage runs together since opening up shop five years ago, and there was simply no way of telling what you were going to float into when you forced open the bay doors into a dark intergalactic tomb. Lana and Mitch had both seen their share of corpses, who's remains were always perfectly preserved and freeze dried in the oxygen deprived vacuum of space. That was until you jump started the engine and the artificial environment kicked in, where upon the corpses, which had sometimes been dead for over a hundred years, would begin to rapidly putrefy into a terrible smelling goop in their EVO suits. That was the ethically tricky part of the job, trying to locate and respectfully dispose of the human remains before you got the power turned back on. They had both learned that lesson the hard and disgusting way one or two times in the beginning, and made sure never to repeat such mistakes.

Keeping this in mind, Lana mentally prepared herself for whatever it was that lay beyond the blast bay doors. It could be totally empty, or they could find mutilated bodies as the occasional space fever made ill selected crew members go crazy and do terrible things. She tried to keep her mind off those grisly memories though as they decelerated and approached the tubular receptacle of the docking bay.

"I'll take care of the doors, you ready to breach?" Mitch asked, but Lana was already depressurizing the small cockpit and preparing to pop the windshield. It was a solid routine they had down pat by now, and muscle memory took over easily. Mitch would get out, float his way around to the small exterior terminal override panel found on the side of every federation standard ship, disengage the magnetic locks and then pry open the doors with a magnetic winch, something he was suited for given his brute strength, and then Lana would gently glide the scout through the narrow gap and bingo, they were in. Find any human remains, relieve them of their ID chips for the database and catapult them out into space or use the ships incinerator if it had one. Take inventory, fire up the ship, and pilot it back to their massive towing station, or if the ship wasn't operable they would take the towing station to it. Just another job.

Except it didn't feel that way, not this time. The interior of the docking bay seemed especially foreboding as the small observation light at the front of the scout illuminated a catastrophic mess of floating debris. Smashed and mangled bits of electronics and cables mostly, she could see the broken windows of the boarding terminal. She could also see her first body floating serenely amidst the levitating chaos as the magnetic receptors on the scout clanked firmly to the metal runway. The corpse's back was to her, but she noticed with a sinking heart how small it was. *Oh god, don't let it be a child* she thought gravely to herself. She tried to tell herself it was just more worksite jitters, which she got occasionally. But this wasn't just excited anticipation. Something felt wrong here, but she couldn't explain what. Despite this she would keep her mouth shut. Mitch was a respectful coworker, but any sign of feminine distress on the job was usually enough to get him in a patronizing *'are you sure you're cut out for this kinda work?'* attitude that she absolutely hated. She nonchalantly gave Mitch the thumbs up as he successfully navigated through the maelstrom of junk that was floating around.

"Jesus, those Ruskies must have had one hell of a rowdy party in here before they shut down," Mitch said through her earpiece, marveling at the scope of random destruction.

"Yeah, also there's a cold one to the north of you, I spotted it coming in. I'm guessing we're gonna have more remains aboard. Let's just focus on getting the bodies rounded up so we can get the lights on," she said, trying not to let the anxiousness come through in her voice. She wanted more than anything for the juice to be on right now. Most ghost ships were dark in principle, but at least with a run close to orbit they could get some backlight in through observation windows of the ship to go with their flashlights. But they were on the dark side of Orion, and there were zero windows on the ship save for the captain's bridge. The darkness in here seemed to hold physical weight it was so dense, as if she could almost feel it's mass pressing in at the narrow cone of light her flashlight emitted, eager to snuff out any and all illumination.

She was getting ready to approach the corpse she saw on the way in and search the flight suit for ID, but she paused for a mo-ment to look to the eastern wall by the entrance to the terminal. Her flashlight shown a bright red message spray painted in Russian on it. The words were quick and jagged, their foreign symbols appeared scribed by a frantic hand.

"...Hey Mitch? Can you read Russian?" she asked, pointing towards the graffiti.

Mitch grabbed onto one of the handrails to stop his motion and studied the words. "Hmmm...nope. But I can snap a picture and send it to the worthless ship AI we have and see if it can translate it for us," which he did so with the helmet mounted camera he had on, which also ran real time biomonitoring stats and live feed to their salvage ship an uncomfortable distance away. "Artemis, can you photo analyze the text in the picture I just sent you into English please?"

"Pr..r...rocessing r...reque...que...uest," a glitchy female voice told them through their suit intercoms.

"I'm sure you are, worthless cheap bitch. Don't get your hopes up with her," he begrudgingly told Lana. "Knew I shoulda nutted up the extra forty grand for the Athena series," he said to himself.

Mitch continued on ahead, sweeping the area with his flashlight while Lana approached the corpse. She slowly turned it over and saw with frightened bewilderment as the flight suit seemed to lose it's shape as she spun it around. As she got a glimpse into the helmet of the deceased she reared back in surprise. Instead of the usual pale, bloated eyed face of a vacuumed corpse there was only the shrunken, shriveled face of someone of unidentifiable gender. The skin was slowly flaking away like ash inside the helmet, and the eyes, no more than small dehydrated gray raisins, rolled around crudely in the cavernous sockets. The hair which was short and cropped, was an ashen gray, as if something had sucked every ounce of color and life from this person.

"Mitch, come back here and take a look at this," she said, unable to hide the tremble in her voice. She mentally cursed herself for letting this benign peculiarity spook her.

But Mitch was nowhere to be seen, and for a moment she panicked as she couldn't find him or hear a response. Then she heard his thick husky voice, but with his own small flavor of fear in it. She couldn't think of a time where she had ever heard Mitch Connell sound afraid in her life.

"What…the…fuck," he said slowly, and she assumed he had discovered his own corpse in the bizarre mummified condition, or worse.

"Mitch? Where are you?" she asked, pushing off a wall and towards his last seen location.

"Down the hall and to the left. I just found someone but they're…they're… I don't know. There's nothing to him but skin and bones, and not even that. I can feel him falling apart in his suit," he said, revulsion thick in his voice.

She frantically scrambled around the corner, losing her grip in the zero gravity and almost crashing into him as she rounded the corner.

"Jesus, watch out!" he said surprised and agitated.

"Sorry," she said, and observed the corpse Mitch held "I found one just like that in the docking bay. Whatever happened to them occurred before the ship depressurized. You wouldn't see this kind of decay unless the corpses were over a thousand years old. But we were still a one planet species back then," she said, desperately trying to rack her brain for some logical reason as to the corpses extremely weathered state.

"What the hell could of caused this? It looks like someone hooked them up to a shop vac and damn near drained them of… well…*everything*. I've never seen anything like this," he said, and there was a momentary uncomfortable silence as they stared at the husk of astronaut.

Finally, Lana spoke, abandoning her tough girl act as she saw she wasn't the only one thoroughly creeped out.

"I don't like this Mitch. I know this place is a gold mine but…Jesus. What happened to these guys?" she asked more to herself than to him.

"Your guess is as good as mine. Let's press on, I got the blueprints loaded in. This place gives me the creeps to, but we came here for a reason. We both got loans to pay back and stomachs to feed. If we hadn't stumbled upon this ship we would be screwed. Let's get the bodies accounted for, and I'm sure we will find a simple answer to this soon enough. Let's not split up though, this place is big and I don't wanna have to hunt you down. I know that's gonna take longer but…something doesn't feel right here," he said. Lana had no qualms with sticking together, the thought of navigating these long abandoned halls alone gave her a chill. Reluctantly, they plunged into the bowels of the ship.

3.

They scoured the first two levels in the dark save for their flashlight beams, where they navigated long, cramped corridors filled with random debris and the occasional floating corpse, each one in that same diminished state. Every corner they rounded was a test in self-discipline to confront the adjacent corridor, but slowly and painstakingly they corralled up all the corpses they could find and tied them up using some rope they found, though by the time they had gotten the bodies back to the flight deck they had basically disintegrated to dust in their suits. When they got to the third level of the ship they had close to ten bodies, if you could call them that, and were coming up on their eleventh casualty when Mitch stopped and shined his light at a hallway legend, all in Russian.

"Hey, I think this might be the generator room, I recognize that symbol, universal for jump drive. Let me see if I can at least get the lights going without turning on the oxygen pumps so we can speed this up a bit," he said and they headed down a T shaped junction where they proceeded left.

They entered a huge room where the large turbines and encased coils of the engine and jump drive were. Mitch did a quick shine over of the hardware and determined it all looked in good shape, despite being archaic engine models. Then he found the small circular console in the center of the room and plugged his HUD into it, where he was then able to jump start the console online using his suit's power pack.

"Now, let's see if I can find an English menu on this son of a bitch," he said, and started fiddling with menu screens. While he did this Lana explored cautiously, shining her light around and observing the peculiar pattern of cracks she had noticed around the rest of the ship. Strange long black crevices that went up the walls and sometimes scaled around equipment, as if though some massive corrosive laser had laid a seared path erratically around the interior of the ship.

She was floating up to one sharp column of the black line, noticing up close it wasn't a crack, it looked more like blackened ice, with a sort of reflective, organic surface, almost like flattened or dehydrated tree roots. She was only inches from it, studying it intently when Mitch yelled "Aha! Mitch the genius, how does he do it?" he proclaimed in a grand boasting voice. A few seconds later Lana shielded her eyes as harsh, white light filled her world. Her eyes adjusted, and she exhaled an amazed breath as she took in the real dimensions of the room and ship, which now felt much bigger. She also got a better look at the black...*stuff* that was laced all over the room, with one narrow tendril reaching on the floor right up to the console Mitch was standing at. It seemed to be concentrated here in the engine room, at least compared to it's traces in the rest of the ship she had seen.

"All right, lets hustle and gather up the rest of the bodies now that we can actually see what the hell we are doing. I can only run the auxiliary power cell for 15 minutes before we run out of enough juice to crank the engines, so let's not waste any time, come on," he said and Lana followed her partner down the final two levels where the cafeteria and laboratory were.

The cafeteria and crews quarters surprisingly didn't have any bodies, just a lot of floating kitchen ware riff raff, although Lana took note of a few floating butcher knives that had what appeared to be dried blood crusted on the blades floating around.

They descended to the bottom level, the laboratory, which featured several partitioned off glass rooms with various geological instruments floating around inside of them. A large digging rover was chained down next to a few other transport rovers, and Lana could see that whatever the black crusty stuff was had almost completely covered the digging rover, giving it a vague shadow quality, as if it had originated and then grew from the vehicle. Over to the far corner they could see where the wall had imploded outwards and they were afforded a jagged view of space.

"Found our hull breach. Looks like it was self contained though. Interesting," Mitch said nonchalantly.

"I keep seeing all this tar like crap around, what is it you think?" Lana asked Mitch, pointing to the black crust encased rover. The crust seemed to cover the outer edges of the tear where the metal had ballooned out, almost as if though it were there to seal it shut, which it almost did.

"Could be chemical flame retardant that was sprayed and then frozen after the power went off. Or busted cooling pipes leaking good knows what and freezing solid. Who knows, who cares. No bodies down here, let's head back," which they did, making their way back up to the flight deck, and corralling the tethered group of suited dust bunnies out the pried open launch bay doors and giving them a shove out to into space. Lana then put the acquired ID bio-tags into a pocket in her space suit and they headed back down to the engine room.

They cleared the area around the console as best they could of debris so as not to be injured by falling material, and then braced themselves for the jarring crash as gravity and artificial atmosphere kicked on and everything floating in the ship came crashing back down. She felt the vibrating of the huge engines start to fire up, and then a hard pulling sensation followed by a thunderous thud as a whole E class ship worth of random derelict crap came crashing to the floor, and gravity pushed their bodies to the floor, a disorienting sensation.

"Oxygen level reading 0% percent. Beginning air cycle," an automated voice told them.

"Should be able to un-suit in about ten minutes. May as well get comfortable while we pilot this beast back to the ship. Im gonna see if I can do a rollback on the pilot's log and figure out what the hell happened to these guys," he said, and began exploring the ship's information terminal diligently.

While he was focused on that, Lana went back to staring at the blackened trails of chemical fluid or whatever it was. It looked slightly different than it did a minute ago, but she couldn't put her finger on what it was. Five minutes of silence passed.

"Oxygen levels at 50%, approaching stasis," the voice chirped from the ships sound system.

Then Lana realized what it was. The black stuff was changing color. Slowly, almost imperceptibly, she saw the glossy black crust begin to slowly bloom into a dark violet, and then from a dark violet into…

"Hey Lana? You should come look at this. I can't make any sense of it. Maybe the translator on this behemoth is busted or something."

Lana walked over, suddenly feeling a strong tension build around her, as if though they were coming to the precipice of some horrible realization.

She glanced down at the rectangular terminal screen and read the captains log, which was dated July 8th, 2125, over a hundred years ago.

4.

WE HAVE CALLED IT RED DRAGON
IT IS SENTIENT
HOME ORIGIN IS EUROPA
THE SHIP MUST BE CLEANSED
OXYGEN MUST REMAIN AT 0%
DO NOT COME FIND US, IGNORE DISTRESS BEACONS
BEWARE THE RED DRAGON
IT MUST NOT BREATH
OXYGEN BRINGS DEATH

They stared at the bizarre log for a minute or so before the on board AI chirped back in and snapped them out of their contemplation. "Oxygen levels at 85%, hull breach detected in research engineering sublevel A. Obstruction detected in flight bay, unable to proceed. Stand by."

"I don't get it. The last captains log sign in before this shit was two weeks prior, and the captain seemed excited. Apparently, they just left some ice titan moon with soil samples they were going ape shit over, literally a ship full of nerds just drooling over—

But Mitch was cut off as Atermis chimed in "Te…Te…text encryption analys…sis c…c…complete. Message rel-rel-relay sent to your h…hud," and suddenly their screen visors were filled with generated computer text which read:

DO NOT TRY AND SAVE US
IGNORE ALL DISTRESS BEACONS
RED DRAGON MUST DIE
SHIP MUST BE CLEANSED
OXYGEN BRINGS DEATH

Suddenly Lana felt an overwhelming dread fill her. "Shut it off, the oxygen. *Now.* I don't know what the hell Red Dragon is but clearly these guys didn't want the place back up and running," she said. Then she looked around and was horrified at what she saw. The black turning purple veins that coated the hallways was now a deep blood red, and they were *moving*. Pulsating and slowly spreading, growing along the walls like rapidly growing tree roots. "Mitch, let's get the fuck out of here. Shut that shit off and—

But there was a scream and a loud slurping sound that interrupted her and she looked back towards the console.

Mitch had been standing on a patch of the previously innate material when he was accessing the terminal, not giving the stuff much attention in his always rational mind. But now the reanimated viscera had completely engulfed the leg of his space suit, and was making it's way up his torso, with one silk thin tendril racing up towards his helmet, lining itself along the thin seal of his helmet baffle and somehow penetrating into it. He flailed and screamed, but was unable to move as his left foot was now firmly rooted to the metallic floor.

"*Mitch! Holy shit!*" she screamed, and tried to pull the growing veins of alien life off him. But they did not tear or give, simply elongating itself like warm toffee as she pulled and pulled, until she herself was covered in thin writhing strands of the stuff. OXYGEN BRINGS DEATH was burned into her mind, and in the chaos she managed to bend over the console and try to shut off the power, but the roots of the red abomination had began webbing itself around the touch screen, obstructing her from inputting any kind of command as if though it sensed what she was trying to do.

"R…R…runnnn," a thin voice emanated from her suit intercom, and she looked over in horror to see that Mitch, a man larger than life and built like a bull, was slowly diminishing in size in his suit, the thin veins of alien life burrowing itself into his ears and nose, pulsating and throbbing as it drank greedily from the man's immense essence. His once broad stone slab face was now gaunt and emaciated, and his whole body twitched and trembled as the thing feasted.

And so she ran, sprinted with all her might, down the narrow corridors, claustrophobia and blind terror coalescing into a maddening energy that sent her rocketing through the ship. The thin strands that

had engulfed her when trying to free Mitch finally reached their stretched limit and let loose with wet tendon like snapping sounds as she exited the room. All around her, the once blackened crust was plumping up and turning red, like some corrupted rose bloom, and the veiny strands reached greedily out towards her as she vaulted up the stairways towards her scout. *It was simply waiting for someone to de-thaw it* she thought frantically as the mysterious cryptic messages left by the Russian research team now held a terrible clarity in their meaning.

She made her way towards the flight deck, hyperventilating, leg muscles burning from running in her heavy suit. She stole one look back before entering the hangar and saw that the entire corridor was webbed in a mass of pulsating red. She took a deep breath and tried to steady herself, she had a good forty feet on the growing mass but was it gaining quickly. She started climbing over the fallen debris towards the scout when she saw with sinking terror that the blast bay doors were shut, the pneumatic winch lay pinched between the two massive doors like a flattened accordion as the power had enforced an automatic reset.

"No, no no!" she screamed and looked around frantically.

She climbed on top of a mound of junk and tried to look for the small circular portholes that meant an emergency life pod station. She wondered if they even had life pods on ships this old, and it didn't help that all the damn labels were Russian. She scrambled around frantically scanning the walls, and looking back towards the terminal door seeing that the red roots were now at the edge of the doorway and spreading.

She ran south along one wall until she found what she was looking for, twelve rows of circular portholes, the red ejection lights lit up on all but one, at the far end closest to the terminal doorway. She sprinted for it, and slammed the green "open" button. The small circular porthole slid away with agonizing slowness, and she could see the human sized pneumatic tube slowly being elevated for entry. "Come the fuck onnnnnnnnnn," she moaned, slamming on the wall trying to will the life pod to make its way faster.

The growth was in the room now, rapidly blossoming on the high walls in great spider web shapes, with one fat straight vein growing slowly but steadily towards her, like a gestating finger eager to devour. It was halfway across the hanger, snaking around debris and closing to one hundred feet. Then fifty feet, picking up speed as if though it sensed her near escape.

There was a cheery sounding chime as the life pod was locked into the launch tube and the clear pod door opened. A pleasant sounding woman's voice spoke to her in Russian, probably telling her the tube was ready and to please enter calmly. She ignored it as she grabbed onto the handrail above the porthole and slid her way into the tube right as the tendrils were about to close in on her foot, immediately closing the small porthole behind her. She didn't notice the small strand that clung to her boot. She strapped herself in and hit the green launch button that hung over her head on a small panel. She watched as the exterior bay door for the tube slid slowly open, yellow caution lights swirling in the narrow metal launch corridor. She looked up and saw that the metal reception door was bulging in as the focused mass of the alien growth pushed against it.

Finally, she saw the circular porthole into the abyss, and hit the launch button right as the reception door caved in. There was a great pushing sensation as the torpedo shot itself away from the ship, G forces slamming her into the seat. She looked up in time to see a blossoming veiny mass of the growth get ripped out into space from explosive decompression, and it began slowly withering back into the black crust.

Lana began to sob hysterically in her helmet as her brain tried to process what just happened, understanding that a man she once thought invincible was now a weathered ghost, understanding that she had just encountered the first known instance of non human intelligent life. She cried hard for perhaps ten minutes while the pod soared through space, waiting for her to engage the rescue beacon. As she pulled herself together, she reached blindly through tear streaked eyes and hit the toggle, which would alert any ship within two hundred thousand miles of her location. Then she looked down as she felt a peculiar tingling sensation in her foot, and saw the red mass blooming around her feet.

SNACK TIME
by Franklyn Searight

It was an arduous ride from Chicago's Union Station to the more leisurely environs of Birmingham, Michigan. With the constant rumble and clickety-clack of the locomotive chewing up the intervening mileage, even a short snooze was impossible for Michael Duffy. He had been unable to sleep for a single moment throughout the entire seven-and-a-half hour trip.

And, adding to the constant noise was the continuous commotion caused by two undisciplined children in the seats behind him, frequently arguing and yacking, both at the same time. They had joined his passenger car with their mother shortly after he had settled in and had not stopped the hubbub for a moment, it seemed, just as they probably never ceased at home or at school, either. The parent, or caretaker, still in her early thirties, was completely oblivious to the obnoxious terrors, seldom raising her eyes from the book she was reading, barely aware they even existed.

Duffy had arrived in this middle-sized community on the outskirts of Detroit to begin a new job, summoned there by his older brother, a carpet dealer by trade and the proprietor of his own developing business which needed a responsible employee to assume the clerical and managerial duties of the clerk who had held the position. This was a job almost designed specifically for Michael Duffy, himself a rug merchant for the last few years and well acquainted with most aspects of the business. The idea of working for and with his older sibling, of course, had made the job offer even more enticing.

Duffy vacated the locomotive at the Troy depot, the mother and her pair of horrors remaining on board, continuing to a distant destination, and crossed a few streets to the city park where he found a hard bench upon which to sit. He placed his single valise at his feet—the remainder of his possessions being shipped at a later date—drew in a deep breath and shook his head, thinking of the impossible twosome he had left behind, their constant clamber and chatter still ringing in his mind. He enjoyed being with children, but too much was more than enough. It was much quieter now, here in the sylvan setting with no distractions to scramble and scatter his thoughts. He extended his legs and bent slightly backward, appreciating the coolness of the breeze.

He considered whether to check into the local YMCA, just a few blocks away, or continue to sit where he was for a spell and recover from what he considered the ordeal of the seven-hour trip. From the side pocket of his suitcoat, he withdrew the remnants of his lunch, a roast beef sandwich, slightly crushed, and a pickle he had chewed off at the end. He could finish these off and consider it his dinner, or leave and walk to the Golden Arches he spied a block away and order something a bit more substantial from McDonalds. He was not a big eater, ordinarily, but even what he had with him might not be enough. He could order a Big Mac and maybe a side salad to hold him until breakfast time the next day.

He made his decision and was about to take the first bite when:

"Hey, Mister," called a thin voice, "you gonna eat it all?"

Duffy turned his head around…and looked down…his eyes coming to rest upon a little boy standing behind hm. He was a lad of perhaps seven or eight years old and not much taller than the back of the park bench. He was dressed in a tattered pair of dark slacks and a wrinkled shirt, white at one time but now smeared with blobs of dirt and an assortment of varied-colored stains. Blue eyes were set in the midst of a cherubic face and peered at him without blinking or noticeable movement.

"Where did you come from?" Duffy asked

"From down there," said the slender lad, pointing with a begrimed finger to a large saucer-shaped iron lid covering a large hole in the ground, presumably a part of the city's sewer system.

"Good one. You're teasing me, aren't you, boy? You mean you live over *there*, don't you?"

"No, sir. I mean from *down there*."

"But it's a sewer, boy. You can't be from down there!"

"Course, I am. It's where I live, ain't it? Me and my sisters come out about this time every day and look for food. It's almost supper time, ain't it?"

"Guess it is. What's your name, boy?"

"Jimmy. What's yours, Mister?"

"Name's Michael. You can call me Mike."

"Ain't you got a last name, Mister? I don't."

"Duffy is the last name. What do you mean, you don't have one?"

"Means I don't have one. No mother; no father; no last name."

"Well, isn't that a shame? And you want the rest of my sandwich—that it?"

"If you don't mind, sir. Me and my sisters are always hungry; I'll share it with them."

"Will you now? You're a very generous boy, Jimmy. Not much here, though. How many sisters do you have?"

"Two of 'em, sir. We always share. It's what we do to get by."

"I guess you'd have to. And do you really live down there…inside the sewer system?"

"Yes, I do. Cross my heart. Me and my sisters."

"Can't be much of a home," Duffy observed, not believing what he was being told, but playing along with the young tyke,

anyway. "Never heard of anyone living in a sewer."

"It's ain't so bad, sir. We found an old couch by the curb one day and drug it down to the big room. Got us a nifty lounge chair, too. Something to sleep on."

"Better than nothing," the carpet seller observed. "Where are your two sisters?"

"Oh, they're around here, somewhere. Probably hiding from you and watching to see you don't hurt me."

"Why would anyone want to harm you, Jimmy?"

"You'd be surprised at what some people are like. Some are good and others are bad. Some enjoy hurting others, some don't; just the way big people are. Guess it's just how they want to live their lives, ain't it? Not easy to tell which ones are which, though."

"Well, yeah. Hard to tell. It's nice you have someone to watch over you, Jimmy."

"Yeah. Mindy and Lucinda, they ain't very far away. Would you like to meet them? You ain't done noffing yet to scare 'em. Probably hiding behind some tree around here."

"Well, sure, I'd like to meet them," said Duffy, not believing for a moment they even existed. "Assuredly!"

"And you won't hurt them?"

"Of course not."

Duffy thought for a few seconds about what Jimmy had already told him and concluded the boy liked to play games with the truth. Did the youngster actually expect him to credit the implausible story of him and his siblings living in the sewer? Of course, maybe they did—anything was possible, he believed—although more likely than not it was a humungous fabrication. But it followed— if he could devise such a whopper, he was certainly capable of inventing the existence of two sisters who shared his dilemma.

"C'mon out!" Jimmy called suddenly, cupping his hands before his mouth, his voice elevated by a few decibels.

And, sure enough, from the corner of his eye, Duffy saw two waifs emerge from behind a large tree, off to the side.

"C'mon over," the boy urged them.

Slowly, timidly, almost reluctantly, the girls advanced toward them. One was taller than her brother, perhaps twice his age and the other was smaller, maybe five or six years old. Both were clad in appalling hand-me-downs which had probably passed through a succession of owners and both had blonde hair flowing about their head and shoulders, uncut, untrimmed and not very clean looking, at all.

"He's okay," the boy said to them. "He's my friend, Mike, and he has some food we can have."

Hearing these words, four eyes regarded Duffy with a more congenial appraisal and their expressions brightened as though he was about to present them with a staggering cake of chocolatey delight.

"This's my family," beamed the lad with a degree of pride.

"I'm pleased to meet you," said the carpet guy, with a nod of his head including all of them. "What are your names?"

"I'm Mindy," said the little girl.

"I'm Jimmy," said the lad, repeating himself.

"I'm Lucinda," said the tallest one. "People call me Lucy."

"Pleased to meet you. My name is Michael Duffy. You can call me Mike or Mikey or Michael."

"I'll call you Mikey," said Mindy, speaking up, her rosy cheeks dimpling.

"I'll call you Mike," choose Jimmy, "or maybe just Mister."

"And I'll call you Mr. Duffy," offered Lucinda, the eldest of the trio, more mature and better mannered.

"Jimmy tells me you have no mother or father. That so?"

Both girls shrugged their shoulders at the same time.

"Ma's gone," said Mindy. "She left one day, leaving us with a box of crackers, and hasn't been back to take care of us ever since."

"We don't know about our daddy," contributed Lucinda.

"Don't know anything about either of them," Mindy concurred. "Daddy left when I was born and Ma didn't tell us anything about him. Didn't seem to even know what his last name was."

"My, my; is that so?"

"Yes, it is," said Jimmy, tired of the conversation being dominated by his sisters.

"Jimmy told me you children live in the sewer. True, is it?"

"Course it isn't," differed Lucinda. "Jimmy was just funning you. Can't you tell he's a huge liar? He tells shameful fibs all the time."

"Well, he sure had me fooled," said Duffy, feigning a reproachful look at the small boy.

Jimmy grinned sheepishly, revealing a gap in his teeth where a baby tooth had been, the space left to accommodate an adult incisor soon to be growing in.

"I didn't really believe him, though. But where *do* you children live?"

"Up there," said Jimmy, changing his original story and using his finger to point to the top of a high apartment building down the street.

"My, my," observed Duffy, "it's a long way up. Lots and lots of stairs to climb, unless there's an elevator. You must live in the pent house, if they have one."

"It's high enough for our needs, all right," said Lucinda.

"You gonna eat your sandwich, Mister?" asked Jimmy again, putting up a brave front.

"No. I've been saving it for you three. Here."

Duffy enjoyed his conversation with the children. His older sister, thousands of miles away, had six of them and he always looked forward to their visits with him. He was more than happy to chat with and share what he had with these three, who were so unlike the brats he had experienced on the train.

He passed the remainder of his lunch over to Jimmy, who studied it for a moment and then passed it to Mindy, the youngest and smallest of the trio, probably the one her siblings took care of first. She took a huge bite from it, severing off a portion, and handed it over to Jimmy, who likewise did the same. What was left, almost a third of the sandwich, was given to Lucinda who bit off a large bite and shoved it into her mouth. She chewed thoroughly, slowly, savoring every morsel before swallowing.

"Thank you, Mister," said Jimmy, in between chews.

"Thank you, Mikey," Mindy murmured, licking her lips, as though she had bitten into an unexpected treat she would enjoy for years to come.

"Yes, indeed," echoed the eldest of the trio. "Thank you, Mr. Duffy."

She swallowed the last of her portion as though it had been the first food she had eaten in days.

"You're very welcome, I'm sure," returned Duffy. "I only wish I had more to offer you."

"This was sure nice of you, Mister," said Jimmy, shifting from one foot to the other.

"Are you still hungry?" the carpet man asked. "It wasn't very much. You must have room for more."

Mindy, the youngest of the three, nodded and said they were.

"Then come with me. I bet each of you would like to have a Big Mac of your own."

"I like Big Macs," said Mindy, innocently.

"Shhh," said Lucinda, taking her hand and pushing her back. "We should be thankful for what we have already received."

"But I do like McDonalds' food when I can get it," the little girl insisted.

"Me, too," said Jimmy with enthusiasm.

"Then come along," invited Duffy, ready to return to the park entrance. He brushed invisible crumbs off his shirt and grabbed his suitcase.

"Hey, you kids," said a rough, virile voice of authority from behind them. "C'mere!"

Duffy swiveled to see, striding toward them, one hand on his hip, a police officer. He was holding a Billy club, or something else of a threatening nature, in the other. A shield, which could not be read at this distance, was pinned to his chest and a peaked hat rested upon his head.

Duffy was surprised. He turned again to face the children, wondering why the policeman would trouble them, but the youthful trio was gone, like the unseen breeze whispering through the trees.

"Now, where'd they go?" the carpet fellow asked of the officer coming to a stop beside him. "And who are they?"

"Dunno *who* they are. Live around here, though. Cause plenty of trouble, they do. Steal food from the grocery stores and lift wallets from unsuspecting folks. Give 'em a good talking to whenever I catch 'em, but not much I kin do about it. Just homeless urchins like you'll find in most communities, I guess. I'd advise you to keep away from 'em."

Duffy stayed around for another ten minutes, hoping the threesome—his welcoming committee to the city—would return once they noticed the agent of the law had gone; he had been actually having fun listening to them. But they did not come back and he eventually left the park, went to the cross streets to get his bearings and began his three block trek to the YMCA, following the simple map drawn for him by his brother.

* * * *

It was not until three days later Duffy was able to return to the sylvan setting near the train depot where he had encountered the three children. He had nicely settled into his little nook at the Y, venturing forth now and then to see something more of the neighborhood in which he now temporarily lived until he could locate more suitable quarters, but he spent most of his free time at his brother's place of business, learning the particular ins-and-outs of the job he had been recruited to fill. It was not a terribly exacting position, but it did require a certain amount of experience, which he had, and study which he was agreeable to do. His lunch and other leisure time were spent on the premises in order to master the expertise he must have.

He had not forgotten his meeting with the youthful trio and thought of them from time to time, wondering how they were getting along and thinking of questions he would ask about their living arrangements and of the comments made to him by the officer which had puzzled him. Once he was acclimated to his job he might be able to assist them in some small way not requiring an exorbitant outlay of currency or time, or place an unfavorable burden upon himself. He would not be receiving his first pay check until the end of the week, however, and until then he had to be careful of how he expended what money he did have. The threesome certainly appeared to be in need of financial assistance, if their skinny frames and slothful attire were an indication of their need, and Duffy was a compassionate man.

On this particular day, his duties at the office now well understood, he was not surprised to find his aimless footfalls taking him past tracts of forested land on his way to the park. His subconscious had been guiding him, he realized, and he found himself looking forward to another tryst with the children if he should encounter them.

Before entering the grounds, he stood for few minutes watching an elderly man and woman, standing in front of a store window, gazing at the display inside before going in. Almost as though it had been prearranged, he turned to see Mindy, the littlest and youngest of the children, sitting on a bench not far away from where he had first met her. She was licking an ice cream cone—strawberry, he guessed—looking at what still remained of the delicacy poking itself above the rim of the cone. She was swinging her legs, too short to reach the ground, and he wondered how she had managed to crawl onto the bench while still holding the treat. Her eyes were fixed on something in the distance and not on the frigid delight which she continued to lick, absentmindedly.

"Hi, Mindy," Duffy said, smiling pleasantly and walking over to her. "Remember me?"

The little girl tore her eyes away from the squirrel she had been studying and looked up to see Duffy gazing at her.

He might have been wrong, but he was willing to swear he had startled her into a state of great surprise; her eyes were wide and her mouth opened into an O. Was she contemplating some nefarious action? Was she fearful she had been discovered?

"Oh, it's you, Mikey," she said at last, the tension in her facial features and the muscles of her physique visibly relaxing as she recognized him and knew he posed no threat to her.

"Are your brother and sister around?" he asked.

"They were," she responded, then turned her head one way and then the other, looking at the nearby people strolling by. Her gaze returned to Duffy and she added, "But I don't see them around anymore. They're probably down the street, begging for a handout."

"A handout? You mean food?"

"'Course, I do. Lunch time, ain't it?"

"So it is. Is the ice-cream your meal?"

"It is," she stated affirmatively, taking another lick from around the side. "I love ice-cream!"

"I think most people do," Duffy observed. "And how did you get the money to buy it? Or did you beg for it like you say Jimmy and Lucy do?"

"Course, I did. How else would I get it? See the ice-cream parlor across the street? I just go in and look sadly at all the mixtures in the bins. When someone comes along, usually an older lady, I look up at her and smile. I don't have to ask for some; usually, they just offer it to me. And sometimes, when no one else is in there, the owner will give me some ice-cream for free.

"Ain't begging, is it? Not if I don't ask for it?"

"Well, maybe not, but if they didn't offer to get you a cone, would you have asked for one, then?"

"'Course, I would. Sometimes, people

aren't so generous unless I do asks, see?"

"Did you thank the lady?" Duffy asked, continuing the conversation.

"I did. Lucy says we must always thank people when they do something nice for us."

"Lucy is a very polite young lady, mature for her age," said Duffy.

"No, she ain't" disagreed Mindy. "Not really. She's a kid, like me; just a little older and taller."

"Are you still hungry," asked Duffy, "or did the ice-cream fill you up?"

"I'm usually always hungry, Mikey, but I already ate half of a hamburger and a handful of French fries when someone walked off, leaving them on the table—probably to go to the restroom. By the time he got back, I had already finished it and was going out the door."

"Tsk! Tsk! The guy was probably pretty mad."

"Maybe not. He might have thought he had finished it himself, or the cleanup guy tossed it away thinking he had left. Maybe he was given another one, if he complained. So, don't worry. I'm pretty full now and I won't ask you for something."

Duffy grinned. "You're a little conniver, aren't you, Mindy?"

"A conniver?"

"Oh, never mind. It's not important. Mind if I sit here, next to you?"

"'Course, you can, but don't ask me questions about my family, okay? Jimmy and Lucy don't like for me to tell strangers about us."

"Oh?"

"They're afraid I'll tell people our secrets."

"Now, what kind of secrets could you three possibly have? You mean like living in the sewer?"

"No, 'course not. Jimmy was fibbing you. No, I mean like the kinds of things we do in the park when it's late at night and the moon is full. Things they wouldn't like for you to know."

"Maybe they wouldn't mind. After all, I know Jimmy and Lucy pretty well now."

"Yeah, I guess you do. Well, late at night we join a big group at a bonfire deep in the woods. We roast marshmallows when we can get some and smash them onto a graham cracker with a layer of chocolate. We call them s'mores. Ever heard of s'mores?"

"Sure I have. Used to make 'em myself, years ago when I was a Boy Scout. Where do you get the fixings from?"

"From the grocery store, of course. You don't know nofing, do you?"

"And how do you get them without having any money? Stand about and beg?"

"'Course we don't. Can't tell you how, though."

"Sure you can. I won't tell anyone your secrets."

"Promise?"

"I promise," Duffy affirmed.

"Well..."

Mindy looked around, satisfying herself no one else was within earshot, raised herself on her knees, leaned over and held her head up for a moment to Duffy's ears and whispered.

"We take the stuff when the lady in charge of the store ain't looking! Jimmy shoves it under his shirt."

Mindy lowered herself, sat back and began to giggle.

"It's funny," she said. "It makes him look like a stuffed Teddy Bear."

Duffy joined in with the laughter, even though he didn't consider it to be funny. He believed children who started off life pilfering would come to no good, meeting up later on with big problems, perhaps ending up in prison—or even worse. The best thing for them to do would be to get a job of some kind to take care of their needs.

"You won't tell no one, will you? You promised!"

He shook his head, no. A promise is a promise and whenever he made one, being gored by wild boars would not force him to break his vow. He did not tell the little tot of his viewpoint, however. Not being their parent, or a teacher, or any other person of authority, he was not in a position to point out the consequences of their behavior, making them feel guilty and ashamed.

As far as he knew, all of the stories they told him were false, anyway. He had heard of fabulously wealthy people, housed in extravagant mansions and living splendid lives of opulent comfort, enjoying the magnificence such wealth could provide. They were known to prowl the streets from to time to time, just for fun, seeking out and mingling with the less affluent and often destitute people they met, later telling tales to their friends of the complete devastation and squalor in which 'those people' lived. For all Duffy knew, the three children were the offspring of prosperous parents who lived a life of affluence and, when he saw them, they were slumming just for fun, just as other children spend their leisure hours playing baseball, or engaging in some other endeavor.

"There they are," exclaimed Mindy suddenly after a spell of silence, pointing to the park entrance.

"Hi, folks," called out Duffy, as Lucinda and Jimmy came toward them, quickening their steps as they saw the two on the park bench. Duffy noticed them slipping something they had been holding into their pockets, but he made no mention of his observation and they were soon standing before them.

"Hi, ya, Mister," said Jimmy in greeting, a salutation immediately echoed by Lucinda.

"Haven't seen you around here for a while," he added.

"What cha up to?" asked Lucinda.

"Oh, just sitting and gabbing with Mindy."

"Yeah? What's she been telling you about us, Mr. Duffy?" Lucinda asked, but directing her inquiry at her younger sibling.

"Nothing, Lucy," Mindy retorted. "I ain't been telling him our secrets."

"I'm glad to hear you haven't," said Lucinda, a frown deepening the lines of her face. "You know much better than to tell,

don't you?"

"Course, I do."

"You shouldn't even tell people we *have* secrets to hide," Jimmy said, his voice tense and a bit cross. "They might imagine all sorts of things."

"But I didn't tell him about … about, you know what," she insisted.

"Shhh," cautioned Lucinda. "The nice man isn't interested in our secrets, anyway. Are you, sir?"

"Wee..ell…" returned Duffy slowly, enjoying the banter and drawing out the word much longer than was necessary. "Actually, I *do* like secrets and I'm good at keeping them, too."

"Shall we tell him, Sis?" asked Jimmy, glancing at Lucinda with a look of perplexity.

"Of course, not," she returned instantly. "For all we know, Mr. Duffy might be a policeman."

"Oh, yeah," agreed Jimmy, "We do have to be careful about what we tell people."

Duffy smiled at him gently, all the while wondering what strange enigmas they did not want others to know about. Their conversation had gone in a direction he had never imagined it would take, forcing the young people to adopt an unexpectedly defensive demeanor.

"She's right, Jimmy," he assured him. "You *should* be careful about what you tell people. I don't have to know your secrets, especially if they're against the law. But, as a matter of fact, I'm not in law enforcement. I work for a company selling and installing carpeting."

Duffy decided he was being a nosey ninny, showing too much interest in their behavior, and said no more.

"We're not breaking the law, Mister Duffy," said Lucinda, drawing a deep breath. "We ain't doing nothing…like…like…that ain't legal."

"No, siree," jumped in Jimmy.

"We don't never stay up late at night to watch *them*," stated Mindy, with conviction.

"To watch whom?" asked Duffy, seemingly unconcerned, but wondering what the little girl was talking about. It seemed to him there was too much denial going on and the children were protesting far more than they should.

"You stop!" demanded Lucinda, addressing her sister crossly, "or I'll give you a good poke."

"I won't tell anyone," insisted the little one, realizing she had crossed the line. She jumped off the bench and cowered back a few steps. Apparently, for some reason, Lucinda's jab was one she had some reason to fear.

"What's this all about?" asked Duffy innocently. "Have you youngsters been drinking too much Kool-Aid lately and seeing pink elephants climbing up the trees?"

"No, no," said Jimmy quickly, but giggled at the absurd picture popping into his mind. Mindy joined in the merriment, but Lucinda remained as silent and as still as a puppet severed from its strings; amusement failed to brighten her face.

"Shut up!" she cried, totally unladylike and completely out of character.

"I won't say no more!" promised Jimmy and drew a straight line across his lips with a finger, as though he was zipping them closed.

"Me neither," promised the littlest one. "Besides, Basil wouldn't want them to know, either."

"That does it!" exclaimed Lucinda. She stamped her foot in unexpected anger, turned around and stalked off in a direction taking her deeper into the park.

"Uh, oh," said Jimmy. "Sis's *really* mad now!"

"Sure is," agreed Mindy. "She's in a real snit!"

"Who's Basil?" asked Duffy, forgetting his resolve to ask no further questions.

The two children burst out giggling again, but Duffy could see nothing to be laughing about. He looked suspiciously at them.

"Basil is a friend of ours," stated Jimmy, forgetting the vow of silence made to his older sister moments ago. "One of the gang."

"He's real nice," said Mindy.

"He is *not*," disagreed Jimmy. "Sometimes he's *real* mean to people...or other creatures he doesn't like—and, sometimes, even to his friends."

"Yeah," agreed Mindy, changing her mind. "He does have an awfully, wicked dispo... dispo... dispo..."

"Disposition?" suggested Duffy.

"Yeah. Disposition. So, we go out of our way to be extra nice when we're around him, and he's good to us, too," she finished.

"'Specially at night," Jimmy continued on, "when the whole flock is sitting around the bonfire."

Mindy finished her ice-cream cone and licked her fingers before wiping them on her dress.

"Probably making s'more?" Duffy suggested.

"Naw," disagreed Jimmy. "Chimeras don't eat s'mores."

"Neither do dragons or gargoyles," stated Mindy emphatically.

"Whoa..." said Duffy. "What is a chimera?"

"It's a creature with a goat's body and a lion's head," said Jimmy, matter-of-factly.

"And it has a snake's tail," added Mindy.

"How did dragons and gargoyles and... and...chimeras get into this?"

"No reason," said Jimmy. "Mindy is just talking silliness."

"Am not!" Mindy declared. "Chimeras eat imps and baby griffins, dragons eat mostly big animals, like lions, and gargoyles eat anything they can dig their claws into."

"Really?" asked Duffy. He knew next to nothing about such fantastic beings. "The creatures you've named are fictitious—make believe, you know?"

"That's what most people think," said Mindy, meaningfully. "But Boris is one. We've seen lots of them singing and dancing while we're sitting around the bon fires. Just at night, though," she added.

"Yeah, way past midnight," Jimmy added.

"I know a riddle, Mikey," said Mindy. "What has to gargle to clear its throat?"

"I give up. What?"

"A gasping gargoyle! Get it?"

Duffy got it, but did not think it was at all funny.

Duffy gave zero credence to what the children were saying. It sounded like a kind of make believe game they were playing, or maybe they were repeating parts of fairy tales told to them at an earlier age. More than likely, however, they were only feeding him a pack of falsehoods. Jimmy was noted for telling them, he remembered, but now even Mindy was willing to make up her own. But their words did arouse his curiosity and he was interested in hearing how the stories ended.

"How many have you seen?" he asked, harmlessly.

"Oh, lots and lots of them," Mindy told him.

"Maybe three dozen of 'em, or more," Jimmy estimated. "Whenever we have our meeting."

"So many fairy tale creatures?" said Duffy. "They must be extremely scary."

"Naw, not a bit," Jimmy disagreed. "They don't frighten me at all."

"Just don't bother them when they're feeding or having fun," cautioned Mindy.

"Sometimes I fall asleep just watching them," said Jimmy.

"Me, too," said his smaller sister, making sure she was an essential part of the conversation. "Sometimes, Lucy has to wake us up when it's nearly dawn and it's time to go home."

"You know, I don't believe I've ever seen a chimera, or any of these other improbable creatures—especially not dozens of them. They're not at all real," insisted Duffy.

"Are so," asserted the little tot. "As a matter of fact, we're…"

"Now you stop that, Mindy!" burst a sharp voice from behind. Lucinda, who had quietly returned to hear what her siblings were saying, was greatly upset. "This good man isn't interested in your nonsense talk!"

"Awe, alright, Lucy. But he's probably seen them on the streets, lots of times, walking around in their human form. The imps, too. Probably talked with them, and had lunch with them, maybe."

"I don't remember meeting any of them. What do the imps look like?"

The two youngsters began to snicker again and it was not until they were able to control themselves Mindy said, "They're very funny looking."

"And they're real small," said Jimmy.

"Smaller than me, even," said Mindy. "It would take five of them standing on each other's shoulders to touch the top of my head."

"You'll be sorry you talk so much," admonished Lucinda, angry her brother and sister did not guard their tongues no matter how many warnings they were given. In a sulk, she left them and made her way out of the park.

"Not very tall, at all," was Duffy's comment.

"No, it ain't." Jimmy bent down and held his hand less than a foot off of the ground. "This's how big they are," he demonstrated.

"Oh, my," voiced Duffy. "Are they really that tiny, Mindy?"

The little girl nodded her head in agreement with her brother.

"They must be as small as little dollies," Duffy guessed, delighted with the imagination expressed by his fledgling friends.

The three chattered for a while longer until Duffy glanced at his watch and realized he had stayed far longer than he had intended. The time allotted to him by his boss had passed and he still had not eaten his lunch. He decided he would have to forfeit it this one time and stood up to leave when Mindy spoke up.

"Would you like to see some of our friends?" she asked, in invitation.

Duffy, who was just about to say goodbye, halted in his tracks.

"What? You want me to come and see the imps sing and dance?"

"Them and the dragons and gargoyles, too. The whole gang is fun to be with. It's like a circus. They have their festival once a month, late at night when the moon is full."

"Lucy might not like for him to come," Jimmy cautioned her.

"So what?" she returned, defiantly. "We just won't tell her."

Duffy neither agreed to attend, nor did he disagree, but was confident he'd rather not waste his time deep in the woods, late at night, for what was almost certainly a wild, pretend adventure at best, or a mischievous children's prank at worst, but he stayed a minute longer to tell the kids how to reach him if they ever wanted to get in contact with him; in turn, they explained briefly, but not quite clearly, how to reach the grove of trees where the festival was to take place, as it always did on the first night of the full moon.

He was noncommittal when he left them, but was quite certain he would not continue to play their game much longer, unable to escape the certainty they found enjoyment with their playful antics. He would not mind seeing and conversing with them again; in fact, he would look forward to it, but under more normal and structured situations, believing he would be rewarded with a degree of fun and amusement while chatting with them. Even so, as far as he was concerned, he would rather they played their childish pranks on someone else.

Duffy happily executed the routine tasks of his position at his brother's shop, and one day, while looking at his desk calendar, he noted the appearance of the full moon would occur this very night.

He had not seen the children recently and had almost forgotten their invitation. For a moment he considered looking for them to find out more about the festival being held, but his decision was already made. What a gigantic waste of time it would surely be and he had much better things to occupy his hours at the YMCA where he was still renting a room, prior to finding more ideal quarters for himself.

But did he really have better things to do?

Duffy knew this night would be one more in a series of lonely evenings when he would settle himself in the large lobby of the Y to watch television, or go upstairs, curl up by himself on the bed in his tiny room, and read a book. This had been his customary routine since stepping onto the streets of Birmingham. He had not seen the children for more than a week now and found himself wondering how they were spending their time. Perhaps sharing a few minutes with them would provide a little variety to the sameness of his life. Not for a moment did he believe in their mythical bestiary or that a gathering would actually take place tonight at the park, but if it did, perhaps a concert or a carnival, it might be of some interest to him.

Attending such an event, however, was doubtful, he thought, glancing at the wall clock as its hands reached to touch the five o'clock hour and quitting time. He did not know where the children were, only that they lived high, high up in an apartment building. He was not at all certain how to contact them, nor did he know of the particulars of where in the park the entertainment would be. He straightened his desk, putting odds and ends away until they would be needed the following day.

"G'night, Max," he called to his brother, looking in at the next cubicle as he passed by.

Max looked up, waved and responded with, "G'night, Mike. See you tomorrow."

Duffy told him to have a pleasant evening and left the building.

Outside, he walked to the corner, looking both ways before crossing the street, when he heard a wee voice coming from behind.

"Hey, Mikey, wait for us. We're not wearing Nikes, you know!"

Turning, he saw rapidly closing the distance, the three friends with whom he had taken such a liking.

"Say, hey, what are you people doing here?" he asked, as Mindy, Lucinda and Jimmy skidded to a stop before him.

"You told us where you work," asserted the boy. "Remember?"

Duffy did not recall doing so, but figured he must have at some point during their conversations.

"We guessed you'd be leaving around five o'clock—when lots of workers do—and you did," explained Lucinda.

"Yeah," contributed Jimmy, "and we wanted to remind you the jubilee is tonight."

"Well…I'm…err…haven't really thought about it very much. So, tonight's the big night, is it?"

"Yeah," said Jimmy, "and we're hoping you'd come."

"I don't think so, but thanks for inviting me."

"Awe, c'mon, Mikey. You'll have lots of fun."

"We've been hoping you'd join us," said Lucinda. "Lots of strange and fantastic creatures will be there."

"You mean the mythological ones, of course."

"They ain't myth..log…cal at all," attempted Mindy. "They're for *real*."

"Yeah," said Lucinda. "The imps and dragons and gargoyles will be there and others. They always are."

"The chimeras, too?"

"Yeah, them, too. But it ain't all," said Mindy, with intense enthusiasm. "Sometimes we get a satyr and once in a while a unicorn shows up…"

"Sounds as though all the beasties come to these assemblies," jested Duffy.

"…and don't be surprised if you see a cyclops or two!"

"We expect a big crowd, Mikey!" said Mindy. "Will you join us?"

"Well, I wasn't planning to…"

"C'mon, Mister Duffy. It'll be tons of fun."

"Well, okay. I'll join you for a little while. Where's it at?"

"In the park, of course. Just meet us at the entrance; we'll be there waiting for you and take you to it."

"Around nine o'clock," advised Mindy, grabbing his hand and pulling on it, childishly.

"Well, okay. I'll try it, just this once."

"That's great, Mikey," she said, joyously.

"We'll see you later on this evening, then," said Lucinda.

Duffy took a step in the street and then stopped. "Oh, I forgot to ask. Do they have concession stands? Sell food there?"

"No," answered Lucinda. "Most of them eat before they go, or after they leave."

"Some of 'em bring their own food with them," said Jimmy, which seemed to strike the others as amusing, for they all began to laugh.

It might be a grand evening, after all, thought Duffy, strolling down the street after darkness had fallen. He had dined moderately and had taken a short nap, expecting to be out later than usual. He reached the park, only to find no one was there but himself. He had expected to find a large, possibly rowdy, partying group, out for a good time in the cool of the evening. But even the children were not at the entrance waiting for him. Perhaps they had not arrived yet, he reasoned, or maybe they had come earlier and decided to go to the clearing without him.

The sky had been washed clean of cloud formations, and a multitude of stars poked out of the heavens in twinkling splendor. The moon smiled down at him as friendly as he had even seen it before, providing amble light as he stood there shifting from one foot to the other. He wondered how long he should wait before going back to his room.

Fortunately, he did not have long to linger before he spied Jimmy coming up the street, hurriedly.

"Hi, Mister," the lad called, stopping

before him. "My sisters have gone inside to find good seats and I've been walking around, waiting to take you to the festival clearing when you got here."

Duffy thanked him and followed him through the entrance and down a winding trail, passing picnic tables and benches and a small pond with water glittering in the moonlight. Their trek along the wooded pathway had hardly begun, when Duffy began to experience unexpected and inexplicable distortions, slowly at first and then more rapidly, as they advanced into the deeper shadows and forested environs. The park, he discovered, was much larger than the two or three block rectangle he had envisioned and he was unable to explain how it had expanded in size so considerably, creating a curious, inexplicable modification in spatial proportions.

An alteration in time was also noticeable. The stroll, which should not have taken more than ten minutes, had already lasted nearly half an hour and perhaps much, much longer. Duffy found he had lost all notion of time and they had still not reached the further border of the arboreal local. It almost seemed to him as though an enchantment had been cast over him, or he had been captured within an unfathomable illusion taking place.

Was he was experiencing a rent in the fabric of reality—a shattering of the space-time continuum itself? How else could such revisions be explained? Either that, or they had not been walking nearly as long or as far as it seemed. He did not believe in such notions, however and finally concluded the distortions were only in his mind. The alternative, and this was far more likely, was they had simply been walking in circles for the last half hour.

Was it possible? He thought not and it did not help for him to realize with each step they took they seemed to be blundering along an alien landscape, an ephemeral area of dreamland, perhaps, and one he had never visited before. His surmise was rapidly turning into a conviction, becoming stronger as

his sense of reality grew denser, more disarrayed, more indistinct.

"What is this place? Where are we?" Duffy wanted to ask of his small companion as they continued along the pathway. Somehow, he was unable to get the words out.

A tingling sensation of unexpected fear began to crawl along his spine.

The minutes passed, their footsteps continued, as Duffy fought against the impression they had stepped from one dimension into another and they were moving in a slower motion along a warp in time and space itself.

Everything seemed to be so...so...surreal!

Eventually, they saw a flickering of light through the trees ahead and shortly reached a large, treeless glade in the shape of an amphitheater. They entered and found they were not the first to arrive. Shadowy, obscure creatures, large and small, walked about or sat on boulders and logs, chattering, joking and laughing with each other. Duffy could distinguish some of the garbled words, but many of the noises uttered were curious grunts and whistling or clicking sounds with strange, alien intonations. A sizeable fire burned brightly in the middle of the clearing and a strange-looking form stood before it, feeding twigs and sticks into the blaze.

Not everyone or everything there was human.

Duffy's confused senses became fixed upon a quivering in the atmosphere as a purplish coloration of the air and landscape pulsed as though something alive. A visible, unaccountable vibration did nothing to free him from the anxiety building in his mind with every passing second. He stepped back a pace, frightened nearly to the very core of his being.

"There they are," cried Jimmy, pointing off to a large tree trunk being dragged closer to the conflagration. On it, their backs turned to them, were two forms; judging by their respective sizes, Duffy thought they might well be Lucinda and Mindy, the smaller one talking animatedly to the larger.

Jimmy led the way over to them pulling Duffy along by the hand and they stood behind them, unnoticed, listening to Mindy's excited voice, energized by her enthusiastic observations.

"Look over there, Lucy," she was saying, pointing to a yawning dragon on the other side of the fire circle. "Who is it?"

"It's Simon," responded the thirteen-year old, "one of the dragons from France where so many of them were exiled."

"Ooh! I haven't met Simon yet," said Mindy. "Is he a good one or a bad one?"

"I've only met him once and when I did, I didn't form a good impression of him. He snorts too loudly and many of his scales are mutilated or missing, as though he's been through dozens of skirmishes. I've heard he's a mean one, but you might enjoy talking with his girlfriend, sitting next to him. I'm told she's quite gentle, for a full sized flame-thrower, and has some very funny stories to tell."

"What's her name?"

"Skelly. If you'd like, I'll take you over later and introduce you to her."

"No thanks, Sis. It'd rather meet Simon."

"Suit yourself, but I wouldn't go anywhere near him. At least, not in his present form."

Everyone there, human and nonhuman, were casual, relaxed and conversational, and seemed to be having a good time. Duffy, however, was in a state of perplexed distress, becoming more and more uncomfortable as the bewitching enchantment held him enthralled, persisting unbroken, and the cloudiness festered in his mind caused his sense of reality to become even more obscured.

He had seen and heard enough—more than enough—and believed leaving sooner rather than later would be best for him to do. He was about to insist the young boy take him back to the park entrance, when Jimmy spoke.

"Hey, you two," he said, announcing their presence, "everyone here yet?"

"Not yet," said Lucinda, as the girls turned to greet them. "Most of our friends are late."

At that moment, a tiny *something* stepped out of the shadows, looking for a place to sit, and walked toward an unoccupied boulder. Carelessly, he got too close to Simon, who opened his long, scaly muzzle and torched him as he might a wayward frankfurter.

"It's just an imp!" exclaimed Jimmy to Duffy, who was now sitting next to him.

"It was an imp," corrected Mindy, as the dragon, not yet satisfied, opened its maw even wider, reached out with its long neck and snatched the little creature off the ground. With masticating swiftness, the massive creature gobbled it down.

"There're so many of them just one won't never be missed," Mindy observed.

"My, my," said Duffy, nearly petrified by what he had seen. "That was…was… *gross*!"

"Not really," observed the lad sitting next him. "It was a small urchin; barely a mouthful for a large dragon."

"I can hardly wait for snack time," said Mindy enthusiastically, leaning closer to the fire.

"S'mores?" asked Duffy, nervously.

"Mmmm! Yummy!"

At that moment an enormous *thing*, bat-like at first glance, swept out of the darkness beyond the fire. It settled on a small log just a few feet away from the foursome.

To his horror, Duffy realized it was not a huge chiropteran, although it had webbed wings folded up neatly behind its back. Its horned head swiveled to glance curiously at the four with a rocky face appearing to have been sculpted out of granite. Its facial construction, with furrowed, grey skin, unblinking eyes and puffy lips, was unbelievable. When opened, scimitar-like teeth were revealed. Its hunched back was curved and enormous talons clung tenaciously to the log upon which it perched.

"Nice evening," mouthed the creature, with a gritty intonation, looking at Duffy and his companions. Its voice sounded like a small avalanche and its grunting mouth moved so slowly it appeared to grind away in slow motion.

"Good grief!" Duffy exclaimed, edging away from it as far as he could. "What's *that*?"

"That's a goyle," Jimmy answered.

"What in the world is a goyle?"

"A goyle," Jimmy repeated. "A gargoyle."

"Oooh," Duffy sputtered and then stuttered, "o-one of those things? But wa-what's it doing here, si-sitting on a l-log? Doesn't it belong on the r-roof of a ca-cathedral?"

"Of course, it does, but not all the time."

"Sometimes they get tired during the day, sitting up there like statues of solid rock," explained Lucinda, "and they transform themselves into their people persona you see on the streets from time to time, not knowing what they really are."

"And during the night," added Jimmy, "they fly around as much as they like. I recognize this one just fine. He's a nice guy; I've seen him around here lots of times."

Duffy began to snicker, approaching a state boarding on total hysteria, unable to acknowledge the reality of the scenario evolving before him and rapidly losing total control of himself.

"Would you like to get closer and pet him?" asked Mindy.

Duffy was quivering now, one baby step away from insanity, he believed, and feeling much as Alice did as she tumbled down the rabbit's hole.

"I wouldn't do it if I were you," advised Jimmy. "Lots of 'em bite. The goyle might take a large chunk out of you if it's hungry."

"All of them bite," Lucinda elaborated. "The smaller ones can take huge hunks out of you, but the bigger goyles can eat you whole in one mouthful."

"The imps and fairies who show up are afraid of them," said Mindy, knowingly. "They disappear in one big swallow if they get too close."

"The big brutes are usually hungry and some of them bring their own meals with them," said Lucinda. "You don't have to worry about *them*."

"Then I'll b-be careful to stay away f-from the goyles," stated Duffy with a childish giggle, adding to what he hoped was playful banter.

"Look over there," said the teenager to her brother, pointing to another animal nearby, perched on a tree branch. "You can just make out its form. It's Estelle, isn't it?"

"I think so," he said, agreeing with her.

"Estelle is a goblin," explained Mindy. "So few of them are left they're on an endangered species list."

"How un-unfortunate," giggled Duffy, dryly, unable to comprehend and accept the existence of the fantastic brutes around them. He studied the animated form a few seconds and then shifted his gaze to four tiny beings entering the fire circle, leaping and gyrating as though they danced to the strains of unheard music. One of them grabbed a backpack another had been carrying, set it on the ground and opened it. Another one snatched from inside a box of graham crackers, and the last one withdrew a stack of candy bars. They broke off pieces of chocolate, placed each between graham crackers, added a blackened marshmallow from the fire, and began to eat.

"How did I ever get involved with this?" Duffy wondered. "All I wanted was to be friendly and helpful."

"What're they da-doing?" he asked, unable to clearly follow their rapid movements.

"They're making s'mores," explained Jimmy. "If you'd like to have one, just raise your hand and they'll bring one over to you."

Duffy thought this was so silly he could not restrain the snicker chortling from his mouth.

"No th-thank you; I'm not hu-hungry. But you th-three go ahead and eat some."

"We don't have to," said Mindy. "We brought our snack with us."

"You did? I don't see any food here for you."

Then it was Mindy's turn to giggle with a

tone sounding far more ominous than Duffy wished.

"You don't understand yet, do you, Mikey? It's because you've only seen us in our human form."

"*You're* our food!" said Jimmy, calmly.

"Whaaaa…?"

"Snack time," Lucinda announced to her brother and sister.

Adroitly, Mindy slipped to the ground and as she did so the structure of her body underwent an unexpected transformation. Duffy watched speechlessly as as her lips bent and twisted and her other facial features and body reassembled itself, shifting and contorting into a form nothing at all like a little girl. Her small shoulders began to broaden and harden; her flesh loosened, then tightened again, its texture becoming leathery and wrinkled before hardening into its new shape. Within seconds, she assumed the features of something chiseled out of granite.

At the same time, Jimmy's body was also altering in size and contour. His head swelled enormously; tiny horns appeared above his forehead; and a smug, self-satisfied grin appeared on his face giving him the grotesque appearance of a leering reptile. The last change to take place were rudimentary wings springing from his shoulder blades and folding back into place.

Duffy stared, his mouth agape, unable to understand the weird conversions. He had no notion of what was happening until Mindy grabbed his leg in her expanded mouth and clamped her grinders together. The pain was excruciating—unbearable—and then he felt the same agony in his arm. Turning, he saw it grasped in Jimmy's cavernous maw, his own alteration now complete. Mindy bit into his leg again, crunching and shearing through bone and causing such pain as might be felt by the ripsaw at a lumber mill.

Barely conscious, blood spurting everywhere as each young goyle quietly fed, Duffy remembered the time when Jimmy pointed to the top of the apartment building to show where they lived and he realized now the boy had not been indicating the top floor, but rather the roof—the place where figureheads of stone congregated and spent their leisure hours.

Duffy lifted his head to see Lucinda mid-way through *her* renovation. The soft contours of her face lost its suppleness as it solidified into a pasty gray, her entire body stiffening and hardening, her mouth slightly open to reveal fangs of stone growing harder and larger as she assumed the structure of a gargantuan goyle.

The final atrocity occurred when Lucinda completed her conversion, pitching him into a paroxysm of horror as bouldered wings fluttered and she lurched at him with craggy jaws opened wide enough to snatch off his head.

AMIRI

by **Nicole Givens Kurtz**

Aurora awoke, sore and stiff, to her dim bedroom's interior. Beside her, the baby snoozed, his tiny hands balled into tight fists. *Already a fighter,* she thought with a mixture of both pride and sorrow. His smooth, soft skin would toughen as he grew, but so would his heart. For now, she relished his warmth and closeness. In the dusty shadows of her room, her son looked so much like Bain, former mercenary, resistance fighter, and lover. Her son's lips curved just like his father's, in an upward smile—*a smile that would seduce many women and break many hearts.*

The thought of him carrying his father's traits chilled her despite the room's cozy warmth. She sighed. The bitterness of Bain's betrayal lingered, souring what should be a glorious miracle—her son's birth. When so many couldn't produce children, Amiri's arrival should be celebrated. So, she pushed her rising anger aside, and focused on the baby's other budding qualities.

His hair was hers: a kinky, curly mixture of tight corkscrews, soft and tender. She fingered them. He had her dark skin tone and wide nose. She snuggled him closer to her, waking him in the process, but he didn't cry out. He already demonstrated strong character by not crying when uncomfortable. This trait would be honed in the years to come.

Despite having birthed four other babies, Aurora had never been allowed to keep them. As a candidate breeder for the United World Council, her babies were taken immediately after birth and given to infertile women called, Mothers. The Mothers would then raise the child as their own, having purchased them outright. As a candidate, she'd been given time to recover before being reassigned to another childless couple. Again. And again.

No longer. Now, living in the hidden Resistance compound, she smiled in the shadows of those painful memories. Nursing, rearing, and parenting a child would be a new experience for her.

"It'll come natural to you," the midwife had said, when she placed a few minutes old Amiri in her arms.

Just like now, the babe sought out her breast and sleepily began to suckle. She closed her eyes and she enjoyed this solidifying of her bond. The interaction made her think of a transfer of power, of knowledge, of love. She'd feed him not only nourishment for his body, but for his mind, his soul. Here lay the secret essence of power—the ability to rear and to mold another human being.

No wonder women were such feared creatures.

In the distance, the automatic doors of her neighbor's apartment opened and Aurora's thoughts turned to Bain. Somewhere across Resistance compound, Bain rested in the arms of another woman. He had been Aurora's lover for little more than a year.

At one point, she thought herself more than bedmate, but a life-long partner. Bound by their shared trauma and enslavement, they'd learned to love, to survive. Yet, those bonds could not withstand freedom. The moment he met someone new, he abandoned Aurora as if leaving her meant leaving behind that uglier, seedier, hurtful life. He sought his newfound freedom in every way, including new relationships.

Aurora's anger ignited as the memories of the past disturbed her inner peace. When she shifted in the bed, the baby's lips dislodged from her nipple. Again, her son refused to yell in distress, instead he made a face of indignation.

"I'm so sorry, little one." She cooed at him and he relaxed.

Once satisfied that Aurora had settled down, the baby found her nipple again, and began to nurse once more.

Aurora extinguished the burning flames of anger and disappointment that ignited in her heart. She didn't want it flowing into the child… her *love* child. Amiri was a child conceived in love, but betrayed by Fate. Had she known that she'd become pregnant when they had arrived, perhaps things would've been different.

She recalled her own actions in her relationship with Bain. As a candidate, she hadn't been allowed to love anyone—not even friends. Lover. Family. Those words had little meaning to her. Once free, she didn't know how to put them into action.

Was it this that drew Bain to the other woman?

Aurora peered outside at the snow-covered landscape surrounding the Resistance compound. She didn't want her little one to begin his life filled with distress and anger. There would be plenty of time before he met his Creator at the end of his life's journey to engage those feelings.

I am free. We are free.

Still, in her experience, freedom could be a fragile illusion.

For if her tenure at the Garden had taught her anything, it was this: One is never truly free.

As her son drifted into sleep, so did Aurora.

And returned to the Garden.

"The goddess, Harvestina, has blessed you with a child, Candidate Browne. It's time to deliver the child to bless the families. You are the great goddess's blessing. Share your fertility with them." The Keeper's smile seemed stitched on with the corners pulled tight. Light eyes gleamed and gloved hands beckoned for Aurora to give the baby to her.

Aurora pulled her baby close to her chest. "No! Not this one!"

Young, often poor, girls were sold into Candidacy by parents or relatives. They had been scrubbed cleaned, checked by doctors, and clothed in these dark, coarse hooded cloaks. They turned their cloaked brown faces toward the shouting, but their heads bowed quickly when a mechanical noise joined the din.

They'd called in the Pale Soldiers!

The Pale Soldiers enforced the Keepers' biddings. The robotic soldiers felt no empathy, sorrow, or pity. They followed orders with rigid precision.

Aurora felt the cold fingers of fear clutch her heart. They couldn't take another child from her. Weakened from the labor, she'd still managed to crawl from the birthing table, snatch up her baby girl and hobble toward the exit door. Agony in every step. Muscles screaming in burning fury.

"No!" Aurora swallowed the lump of fear in her throat.

The Keeper nodded. "You know the Garden's rules, Candidate Browne."

The Garden grew babies, and pruned freedom.

* * * *

The Keeper inched closer to her. Aurora could smell the hint of tobacco on the woman's breath. "Candidates aren't fit to keep a child, Browne. Your bodies are only good for planting human seeds. Even your skin is dirt brown. The Goddess has decided this path. What's sowed within you is reaped for the parents. Your womb is fertile ground, and as such, you grow beautiful children for the world."

Aurora wanted to run, to fight, but terror pinned her to the spot. The two Pale Soldiers entered and closed rank around her, kicking and stepping on women in their path who didn't move fast enough to avoid them.

The Keeper held out her arms out for the child. The Pale Soldiers' shadows fell across Aurora's face and that of her babe.

"The child! Now!" The Keeper beckoned.

The whirring of the Pale Soldiers' machinery grew louder. Aurora watched as one of the soldiers raised a hand, an electronic baton in his fist, poised to beat her.

"The baby!" The Keeper gestured again. The smile on her face was broad, cold, calloused.

Aurora stepped back into the wall. They wouldn't hurt the baby. The new parents wouldn't want the baby battered or bruised.

Only her baby's life mattered to them.

Not that of the woman who bore her.

"You can't have this one!" Aurora shouted back. Tears burned her eyes, and then splashed down her cheeks.

The Pale Soldier's baton fell.

* * * *

The scream tore through Aurora's throat with anguish and urgency as she bolted awake. Heart pumping, she fought to catch her breath. With arms flailing and fists fighting, she had become entangled in the covers of her bed. Adrenaline roared in her ears as she fought to get clear. Once she oriented herself, she scanned the room.

Safe.

The snow gleamed through the window.

"I'm at Resistance headquarters. Not the Garden." She wiped the sweat from her brow.

No Pale Soldiers. No Keepers.

They weren't taking her baby. Not this time.

"Are you all right?" Bain stood inside the doorway. His uniform looked like he'd slept in it, and his shoulders sagged. His dark curly hair had been shorn. He didn't look like himself.

"What are you doing here?" She adjusted the covers around her waist, and reminded herself to change the access code to her quarters.

Aurora tried to regain control of herself by slowing her breathing. The memory had been so real. Her heart still galloped in her chest.

"I called your name, but it looked like you were having a night terror." Bain came further into the room, toward her.

Aurora climbed out of the bed and wrapped her robe around her, crossing her arms. "What do you want?"

"I'm here to see him." Bain nodded at the baby, still asleep in the bed.

Bain walked over to the bed, and squatted down beside it.

Her son—*their* son—slept on, unaware. He'd managed to avoid the nightmare's violence.

Safe.

Free.

Something she'd never experienced as a child. She sighed. How could she, a damaged, used-up candidate, raise a baby? The Keeper's words came back to her and she shuddered.

"He has your eyes." Bain whispered.

Her eyes?

"You can't know that. He's asleep." Aurora folded her arms.

It sounded so strange. She never thought about how her children would have parts of her. In the past, they'd been a part *from* her. Taken. Given to other women.

Now, she was Mother.

Bain shrugged. "I've seen him before, Aurora. Anyway, look! I think he's trying to turn over."

"It's too soon." Aurora joined him at the bed.

Wrapped in the blanket, a mop of black curls plastered to his head, the baby slept on but had begun to rotate his body as if attempting to roll over.

This close to Bain, Aurora smelled the machine oil and fire. It made her nose itch. He must've come directly to her from his detail.

Bain shifted his gaze from the baby to her. When he reached out and cupped her face, she flinched.

"Don't touch me." She shoved his hand from her face.

"Aurora," Bain sighed.

"I don't want you here."

Bain threw up his hands. "Look, I know you're angry about Maria."

"Angry?" Aurora quirked an eyebrow.

"You don't know how I feel."

Bain held his hands up. "I'm sorry."

"I don't want you to come here without making arrangements beforehand." She needed time to emotionally prepare for his visits.

"He's my son, too! You won't keep me from him." Bain's face hardened as he stood.

"I won't?" She met his leveled glare.

It became clear in that moment. He meant to keep the child for himself. He and Maria would do what all couples did—take the child for themselves and leave the candidate with nothing but emptiness.

"No one is taking anything from me, again." She leaned in close to him. He needed to see the ferocity in her eyes.

Bain studied her expression, before falling back a step. "You think I would? I know what happened before. I was there, remember? I know the Keepers…"

He looked away, and then sat down the edge of her bed. "Even though we aren't together, we'll raise him *together*. You and me."

"I can't believe anything coming from you." Aurora leaned down and covered their son. He'd kicked off the blanket.

Bain hesitated and avoided her eyes. "The United World Council still controls much of the world—the Gardens, and other places like it. Even if we die fighting, we did manage one miraculous thing. Our son was born *free*."

Aurora sat down beside him on the bed. Even after the horrible time she spent in candidacy, the fact she had escaped, continued to exist, and brought another life into the world defied most of the UWC's rules.

"He knows nothing of the oppression he will face. Simply because of how he was born, his appearance, and who his parents are." Aurora looked at her son's peaceful slumber.

"Not yet he doesn't." Bain agreed. "We will teach him to be strong."

"It may not be enough." Aurora acknowledged, her heart heavy. She swallowed the rest of the words, unable to speak her greatest fear aloud —that the Garden, or even worse, the United World Council, would take the child from her, even when he becomes a man.

He nodded. "It may not. We'll prepare him as best we can."

"Yes."

"After all, he's got you for a mother." Bain shot her a grin.

Aurora drew her knees up to her chest and hugged them. The mention of the word 'mother' made her quiver inside. *Mothers* had been harsh, unsmiling women who looked on during the coupling sessions as their husbands climbed on top of candidates and with force, planted their seeds.

At this, Aurora rushed to the bathroom and threw up. She couldn't be like those *Mothers*. The resentment and outright bitterness on those women's faces tore through Aurora. They hated her.

Not just her, but *all* candidates. They couldn't bear their own children, and because of the last series of wars, medicine to assist with infertility had been denounced by the Harvestina religion, and by the rise and global domination of the United World Council. Instead, candidates had been shipped all over the world, from one Garden to another to help with repopulation.

Bain handed her a wet cloth as he squatted down beside her in the tight, tiny bathroom. Kneeling before the toilet, Aurora wiped her mouth, but refused to look at him.

Perhaps he held too many memories of that horrific time as well.

Bain had been the manservant of one of the Mothers. As servants to that couple, they had fallen in love. But nothing as fragile as love survived in this brave new world beneath the United World Council's governance.

Even when she resisted.

"I'm sorry. I didn't mean you'd be like *those* women." Bain stood and offered his hand.

She avoided his hand and got to her feet

on her own. When she discarded the towel, and wiped her face, she caught Bain staring back into the bedroom. He had anguish inside him and his body language betrayed it. Lean, athletic and tall, he'd been a popular manservant. Farmed out to women as anniversary gifts and bachelorettes' toys, Bain held emotional scars of his own, no doubt. When he didn't see her looking, he would drop the mask he wore. Then Aurora saw the real him.

"Bain." She reached for him, and he let her pull him into a tight hug.

In these moments, nothing could touch them—not the UWC's continuing domination, not the other woman in Bain's bed, nor the horror of their pasts.

They were two freed human beings who had created a freeborn child.

Out of the terror of forced candidacy, Aurora saw the path ahead of her. The fight the Resistance waged had become more personal. She'd fight for the freedom of all people, not just her son. All the enslaved were sons and daughters.

Their baby cried. It interrupted the hushed silence and quiet communication that passed between herself and Bain.

"Amiri," Bain whispered, wiping his eyes with the corner of his uniform's sleeve as Aurora broke their hug.

"Amiri?" Aurora went into the room, picked the babe up, and held him close, rocking him.

"It means commander, leader…prince."

"He's not a prince, Bain." She adjusted her robe, freeing one of her breasts.

As the baby suckled, she studied his round, brown face. The peaceful look of bliss.

Bain came in from the bathroom. "If we raise him as a leader, he will become one."

Aurora watched the baby's tight fist. *A fighter. A leader.*

"Amiri."

She would be a good mother, because she *had* to be. The world didn't pull any punches for people not ready to bow beneath the UWC's boot. After all, she had to rear a leader who would help bring freedom to the world and throw off the chains of oppression.

"Yes. It suits him." Aurora kissed her son's fist.

Bain came over and kissed Amiri's forehead. Then, to Aurora said, "May I come after my shift tonight to see him?"

Aurora looked up at Bain. "Yes."

STICKS AND STONES
by John B. Rosenman

What would make a member of a species that abhorred violence not only kill, but savagely rend his victim's body until it was barely recognizable?

Lee Chang, a human, pondered the question as the towering Brynn guard led him down the hall to a well-lit cell in Estaban's central prison. There, his closest friend sat on a bed, staring down at his clawlike hands.

"Hello, Rizan," Chang said.

Rizan raised his gold, multifaceted eyes and met Chang's through the bars. Like many adult Brynn, Rizan was well over two meters tall and had a superbly muscled blue body. His massive, armored head was set like a block on shoulders twice as wide as Chang's own.

Ever since they were roommates at school twenty-five years before, Rizan had displayed the kind and nonviolent temperament of his species. Though the Brynn's peaceful disposition differed radically from that of humans, the two species had complemented each other beautifully in the thirty years since they had met, governing not only Estaban effectively, but other League worlds as well. To their partnership, humans contributed imaginative daring and boldness. The Brynn, in return, offered a genius for organization and administration, and a calm, productive thoughtfulness that often served to guide human impetuosity into constructive channels.

Calm, productive thoughtfulness. Studying his friend, Chang remembered the mangled, mutilated corpse he had recently viewed. He shuddered and nodded to the guard.

"Please open the door."

The guard cast a worried glance at Rizan. What must he be thinking? Chang thought. In all my life, I haven't heard of one of his people ever harming anyone unless attacked. He nodded again.

"Please open it. I'll be safe." Gazing at Rizan, he explained, "Rizan's my friend."

"Yes, sir," the guard said. He tapped the code-lock a few times and the door opened. Chang entered, hearing the door slam shut behind him.

"Hello, Rizan," he said again.

Rizan's lips twitched, his gold eyes bleak. "Lee, my old friend."

"Mind if I sit down?"

"Please."

Chang sat on the cell's solitary chair and drew a deep breath. The room smelled clean and looked spotless. Through the window, he could see it was late. The night sky glittered with stars, and Malvo, one of Estaban's two moons, was barely visible, sinking fast toward the horizon.

"Is it true?" he finally asked.

Rizan shook his head from side to side, a Brynn gesture indicating assent that was still confusing to some humans.

Chang's heart sank. "But it must be some crazy mistake! The report said you weren't threatened in any way, and yet you deliberately tore ex-councilman Perry's body to pieces, then turned yourself in to the authorities."

Another lateral nod. "Yes."

"But...but *why*? There must be a reason."

Silence.

"There must be a reason," Chang insisted. "There must! I *know* you, Rizan. Something terrible must have happened to make you do such a thing!"

Rizan raised a hand to rub his great blue skull. "Marcus Perry is…was…a most offensive human being."

I don't believe I'm hearing this, Chang thought. Did he say 'offensive'? Can this be *Rizan* talking?

"Rizan," Chang said, "our side held a fragile majority on the Council. Now Merrit's forces will seize control."

"I know that."

Chang gaped. "Damn it, Merrit doesn't understand that the Sunac are the most violent race in the galaxy. He wants trade concessions from them and will do anything to muscle in on their markets! And you know what the Sunac will do at the first sign of League aggression. They will attack and shatter the peace we've struggled so hard to preserve."

"Yes. It will almost certainly lead to war." Rizan sighed. "Even before I…killed Perry, I realized that Merritt sent him to provoke me. I also saw that Merrit had duped Perry, for he did not understand what his behavior would cost him."

"Then *what* made you do it? What made you ruin the peace we've fought so hard for and start a war that will kill *thousands*? A war, I might add, in which even your people will be forced to fight?"

Rizan was silent.

Chang persisted. "I've known you half my life. Even for a Brynn, you're a pacifist. You wouldn't hurt a flea if you could avoid it. Remember hazing at school? The upperclassman who, day after day, called you names?"

Rizan's lips twisted. "I remember. His name was Starling. Even for a *human*, he was irrational. I pitied him and found him to be mildly amusing."

"'Amusing'?" Chang stared. "What could you possibly find amusing about him? Starling was a bigot!"

"Yes, Lee, but his excesses were so droll."

The remark sounded like a page from a study on Brynn humor and irony. Under the circumstances, it served to make his friend seem stranger, even more unlike the man he had known.

Chang rose. "In God's name, what could Perry possibly have done that was worse than what Starling did to you? What was so bad it made you recklessly throw away everything we've fought for?"

"'In God's name' you say?" Rizan rose too, towering over Chang, his gold eyes flashing, his mighty body bulging with armor-like muscle. Moving to the window, Rizan gazed up at the night sky through the cold, rigid bars.

"The Universe is so beautiful, you know," Rizan said. "And so, too, is everything in it. The trees, the grass, the flowers. The microscopic worlds in a drop of water." He nodded up at the stars. "Did you know that one of our greatest poets once called the stars 'the shining thoughts of God'?"

"Yes, very pretty." Watching him, Chang repressed an urge to scream. Didn't the fool know what he had *done*?

Rizan turned from the window with a feeble smile. "Too often, humans think that despite our size, the Brynn are sentimental cowards afraid to fight. But we evolved our massive bodies in order to survive against a brutal enemy. After we finally destroyed the Jahanan, we no longer had a reason for our size and strength." He turned back to the window and gripped the slender bars with his great, clawlike hands. "Ever since then we have preferred peace."

"And valued life."

"Yes. Our remorse for destroying the Jahanan has made us come to revere all living things. Never again do we want to erase any beings from the sacred Scroll-stone of life."

A large, hairy spider crawled through the bars. Chang stepped back. He had always loathed and feared spiders, and they were especially common on Estaban. His nostrils crinkled. Ugly, filthy beasts, and here it was, invading this clean cell!

"Do you find spiders repulsive because they have multiple legs and scurry about?" Rizan held out a huge blue hand and smiled as the spider crawled onto one of its curved, razor-sharp nails. "But they are beautiful too, Lee. Just as all living things are beautiful."

"And was not Perry beautiful?" Chang asked, gazing at Rizan's sharp, immensely powerful fingers.

Rizan's hand froze, the spider crawling over it. "In the thirty years since our peoples met, the Brynn have kept a secret. To conceal the fact that for us, there is one unforgivable insult. Despite our antipathy for violence, this insult triggers our worst, atavistic tendencies, filling us with a primal rage that we are powerless to resist. And now, some humans have discovered that secret and sought to exploit it."

"What is this insult? Tell me!"

Carefully, Rizan set the spider on the window ledge and returned his attention to the stars. He opened and closed his mouth a few times, then shrugged, apparently realizing the secret had already been discovered.

"Perry told me that he had desecrated the grave of my First Ancestor by smashing its sacred Scroll-stone to pieces and smearing its carefully tended grass with filth and excrement. To make certain I believed him, he even showed me a holex of the despicable act. At first I was numb with shock and could only watch him cheerfully defile my Progenitor's resting place in the most abominable and infuriating of ways. And then—and then—as my paralysis wore off and I struggled to restrain myself, to keep myself from striking him, Perry did the worst thing of all, the one thing I could *not* tolerate!"

Chang stared in disbelief at Rizan's bulging eyes and twisted features, which emotion had darkened to purple. He was breathing hoarsely and a tic had appeared on his right cheek. Could this be the calm, rational man he knew? Was this mad killer actually Rizan?

"What did Perry do?" Chang finally

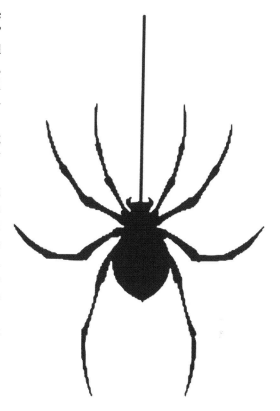

asked. "Tell me."

Rizan's gold, multifaceted eyes burned into his, and he raised his great, clawlike hands. "He threw his head back and—and—he *laughed* right in my face!"

"He *what*?" Chang paused, trying to make sense of it. "But so what if he did, Rizan? It was an obscene, upsetting thing to do, but surely you must have realized he was only trying to provoke you, make you do something that would weaken our side's unity. Look, do you remember how Starling used to bait you at school because he figured you wouldn't fight back? He even called your mother *a cheap whore* and you didn't even blink!"

"I see you don't understand," Rizan said.

"No, I don't," Chang admitted. "So he tore down your ancestor's Scroll-stone and crapped on his grass. So what?"

"My *First* Ancestor."

"What *difference* does that make? Your First Ancestor must have lived five thousand years ago. He's mere dust by now! You should have simply filed criminal charges against Perry and arranged for the grave to be repaired and cleaned up. That would certainly have discharged any offense to your clan's honor."

Rizan raised a mighty arm and took Chang's in his clawlike fingers. Though he could have snapped it like a straw, his touch was gentle.

"Your people are so smug and complacent, Lee. They think they have all the answers and know the Brynn well. But they don't. While my people are like yours in some ways, we are vastly different in others."

"Explain!"

Rizan's face flooded with emotion. He stepped back, breaking contact.

"When Perry desecrated my First Ancestor's resting place and laughed insolently in my face, he was saying that my entire clan, including its very root and foundation, was weak, cowardly, and undeserving of either respect or honor. He was boasting that *his* line, *his* genes, had a far better right than mine to survive, and to be engraved upon the sacred Scroll-stone of life."

"But Perry was *human*, a Pygmy compared to you! You could have crushed him like a grape. In fact, you did!"

"I know, but I was powerless to resist. Once he'd shown me what he had done and arrogantly, mockingly *laughed* about it, I *had* to act. It was madness in my blood. It was my deepest, inborn, primal nature, m-m-my...physiological imperative." He stopped, breathing hard, his great chest rising and falling as his face darkened to purple again. "Indeed, the act was what the Jahanan always used to do to enflame us, to assert their supposed racial superiority over the Brynn."

Chang tried to understand, but all he could think of was a childhood rhyme. "When I was a kid, there was something we used to chant when someone insulted us. 'Sticks and stones may break my bones,/But names will never hurt me!'"

"Even if it seems harmless, there is always something that one cannot bear," Rizan said softly.

"I cannot believe that. You would rather go to war—"

Rizan nodded his head up and down, indicating disagreement. "You simply have not experienced it yet."

Chang moved closer. "If...if *I* had desecrated your First Ancestor's grave, and then laughed in your face, what would you have done? Killed me as you did Perry? My God, Rizan...you *ripped his entire head off!*"

Rizan's complex gold eyes darkened. "I don't know what I would have done. I hope that I would have been able to resist."

Chang felt as if he would explode. "But I can't forgive you—not for this!" In despair, he went to the door to signal the guard. Then he looked back. "If you *had* to kill him, why, *why* was it necessary to confess? You could have saved your honor or whatever it was, and we could have avoided war!"

Rizan hesitated, his face etched with sorrow. "It would have been wrong to lie and conceal my act. If I had done so, I would only have proven that Perry was right."

"But thousands will die! Perhaps millions! The very peace you claim to cherish will be shattered by your act, and your peace-loving people will be forced to fight too!" Chang swallowed. "Rizan, my *son* is stationed on Sunac. Yours is too. They could both die!"

A tear ran down Rizan's thick, armored cheek. "I am sorry, my friend. I knew the terrible consequences of my act, but I tell you again that I had no choice."

Chang raised his fist, then weakly dropped it. Rapping the cell door, he waited till the guard came and freed him, then followed him numbly down the hall.

Outside he entered his ground car and drove till he was well beyond the city. Repeatedly he tried to understand the man who had been his closest friend. But he couldn't. Thousands—no, millions—would die because of this senseless war Rizan had caused! Desecrate the grave of his First Ancestor? Was that anything to kill about? To Chang, it was insanity, the raving gibberish of a mad alien.

At last he stopped his vehicle. Leaving it, he began walking across a field. Then he stopped.

Slowly, he fell to his knees in the deep grass and gazed up at the starflung reaches of the universe. "The shining thoughts of God." *Oh, God, if You really are up there, what are You thinking NOW?*

Something tickled his hand. He raised it, squinting in the starlight at a large spider. Almost immediately, he felt others on his legs and stomach. He looked down.

His entire body was covered with them!

This was not merely one odious creature—but hundreds! He wanted to run, scream, but found himself paralyzed by fright and revulsion. All his life he had feared these filthy beasts, and now they were swarming all over him!

Even if it seems harmless, there is always something that one cannot bear,

Rizan had said. *You simply have not experienced it yet.*

Chang shuddered, feeling the spiders burrow beneath his shirt and race across his skin. Their hairy legs probed his mouth, crawled through his hair. No, it wasn't the same as what made Rizan snap—it wasn't, it wasn't, it wasn't! The insult to Rizan's line was an imaginary trifle. But these…these *things*, though physically harmless, were supremely horrible!

Then, despite his terrible, mind-crazed fear, Chang suddenly realized something. He was deluding himself. It *was* the same and Rizan was right! At that moment, he would gladly wish a dozen men dead or start a *hundred* wars if it would only help him to escape these disgusting, repulsive creatures!

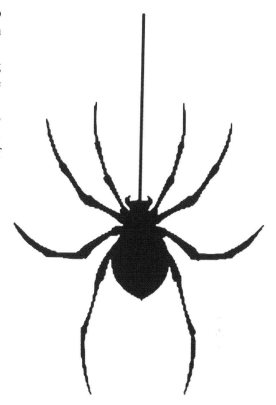

Screaming, Chang broke out of his paralysis and started to smash the spiders in a mad ecstasy of fear and rage. Again and again he raised his fists and brought them down, crushing the scurrying beasts to pulp. He stamped furiously at those on the ground and clawed at the ones on his body, ripping them to shreds and flinging them wildly in every direction.

Finally, his entire body coated with a black, seething mass, Chang managed to recover a little sanity and lurch to his feet. Tearing off his shirt he staggered toward his car, slapping the spiders from his body with weakened, gore-stained hands. Above, the stars blazed down, burning not with divinity, but with the bright cold promise of war.

✳

T. GIPS AND THE TIME FLIES

by Ahmed A. Khan

No one knows his real name. At one time he had been called The Great Problem Solver or TGPS for short. Then the TGPS got transformed into T. Gips, and this name had stuck.

Whenever and wherever in the known universe there is what appeared to be an unsolvable problem, the first (or sometimes the last) person people think of is T. Gips. He charges a lot but, more often than not, he delivers.

T. Gips had just solved a problem of grave proportions on the planet Sisimak and was on his way to his homeworld of Elbracket when he received an S.O.S. from Space Colony #203, the planet known as Enbond He sighed and changed his flight plans. He was now on his way to Enbond to help the colonists there about some trouble caused by native insectoids called—such a strange name—time flies.

Dreading every moment, he called his wife, Jojo, on the Intergalactic Communicator.

Jojo's youthful, smiling face appeared on the screen. She looked so ravishing, T. Gips fell in love all over again.

She came straight to the point. "When are you coming back home?"

"I—I was on my way home." He stopped, took a deep breath and continued. "I have received an S.O.S. from Enbond."

Jojo's smile vanished. "Mr. Gips, you are dead," she said icily and disconnected.

T. Gips sighed. Getting back into Jojo's good books would be a problem, probably greater than the one he had just solved on Sisimak or the one he would attempt to solve on Enbond.

His thoughts moved back to Enbond. He hoped he would not be bored there. He hoped he would at least be able to practice his archery—one of his many hobbies.

His ship emerged from hyperspace. Enbond was close at hand.

An hour later, Gips was sitting in the main dome, in the office of Administrator Robb Javins, discussing the problem of the time flies with him. "We had some time flies in our bio lab in this dome," said Dr. Javins, a portly man with a face that would have been called merry at normal times. Right then, all it showed was stress. "They were kept in a stasis chamber. They got out. Sheer negligence of a lab assistant, you know."

The dome was constructed on a hillside at quite a high altitude. The clear windows of the office overlooked a huge forest way down the hillside. Enbond was a forest world, full of interesting life forms.

"Why are these insects called time flies?" Gips asked.

"Because anything they touch is transported through time," said Javins.

A startled, "What?" escaped Gips' lips.

They were interrupted by sounds. *Buzz-crackle-pop, buzz-crackle-pop*, the sounds went, starting low but slowly increasing in volume. Even as they watched, the wall on one side of the office developed fly-sized holes through which some flies zoomed in. Some of them landed on the table, and as Gips watched, parts of the table started vanishing. Very soon the table surface was pock-marked.

Meanwhile, Javins had jumped out of his seat and was heading with great speed for the door. His speed was truly admirable in view of his girth.

"Run," he shouted, even as he put his words into practice.

Gips ran.

"So where does the time-transported matter go?" Gips asked while he ran beside Javins. "Forward or backward in time?"

"Forward. That is how they feed."

"Explain."

"There is a release of energy related with transporting matter forward in time. The flies absorb this energy."

"Indigenous?"

"Yes, and thank God, they remain at lower levels and never move to higher altitudes, else our dome would not have survived."

"Interesting. What do you expect *me* to do?"

"Catch the escaped flies."

"Can't you kill them?"

"How? They are virtually untouchable. Anything touching them gets transported in time." They had to stop running because they had reached the end of the corridor.

"And," Gips prompted.

"And we are hoping you can find a way to get them back into the stasis chamber."

"How?"

"Aren't you the great problem solver? So solve."

Gips thought hard, and thought fast. The time flies were following them. He could once again hear the *buzz-crackle-pop.*

He snapped his fingers. He had the answer.

"Come with me," he said and raced toward the room that had been assigned to him as his living quarters.

Inside the room, he opened his bag and pulled out his archery set. He grabbed an arrow and handed it to Javins.

"Quick, put this arrow in the stasis chamber."

"What?" Javins exploded.

"Quick, man. Don't waste time."

Uncomprehendingly but with a what-the-hell air, Javins hurried toward the bio lab, closely followed by Gips. They entered the lab. Sounds indicated that the time flies were close behind them. Very close behind them. Almost upon them, actually. Javins turned to look. The flies had entered the lab and seemed to be making straight for them.

Still not knowing how it could save them, Javins threw the arrow into the stasis chamber. Immediately, the flies changed direction and homed in on the arrow. Within moments, they were all safely inside the chamber, and Javins sealed it.

"What was it all about?" Javins, still incredulous, asked Gips once they were back in Javin's office and had got their breaths back. "What made you so sure that an arrow would lure them into the stasis chamber?"

"Haven't you heard," explained Gips, "that time flies like an arrow?"

T. Gips left. Watching Javins bang his head repeatedly on the office wall was not a pretty sight.

❁

THE ANGRY PLANET
by DJ Tyrer

Vinn Mazell was startled by the sudden announcement by Siri that the ship had picked up a distress call. He was sitting alone in the stark familiarity of the vessel's bridge.

"Say again," he said.

"I have picked up a distress call," repeated the perfectly-modulated voice of Siri.

"Details."

"Standard Colonial Service format. Originating from the planet designated XC-23. It began broadcasting 32 hours ago."

"Play message."

A man's voice replaced that of Siri: "This is the Worldbuilder colony on planet designated XC-23, known as Red Eden. We require immediate assistance. The—" The message cut off, incomplete.

"Is that all?" Vinn asked.

"Affirmative," said Siri.

"Set a course for XC-23."

"Affirmative. Setting course for XC-23. Estimated time of arrival: Two hours."

Most of that time would be that spent travelling in-system from the jump point.

"Send a message to the Red Eden colony, as follows: 'This is Vinn Mazell of Z Patrol. Have received your distress call and will reach you in approximately two hours.' End message. Repeat twenty times."

"Broadcasting message."

Travelling through subspace, the message would reach the system in minutes.

"Give me all the information on XC-23, colony, planet and system."

"Accessing data." There was a pause of a few seconds, then Siri spoke again: "XC-23 system consists of a red giant star and three surviving planets: two gas giants and a small, rocky planet on the system fringe. Primary world is a moon of the second gas giant. The settlement of this planet began

one Standard Year ago with a standard terraforming outfit consisting of 152 personnel and dependents. No further data."

"Thank you, Siri."

"You are welcome." Another pause, then: "We are ready to jump, Commander."

"Initiate jump."

He felt the lurch as the ship sidestepped from the universe of everyday experienced to the tortured realities of hyperspace. No matter how many times he jumped, he always felt as if his intestines and lungs were attempting to swap places and his spleen was trying to escape via his mouth. But, as they did every time, his innards settled down after a minute or two and he could almost enjoy the darkness and silence of the jump as the ship powered down non-essential systems.

Then, a few minutes later, came a second lurch and the ship returned to realspace and, after a moment, the systems came back online.

"We have reached system XC-23." He rolled his eyes at Siri's habit of stating the obvious.

"Scan system. Any further data on the colony."

"Scanning." There was a brief silence. "Scan indicates colony world is approximately 30% terraformed. Further data on world and colony unavailable due to interference."

"Interference? What sort of interference?"

"Unknown. Insufficient data. Unknown energy is preventing a more detailed scan."

Now, that was interesting.

* * * *

The ship was in orbit about the moon that the colonists had dubbed Red Eden. Vinn could see why they had chosen that appellation for their new home: whether due to some element of its atmosphere or merely the reflected light of the crimson star, the planet-moon had a distinct red hue to it. The depowered colony jumpship hung in orbit like a satellite of the planet-moon, having deposited its human cargo.

"Siri, have you managed to scan the surface?" Vinn asked: little of the surface was visible from orbit.

"I have located the colonial settlement and the primary atmospheric generators, but further examination is still precluded due to an unidentified energy signature."

Shapes indicating the sites in question appeared upon the otherwise undistinguished image of the planet.

"Is the atmosphere breathable?"

"You will need a breathing mask, but no other precautions."

"Prepare the lander for launch."

"Affirmative."

He fetched his facemask and other equipment he might require, then headed for the newly-readied lander, a small shuttle intended for in-atmosphere flight.

Grasping the controls, Vinn launched it and guided it down towards the surface, following the coordinates supplied by Siri. The lander bucked like a Vendulian Kickster as it entered the roiling atmosphere where intense winds buffeted it. It was always the same with these partially-prepared planets, the terraforming of the atmosphere always seemed to send the air into turmoil.

On the viewscreen, all he could see was a swirl of orange-and-red cloud. Then, suddenly, he was through the thick layer and the ruddy surface of the planet below was revealed. He could see the various prefabricated structures that made up the colonial settlement and, flanking it, two great towers that were part of the network generating an atmosphere more suitable to earthly life. These ones appeared no longer active and one was leaning at an angle.

Vinn brought the lander down on a land-

ing pad on the edge of the settlement, beside the mangled remains of a VTOL craft that looked as if it had been tossed about by a storm. He wondered if the powerful forces that had been unleashed by the rebuilding of the atmosphere had brought disaster down upon the colonists.

He put on his mask, along with a pair of goggles that would not only protect his eyes, but allow Siri to feed him data, and attached a holster with a laspistol to his hip: although he was working on the assumption the colony had been hit by a storm, he knew that assumptions without preparation for other possibilities generally got people killed.

"Lower the ramp," he told Siri, "then raise it behind me." Vinn had heard plenty of tales about pilots who had left a ramp down only to find something nasty waiting for them inside.

He walked down the ramp onto the landing pad. The wind buffeted him. it wasn't as angry as those in the upper atmosphere, but it was still pretty powerful. Vinn was grateful for the goggles as the wind was kicking up plenty of dust: XC-23 was less a Red Eden and more of a red wasteland; there was some native plant life, but not until the transformation was complete would it be lush.

"Siri," he shouted over the sound of the wind, "can you access the colony mainframe?"

"Affirmative," he heard her say in his ear, through an earbud. "Unfortunately, it has been severely compromised with significant data and hardware loss."

"Can you locate any of the colonists?"

"Negative."

Vinn walked along a metal walkway raised above the ground towards the settlement. Like all such colonies, the buildings were basic and prefabricated from lightweight plasteel. A few had signs, such as a bar and a workshop, but otherwise looked alike.

He began checking the buildings, but each one was empty. Some were pristine, even down to the half-finished mugs of mycobeer in the bar, as if the colonists had just stepped outside for a moment. Others were smashed open or were askew as if the wind had partially-overturned them.

"How can this be?" he asked Siri. "How can one building be untouched, while the one beside it looks as if it has been struck by an earthquake."

"I possess insufficient data to answer that query. However, it does seem as if some sort of tectonic event had taken place here, affecting certain of the buildings."

"An earthquake and not a storm?"

"It would appear so, yes."

"Odd."

Vinn headed towards the main building, which once would have been the hub of the colony. It had a shape reminiscent of an egg on its side and appeared to have been cracked open, just like an egg, too.

It only took Siri a moment to override the security barring the doors to him; not that the sealed doors appeared to have done the people inside much good.

Vinn entered, a helmet-mounted torch lighting his way. The interior was quiet and dark like a mausoleum and put him in mind of a vintage movie he once had watched, the utilitarian design now buckled and twisted into a peculiar creepiness. His footsteps echoed eerily.

"Anybody home?" he called, voice muffled by his mask.

There was no reply.

"Can you connect me to the base communications system?" he asked Siri.

"Negative. Communications offline."

He was going to have to do this the old-fashioned way—floor-by-floor, room-by-room. There was nobody present and no clues as to what had happened here: the building had clearly been overtaken by some disaster and there were hints—laser burns, discarded weapons, the scorch of explosives—that an act of violence must have preceded or followed it, but no bodies, no blood, nothing to indicate where everyone had gone or why.

Vinn paused in operations, hoping to salvage some sort of information, but the story was the same as Siri's attempt to access the mainframe wirelessly. The only clue, if it were a clue and not a red herring appropriate to the world, was a printout that, from what he could read, it having been torn and burnt, gave the coordinates of...something; possibly nothing.

He continued his search through the building.

Suddenly, something burst out of the darkness ahead and lunged towards him. Vinn raised his laspistol and fired, dropping the loping monstrosity.

He moved towards it. It twitched and he fired a second shot to still it. Had the colony had a simian labour force? Siri had made no mention of simians. Nor was there any record of higher native life-forms.

Then, he looked closer: the creature was wearing a shredded boilersuit. He rolled it over and stepped back in shock. Although twisted and horribly changed, the thing was unmistakably a man. It was one of the colonists, yet one who had somehow become feral, almost alien in form. What had happened to him? Had the base's medical bay been functioning, he might have been able to get some answers, but he would have to get the body back to his ship to examine it.

He finished exploring the building, and then exited it.

Even weak and ruddy as it was, the sunlight that hit the surface of XC-23 was preferable to the darkness of the base interior.

Having found nothing but questions at the colony site, Vinn decided to head for the coordinates he found in the operations room. It might be nothing more than the location of a mine or for a proposed geological survey that had never taken place, but it was the only lead he had. Other than one that had been destroyed by whatever disaster had overtaken the place, he had seen no ground vehicles, meaning he would have to either take the lander or proceed on foot. The former being too obvious, he decided to stick to his own motive power.

After walking for some time, he found himself following a ravine. Sheltered from the worst of the winds, he could see tyre tracks in the dust and the occasional boot print: it seemed as if the colonists had come this way en masse. It seemed he had chosen well.

The ravine led to a crater at the coordinates he had found, a rough ramp leading down into it. The crater was crowded.

Vinn stood on the lip of the crater and gazed down at the vehicles and people that were assembled below. None moved. Everyone was standing in rank and file as if waiting to be inspected. Then, as he watched, a hole seemed to collapse into existence at the centre of the crater and things, vaguely humanoid, yet crudely-formed and featureless, poured out of it like ants from an anthill. They scattered amongst the regimented host of humanity and moved between them, pausing as if to examine individuals, then seizing hold of certain unresisting figures and dragging them towards the hole.

Vinn knew he ought to intervene, but there were too many of them. Then, as he watched, the hole closed up behind them as if it had never existed. It was, he realised, a little like a mouth closing.

The other people who had not been taken remained in their ranks, unmoved by what had just happened.

"Siri, can you tell me what is under the ground here?"

There was no response. Clearly, whatever had been affecting the scans had cut the signal off completely.

Vinn began his descent into the crater, but halted after only a short distance, having spotted more movement below. For a moment, he thought it was the alien things returning, but it was one of the settlers, a woman dressed in dust-stained khaki slacks and blouse. She appeared to be searching the vehicles, glancing over, occasionally, to where the hole had briefly appeared. She seemed unaware of his presence.

Slowly, he crept down into the crater and made his way over to her.

"Hey! Psst!"

She span around, eyes wide with fear, only relaxing a little as she saw him. Her entire body was tense, like a gazelle that was ready to run. Her eyes were red and damp, but whether from tears or the stinging dust, he couldn't say.

"Hi. I'm Commander Vinn Mazell of Z Patrol. I got your distress call and have come to help you. Can you tell me what has happened?"

"I'm looking for my children," she said, not really answering him.

"Okay. Are they in the vehicles?"

"I don't know..." She began looking inside them, again, and he joined her.

"They aren't there," she wailed. "I don't know where they are."

"Look, if you can tell me what's been going on, I'll be able to help you and, maybe, we can find them. What's your name?"

She ran her hands through her hair, as if doing so would collect her thoughts.

"My name is Carolyn McKie. I'm a colonist here. Oh, you must help me find my family!"

"Just start at the beginning."

She repeated the action of running her fingers through her hair, calming herself.

"Um, well, things haven't really been right since we arrived. It was, uh, just little things at first—earth tremors and the like. Then, as we began transforming the atmosphere, things got worse and there were storms and stronger 'quakes. Then, one day, a powerful storm struck us, followed by an earthquake, only..." She lapsed into silence.

"Only?"

"Only, it didn't affect everything the way a normal 'quake would. It was...directed. Yes, directed. Then, those things came and seized people and dragged them off. Only, not all of them: some just went, walking or driving. I hid and, somehow, wasn't taken, but I followed them...here."

"I found the coordinates to this place in operations. Can you tell me anything about that?"

She shook her head. "Sorry, no. I worked in HR. Anyway, I followed them here and watched some of them being dragged into that...that *maw*. Those who had been brought here, struggling. They were the first to go, although others were taken later. My husband was in the second batch, but I haven't seen my children. I try to tell myself they got away like I did, but..."

He understood. "Do you know what is taking them, and why?"

Carolyn shook her head again. "All I know is that, sometimes, that maw opens up and these weird rock-people come and drag folk off with them. They don't act intelligently, but I suspect they *are* directed, like the earthquake. Something down there controls them."

"What happens to those taken away?"

She shrugged. "Most never return, but some came back more like creatures than human beings."

"Feral," he said.

"Yes, feral. Look, I've got a theory."

"What is it?"

"The planet is alive and it's angry. No, wait, don't scoff. Look, that...hole is like a mouth, swallowing people up, and something has to be guiding the aliens. Put that together with the storms and 'quakes and, then, it all comes together to make sense."

He listened as she explained her theory and found himself nodding in agreement. It all had an awesome sense of logic to it.

"Sometimes," she added, "people come back different, as I've said, but most haven't. Maybe they're hostages, but I suspect they're being used to study us. I'm certain the planet is alive, sentient, and it wants us gone. It's studying us, like a doctor studies germs so he can kill them."

He had to nod his agreement there: it made a lot of sense, seeking your enemy's weaknesses, but the idea of an angry planet just seemed crazy. Nothing like it existed in human-explored space, but there was always a first time.

"The way I see it, we need to go down there, too, see what's going on, see if we can rescue them."

Even as he said it, he wasn't too keen. Although he didn't share her certainties, he found the lack of knowledge about what they faced almost as terrifying.

"Weren't you listening?" she snapped back. "Everyone who goes in there is swallowed up."

"*No*, you said some come back: They don't all die. We won't die. And, maybe your kids are down there..."

That was the right thing to say and she nodded and said, "Yes, they could be. Could be...I'm going to save them!"

They hid themselves behind the vehicle nearest to where the hole had opened up and waited.

"How long are the intervals between the openings?" Vinn asked Carolyn.

She shrugged. "Anywhere between one and six hours, or so."

He took her through the events that had befallen the colony again, twice, but could learn nothing more. Then, the hole opened again and the rock-like beings swarmed out. They waited for them to disperse amongst the assembled colonists and, then, moved quickly towards the pit, crouching low and hoping not to be seen. The entities seemed intent upon their work and paid them no heed.

Although an opening in the crust of the planet, the hole looked disturbingly like an orifice belonging to a living creature. Vinn felt nauseous and really wished he didn't have to enter it. Carolyn, driven by the thought of her children, seemed unconcerned. A tunnel sloped downwards from the hole and led them deep beneath the surface of the planet.

They walked in silence, each pondering what awaited them and not daring to voice their thoughts.

Suddenly, two of the rock beings appeared out of the shadows ahead of them and charged towards them. Vinn raised his laspistol and fired, but it appeared to have no effect.

"They're stone!" Carolyn shrieked at him.

He tried to think what he carried that might affect them, then Carolyn raised an object that he recognised as a rivet gun. She pulled the trigger on it and there was an explosion of compressed air and a rivet spat towards one of the figures. Chunks of rock were blown free from it. she fired again and again, blowing them apart until nothing was left but fragments.

"Impressive," he said.

"I came prepared. Come on."

"I wonder..." he murmured.

"What?"

"They're like white blood cells, protecting..." He trailed off.

They went deeper and reached a series of galleries branching off from the main tunnel. In some, human bodies were laid out upon slabs where they were being examined by more of the rock beings, while, in others, hypnotised people stood about, unresisting, appearing to undergo some form of examination or conditioning.

"It, whatever it is, wants to understand us," said Vinn.

"But, we didn't detect anything when we surveyed the world," Carolyn said, her voice strained as she fought to control the panic rising within her.

"It must be the entire planet, something quite beyond the parameters of your scans. Clearly, your terraforming process affected it and it set out to purge you; cure you, like a disease. I suspect..."

"What?"

"There figures didn't exist before. Not in this form, anyway. I think their form reflects ours. They are a direct response to our presence."

"That's all very interesting, but it doesn't rescue my kids. Where are they?"

They were searching the galleries, the stone humanoids seemingly unconcerned by their presence.

"Well, if we can understand what's driving it, maybe that can help us find them, and save the others. Unfortunately, between your terraforming and our forcing our way in here, it may just assume we're hostile."

"I don't care. I just want my kids."

Suddenly, Carolyn stopped and pointed: "Look! There they are!"

There were two young children standing hypnotised. Vinn was glad to see they appeared physically unharmed.

"Get them," he told her; "I'm going lower."

He left her as she ran to them and continued down the tunnel.

Deep below the galleries where the colonists were being held was a vast chamber, the walls of which glittered with quartz. Columns and outcrops of quartz jutted out throughout it. *Things* moved amongst the clusters, not the humanoid figures he had seen above, but things that had no real analogy in his experience. They were also composed of rock, but, he guessed, predated the figures that had come for the colonists.

Was this the brain, or what passed for the brain of the planet entity? Perhaps only one of many scattered throughout the world working in concert?

Could he...? Vinn headed for the nearest outcropping and laid his hands upon it and felt something like an electric shock as he was struck by a surge of...consciousness was the word that came to mind.

Images crashed violently through his mind as he attempted to project those he wished it to understand. His head hurt. There was anger. Fear. Or, at least, those were the analogues he could term the immense feelings that flooded into him. Was the problem of scale insurmountable? Could a planet understand a human or vice versa, anymore than a human could understand an amoeba?

Suddenly, he staggered back, releasing his grip on the node, pain and nausea racing through him. He turned and ran.

Somehow, Vinn found himself staggering back out into the ruddy sunlight. He couldn't recall the details of his ascent.

He was startled by the sound of voices and looked about in confusion: The colonists were no longer hypnotically regimented, but were stumbling about, asking one another what was going on.

Someone was calling his name. Vinn turned around and saw Carolyn leading her children out of the hole.

"What happened?" he called.

"I couldn't get them to move—they were like statues—then, suddenly, they were themselves again. Everyone came back to normal."

Carolyn gestured behind herself and he saw more colonists stumbling up out of the pit.

"I think… I think I managed to convince it to let us go. We need to gather everyone together."

She and a couple of others helped him to gather the surviving colonists together.

"We have to strike back," one said.

"No, it means us no more harm," Vinn replied.

"It killed our people!"

"It reacted to us how we react to germs. It wasn't malicious. It was angry, but I think I've managed to assuage its anger. But, if you attack it now, it will respond and it will destroy you. It is too powerful."

"Then, what do we do?" Carolyn asked.

"You need to leave. Summon the shuttles from your jumpship and ferry yourselves and whatever you can salvage off-world, then go and never come back. Leave XC-23 to itself."

Carolyn asked, "It will let us go?"

"Yes, I believe so. It released you…"

"Then, we should go," she said. "I thought I'd lost my kids, my husband, but they're alive and I don't want to risk them again. We must go."

Vinn nodded. "Leave, find another world to settle; there are plenty of planets in the galaxy. XC-23 is something unique. Perhaps, one day, we'll understand it, maybe even live in harmony on it, but not yet. For now, we have to leave it alone."

From orbit, Vinn Mazell watched as the planet brought the atmospheric generators crashing down, breaking them up and absorbing the wreckage of the towers and the remnants of the colony until there was no visible sign that humanity had ever been on the world. XC-23 had returned to its pristine, untouched state, angry no more, but he had to wonder how the encounter with humanity had changed it—and how it would change humanity.

The colonists had already jumped out of the system. They would doubtless be allocated a new world to colonise, although he doubted many would relish the task. They had suffered already.

But, humanity would continue to spread out across the expanse of space, colonising new worlds. Perhaps the being that was XC-23 would provide new insights that could help them. Already, he felt new thoughts within his mind, echoes of his communion with XC-23; strange thoughts with a meaning he couldn't quite comprehend, insights far beyond any he had felt before. Somehow, he knew he had much to learn.

"Siri, set a new course."

"Coordinates?"

He provided them: they had come from that inscrutable, alien mind. He wondered what he would find.

"Affirmative. Setting course. Six jumps. Estimated time of arrival: one week."

Vinn sat back and relaxed. One week and he would know.

❈

THE HEART OF A HITMAN
by Rie Sheridan Rose

Flannery Quinn glided through the dark, silent London streets like a cat. The centuries had not been kind to the Earth. Despite the Global Unification Treaty of 2384, which ostensibly created a duly elected central government, undercurrents of unrest ebbed and flowed.

Only the occasional sweep of a guard team searchlight as they made their rounds disturbed the deserted streets. The Resistance was worrisome enough that strict sanctions closed the cities at 1900 hours. It was well after the curfew—a hollow edict easily flaunted by a well-placed credit or two but effective for keeping the poverty-stricken penned up at night. Standing orders were to shoot on sight, and if you had no credit case to hide behind, the Guards' aim was exceptional.

Dressed in unrelieved black, Flannery carried his disrupter drawn as he moved through the streets. The heavy sidearm was an antique compared to the slimmer models that most field agents preferred. However, Flannery found comfort in the fact that if they forced him to carry a gun at least his weapon looked like one. The entire function of a disrupter was to damage or destroy the integrity of the cellular structure itself. It should look dangerous, not like some toy off a vidreel.

A pulsing microcircuit in his left wrist masked his progress, rendering him invisible to ordinary sensors. If they had no lurking SkyBirds, he was safe—though an observant human eye might spot him in the shadows…

As if conjured up by his thoughts, his ears caught a high-pitched whine from the darkness overhead. Throwing himself under the projecting servosteel overhang of a nouveau chic boutique fronting the street, he jammed his gloved hands deep into the pockets of his thick jacket. Scarcely daring to breathe, Flannery traced the passage of the airborne surveillance globe with his eyes. The device was a standard mechosentry; electronic scanning detectors housed in a round servosteel casing and set into a predetermined flight pattern. Any physical movement and biomolecular feedback filtered through the globe's detectors for threat analysis. The sentries were programmed to automatically destroy any unauthorized sensory devices detected by such a scan. While a SkyEye might herd a harmless wandering human in for interrogation, it would fire an energy beam at a passing aircar that strayed outside the pre-programmed road system. Or a potential two-legged spy armed with data retrieval or collection equipment.

Falling as he did into the latter category, and unable to rid himself of his tell-tale sensors, Flannery prayed to the Son that the metal surrounding him would distort the SkyEye's data. After what seemed an infinite space of time, the SkyEye passed out-of-sight, never even slowing in its movement. Letting out a shaky sigh, Flannery stepped out into the street once more. That was too close for comfort.

He tugged off one of his close-fitting black gloves. "I hope this soddin' weather hasn't affected me readings," he sighed aloud, staring down at the sleek craftsmanship of the silver cybernetic device revealed in the dim starlight. The sensory equipment he couldn't conceal from the SkyEye was built into the slim artisan fingers of his artificial hands. With a sigh, he replaced the glove. If the readings were off, there wasn't much he could do about it in the field.

He had lost both hands at thirteen to the Discipline Tribunal—the judicial branch of the planet-governing Lords of Discipline. Accused of theft, the penniless orphan had been unable to buy defense, and the supreme punishment had been inflicted as a lesson to the other street denizens. He had been dying in an alleyway when his team leader Ace Kilcarney, had found him and unofficially adopted him.

Through the golden persuasion that was his trademark, Ace had convinced the scientists at Uniglobal Surveillance that Flannery was a perfect test case for their latest developments in cybernetics. And so here he was—fifteen years and twelve sets of appliances later—carrying out yet another in a never-ending series of missions as Uniglobal's favorite hitman.

A rime of frost crunched softly beneath his boots as he slipped forward. The clear January night was bitterly cold, and Flannery shivered despite his heavy jacket. Above him, the brittle Heavens glittered with stars in spattered profusion, no longer paled by the pre-curfew lights of a restless city.

He had roamed the London streets for hours. It was safer to berth the aircar outside the city perimeter and walk to his goal deep within the sprawling metropolis. He didn't mind. The frigid beauty of the night walk helped him to forget its inescapable conclusion. After he accomplished the mission, he'd hole up somewhere and sleep before returning home.

Chewing his lip out of nervous habit, he winced, exploring the painfully lacerated area with his tongue. The entire inside of his mouth was in shreds. He chuckled bitterly— more air than sound. This was all so stupid.

He reviewed his mission objective one more time. A minor official on the London Lord General's staff had indiscreetly voiced his dissatisfactions in a public house, and had been brought to the Board of Rule's attention. Flannery's assignment was to silence the man's complaining. There was no room for dissension in the governmental ranks; Lord and Council eliminated any individual they found was not absolutely loyal—for the good of the State.

He wheeled toward a flutter of sound emanating from a nearby alleyway, finger convulsing on his disrupter. A brief burst of silent death lit the night—the writhing form of a squalling cat pinned by the beam. Flannery's held breath whooshed out in a sobbing exhalation of sound.

God's Son, he despised himself for the death he dealt. He wasn't sure why he continued… Was the true reason he accepted these assignments because he would lose his own life if he did not—and it was more precious to him than he realized? Or that he feared the reprisals that would come to others if he failed.

He fingered the scar at the base of his windpipe absently. Even as he slit his own throat hadn't he subconsciously hoped someone would stop him? He sighed. Philosophizing served no purpose. He was what he was—his only other choice was death, and he couldn't quite take that final step. Especially since he would probably not die alone.

At length, he reached his destination in an old section of town, quietly scaling the outer wall of the compound. Daggers built into his fingertips dug into the soft mortar between the bricks like cat's claws.

Reaching the top of the wall, he paused to reconnoiter the grounds. His sensors swept the air, seeking a security system. He snorted derisively—either this civil servant was so lowly that he didn't rate protection, or the Board of Rule had withdrawn it to make the hit easier. Knowing his masters, he bet on the latter.

Leaping lightly from the wall, Flannery crouched at the bottom, adjusting to the darker shadows of a snow-covered garden. He breathed in the heady scent of living greenery sleeping beneath the snow. Fir and pine, a touch of cedar…evergreens hardy enough to survive and thrive even in the London winter. Concrete, cobbles, and servosteel

covered the majority of space in the European states. Gardens were the playthings of the rich and powerful—or, as in this case, their stooges. As a child of the Dublin docks, the beauty of living growth always stirred Flannery's soul, even in winter.

Stealing through the garden to the rear of the house, he searched for a way in. He touched a wrist control and a panel opened beneath his hand as he reversed its magnetic catch. He slipped inside the residence like a shadow.

Flannery swore under his breath as he registered three human forms within the house. The mission profile assured him that the man would be alone! He almost walked out of the dwelling—but the bitter realization that such action would rain down retribution upon the rest of his team kept him moving.

In one room, he found a sleeping boy about seven years old. His teeth grated together as he pondered what would happen to this child when they discovered his father's body. The scandal would ruin the boy's future. Another innocent victim of the Lords. Flannery wished he could do something… anything…for the boy, but knew that nothing would change the future.

In the main sleeping chamber, he discovered the bureaucrat entwined with a woman upon an antique bedstead. There wasn't a clear shot at his target. Any blast would awaken the companion, and Flannery refused to kill her too.

He carefully eased off his right glove and stared down at his prosthetic in disgust. The scientists had long ago dispensed with the syntho-skin that would have disguised the missing extremities because they felt it was "non-cost-effective". The gleaming silver of his appendages was a jarring reminder every time he began to feel normal. He wore his gloves at every possible opportunity.

In the years that he had been without his real hands, the period of adjustment he had with each new pair of prosthetics had been declining. These appliances were less than three months old. He wasn't even sure he'd completely explored all their functions.

In addition to the sensitive sensory devices, his hands had a number of other uses. One of the favorites among the controlling body of Uniglobal was the built-in laser-scope that made it a near impossibility for him to miss with his disrupter. It made him a very good hitman, and he was expected to like it. He did his job...but they couldn't make him like it.

He flicked out the hidden needle in the thumb of his hand. While his fingers housed daggers, the thumbs had other functions. There was the syringe in the right—with the tiny vials of various lethal compounds stored in the wrist, and within the left, a single strand coil of adamantine wire strong enough to lower him down a four-story height—or function as a garrote that could remove a head from the body as cleanly as a guillotine. That was messy though, and he was trying to avoid that in this case. Quick and clean, and get out before the family awoke. That was the hope.

He slipped a vial into the syringe and stepped to the side of the bed. Leaning over the sleeping diplomat, he jabbed the needle home in the man's neck, eliciting a tiny cry of pain. He activated the plunger instantly, but the faint noise had been enough to awaken the woman. Seeing Flannery bending over her lover, she screamed.

He ripped the needle free and vaulted the corner of the bed, heading for the hallway door. Standing in the opening was the sleepy child, roused by his mother's continuing screams. Flannery drew his disrupter, gaze raking the room for a way out. Peripherally, he registered that the woman was sobbing hysterically into an activated vidphone. A well-placed blast from his weapon blew out the screen, but he knew instinctively that it was too late.

He had only two choices—kill the pair of them or flee the scene. He leveled the disrupter on the boy and then pulled it out-of-line. He would not kill the innocent!

The only weak spot in the room was a double window overlooking the garden. A heavy gauge servosteel mesh, designed to keep the ordinary intruder out, screened the window—but Flannery was no ordinary intruder, and it had no prayer of keeping him in.

He ripped out large sections of the wire with his daggers. The window itself was five centimeters of heavy glass, and he kicked at it desperately, heedless of the noise. A security squad would doubtless be here any moment—he had no time for niceties.

In the back of his mind, he realized he was a fool to leave the woman and child alive to identify him, but killing them was not in his orders. He refused to commit cold-blooded murder. Of course, some might consider that his job...but he never caused collateral damage—not even to save his own neck.

Diving through the remains of the window, he rolled to his feet and sprinted through the frozen garden towards the wall. He no longer cared as his boots trampled carefully bordered beds. He scrambled up the wall and dropped to the street.

In the distance, he saw the sweeping beam of a Security transport heading his way with a juggernaut's steady implacability. The distance to his aircar stretched infinitely before him, and he began to run. He longed to keep to the deep shadows near the buildings, but knew he could make much better time in the empty street. His sensors warned him that the transport was closing the gap behind him. Any instant now, the blinding beam would pin him in its pitiless glare—just before the Security disrupter shot him from behind.

Flannery poured his heart into his running, spurred forward by the thought. Images of bodies flashed through his mind, twisted in agonized attitudes of death. The cat's death squall rank in his ears. He had to get somewhere safe....

The search beam flared about him with a sudden brilliance. His heart threatened to choke him as it leapt into his throat. Willing his feet to go even faster, he forced himself onward.

A burst of familiar blue fire struck the street scant inches to his left, leaving an ugly scorched burn in the pavement. He dodged instinctively to the right and a second flash singed through the heavy sleeve of his coat.

His breath tore from his throat in a ripping gasp. There was no greater fear in Flannery's heart than death by disrupter. Intellectually, he realized that with his lifestyle it was a high probability, but emotionally, the thought terrified him as nothing else.

He put on a final spurt of speed and threw himself into the shadows along the edge of the street. As God's Luck would have it, there was a gap between two buildings, too narrow for an alleyway, but wide enough for him to slip into.

Hugging the wall of the building before him, Flannery fought to catch his breath. His cheek pressed tightly against the rough surface of the synthobrick. His sensors told him that the transport had stopped and was disgorging Security troops. In seconds, they would locate his niche. Guided by the instinct to survive, he drove his blade tips into the wall before him, scrambling catlike up the surface until he hung suspended several meters above the pavement.

He jammed the blades of both hands into the mortar up to their housings and allowed himself to dangle. He turned his face into the crook of his arm; a black shadow clinging to a shade. The entire operation took him less than ten seconds.

Flannery held his breath as the search team pounded into the passageway, armed with rifle-model lasers and disrupters. He swallowed hard, closing his eyes and willing them to go away. His cloaking sensors continued to mask his presence on the portable tracking unit one of the guards carried. Flannery held himself perfectly still and silent while the Security men called back and forth, searching the crevice with a fine-toothed comb. Mercifully, none of the searchers looked up.

Nerves and sinews of adamantine and carbonite augmented Flannery's muscles from his wrists to his shoulders. Even so, after several minutes of supporting his dead weight, his arms were numb. For once, he thanked the Son for his tireless hands and wrists—not daring to move until his sensors registered the departure of all Guards within a kilometer radius.

Setting his boot tips against the wall for purchase, Flannery gingerly yanked one hand free of the synthobrick. He tried to re-insert his blades further down, but there was no force behind the effort even with his enhanced strength. He couldn't overcome the fatigue in his tortured muscles. Gritting his teeth, he jerked his other hand free, letting himself fall.

He hit the pavement and rolled automatically, coming to his feet and staggering further down the crevice. Cradling his numbed arms to his chest, he knew he had to hide somewhere until he could continue to the airfield safely. It would be stupid to go on until he had a prayer of defending himself.

The narrow passage took a downturn, and ended in a slightly wider courtyard cut off by a third building. There were several doors opening into the space, but a quick examination found them all locked. It appeared that he had stumbled into a refuse pit—garbage littered the wet, slippery pavement of the alleyway. The sickly-sweet smell of rotting meat and vegetation almost made him gag.

Flannery sank into the recess of a doorway, with his arms folded across his chest protectively. He let his head fall back against the solid comfort of the door panel behind him. Hell's flames, what a bloody mess.

He was sure that he'd accomplished his mission—but under circumstances that a raw cadet would have scorned. The Guards had nearly taken him. He'd let witnesses live. He'd used a method of disposal that could potentially pinpoint him as the perpetrator. To top it all off—he mused ruefully, staring down at the gleam of silver in the moonlight—he'd left his glove at the scene of the hit. Thank the Son none of the Security detachment had seen a glint of metal against the brick.

He banged his head repeatedly against the door—self-imposed penance for stupidity. Ah, well...it wouldn't help to continue going over and over it.

What he needed now was ten hours sleep, and a good, hot bath—not necessarily in that order. He huddled into his heavy jacket, shivering miserably as the dampness of the doorstep began to penetrate his clothing, his forehead resting on his bent knees.

Maybe he could catch an hour's sleep—that should guarantee that the chase was long over, and his sensors would alert him if anyone approached. No one would be looking too hard for the murderer of a suspected traitor, as long as he wasn't caught red-handed.

It should be easy to avoid the Security patrols now that he was behind them, and the return to The Deck should be strictest routine from here on.

Mentally setting his mental alarm clock to awaken him in an hour, Flannery let himself drift off. Years of field agent work had given him the ability to sleep any where at any time, and he welcomed the peace.

Exactly one hour later, he snapped into wakefulness. Carefully testing his arm muscles, he found he had full control of them again and rose clumsily to his feet. The chill damp had done its work—his entire body was stiff and sore.

Slowly and painfully, he made his way back to the aircar, crawling inside and gratefully setting the autopilot to take him home.

Flannery berthed the aircar in its accustomed spot just as the first rays of dawn tinged the sky with blood. He leapt from the vehicle, barely catching himself as he stumbled from weariness. God's Son, he was so very tired...

The Dublin streets were ill-lit in these neighborhoods, the buildings ramshackle constructions of servosteel and concrete, mixed with a few ancient wooden structures from the days when lumber was plentiful and cheap. Desperate men and women fought to eke out a living amid the squalor of centuries in the surrounding slums.

Flannery put himself on automatic pilot now, trusting his sensors to alert him to any incoming danger. When they automated the docks, the government seriously curtailed one of the region's traditional means of employment. They still needed human beings to run the equipment, but it now took only one person to handle work that would once have occupied a dozen. Many of the women—and some of the men—had turned to the vixen trade as a means of staying alive. Other individuals roamed in packs like vicious dogs, pulling down stray travelers foolish enough to venture forth alone after dark.

A noise to his left broke his reverie, and Flannery nonchalantly eased the side of his jacket back to bare the heavy disrupter slung on his hip. It was illegal to carry a weapon on the streets, but unless those trailing him were Guards, they were unlikely to dispute with him about it. The citizens of the docks knew Flannery's face well, and all acknowledged that one did not trifle with him. The tingling in his sensors dissipated as those following him drifted off, and his thoughts turned inward once more.

He might as well get home and get some more sleep. There would be repercussions to tonight's affair. Like as not bad ones. He'd best be ready to meet them.

Compassion really had no business in the heart of a hitman.

❈

THE KIDNAPPED PRINCE
by Cynthia Ward

Through the smoke of sennet-spice and drü-weed, a woman with ice-pale eyes watched the door open on the far side of the room. The light of the triple moons spilled into the dimly lit space, outlining an androgynous figure swathed in render-ant silk. The glow of fire-beetles in the cage near the door revealed the figure's dark eyes. They moved nervously above the veil, trying to pierce the gloom of the Low-Port bar.

Rising, the dark woman with ice-colored eyes moved past the crowded tables and the stinks of sweat and garkha-grain beer and cheap canal-vine wine. The woman was slim and rangy, short even for a descendant of the Terrans who crossed hundreds of light-years to Shioma before their experimental star-gate exploded and stranded them. The woman wore a light linen tunic and Zhemish infantry sandal-boots, and cords of locked black hair fell over her shoulders and bare arms. She had a dagger sheathed at her left hip and a particle-beam pistol in a flapped holster to the left of her belt-buckle, positioned for a right-hand draw.

With the grace of the purple panther of the Nergolian Hills, the ice-eyed woman came up to the slight figure who stood in the doorway, waiting for moon-dazzled eyes to adjust to the low light.

"Come." The ice-eyed woman spoke in the trade-tongue of the equatorial nations of Shioma. Her voice was low, her accent faint and strange. "Sit with me," she said, raising her left elbow slightly, "and tell me why a high-born of Sarkanarr comes to a Low-Port bar."

The eyes flashed above the veil. "You mistake me—"

"No one in the bar mistakes you," the ice-eyed woman said, keeping her voice soft.

"Your presence here would hardly be more peculiar if you were a furred tunneling-snake of the Northlands glaciers." She raised her bent arm a little higher. "Act as if you've come to see me, because you have."

"How can you think such a thing?" demanded the veiled figure.

But the voice was low, and a slim hand rested itself on the ice-eyed woman's arm; and the pair crossed the dimness of the Low-Port bar steadily, as if the slim hand did not tremble like a zhusha-leaf.

The ice-eyed woman smiled. "Were I not your target," she said, "you'd have immediately informed the only child of Lost Terra in the bar that you were meeting someone else."

The veiled figure made no reply, and they came to the ice-eyed woman's table. She pulled back the nearer chair, and the veiled figure sat. The ice-eyed woman took the other chair, putting her back to the wall.

She murmured, "A veil draws attention, where devotees of the Thousand-Armed Goddess of far-Southland Xarre are scarce. But no child of the great merchant-houses of Sarkanarr can venture bare-faced and alone to the Low Port without arousing attention that may end badly. If you plan future excursions, you may want to bring some of your house-guards in the leathers of spacers, and not wear your favorite servant's garments."

"Why should I not," said the veiled figure, "when my own garments must mark my status?"

"Your servant's garments do the same," says the ice-eyed woman softly. "Have you not noticed how much finer they are than the garments of anyone else here? Now, if you were used to coming to the Low Port to make assignations with outlanders or offworlders or rough trade, you would have the costumes for it, and you would not be searching for Leigh Silence. You seek to hire me for an enterprise of dubious legality, Ait, Secondborn of the House of Balgair."

The dark eyes narrowed above the veil. "How do you recognize me?"

"Be quiet."

A slim young androgyne with the black eyes and skin and flame-colored hair of Sarkanarr, wearing a scrap of Esran spider-silk and bearing a stoneware bottle, came up to the table. Silence tilted her chin. The server refilled her small crystal goblet from the bottle of resinous Bhesrecian brandy.

"Bring the blue wine of Gegrevot for my friend, and leave the bottle for me," said Silence, and the server placed the bottle gently on the table and departed.

Silence's gaze swept the room and returned to the veiled figure.

"I know you, Secondborn Ait, by the brown of your skin and the shape of your eyes, which are as outlandish in Sarkanarr as my rounded Terran chin or the pale features of your Northlandish father," Silence murmured. "And if I'd forgotten the existence of your family, I'd have been reminded by the death of your mother, the *jek* of Sarkanarr, and the discussions of your elder brother's duty to face the Firstborns of the other great merchant-houses, three days from now, to accept the challenge of any who would contend for the crown of Sarkanarr."

"You know so much about my family, exile!" said Secondborn Ait in a low, scathing tone. "You must fancy you also know why I'm here."

"It's difficult to accomplish in the close-guarded palaces of the great merchant-houses, with their private armies," said Silence. "But, with the *jek*'s challenge so near, I deduce your elder brother has been kidnapped."

The veiled androgyne drew hser head back, as if Silence had thrust a venomous tricorn-asp in hser face, and said softly in despair, "Have I delivered myself to one of his kidnappers?"

"If that were my reputation," Silence said, "you'd never have come looking for me."

"You are smuggler and mercenary, I know," retorted Secondborn Ait in sudden anger. "But an outlaw like you must know who the kidnappers are."

"I know some who are rumored to engage in such work. That doesn't mean they do." Sipping brandy, Silence took a look around the bar and returned her attention to the Secondborn. "Why do you want to hire me?"

"You found the Golden Casque of Ahzé."

Silence placed her goblet carefully on the tabletop. "An expedition found Ahzé. All in the expedition died—"

"—save you, who returned with the Golden Casque."

"I returned," said Silence, "and count myself lucky."

"I think you brought the Golden Casque out of the Valley of Ahzé and sold it," was Ait's rejoinder. "What does it do?"

Silence smiled. "You ask a child of Terra what an ancient artifact of Shioma does?" She shrugged. "I've heard hser great technologist made it for the last Supreme Monarch of Ahzé, so hse could strike down hser enemies with terror."

"It's said only someone of the Supreme Monarch of Ahzé's bloodline can use it. But hse went mad, they say, when hse used the Golden Casque."

Silence sipped brandy. "It's also said hser technologist knocked down some of the mountains surrounding their high valley, so all the passes to Ahzé were blocked, and outsiders could enter the valley no more."

"Yet you got in with the treasure hunters," said Ait.

"The ways into the valley are all blocked—the rumors have that much right," said Silence. "We had to climb over the Mountains of the Clouds, which are higher than the atmosphere of Shioma. We had air in bottles and warm clothing, yet the mountains killed half of us in our approach, and—" She drained her goblet and looked at Ait. "Better if we had turned back."

Ait said, "Is it true the technologist turned the people of Ahzé to ghosts so they might live forever?"

"The expedition found nothing in the ancient ruins that you or I would call human," Silence said. "But you see people sometimes with the vivid purple eyes of Ahzé, that no other race has, on this world or any other we know."

"The Beast-Trainer Zursian has purple eyes," said Ait, speaking of a gladiator popular in Sarkanarr. "Now, we need to discuss your payment. You'll receive half in advance—"

"I take seventy-five percent in advance, if I take a job," said Silence. "If I take yours, you will bring me into the palace of your family—for the lack of news or rumor about your brother's disappearance says he was taken from home, where your family could keep it quiet—and when I finish my investigation, I will search for your brother. Now, the server returns with your wine. Pay for our drinks."

When the server was gone, Silence refilled her goblet with brandy and glanced about, then spoke again to the Secondborn.

"If you would have me consider your offer, admit why you sought this Terran for your work."

"You exiles are stronger and faster than anyone native to this world."

"Terrans have that potential because our lost world had slightly greater gravity than Shioma, or so it's said." Silence smiled. "There are living planets and moons of the saffron star-system with higher gravity than Shioma, so there are many outworlders in Sarkanarr who could fulfill this need."

"You will not double-cross me."

"Many will not double-cross you," Silence replied, "for dishonest outlaws don't long survi—hold quiet."

Silence looked directly at three hulking figures with the black eyes and skins and flame-colored hair of the dominant race of Sarkanarr. They approached the table, woman and man and androgyne, clad in the uni-

forms of a rival sea-navy. The insignia was torn off and the garments were gone half to rags.

Silence rested her left arm on the little table, her fingers curling over the edge, as she addressed the trio.

"Don't bother us."

The trio spread out so the woman came to one side of the table and the man and androgyne stood on the other.

"We're not bothering you, runtish exile scum." The woman tilted her sharp chin toward Ait. "We're taking your bit of silk."

"You're new here," replied Silence, "so I do you a favor by telling you to leave us now."

The three exchanged smiles; then the man reached for his cutlass and the androgyne reached for hser shock-baton and the woman reached for Ait's shoulder.

A flick of Silence's right wrist and the smell of resin intensified as the dark brandy streamed through the air to strike the deserter-woman's eyes.

Her lips were parting to curse, her arms rising to dash the liquor from her eyes, the goblet falling, as Silence seized the neck of the brandy-bottle in one hand and used the other to pull on the table-top.

The edge of the table drove into the deserter-woman's thighs. As she staggered back with an oath, Silence twisted around, swinging. Her bottle broke across the side of the deserter-man's head and sent him slumping, cutlass half-drawn, against the deserter-androgyne.

The deserter-woman's hands closed on Silence's neck.

Her swinging arm changed direction, rising to send her fist above her shoulder and into the woman's face.

As the woman collapsed, the deserter-androgyne thrust hser crackling shock-baton at Silence. She found hser weapon knocked aside by the length of broken bottle in the Terran's right fist, and her temple slammed by the left fist.

Ait rose from hser chair. Hse alternated

hser attention between the three deserters stretched motionless on the floor. Hse was shivering like a twig in the wind.

"Sorry to spill your wine," Silence said to the Secondborn, "but it's time to leave."

She raised her arm.

Ait glared. "Leave off reaching for me, before someone thinks I take offworlders to my bed."

"Better that, perhaps," Silence murmured, "than leaving them to wonder just what *did* draw a high-born to a Low-Port bar?"

Ait hooked hser arm around Silence's elbow.

Hse was silent through several narrow, crooked Low-Port streets. It was midnight, but the streets were as busy as an Upper-City high street at midday. The pair passed sailors and spacers, privateers and mercenaries, prostitutes and procurers, gamblers and duelists, buskers and artists, athletes and gladiators, beggars and pickpockets, drunks and smokers, dancers and bar-servers, slummers and bodyguards.

"We never climb the hill," Ait muttered.

Hse tilted hser head to indicate the miles-long slope revealed by the age-long shrinking of the equatorial Girdle-Ocean, and covered again by warehouses and apartment blocks as the city of Sarkanarr expanded to follow the retreating water.

"I don't need to know the byways of the Low Port," Ait continued, "to know this isn't the way to my home."

"I'm making sure we're not being followed," Silence murmured. "Now, tell me why you sought me, or I'll leave you at your family's gate and your brother to his fate."

"I sought you," answered the Secondborn sullenly, "because you were the babe raised for five years by animals, and have the strength and senses of a wild beast."

* * * *

As hse removed hser veil, Ait whispered, "I've never been in my brother's rooms before."

"Yet you brought me here without hesitation through a complex of secret passages," Silence remarked.

She moved through the vast bed-chamber, observing the disorder. The bedclothes were torn half off the bed. Pillows were scattered about, one spilling the down of the xerex-bird. A light chair was overturned. As Silence examined the room thoroughly, floor to ceiling, her nostrils often flared.

"Why is your brother's room still in disorder?" she asked Ait.

"I asked the servants to leave it unchanged," hse replied. "How would you learn anything otherwise?"

"Who else knows the secrets of your hidden passages?"

"Only the Firstborns of our bloodline," Ait said.

Silence studied her with raised eyebrows. "Only?"

Ait's eyes narrowed. "My brother Ajassi secretly taught them to me, when we were children. Now that our mother is dead, no one else alive knows them."

"Well, if no one in your palace saw the kidnappers, as you've told me—"

"They did not!" Ait sounded half in despair. "Hundreds live in the palace, and of those who were here last night, no one saw anything to suggest any strangers were about. My family knows this because the head of our security force is a mind-speaker, who gave everyone the drug pakti to remove their mind-shields before questioning them."

"—then whoever kidnapped your brother knows the secret passages."

"Or someone was able to resist the drug."

"Resistance to pakti is a talent even more rare than mind-speech, but it happens," Silence said. "There are many scents for men in this room."

"Ajassi has a number of man-servants."

"Two scents are new to this room, about a day old."

Ait stiffened. "He has no new servants."

"One of the new scents belongs to a man and the other to an androgyne."

"Then you *can* track Ajassi's kidnappers

by scent!"

Silence smiled gently. "After so many hours, that's unlikely, in a city with millions of inhabitants and billions of smells," she said. "Has a demand for ransom been made?"

"If it has," answered Ait, "I haven't been told."

"Perhaps there hasn't been one," Silence said. "It's possible a rival merchant-house might think it advantageous to hold your brother prisoner until the challenge-day has passed, so your family will lose any chance of keeping the crown of Sarkanarr. Have you heard of other missing Firstborns?"

The Secondborn frowned. "I saw the Firstborns of the other nine great merchant-houses at the Banquet of Rain Flowers, earlier this evening," Ait said. "My father excused my brother's absence by saying he was taken with a sudden attack of ague." Hse smiled ironically. "At this evidence of weakness, they did poorly at disguising their pleasure."

When Leigh Silence finished her examination of Firstborn Ajassi's private suite, Secondborn Ait opened the secret door again. Hse led Silence through a series of secret passages to the outside world. They were not the same passages which Ait had taken to lead Silence to hser brother's bed-chamber.

The door closed behind Silence, leaving her alone at the edge of a deserted street in the hour before the rising of Scatch, the saffron sun. Silence remained in the dark, narrow doorway, her hand on the beam-pistol, loosened in its holster. She looked about, tilting her head to listen, inhaling the scents.

Across the well maintained street, with its glowing lamp-posts and bloom-filled berms and trumpet-flower trees and occasional parked groundcar, rose the palace of the House of Balgair. Silence was unsurprised. The hidden passages had gone up and down and wandered widely to one side and the other. She wondered if secret passages wove all through the district of the city controlled by the House of Balgair.

The sky was clear and the stars showed faint and few above the blaze of the Upper City. A cool breeze moved through the street. The breeze carried the smells of the flowers and irrigated earth and wood-smoke and baking bread and a thousand, thousand other scents.

As Silence stepped out of the unlit doorway, the day-old scent of Firstborn Ajassi and the two individuals who'd been in his bed-chamber dissolved into the thousand, thousand scents.

An image filled her mind:

A caped figure with raised cowl, seen from above and behind, crouching in the mouth of a dark alley to aim a beam-pistol across the brightly lit street, targeting Silence.

The noiseless beam seared her forearm as she threw herself behind a parked groundcar.

Drawing her beam-pistol, she peered cautiously around a tire. She saw the alley, and glimpsed a cowled figure leaning into sight with beam-pistol raised. She fired.

A new image filled her mind:

The shadowy figure who'd fired at Silence dropping the beam-pistol damaged by Silence's shot, then turning to run out of sight down the dark alley.

Silence's searching gaze found the creature which had sent her the images. It blinked at her from where it rested like a bread-loaf on the edge of a roof overhanging the alley. It was a canal-cat with eyes as golden as the largest moon and fur as silver as the smallest. No one remembered what the breed was called, before the canals were built and the little felines spread from pole to pole, but they were sleek-pelted fishers and swimmers who adapted readily to city life. Occasionally, a canal-cat showed the ability to touch the mind of a person born with the same talent; but some said all cats of Shioma, large and small, possessed this ability, and kept it to themselves.

Sprinting across the deserted street, Silence mind-bespoke the canal-cat. *Why are you helping me?*

Another image came: *Herself, dropping flat on a bridge to reach down and pluck a silver kitten from the canal where it swam, trying to reach land before a river-shark caught it.*

Then the cat sent the sensation of tastes and textures, raw flesh and hot blood, which Silence knew meant *good hunting.*

She didn't see the cowled figure in the shadowy alley, but by scent and sound she followed the figure through several twists and turns and forks. As the sound of labored breathing joined the sound of the running footsteps, Silence knew she was closing the distance; and she knew her prey could hear her pursuit.

Then she rounded a corner to find a busy boulevard, and the cowled figure darting into traffic.

Under a predawn sky paling to lavender, the walkway bustled with litter-bearers and foot-messengers. On the other side of the walkway and a line of parked vehicles, costermongers pushed laden handcarts. Beyond them, the boulevard which ran along the Great South-North Canal was packed with mounted *thrun* and *thrun*-drawn wains and bicycles and tricycles and rickshaws and motorized vehicles. Most of the last were trucks, transporting goods to and from the sea-port and the space-port.

The morning traffic crawled, and stopped, and at erratic intervals lunged abruptly forward for several yards. Despite the risk of being crushed by a sudden movement of vehicle or beast, the cowled figure dodged and darted across the ten lanes of traffic. If the figure reckoned hser pursuer would not fire into a crowd, hse reckoned aright.

Gaining the far side of the boulevard, where a walkway ran beside the canal, hse ducked out of sight.

Then from the place where the cowled figure had disappeared, a small aircar with an enclosed cab rose soundlessly into the paling sky.

Silence made her way carefully across the thoroughfare, which marked the boundary between the district of Ait's House and that of another great merchant family. Finally, Silence reached the side of the canal, a broad straight waterway as thick with passenger and shipping craft as the road.

As quickly as the crowded walkway allowed, she strode to the space from which the aircar had risen. It was already filled by a groundcar whose occupants were gone. The cowled figure was gone. Hser scent ended here.

Silence holstered her beam-pistol and looked at the androgyne's footprint in a patch of mud.

The hired aircar left Silence by the arena. The vast structure stood in isolation beyond the southwest edge of the Upper City, where the land grew rough to the west, and gave way to rain forest in the south; Sarkanarr had expanded eastward, past the spaceport, and followed the retreating sea north. The rising sun gilded the pale stone of the arches and columns and caryatids and idols of the upper stories and the blank lower wall of the structure.

The amphitheatre had been ignored for millennia after the Zhemish Empire fell, losing its hold on Sarkanarr and other lands which bordered the Girdle-Ocean. Then, five centuries ago, the ten great merchant-houses of Sarkanarr grew more powerful than the elected council, and they restored the Zhemish arena and underwrote operas and theatrical plays and athletic competitions there. In the last two centuries, the merchant-houses added blood sports, in which criminals and volunteers fought one another or great beasts brought from every continent of Shioma, and even from the dying seas.

A broad walkway circled the amphitheatre within a great ring-road. On the wall of the amphitheatre hung banners that unspooled nearly the length of its two-story height. Some banners portrayed bouts between duelists or bare-hand combatants, or battles between human and beast. Other banners were woven to portray an individual athlete or actor or orator or gladiator. Each gladiator was armed with a sword or dagger, trident or spear, whip or shock-baton, and wore a costume that sometimes included an open-faced helmet or pieces of plate armor, but always left most of the body bare. Silence did not attend events at the arena, but she knew the banners portrayed the most famous entertainers.

As she started across the broad walkway, she examined the nearest banner. It portrayed a nearly naked androgyne with brown skin and powerful muscles and tawny eyes. Hse held a fighter's stance and gripped a beast-trainer's shock-baton. Hse scowled, rendering more fierce a face tattooed with white stripes resembling those which marked the pale lavender pelts of the tigers of the southern ice. At the lower edge of the banner, the script of Sarkanarr identified the figure as Beast-Trainer Told.

A woman strode around the curve of the amphitheatre. Silence halted and turned to face her. She looked Sarkanarrese and wore the uniform of the arena-guards, with a beam-pistol at one hip and a shock-baton at the other.

Seeing Silence, she called: "There are no entertainments today, or for another ten days. Haven't you heard?" She raised her left hand to touch forehead and breastbone. "The *jek* is dead, may her rest be unbroken."

"Deities grant the *jek* sweet oblivion," Silence replied, imitating the gesture. "I've been summoned by Beast-Trainer Told."

"Begone," said the city-guard. "You have no look of the whore about you. Anyway, the Beast-Trainers Told and Zursian take only one another to bed."

Silence looked at the guard uncertainly. "My employer is very specific about whom I should see here, and what I should wear, and when I should arrive."

The city-guard scowled as fiercely as the tattooed beast-trainer on the wall-banner, perhaps because Told and Zursian were among the city's most popular entertainers,

and their displeasure might end a mere arena-guard's job.

"Stay where you are," the guard told Silence finally, "and I will ask."

The guard turned away, taking a large ring of iron keys from her belt as she approached the closest admission-gates.

Soft-footed as a cat, Silence crossed the broad walkway and came up behind the guard. Pressing the muzzle of her beam-pistol into the bare flesh of the guard's neck, she murmured, "Make no sound."

The guard inhaled. She hadn't seen Silence's beam-pistol or dagger. In the aircar, Silence had moved the handgun in its holster and blade in its sheath to the back of her belt, tucking them between the leather strap and her tunic.

Silence shifted her weapon so the muzzle pressed into the guard's back and said, "Stay quiet and unlock the gate, and you won't get hurt."

The guard unlocked the little door in one of the pair of vast tsen-wood gates, and obeyed Silence's direction to walk slowly into the arena. Keeping the muzzle to the guard's back, Silence followed her into the dimly lit entrance hall. Silence halted the guard with a word and closed the door, then looked in the pouch on the guard's belt. With her free hand, Silence withdrew a pair of fine, coiled plant vines.

She told the guard, "Put your wrists together behind your back."

The guard stiffened.

Silence pressed the muzzle more deeply into the flesh beneath the guard's tunic.

The guard moved her arms behind her back and crossed her wrists. Silence let one of the violet-hued vines fall open and then snapped it suddenly against the crossed wrists. The thin, tough vine wrapped itself several times around the wrists.

"Lie down," Silence added, "or the uki-nik-vine will knock you off your feet."

A snap of the second vine bound the prone guard's ankles together.

Silence placed the guard's key-ring in her

belt-pouch. She removed the helmet from the guard's head, then used strips of linen torn from the hem of the guard's tunic to gag her. Silence placed the guard in the shadow of a ticket-seller's booth near the wall.

"Stay still," Silence told the guard, "and I'll let you live."

Restoring her gun and dagger to their accustomed positions on her belt, Silence proceeded to the nearest of the broad stone staircases at the back of the cavernous hall. Ascending, she came to a wide opening. She looked out on stone tiers of seating that rose toward the brightening sky.

She studied sky and seats with sight and smell and hearing. She didn't reach out with her mind-talent. It couldn't detect shielded minds, and a few minds could sense such attention even while shielded.

Seeing no life beyond some distant birds, Silence crossed the walkway and looked over the low rails lining the outer edge. Below, the sands covering the oval floor were clean and neatly raked. The floor was empty.

The barrier was low because no sane or sober spectator would jump into the arena, where she would be killed by beast or arena-guard. And if any were incautious or insane or inebriated enough to fall or jump over the barrier, they could not jump or climb out. The wall around the floor was two stories tall, and it was coated with an opaque helio-trope material that was as smooth and resistant to damage as diamond.

Silence sprang over the rails.

Landing on the sand with a roll, she came nimbly to her feet and turned in a circle, examining the arena from its lowest exposed point.

One of the pairs of great tsen-wood gates lining the wall swung open.

A massive, slope-shouldered figure with a low, jutting brow burst onto the sands. Almost seven feet tall, the figure wore a linen tunic. Where his skin was visible, it was the hue of sand and thick with magenta hair. Raising his long arms and parting his prognathous jaws to bare three fangs, he uttered a furious sequence of grunts and growls and raced toward Silence.

Silence uttered a rapid series of sounds which resembled the figure's guttural syllables.

The figure paused, shifting his weight back and forth on short, bowed legs as he examined Silence with narrowed eyes.

"I am Stranger of the Band of One-Arm," she repeated in the language of the People of the Nergolian Hills. "Do you understand me?"

The figure said, "I, Broken Fang, understand you."

Some Shiomans said the beings known as half-apes had been human, once, but regressed because of forbidden acts, or because they had mated with apes, or become inbred, or earned the curse of a deity or demon. Other Shiomans said the half-apes, who kept to the most remote wilderness regions of Shioma, were the surviving remnants of an intermediate stage between the native races of Shioma and the animals from which they'd evolved. Some scientists had come from Terra to study the hominids and humans of Shioma and other living worlds of the Scatch star-system, hoping to determine whether their close resemblances to Terrans and one another arose from a common ancestor; but that research had ended with the destruction of the Terrans' star-gate.

Silence called again to the hominid.

"Let me enter your cave in peace, Broken Fang, and when I am finished there, I will open the gates and help you escape the hairless ones."

"You are the first hairless one to understand our language," replied Broken Fang. "But hairless ones make us fight, again and again, so one by one we die and I am the only one left. Hairless ones want me to die, too. So I know you are a liar. But you are not quite as ugly as most hairless ones, so I will make you my she."

Orphaned in babyhood, Silence had been raised among the half-apes of the Nergolian Hills, where the females led the band and made the mating decisions. Then her foster-family was slaughtered and she was found and raised by a woman from the Terran colony, where androgynes were unnervingly uncommon, and all the sexes participated in decision-making. The humans of Shioma and the neighboring worlds had vastly differing arrangements of roles and hierarchies. After so many years spent wandering the Scatch star-system, Silence almost didn't find this behavior by a male hominid odd.

"I am one of the People," Silence told Broken Fang, "and you approach me at your peril."

Broken Fang lunged toward her, reaching with clawed fingers. Silence knew the wilderness-forged strength of her muscles surpassed that of many humans, Terran or Shioman. She also knew that, if this immense hominid got his hands or hand-like feet on her, the fight would end immediately in her defeat.

Silence had time to free and aim her pistol. She left her weapons untouched. The People saw no honor in using a weapon in single combat.

Silence leaped into the ambit of Broken Fang's reach.

As his arms closed about her, her knuckles met his throat with a crunch. The hominid staggered back, gasping for air with a crushed windpipe. He sank to his knees, clutching his throat, and fell, and Silence smelled the approach of his death.

Kneeling, she took the sides of Broken Fang's massive head gently between her hands and, with the resting-prayer of her foster-parents' band and a quick cracking twist, she granted the hominid the mercy of immediate death.

Rising, she drew her beam-pistol and approached the open gates warily. From the opening came the smells of carnivores and dung and blood, and the sounds of mastication, and bones breaking in powerful jaws. The electric light in the space beyond the opening revealed great beasts in two rows of cages. Silence saw panthers and slekkars

and yugons and ice-tigers and immense lizards and serpents.

In the most distant cage on the left, a young man stood, gripping two of the vertical bars. He wore the finery of the high-born of Sarkanarr. He had the eyes and skin of the children of the House of Balgair.

As Silence reached the entrance, two figures appeared in the doorway.

Silence dropped to the ground, stricken by a terror so vast, she could make no sound.

Her heart pounded as if it would burst like a star going nova. She shook violently and sweat sprang out all over her body. She panted and couldn't draw a breath, and the world wavered, darkness pressing in from the edges of her vision.

She was a baby animal, and the Nergolian panther stalked toward her, where she crouched at the base of a high tree with a mauve bole too smooth to climb. She had crawled away from One-Arm's band in the search for sweet shadowberries, and the rest of the People were too far away to help her, even if they flung their crude spears with fire-sharpened tips. The trees with rough bark or low branches seemed too far away to reach with her trembling limbs.

She was a little animal, clinging to her foster-mother's back as the storm filled the world. It lashed the forest with rains that must drown the People, and winds that tore up even the thickest of trees, casting them about like twigs, so they shattered other trees and unlucky beasts and hominids like fragile snail-shells. The band of One-Arm fled the forest, only to discover lightning playing in the spaces between the high barren peaks of the Nergolian Hills. The lightning spread across the sky with a thunder so tremendous, it shook the rocks of the high places into an avalanche.

She was an adult, alone in the age-old ruins of Ahzé. The city was uninhabited by any living person, and it had no ghosts. Yet it had patches of raw light which hovered above road and floor at about the height of her midsection. The lights were nearly the size of an adult Shioman's torso, and they crackled like electricity and wavered in and out of visibility, like flickering flaws in the air.

One of the lights moved suddenly toward Silence. She darted away, her heartbeat growing more rapid. But the light followed, engulfing her left hand, burning it like an electric shock. She heard the mind-voice of the light in her head, and knew suddenly that it was an inhabitant of Ahzé, turned like all the inhabitants of Ahzé into a being of deathless energy. And the mind-voice screamed endlessly in Silence's mind, because the light's life was alien and inexplicable to it, and there was no end to that life, and no way to bring it to an end.

Silence grew still on the sands of the arena floor.

She fired her beam-pistol.

Just inside the gates, a man in a beast-trainer's leather kilt and metal belt and a gold-gleaming helmet which hid his face fell against the androgynous beast-trainer who stood next to him, with a little burn on the bare skin above his heart.

Supporting the man with hser left arm, the androgyne snarled like the ice-tiger whose white stripes tattooed hser face and snatched hser shock-baton from hser belt with a wrathful cry.

"Why did the Golden Casque of Ahzé not kill you!"

Silence reeled up, gasping for air, and the androgyne whose scent she'd followed through the Upper City shoved hser weapon into Silence's gut and shocked her so she could not breathe.

She snatched the gold helmet from the head of the sagging gladiator, exposing glazed purple eyes. In the same movement, she swung the heavy object into the side of the androgynous beast-trainer's head. Bone gave with a crunch, and skull and casque both were distorted suddenly. The beast-trainer's tawny eyes rolled up and hse sank down, the shock-baton slipping from hser hand. The other beast-trainer fell beside hser

so each lay motionless with an arm around the other.

Sucking in great breaths, Silence laid the helmet aside and checked the scents and pulses of the fallen gladiators.

Both were dead.

Silence stepped over the bodies, entering the large room beyond the gates. She stood, surveying her surroundings by sight and scent and sound. The space was large enough to hold a score of sizeable cages. Half were empty. There were living quarters behind the cages to her right, and storage space, with a meat locker and stacks of boxes and a familiar hovercar, beyond the cages to her left. In the cages, the beasts roared and snarled at her.

Finding no uncaged threats, she holstered her pistol and picked up the casque. She looked inside. Then she lowered her left hand into the helmet and pulled out all the wires and electrodes and everything else that was not part of the shell. She let the pieces fall to the floor, and broke everything she could crush beneath her heel.

Then she slammed the casque against the stone of the floor until the shape of the helmet was unrecognizable.

Abandoning the casque, Silence removed the heavy key-ring from the broad metal belt of the dead man and walked to the last cage on the left.

"Three people dead, who should be alive," Silence said to the man in the cage. "All because you didn't want to tell your family you have no interest in becoming the ruler of Sarkanarr, Firstborn Ajassi."

"What are you talking about?" cried the man in the cage. "I was kidnapped—"

"I knew whose agent purchased the Golden Casque of Ahzé, when I sold it last year," Silence said. "The great merchant Houses of Sarkanarr like to collect ancient artifacts, and when you can get them to work, you use them on one another—but none of your family has the blood of the last ruler of Ahzé, and so none of you has been able to use the Golden Casque. Yet never were any of your

House willing to part with it, until now."

"Why should I care about fantastic artifacts or Ahzé bloodlines, when I'm trapped in this cage—"

"You slipped away to the arena on a night when there were no events, so you could approach Beast-Trainers Told and Zursian, who were the best of your family's arena-fighters, and stayed with their animals in the arena instead of living elsewhere," Silence said. "And you tried to hire them to kidnap you."

"Hire *animal trainers* to kidnap *myself*?" Firstborn Ajassi burst into incredulous laughter.

"Told and Zursian balked at your proposal, though the pay you offered must have been great. They had no reason to risk their fame and fortune, even for a high-born of their patron House. But you took note of Zursian's purple eyes, and offered the fabled Golden Casque of Ahzé—and *that*, they could not resist."

"That's the most ridiculous story I've ever heard."

"But you failed to understand something important, didn't you?" Silence continued. "You failed to realize Told and Zursian would never have freed you, once the Firstborns' challenge for the crown of Sarkanarr was past."

"They would never have kept me after—" Ajassi's jaw snapped shut with a click.

Silence said, "How could they trust a man who'd get himself kidnapped not to reveal the identities of his kidnappers to his powerful family, who might covertly kill them and take back the Golden Casque of Ahzé?"

Ajassi's eyes narrowed.

"Who are you, and why are you here?" he shouted. "To steal the casque?" His eyes widened with a new thought. "How did you know who kidnapped me?"

"Your kidnappers didn't trust you, so one watched your House. Told saw me leaving by the secret door you revealed to them, and deduced some member of your family had hired me to find you. And, though I never attend the games, it's possible Told recognized

me as Leigh Silence."

Firstborn Ajassi's face grayed, and he whispered, "The Terran beast-woman?"

"Whether hse recognized me or not, Told fired hser pistol at me, then fled. Perhaps Told assumed hse'd killed me. Perhaps hse wanted to warn hser lover about me."

Ajassi's breathing grew harsh.

"Mind-speech is common enough in the Scatch star-system that its peoples never developed long-distance communications technologies," Silence said. "But mind-speech is so rare among Terrans that most thought it a myth, and they developed long-speech technologies everyone could use. Told had no mind-speech or Terran communication device, so hse had to come here physically to communicate hser discovery with hser lover."

"Told burst in here suddenly," Ajassi whispered, "and hse and Zursian moved far from me. I could see they were talking, and they spoke for a while, but I couldn't hear them."

"Discussing me," Silence said. "Told must have known I never got a good look at hser before hse escaped in an aircar, and I was on foot. They must have concluded I'd never find them—"

"How in the names of all the deities *did* you follow Told?"

"Hse didn't realize hse'd left his footprint in a patch of mud, or didn't care, assuming I wouldn't recognize the pattern of hobnails and tread on the underside of hser sole. But some gladiators enjoy the pleasures of the Low Port, and they arrive in full regalia." Silence smiled. "The print of their footgear, designed for good purchase in the sands of the arena, is unique."

Her smile grew grimly humorous.

"Telling Zursian about me wouldn't have taken much time," she said. "Why do you suppose Told and Zursian spoke at length?"

Ajassi shrugged. "Love talk. Or gossip. Or a fondness for prolixity. What does it matter?"

"Once they were done talking about me,"

Silence said, "Told and Zursian discussed whether to kill you immediately, or enjoy keeping a high-born in their power for a few more days, before killing you and feeding your remains to their carnivores."

Ajassi's head jerked back, eyes widening.

"This brings us to another concern," Silence said. "The Firstborns' challenge for the crown of Sarkanarr is tomorrow night."

Ajassi began to shake.

"Zursian used the Golden Casque of Ahzé to fell you with terror." His tone was bitter. "Why did it not destroy you?"

"I've been terrified more times than I can remember," Silence said. "You keep going. It's just part of life."

"For a wild offworld animal," Ajassi snarled.

Silence laughed.

"The person who hired me had the shakes and scent of fear, but still came to the Low Port and hired the wild offworld animal to rescue you," she said. "It's regrettable that person cannot be proclaimed Firstborn of the House of Balgair and defend the crown of Sarkanarr."

Turning away from Ajassi's cage, Silence continued across the room to a pair of tsen-wood gates in the outside wall. She opened the gates, revealing the empty walkway and ring road and a sunlit view of rough hills and purple forest. The mild winter breeze carried the scents of city and dust and weeds and distant blooms and trees into the space.

When Silence turned from the doorway, the beasts' muzzles were raised, sniffing the air. They turned their heads toward the opening. They began to pace in their cages.

Silence spoke to the beasts in the tongue of the People and sent an image with her mind-speech, and wondered if any of the beasts understood her.

She took Told's shock-baton in her left hand, holding it ready as, one by one, she unlocked and opened the cages.

The animals stared and sniffed at her. They bounded from their cages. Then they went through the gates she'd opened, and she saw them running toward the wild places.

When the animal-cages were empty, Silence flung Zursian's key-ring down with a heavy crash at the base of the barred door of Firstborn Ajassi's cage.

"Free yourself," she said, "or huddle here until the challenge is done."

Leigh Silence turned and followed the beasts out of the arena.

THE OUTPOST, OUTSIDE
by Larry Hinkle

Erik had just finished updating the entry logs when the alarm sounded. Movement in Quadrant Three. The ground sensors hadn't been tripped, but something in the area must have startled the bird. He rewound the footage again and watched for any signs of the infected.

Jerry rolled his chair over to Erik's desk. "What do you think it is?"

Erik shrugged. "Probably nothing."

"I hope so," Jerry said. His voice trembled a bit at the edges. "Ain't no way I'm going out there."

"Don't worry about it. I'm sure everything's fine."

"You don't have to tell me twice." He got up and headed for the door. "I'm going to the cafeteria. You want anything?"

"Nah, I'm good."

"Suit yourself, man. Your brother's making Cheez Whiz casserole."

"No thanks. I ate enough of that stuff growing up." Erik turned back to the monitor. Once he heard the door shut behind him, he breathed a sigh of relief. The last person he wanted to take outside was Jerry. If you wanted to know the similarities between string theory and string cheese, Jerry was your man. But if you wanted someone you could count on when the crap hit the fan, Erik would sooner trust his back to HAL 9000.

Erik rewound the footage and watched it again. He zoomed in. There, in the upper left corner of the screen, he thought *maybe* he saw something in the trees move right before the bird took off, but the footage was too blurry to be sure.

He leaned back in his chair. Maybe the bird was just hungry. Or horny. Do birds even get horny? He knew they laid eggs, but that's where his knowledge of avian reproductive practices ended. He couldn't remember any of his friends ever bragging about doing it "birdy-style," but that didn't mean birds never let their freak feathers fly. Too bad Doug hadn't recruited an ornithologist for this mission. Or even brought a bird book for that matter. He made a mental note to request a data search on the subject. It might take a couple days, as net access was spotty this far out. And when it was up, everyone wanted on. *That's what she said!* He snorted at his own lame joke, and then watched the footage again.

* * * *

Although they were only born four years apart, Erik had never been close with his little brother. So he was shocked when Doug asked him to join the mission.

"We could really use someone like you this time out," Doug said.

"Someone like me?" Erik cracked his knuckles. "Aren't you worried about getting your butt kicked in front of your team?"

"Not as worried as I am about them getting their butts kicked."

"By who?"

"That's classified. I just need you to protect them."

"From what?"

"That's classified, too."

"Then I'm gonna have to say no." Erik pushed his chair back from the table.

"Erik, wait." Doug looked around the room. "Look, I can't go into all the details right now, but there's been an outbreak in Sector Five. Roughly half the population is infected."

"Infected with what?"

Doug didn't answer.

"Let me guess. That's classified too,

right?" Erik ran his hand through his hair. "Fifty percent? That seems pretty high. Are you sure about those numbers?"

"Plus or minus two percent, but yeah, we're sure." Doug paused. "I've probably said too much already, but you *are* my brother, so I'm gonna bend the rules a little bit more."

"Gee, thanks."

"Reports from the field indicate the infected seem to share some sort of hive mind. They seek each other out and travel in groups, spreading the infection as they go. It's up to us to find a cure, or at least contain the outbreak."

"Sounds like you need more bug hunters," Erik said. "Not someone like me."

"You're right. I don't need someone *like* you," Doug said. "I need you." He slid a file across the table. "These are the guys I've recruited so far. They're experts in their fields, but do you really think any of them can handle themselves outside a lab?"

Erik flipped through the file. He didn't recognize any of the names, but he could tell by their headshots that his brother was right; it looked like half of them hadn't even hit puberty yet. Plus or minus two percent.

He knew Doug would never admit it, but something about this mission had him spooked. It's the only reason he would ask for help.

Erik closed the folder and slid it back. "What's in it for me?"

Doug smiled. "Besides the joy of us hanging out together for a few weeks?"

"Yeah, besides that."

"How about the chance to protect some of the brightest minds of our generation?"

"Not good enough."

"How about we really need you on this one, Erik? *I* really need you." A flush crept up Doug's cheeks. "Would it help if I said please?"

Erik mulled it over. His gut said to walk away, but he knew their mom would expect him to take care of his little brother. Life would be so much easier if he were an only child.

"Okay," he finally said, "I'm in."

It only took a couple days for Erik to second-guess his decision. He could handle his brother, but the other guys were way too Poindexter for his liking: plenty of booksmarts, but the social graces of a herd of flatulent goats. If they weren't fighting over who dealt it, they were arguing over who smelt it.

Baby brother was definitely going to pay for this if they made it back.

Erik debated whether to tell his brother about the bird, but decided against it. Base security was his responsibility. Anything out of the ordinary, he had to check it out. In person. You don't trust a mission like this to a monitor: other outposts had made that mistake in the past; his wouldn't.

Besides, Doug would want to tell the others, and then they'd spend the next three hours arguing about whether the infected were nearby and what to do if the outpost were overrun and whether the Flash could outrun Quicksilver and whether the element quicksilver was poisonously beautiful or beautifully poisonous and in the end they'd agree to send Erik out to investigate, but by then it'd be too late.

He took a last look at the footage, checked the coordinates, and stepped outside. The pneumatic door, designed to shut silently, still sounded too loud to his ears out here under the overcast grey sky. He scanned the vines and deadfall at the edge of the woods, and waited.

Nothing moved.

Without taking his eyes off the woods, he reached into his pack, pulled out the microsprayer, and coated himself in a protective mist. The boys in the lab thought this new aerosol would give him about thirty minutes of protection from the contagion, but they had no way to know for sure until it was tested in the field. Which technically made him a guard *and* a guinea pig.

He was getting too old for this crap. Still, *something* had spooked that bird. And he was pretty sure it wasn't a birdie booty call.

He knew opening the outside door had triggered an alarm back in the control room, so the lab monkeys were probably watching him on the monitor by now. He also knew none of them were brave enough to join him, so he was surprised when the door opened and Doug walked out. Maybe little brother was finally growing a pair after all.

"You actually gonna join me?"

"Out there?" Doug stole a quick glance at the woods, then turned his attention back to Erik. "No way. I just came out to get the sprayer back. We can't take a chance on you losing it."

Erik spat. "Should've known you couldn't hang." He handed the bottle to Doug.

Doug tucked it into his pack and gave Erik a vidcam. "I need you to wear this. It'll stream everything back to the lab in real time, so we can see what you see. It streams audio, too, so watch your language."

Erik held the vidcam at arm's length and stuck his middle finger up toward the lens.

"Really? You better hope Mom doesn't see that."

"You better make sure she doesn't," Erik said. "Or this contagion will be the least of your worries."

Doug handed Erik an earpiece. "I need you to wear this, too. If we see anything we want you to check out, I'll let you know."

Doug went back inside. Erik was on his own. He put the earpiece in and gave the vidcam a final one-finger salute before clipping it on his hat.

Part of him wished his brother were a little braver, but the more rational part was glad Doug hadn't wanted to tag along. Going out by himself like this was dangerous enough, but taking his brother would only make it worse. He could move faster on his own, and he wouldn't have to worry about being a babysitter.

He was just a few yards into the woods when his earpiece crackled to life. *"Hey Erik, you doing okay?"* Speak of the devil. His brother's disembodied voice sounded even younger in his ear.

"I'm fine, numb nuts. How's life back in the nursery? Mom come by to tuck you babies in yet?"

"Very funny. She did call earlier, though. Wants us to come home for dinner sometime."

"Finally, some real food." Erik's eyes narrowed. "Now shut your face hole. Time to show you boys how it's done."

Erik followed the trail deeper into the woods. He was only a few hundred yards away from the outpost now, but already it felt like a different world. The wind had picked up. Branches swayed overhead, swallowing the light. Shadows pulsed and danced along the edge of the trail, playing havoc with his depth perception.

He stopped.

"I'm starting to lose the light out here. You knuckleheads see anything?" He tried to keep his tone light. Couldn't let the lab coats know the shadows were getting to him.

"Vid feed's pretty dark, but we're also tracking you on GPS. It looks like the path forks up ahead. Go left."

"Roger that." Erik continued forward, slowly, his eyes constantly checking for movement, his ears cocked for any sound that would indicate the presence of the infected: an errant twig snap; rustling underbrush; or, worst of all, the high pitched, maniacal giggling that signaled an oncoming horde.

He reached the fork. The path to the right headed up, toward daylight. The path on the left tracked down and disappeared into darkness about twenty yards from his position.

"You sure you want me to go left?"

"Did I stutter? Wait, you're not scared are you?" He could hear the grin in Doug's voice. *"Do I need to send Jerry out to rescue you?"*

"That's pretty brave talk coming from someone who still sleeps with a nightlight." Erik gritted his teeth. "Don't think I won't forget this."

"Sorry man, just busting your balls. Be careful out there, okay? Don't make me tell

Mom I lost you."

"You won't get rid of me that easy."

Somewhere in the darkness, a twig snapped.

Erik stopped in his tracks. "Did you hear that?"

Someone was down there. Maybe a *bunch* of someones. And they clearly weren't concerned with stealth.

"Hold on, we're running a scan."

Erik wiped cold sweat from the back of his neck while he waited. Did Doug sound worried?

A single, manic giggle floated up from the darkness. Then another, and another, and another, each building on the last, until the laughter echoed throughout the woods just below him.

"Talk to me, Doug!" Erik shook while his mind fought against his body's flight response. His mind was losing. "What's going on?"

The infected were getting closer.

"Erik, they're coming!" Doug's voice screamed in his ear. *"Get out of there! Now!"*

He ran, all the time looking for somewhere to hide. No place looked safe.

The laughter was all around him now. Had they circled around behind him on his way in? If so, Doug's team had severely underestimated any affect the infection had on intelligence. Could the hive mind actually make them smarter?

Erik was near panic. The trail hadn't been this long and narrow coming in, had it? The light was almost gone, and he tripped over rocks and roots every few feet. A branch hit his face, raked his eyes and knocked his hat off. *Shit!* He'd lost the vidcam. Doug couldn't help him now; he was on his own. He ran off the path and crouched behind a tree. He needed to get his bearings, but things were moving too fast to process. The infected could be anywhere—hiding behind that outcropping of rocks, lurking in those bushes to the right, coiled on a branch right above him!—just waiting to strike.

Waiting for a chance to spread their disease.

To infect him with their cooties.

Erik swore this was the last time he'd ever go camping in a Boy-Only fort built by nerds.

THE VAULTS OF BAN-ERACH.

by Steve Dilks

I

The dark stranger stood like a statue, framed against the megalithic ruins of the prehistoric city. No breath of wind murmured through the streets lying beneath the pale sun. It was as if the very gods had abandoned and forsaken this place.

To Matt Randall it seemed he was the lone survivor on a dead world. As he came down the main avenue one hand fell to the butt of a heat-gun holstered at his thigh. His eyes, suspicious and feral, scanned the architecture. It towered all about him, leaning at bizarre, disjointed angles.

Columns reared from the sands and reeled drunkenly into the sky. Shattered domes in ghostly splendour lay forgotten in the ochre drifts; forgotten to all but the unknown hands that had reared them.

Behind him his mount groaned irritably and he pulled its leash. The surly beast lumbered forward again, feet padding in the

heavy sand.

His departure from the Zuethii nomads had been in haste, leaving him little time to equip- but, in addition to two days drinking water, a battered rifle leaned from his saddle bow. From the opposite flank jutted the hilt of a Vaithor long-sword. Out here the better armed the man, the better his chances. Randall knew this better than most. The deserts of the Gabahar were fraught with danger.

Until recently, he had been chieftain of those Zuethii—bloodthirsty reivers who, with flame and steel, were the terror of the trade canals. As the Blood Hawk, his name had struck fear into the hearts of the colonies. But betrayal had made an outcast of him. Those reivers bayed just as mercilessly for his blood now as when he had led them against their hereditary foes. They had not given up their pursuit of him, even though it had ranged far out into these barren wastes.

Just a few hours ago a storm had passed, serving to cover his tracks. It had been one of many that whipped up without warning in the desert. Evidently, it had also uncovered these ruins.

 Yet, not even in scraps of legend, had Matt heard tales of a city buried this far east of the Gabahar. There was mystery here buried in more than just sand. At his feet lay a riddle of the very eons.

Alone, as he walked, he thought to hear a lament of the dead calling out to him from the desert- but it was only the wind sighing through the doorways of buildings whose edifices gaped along the avenue in silent rows. Like bleached skulls those buildings stared at him through hollow, accusing eyes. They screamed at him from sand choked mouths then cursed him from toothless maws full of darkness and decay.

Randall blinked and wiped a leather gloved fist over his brow. Turning, he reached for the water skin tied at his saddle. The beast snorted as he began loosening the thin leather straps. Mumbling soothing words, he lifted the skin. As he did the beast let out a bellow and jerked back, eyes rolling

in fear. Behind him, something monstrous had exploded up from under the sand. Randall whirled, reaching for his gun.

All he had was a fleeting glimpse of blackness as a deep shadow fell over them. Then he was buffeted violently aside to come crashing down on his shoulder some yards away. He rolled, coming up dizzily against the side of a building.

Watching in horror, he saw his mount snatched bodily into the air. It let out an ear piercing scream, held fast as it was, in the grip of mighty pincers. Randall's unbelieving eyes caught sight of titanic jaws just before they crunched down.

Bone snapped and blood sprayed, splashing him and the surrounding buildings in a deep scarlet burst. Randall jerked twice on the trigger, feeling the weight of the silver heat-gun's recoil along his shoulder. A trumpeting bellow split the air.

More in anger than pain the creature hurled the mount from it. As the shredded carcass slapped wetly against the side of a building, it turned to face him. Scaled reptilian legs stamped in the dust as it squatted on thick set haunches, mighty pincers playing the air like some grotesque monstrous crab.

 Randall saw a hunched body housed in an impenetrable disc shaped shell. Small red eyes burned as the jaws elongated down, displaying sabre curved teeth, freshly stained with blood.

Crouching low, Randall pressed his back hard against the wall behind him then leaped out from it in a single cat like bound. Feinting to his left, he veered to the right, sprinting full tilt across the sand strewn avenue. He made for one of the lesser streets, hoping to lose the creature in the jumbled confusion of the city monuments. He began zigzagging down the shattered pathway, past columns of alien design, through strange frescoed archways, in an attempt to throw off his scent. In navigating the unfamiliar terrain he dared not risk a glance behind. His imagination already had the creature's fetid breath on his nape. As it was he could hear the steam engine fuel of its hiss; the stamp of splay toed feet in the dust.

Gritting his teeth, he drove himself to greater efforts, heart pumping piston like beneath his leather armour.

He came to an intersection. At its centre, thrusting up through the sand, was the tip of what appeared to be a black pyramid. He made for the structure and began climbing just as the beast rounded a corner and came into the clearing behind. At the pinnacle, Matt climbed around the apex, pressing his back against the rough surface. Raising his gun in one hand, he stood motionless and waited. He could hear the creature's measured tread below as it tried to fathom out where its quarry had gone.

Swallowing down a rising surge of hysteria, Randall inched along the narrow stair, feeling his way with an outstretched palm. Presently his groping fingers came across something other than the hewn substance of the pyramid.

Wonderingly, he twisted his head round. His hand had found a metallic door set in the stone. Of a light silver hue, it gleamed in the sunlight. The surface was inscribed with strange hieroglyphs, written in a language he did not know. Shifting his weight onto it he pressed hard and was rewarded when, with a deep compression of air, it opened-sliding noiselessly into one side of the wall. Incredulously, he stared in.

Only darkness met his gaze but he did not hesitate. With one last look behind he stepped over the threshold and into whatever mysteries lay beyond.

II

He found himself standing in a tunnel. Ridges, little more than worn bumps, lay beneath his feet. He slipped down the incline and, as he did, one hand groped in a thick slime that coated along the walls. He had little thought for what lay ahead, only an instinctive fear of the creature behind. As he plunged further into that strange structure he realized that a soft, luminescent glow was lighting the way. It came from the slime dripping along the bone like ridges of the tunnel and, as Randall followed the path down, his feet slid on a stair too narrow for human feet.

How long he followed that winding, worm like hole he had little idea but, after some time, surmised that he must be deep inside the heart of the pyramid.

Then, without warning, he had rounded a bend and found himself gazing into a chamber. Not a cold, dark chamber, as one would expect from being buried under timeless sands, but a hall; vast and sweeping, lighted by an uncanny silver glare that reflected from each facet of the oddly carved walls.

There were machines here. Vast and slumbering; forgotten relics of an unknown race. They hunched like sleeping giants, covered in the thick dust of centuries, as if waiting to be roused into life by unwitting hands.

Randall stared at them, his mind dazed. Then he had stepped out slowly onto the floor, his heat-gun hanging forgotten in his hand. He passed down long lines of those squatting machines, wondering what purpose they could have served in the long ago. He walked through them, feeling dwarfed by the antiquities of the past. At length he came to the far end of the hall. There he found himself confronted by strangeness such as he had never encountered in all his long wanderings among the interstellar gulfs of space.

Across the entire length of the far wall was a great curtain. It shimmered and undulated like liquid silver as if imbued with some protoplasmic life force. Emblazoned across its surface was a symbol. A great black circle lined with runes. Matt came toward it now and, as he did, he felt static waves of energy emanating toward him. Mesmerized, he stepped forward, reaching up with one hand. As he did his eyes flew wide. He gasped and tried to fall back but found himself unable to move.

Something had reached out to him from beyond that curtain—something that touched and slid around his mind, probing with alien fingers of clammy dread!

Then a voice spoke a word. A word that echoed in the furthest recesses of his brain...

"MATT."

His jaw slack, Matt Randall lifted his hand once more. He reached out, his fingers brushing the black symbol. They touched lightly in the liquid pool of the curtain and, as they did, he felt tingling waves of ecstasy surge deep inside his body.

Mechanically, he stepped forward. One moment he was there and the next, he had plunged out of the world he knew and into the depths of those silent, shimmering waves...

III

There was nothing in the void. Only a seething mist billowing against a backdrop of inky darkness...

Here was the infinite. Not the infinite of limitless horizons, but an infinity devoid of all shape, colour and sound.

For unguessed eons he drifted; both formless and nameless, knowing no sense of self or purpose.

Then thought. A vague impression. An understanding of awareness.

"MATT."

The word, calm and commanding, awoke him. Dimly, he felt something else stirring. Something that crawled along at the edge of his consciousness as if seeking to burrow in. Instinctively, he fought against the urgency of that sensation.

He saw streamers of light coming toward him, streaking silently across the void. They played around him and gathered him to them. Then he was borne along with them, streaking impossibly fast though the smoky dusk.

He knew no fear only a sense of serenity. Wrapped in their energy, they hurtled on, ribbons of limitless light. Then something reared up out of the void, coming gradually closer. Matt had a glimpse of ethereal spires and towers, translucent domes and delicate spanning archways.

It was a city; but a city glimpsed in the midst of a dream, floating in the nether of un-space.

Toward it they dropped down. Wraith like, they sank through the curve of a huge dome and Randall found himself in a vast megalithic hall with smooth ghost like curving walls that became indistinct when he tried to focus on them.

Those ribbons of light contracted and stood wavering before him in a circle. Without form or body, Randall looked on them. A voice vibrated inside his mind.

"You found the ancient city. The city that we once called Ban-Erach in the long ago."

Randall formed thoughts. Reaching out, he touched those ethereal beings with his words; "What happened there? Who are you?"

"Once we were the inhabitants of that city. Long ago we, too, were formed of flesh and bone. Our cities stood proudly on the sands of Harmakhis; our jewelled towers rearing against the light of her ancient moons. We lived long, peaceful lives and were given to study. But we saw new races coming. Races that came from the stars to exploit the old worlds—men in rocket ships, come to strip mine us of our wealth and traditions. Humanity... how we feared him! He forged alliances with the young barbarians, whom they tricked into casting us out. For man is weak of spirit and craves to destroy that which he can not understand. He drove us into the harsh lands, hunted us down and killed us. Slowly, our numbers dwindled... In those last days, we forged our efforts into developing machinery to build a gateway that would take us into the great unknown, into dimensions beyond the realms of physical being."

"Then—why did you call me?"

"We did not. We were alerted to your passing through the barrier by energy waves. Your passage created a ripple through our continuum. There are others here. Others that mean harm to the world we left behind... Others that want to return in the name of conquest and war. It was they, feeling your presence that called you through the curtain. They need your body to pass through. Otherwise, there is no return for us. Unless a body steps over willingly and becomes a physical host, we must stay in this realm."

"So... I was tricked into passing through the silver curtain?"

"Yes. We must return you quickly. The longer the delay, the less you will be tied to the plane of existence you came from. Your physical presence will become undone and there will be no turning back. You will be stuck here forever, unless another takes you over first."

Randall fought down a rising surge of panic.

Then, suddenly, those beams of light wavered. Another voice spoke and its stress patterns were audible. "They come," it said.

Instantly, the beam beings contracted around him in a bright, singular band. Gathered amongst them, Randall felt himself filled with a strange energy. His consciousness expanded. It reached out through the dome above him and encompassed the void.

He saw other streamers streaking toward the city.

They came bending down through the un-space, corporeal beings of eldritch light.

Waves of their energy reached out, searching for him. Randall felt something beating against his will and he was filled with a cosmic dread. Something alien touched his mind with grasping talons.

In that moment something broke in Randall's brain. He understood now who they were and what they wanted of him. He screamed in mute knowledge of that understanding.

Light exploded and became darkness once more.

Randall felt himself slipping, falling eternally into a blind abyss. He was vaguely aware that he had a gasped in a lungful of air, as if he had been holding his breath. Back through the shimmering curtain he fell and, as he did, he reeled away from it. He

ran and, in his headlong panic, he did not pause. Down those long lines of slumbering machines he fled.

Then he was groping his way back up through the tunnel, falling to his knees in the phosphorous slime as his hands reached out against the fleshy substance of the organic ribbed walls. No thought or purpose guided him, only a blind instinctive fear to be away from that terrible place.

He came up through the metal arched doorway and out onto the crumbled steps of the pyramid. He stood there a moment, gasping in of the cold desert night air. He slid wearily down the stair. Falling to his knees in the soft sands, he looked up. A pale moon stared down at him, a cracked and leering face. Randall stared at it. He felt the cold numbing chill of the stars as an almost tangible thing.

He laughed insanely. A deep knowledge was branded into him and he raised his hands to his head. He staggered up and, as he came reeling into a clearing, a pale face reared up at him out of the darkness. He had a fleeting glimpse of rolling eyes and bared teeth above a forked beard before a rifle butt crashed hard against his temple.

He knew no more.

IV

He came to slowly, lances of pain sending waves of agony slamming into his temples.

He opened his eyes and lifted his head.

Above him, the sun stared down in merciless defiance. He blinked, spitting sand from his mouth, and retched into the dust.

He found that he was lying on his side in the middle of a clearing. Through narrowed eyes, he scanned the clustered tents of nomads gathered about him on the ancient ruins. Beasts of burden crouched before hide awnings as warriors swaggered to and fro. They were Zuethii. Having caught up with him at last, he knew he could expect no mercy from them. He shook his head. The delirium of the night before had passed and, for that, he was at least thankful. He rolled over, hands twisting painfully in the bonds tied behind his back.

A shadow moved over him and Randall jerked his head round to see the silhouette of a man standing there.

"*Savoryi*, Matt Randall," a voice said in the ritual desert greeting, "Apologies, my friend, for the nasty bruise. You gave the sentry quite a fright last night, reeling out of the darkness like that."

He squatted down and Randall, grimacing, strained futilely against his bonds.

"Vallitch!" He spat the word.

The tribesman grinned. Rubbing a sinewy hand over his jaw, he reached for a haunch of meat in a nearby pot. Strong white teeth bared in the crag of a weather beaten face as he chewed. Eyes, black and hard as stones, regarded his prisoner thoughtfully.

Randall stared back.

Here two men, born worlds apart, faced each other. Men different yet, intrinsically, the same. Both were reared in harsh environments and were toughened by the extremities of existence. Vallitch lived a wild life in the Harmakhisian drylands, his skin darkened by the light of an unforgiving sun. He lived according to the code of sword and rifle and could trace his ancestry back a thousand years. When he raised his head to the wind he heard the spirits of those ancestors whispering back to him in the sands that sighed eternally across the bleak, unending plains.

By contrast, Randall was a lone wolf.

A half son of earth and a pariah breed of outlaw starmen, he had been reared in the voids of outer space. The burn of a thousand heat gun rays crisscrossed his lean, wolfish frame; a frame burned dark by the radiation of interstellar suns. He followed no man and the only spirits he listened too were the cold winds that blew between the vacuums of the stars.

"You are a good fighter, Randall. But you cannot lead us. That privilege belongs to the Zuethii alone, by birthright," said Vallitch, tearing at the mutton. Juice dribbled into the fork of his beard.

Randall glared. "You took matters into your own hands. No man appointed you leader. Where were the council of elders? By flouting tradition you betray your people. As soon as these dogs realize their mistake they will tear you to pieces. How long do you think they will follow a cheat and a liar? Pah!"

Vallitch, dropping the meat bone, started angrily to his feet. He raised his hand in quivering rage, as if to slap Randall across the face. The jewelled rings on his fingers flashed in the sunlight. Then, regaining his composure, he forced his lips into a wry smile. Looking around he shrugged and, lowering his hand, crouched down again.

"I like you Randall, but desert law dictates I kill you." He grinned. "Unless..."

"Unless, what?" growled Randall.

The tribesman leaned in close. "Unless you give up to me the secrets of this city. I know there is treasure here. You fled here in the hope of carrying much of it away as you can. Where is it?"

The star farer stared at him a moment then threw back his head and laughed. "I didn't come seeking here, you fool! The city was uncovered in the storm. A sand creature ate my behmon for lunch and damn near got me, too. I fled—"

"We found the pyramid. What is in there? Show me and I will let you live. I swear it by Ahzruhl."

Randall recoiled inwardly at the thought of entering that strange structure again. Yet, as he stared into the greed lusting eyes of the nomad, the seeds of a desperate plan began to form in his mind. He swallowed thickly. Fixing the Zuethii chieftain with a level stare he heard himself say; "Alright, Vallitch. You win. I will lead you to the treasure. Though I warn you—it is one far stranger and greater than any you have ever known."

V

Once more Randall found himself standing on the pyramid. Beside him the black doorway gaped open like a throat yawning to the gates of hell. As he stood before it he turned, looking at the fierce bearded faces gathered below him on the stair. A breath of icy wind blew up from behind and he shuddered. Vallitch came up the steps. At his side was a tall woman, lithe and strong. Her hair was bound into a warrior's top knot. Black swirling whorls were tattooed into her dark skin and, as she stared at him through almond shaped eyes, Randall's lips bent in a tight line. From her belt she drew a curved knife. Reaching up behind him, she freed his hands with a single slash and stepped back. No expression showed on Randall's face.

Rubbing life into his numbed wrists, he stared at her and said; "Nuri. I'm going to give you one last chance- get out of here while you still can."

The woman called Nuri laughed. Spinning the blade deftly in her fingers, so it flashed in the sunlight, she sheathed it and, leaning forward, gripped his chin with one hand. "You are too soft, Randall. That's why Vallitch is leader and I am his woman now. You were always weak." She laughed again and the space farer, jerking back from her, said nothing. His eyes burned with fury.

A hand gripped his arm and spun him round. With a grunt, he was pushed toward the opening, a heat-gun pressed into his back. Gritting his teeth, Randall stepped over the threshold. Then he was groping, once more, into the winding depths of that worm like hole.

The nomads pressed behind, cursing as they slipped in the gelatinous slime of the walls and stair. Hairy hands gripped rifle and sword hilt; dark eyes scanning wildly around. Used to the wide open spaces of the desert, they hated the claustrophobic interior of that strange burrow. Behind them, Vallitch urged them on with muttered oaths and threats.

Finally, they stepped out onto the glassy floor of the great hall and they spread out, looking around them in wonder.

Matt walked slowly forward and, behind him, the Zuethii pressed close. Directly to his left, Nuri held a heat-gun poised at his back. Vallitch stalked to the other side of him. His long curved sword was in his hand and the hem of his dusty robes swept over the floor. Towering above them, the monstrous machines leaned down, waiting, as they had waited in silence down the long centuries. Then they had passed through them and came up before the silver curtain swimming across the whole length of the far end of the hall.

When they beheld it, the tribesmen fell back. There was an audible intake of breath. Some warded themselves in superstitious dread. Vallitch turned. Did Randall see a glimmer of doubt, a cold touch of fear in those eyes at that moment?

Grumbling a curse and throwing back his robes, the Zuethii chieftain lifted his sword.

"Dog brothers!" he cried, "The depths of the off-worlder's treachery is at last revealed! Here is a treasure your former chieftain sought to hide. He led you, gaining your trust—the proud and honourable people of the desert, just until he could find this city... Aye! He hid this place from you, the Zuethii, who's birthright this land is! Once he had the treasure in his hands, he would have betrayed you to the authorities."

All eyes lifted toward him as he spoke. The nomads drank in his words and, slowly, he lowered his sword.

Inwardly, Randall felt a grudging admiration for the cunning of Vallitch. He was no fool that much was certain. Only a man of iron demeanor could lead these wayward sons of the desert.

Turning to face him in a whirl of desert robes, the chieftain fixed Randall with a dark hooded stare and, in that stare, was the gleam of a secret triumph.

Outflinging a drape sleeved arm, he indicated the curtain shimmering behind him.

"Show us, great leader. What is this thing? Where is the treasure that you have held back from us, the rightful sons of the desert?"

It was then that the whisperings began. A shuddering thrill went through Randall's body, like a mild electric jolt. Once again he felt himself drawn toward the protoplasmic waves of the shimmering curtain. But this time he was prepared. He steeled himself mentally and his mind clamped down like a vice, shielding him from the mesmerizing pull of its alien power.

He knew that he had only a slender moment of time with which to work with and he had to move fast. The tribesmen, shocked at the alien touch washing over them, stood in slack jawed amazement. All eyes turned glassily to the curtain. Vallitch stiffened.

A tribesman came, lumbering up through the ranks of his companions. Slack jawed and glassy eyed, he reached out, even as Randall had done before him, for the rune on the curtain. All eyes turned and watched in fascinated wonder as he lifted his hand. The tips of his fingers rippled the surface. A shudder of ecstasy swept over him. He moved forward and, as he did, those silently lapping waves seemed to part eagerly before they shrouded over him.

There was a brief waving ripple and he was gone.

In that moment, Randall struck. His left elbow shot out and, behind him, Nuri groaned as her head snapped back. Just as her legs began to buckle, he grabbed her wrist in both hands, wrenching the heat-gun from her grasp. He whirled quickly behind her, his left arm encircling her neck. Pulling her close, he pressed the silver snout of the gun hard against her temple.

Too late, Vallitch staggered toward them. His limbs seemed leaden, as if he were wading through water.

Randall pulled back, away from the mesmeric influence of the curtain. The tribesmen parted from around him until he was brought up short, his back pressed against the bulk head of one of the great machines. He glared around him like a cornered wolf.

"Back!" he snarled, "Or I blow her head off!"

Vallitch, shouldering through the press, threw nomads aside as he approached. He shook his head. Outside of the influence of the curtain, a semblance of normality returned to his eyes. Lifting his curved blade in a trembling hand, he indicated the space farer.

"For this you will be flayed alive, your eyes torn from their sockets! I will leave you to rot in the sun!" he hissed.

Randall laughed. A dry, hollow sound.

"Then we all die together, Vallitch. Your greed has brought your doom! This place is cursed by an evil only an off-worlder can understand. You have led the Zuethii to their deaths!"

The tribesmen hesitated. They looked around; first to each other and then to their new found leader. Uncertainty and loyalty for each man tore at their hearts. The bond they had for their old chieftain was still an open wound. Vallitch knew this. Sweat formed on his brow and dripped down his face from beneath his *keffiyeh*. His teeth gleamed fiercely in the spike of his beard.

"Kill them both!" he snarled.

Reaching down, Randall grabbed for the hilt of the long-knife sheathed at Nuri's hip. He jerked it out and flipped it through the air, hurling Nuri aside with his gun hand as he did so. Vallitch leaned back, his sword sweeping out as the deadly blade flashed toward him. Deflecting it in a clash of sparks, the knife sank into the throat of a warrior stood beside him. The nomad gurgled, reaching up to his throat as he died, a thin red line of blood sprouting from his opened jugular.

Randall was already moving. He dived, sliding out across the floor as a shot whined above him, piercing the plating of the machine behind. He hit the ground hard, the heat-gun hissing concentrated waves of sonic energy from his hand. A tribesmen howled, his ear ripped away; one side of his face melting from the assault of the static plasma blast. Matt rolled to his feet. He lashed out, the butt of his gun crunching into the face of another nomad fumbling for a sword hilt. The man reeled back, spitting blood and broken teeth from a shattered face.

Like a raging sand cat, Randall tore through the press. Reaching out, he grabbed the barrel of a rifle being aimed at him by a kneeling tribesman. Wrenching it toward him, he kicked out with his heavy boot, grinning fiercely as that man catapulted away.

Randall whirled, ramming the butt of the rifle into the face of another who came in from his right, a dagger ripping up murderously in his hand. The nomad's blade tore against the chest plate of his leathers before he was driven to his knees, his features dissolving into red ruin as the rifle butt slammed into his skull.

Shaking his head, Randall saw Vallitch wading toward him through the press, a heat-gun in his hand. Flinging aside the bloodied rifle, he made to raise his own gun. Then suddenly, from below, a hand reached up and clamped onto his arm.

Looking down in horror, he saw the blood stained face of the man he had just beaten with the rife clinging in fierce determination to his gun hand. Randall's blood froze. Raising his head, he watched as Vallitch slowly lifted his heat-gun, eyes blazing with fanatical hate.

VI

If eternity could be measured in time, Randall lived a thousand lives in that instant. His fear was replaced by a calming sense of the inevitable.

Suddenly, a shot rang out and Vallitch spun away, a yell torn from his lips. He hit the ground, the heat-gun sent spinning from his hand.

Randall leaned down, knotting a fist in the hair of the nomad clinging to his arm. Cupping his other hand under his chin, he wrenched violently. The man fell back, his neck broken. Stepping over the flopping corpse, Randall raised his heat-gun, aiming at Vallitch as he lay writhing on the floor.

It was then that Nuri, moving in from his right, swung the butt of her rifle. Knocking his arm aside, she spun round to face him, eyes blazing dangerously.

"No, Randall. Not like this. I know he ordered my death- but not like this."

Randall stepped back, lowering his gun. There was a breathless silence.

"Then why did you stop him?" he asked.

Conflicting emotions warred on Nuri's face. Turning on her heel, she addressed the nomads gathered around them. "We decide this once and for all," she cried and her voice echoed in the silence that had fallen over the chamber. She gestured impatiently at Vallitch. Her lip curled in contempt as she indicated him with her rifle. "Give him his sword," she said.

Holding onto his left shoulder, Vallitch climbed stiffly to his feet, teeth gritted with pain. Blood seeped between his fingers and ran in scarlet rivulets down his dust stained robes. As he lifted his right hand, his eyes swept the throng gathered before him. A nomad handed him his sword. Turning it this way and that, he looked to Randall standing across the way. Tribesmen parted before them, clearing a space.

Randall, tossing the heat-gun aside, reached for the hilt of a sword offered him. He took it, hefting its weight in one hand. He was an indifferent swordsman. Vallitch had been born to the blade. Even with his left shoulder injured, the nomad was still a formidable adversary.

Crouching low, the spaceman moved into the clearing as the tribesman came forward to meet him. Every eye was fixed on them in tense expectancy.

Vallitch came in at a rush, his head thrown back, a Zuethii war-cry on his lips. Steeling himself, Randall raised his blade and braced to meet the charge.

Just then, behind the expectant throng, something materialized. It flopped through the barrier of the silver curtain and oozed across the floor. A strange bellowing cry split the air and, as every head turned toward the sound, they gazed on a sight of mind numbing terror. Even Vallitch paused in his head-long charge, the war-cry frozen on his lips.

The tribesman had returned from behind the curtain. But he had not returned unchanged. His body and form were grossly distorted; warped and bloated beyond shape. Under his skin, shapes writhed and moved as if seeking to break free from their prison of flesh. He reared up gigantically now and every feature and limb was hugely exaggerated. As he flopped toward them, one huge bulbous eye was distended, pleading with mind shattering terror. A giant, slobbering mouth yawned cavernously, as if to scream its horror at the world but, instead of human words, myriad alien sounds babbled forth.

"Wh—what is that thing?" whispered Nuri, moving back slowly.

"Destroy it!" exclaimed a tribesman. Rifles cracked and the hiss of heat-guns filled the chamber.

The monster screamed and recoiled under the fury of those blasts. But their respite was short lived. The entity moved forward again, with a dexterity that belayed its bulk. A huge arm lashed out and a boulder sized hand gripped a nomad by the head. There was the sound as of an egg being crushed then the monstrous bulk had dragged itself toward them, leaving a man sized trail of blood smeared across the floor. Before its advance, tribesmen scattered in terror.

Randall swore and threw down his sword. Looking around him, he snatched up his discarded heat-gun and moved back through the machines.

The monstrous bulk swept toward them, a huge blubbery mass. At each flick of its mighty arms, a tribesman was sent hurtling and screaming through the air. Directly in its path, Vallitch stood frozen. Nomads ran past him, but he stood as one transfixed. The huge face of the monster swung toward him, fixing him with that terrible stare of suffering. A huge arm swept out. It opened its mouth.

Who can say what thoughts were meant to be expressed and put into words at that moment? Did the creature, perhaps, recognize his chieftain then? Did he wish to convey to him his suffering, his torment at the hands of that alien possession? Only a bellow of despair sounded from between bloated lips and, in that final dread instant, Vallitch woke at last. Raising his arms, he cried; "Ahzruhl! Protect your servant!" Then a giant fist swept down, smashing him to the floor.

Nuri cried out in wounded pain.

Randall whirled. Dragging her back from the creature's path, he shook her violently.

"Damn it! He's dead! Get out of here!" He pushed her forward and, as she stumbled back toward the tunnel, he turned. The monstrous entity had made it to the first of the great machines now. As nomads fled down the hall from it, a giant arm reached up. Monstrous fingers moved over the machine's surface and hidden ancient engines grumbled into life. An ominous whirring noise filled the hall. The huge bulk slithered down again, turning to face the curtain.

Randall watched in morbid fascination.

Shimmering waves began to undulate across the curtain's surface. A whirling vortex formed, spiralling out in concentric circles from the lines of the black rune.

"He's opening the portal," Randall hissed through gritted teeth.

The vortex widened. He thought to see terrible things groping there in the abyss beyond.

He averted his gaze. Lying at his feet was the figure of a dead tribesman. His brains oozed down the side of a machine where he had been slammed viciously against the side of a dented bulkhead. Strapped to his back was a rucksack. As soon as he saw it, Randall kneeled down.

Imprinted on the camouflage and highlighted in bold, were three letters—H.U.P.

Harmakhis Union Protectorate.

Some months ago, Randall had led the Zuethii in a successful a raid on a munitions base. It belonged to a security company the Harmakhis world government had set up to quash the uprisings of dissatisfied natives.

Among the items they had seized were state of the art off world weapons.

Heart thudding in his ribs, Randall tore the pack open, hoping against hope that it contained something within. He groped around for a moment and, when his hands came out again, they held three small, black plastic boxes. He stared at them a moment. Then, wrenching the heavy sack from the mangled corpse, he was moving forward. He glided in a half crouch, down through the long lines of those awful machines, until he came up to the one throbbing with life.

Before it, standing out between the floor and the curtain, squatted the amorphous entity that had once been a Zuethii tribesman. It crouched on trunk like legs, staring intently at the curtain. Beneath hideously bloated flesh, alien life forms moved. Even though its back was toward him, Randall shuddered in revulsion.

He moved stealthily over to the machine, twisting a dial on one of the boxes in his left hand as he did so. A button lit up and he swung the heavy rucksack in both hands, wedging it deep under the bulk housing. Then he turned and fled, quietly as he could, up that long corridor of machines. Behind him he thought to hear an ominous keening noise, rising in a tidal wave of sound. He did not look back. His foot snagged in something. Stumbling, he looked round. A nomad groaned, reaching up to him from the floor with a clawed hand. Randall hesitated. Bending down he pulled the man up, slinging him over his aching shoulders. Then he was moving on, staggering over toward the dark mouth of the tunnel. Reaching the worm like hole, he bent down as the nomad flopped bloodily into the opening.

"Can you climb?" he panted.

"*Sabihb*, leave me. You can do no more..." the nomad gasped. A bloodied hand reached out and flopped weakly on his shoulder. Shaking the sweat from his eyes, Randall grasped his robes in both hands.

"You fools may have deserted me in favour of that treacherous dog," he snarled,

"but I'll be damned before I leave any man I once called brother in this forsaken hole."

Bracing his feet, he turned and began hauling him along over the worn ridges of the tunnel.

Behind them, the keening sound grew to an unbearable pitch.

VII

Reaching the opening, Nuri pulled herself into the sunlight as a struggling knot of tribesmen came pouring out around her. She half fell down the pyramid steps and, as robed forms pressed her in, she threw men aside and staggered into the camp.

Seeing the frightened mob running toward them, the guards leapt to their feet and snatched for their rifles. Among the tents, saddled lizards stamped in the dust.

"Move out!" Nuri shouted, striding toward them and waving an arm in the direction of the desert.

Swarming past her, warriors began groping for their mounts. Short horned, rusty haired behmon pawed nervously in the dust as nomads clambered up their flanks. Lizards hissed as their riders, swinging into the high peaked saddles, swung them around and headed out into the drifts.

Nuri leaped into the saddle of a two legged reptile. Grasping the reins, she jerked its head around. Before her stretched the limitless wastes of the Gabahar. She paused, turning back to face the pyramid. A tribesman reined up beside her.

"Sabihbya?" he asked.

She looked at him a moment. Then, with one last final glance at the pyramid, she swung her mount round and was heading into the desert.

They were some way off when the explosion hit. A heavy thump sent a shockwave rippling out from the center of the ruins. On its heels, a vast tremor shook the ground. Riders were hurled from their saddles as the whole desert erupted beneath them. A tribesman, thrown clear of his mount, climbed unsteadily to his feet. Groping for his halter, he lifted his arm and pointed back the way they had come.

Every head turned to where he indicated.

A red plume of dust was mushrooming into the sky. Below it, the city was disappearing into the sand, dragged into an abyss that had opened up beneath it.

The desert winds howled and, through billowing clouds, they raised the cloths of their *keffiyeh* against the sand gritting their eyes. Then it had passed and, through the red settling dust, they saw a silhouetted shape approaching toward them.

Squinting, they saw that it carried another form in its arms. Even as they murmured to each other in amazement, that figure, burdened by its weight, sank down and collapsed in the sighing drifts.

VIII

The sun was a blood stained smear hanging low on the horizon. In the east, rising above the ochre drifts, the moons of Daros and Pehma swung steadily into a tinted sky.

From a high crested ridge of dunes, mounted on a sleek lizard, Matt Randall breathed deep of the cold Harmakhis air and pulled his robes closer about him. He watched those distant moons rise above the domed bubbles of Zenabel as the lights of that city glowed softly in the gathering twilight. As he gazed on her concrete towers and spires of outthrust steel and heard her cold thrumming industrial dirge a sadness swept over him at the sights and sounds.

There was sorrow in Matt Randall's heart; sorrow for all dreams and glories turned to dust. No longer would the wings of the Blood Hawk sweep across the red wastes, his cry echo down the valleys and dried canal bottoms of ancient Harmakhis.

He sighed and, turning his head, looked out into the desert.

Behind him, sat as close as they dared come to the domes of the hated off world city, were the Zuethii. A hard bitten, rag tag lot they were, harsh and cruel as the desert winds, but Matt Randall loved them to a man. That they dared come this far was a sign of the respect and awe they had for him. But there would be no farewell song. No lament for the loved departed. He was an outcast now. He grinned a bitter grin and lifted his reins.

"All things come to an end," a voice said.

Randall turned to stare at Nuri sat on her mount. She lifted herself boldly under his gaze, this fierce nomad woman who had once been his lover.

"Are you sure you can lead them, Nuri?" he asked.

"They accepted you, didn't they?"

Randall smiled and nodded. There was silence.

"Where will you go?"

He shrugged. "I'll see if there's a ship heading out to Kronos... Senuvia, maybe."

They stared into each others eyes a moment as a wind sprang up. Sand hissed about them.

Randall, turning his mount, headed down the incline toward the glowing lights of the distant city. Behind him, the wind whipped wildly through the robes of the desert men. A plume of red dust spun from beneath the feet of their mounts and lifted into the sky.

A nomad gasped and pointed.

Outlined against the sky for a moment, it seemed that the spirit of the Blood Hawk was beating its wings against the darkness.

But it was only dust.

TOTALITY

by Andre E. Harewood

July 1st, 2037

"Only twenty?"

"You were hoping for more?" the woman asked her incredulously in response. Carol Annis was one of the counsellors talking with XNX Flight 246 passengers today, and most of said passengers expressed emotions from rage to hope to horror. The woman before Carol was the first seemingly expressing disappointment.

"Corinne," she continued, "I'm afraid I don't understand."

"Sorry to scare you," Corinne said. The phrase should have been a joke but it sounded matter of fact and cold. "It would be easier if I was a hundred years in the future, not just twenty. You can escape anything in a century."

There were subtle hints of vanilla in the air though there were no visible candles or air ducts or devices to emit such a scent. Corinne Cohen adjusted her glasses, inhaled her favourite fragrance deeply, not caring where it came from, caring only that it was there and it was barely calming her. The walls of the interview room originally had a vista of blue skies and lazily drifting clouds that made the small area seem larger but had the unexpected effect of freaking out most Flight 246 passengers because the pictures were moving. The walls were now a calm-

ing and static blue. Corinne, a tall woman with brown skin and a shock of black hair, sat in an office chair that had subtly moulded itself to her lanky frame; the woman across the uncluttered mahogany desk from her sat in similar comfort. Corinne's seat on the plane, 12C, felt much like this in its ergonomic comfort but the 20 year old technology wasn't made from 2037 smart materials. Corinne wondered if this would be considered an ill-fated flight, and if he and the other passengers were its survivors.

"I slept through it, you know."

"A few people did," Carol informed her.

"The most miraculous thing to ever happen to a human being...and I was dreaming about...things that don't matter anymore, things that haven't mattered for two decades."

"They still matter to you."

"They'll always matter to me," Corinne said in a tone that showed the first sign of breaking but she quickly shifted to another topic with a renewed detachment. "I wondered if I should check in like people do after disasters or terrorist attacks. Then I wondered if any of the social media sites from my day still existed. If they did, what would I write? 'Hi! Back after a longer vacation than expected! What did I miss?'"

Corinne scoffed, taking out her 2013

model smart phone.

"Can I even charge this now, Carol? I haven't seen any plugs or outlets."

"Most of our devices are charged remotely these days."

"Of course. Can you tell me what happened exactly?"

"I'd like to talk about you for a bit first."

"I'd like to talk about what happened for a bit first."

"We don't know any more than you've already been told, Corinne. Your plane passed through a..." she broke off as she checked the blue writing on an otherwise transparent handheld device. "Your plane passed through a space-time vacuole, a stable corridor between Wednesday June 28th, 2017 and Wednesday July 1st, 2037... Today."

"Are there many of these corridors? These vacuoles?"

"There have been other incidents, yes. The United Nations has a special team investigating the various phenomena in conjunction with Sexton Industries' Temporal Mechanics. I can give you all of that information after we talk about you, OK?"

"OK."

"You're from the Caribbean?" she asked despite having all of Corinne's personal information at hand.

"Just beyond your imagination, yes."

"I take a vacation there every other year or so. My husband and I love taking the train from Florida."

"The what?"

"Ah, sorry. You have a lot of catching up to do. You worked in media?"

"Lead content producer for my company's three radio stations."

"Were you born in the Caribbean? I can understand everything you're saying."

"I was raised to speak 'proper' English as some people call it. Growing up on a steady diet of American and British TV shows probably helped, too. I switch into speaking dialect when I'm around others speaking it, but this is my default voice."

"It's a beautiful voice."

"Thanks, but I'm sure my voice and my creative skills are useless here in your future."

"You'd be surprised. Real human interfacing is making a comeback."

"I got into production work to get away from interfacing with too many real humans."

"That's still very possible now, too."

"You're supposed to ask me about my loved ones next, aren't you?"

Carol put down the transparent pad.

"You have some experience with situations like this, Corinne."

"There was a terrorist attack on a plane a few yea...many years ago. I helped cover it. I put together a five-year retrospective on it, too. I know how counsellors work their way up to the hardest topics with victims."

"Is that what you think you are? A victim?"

"You know. You have the information about my family. You tell me."

"No children, not married..."

"They hadn't legalized that kind of marriage back home last I saw, and my kind of recreation doesn't lead to procreation. If either has changed in the last two decades, I'd be surprised...more so by the marriage equality, to be honest."

"Your parents, Corinne," Carol began as she searched her face for signs of emotion, "they passed away."

Carol noticed Corinne's fingers digging into the smart foam of her chair's hand-rests but her face remained icy.

"Your father died five years after your plane disappeared. Your mother died two years ago."

There was silence as Corinne stared directly at her, causing Carol to avert her eyes at the intensity.

"Did they suffer?"

"The report says they both passed peacefully in their sl..."

"Did they suffer while they were alive?"

"I'm afraid I don't..."

"Stop being afraid and answer the question!" Corinne said commandingly in that voice Carol had previously loved. "I was the one making all the money, taking care of everything from rent to food to doctors' appointments. It was only ever the three of us. Did they suffer?"

"Once you were officially declared dead a year after Flight 246 disappeared without a trace, XNX's travel accident insurance payed out £50,000,000 to them. No, Corinne, I don't think they suffered materially. I don't know what the status of their estate is. I can have an attorney help you find out about that once you're settled at the ho..."

"It doesn't matter."

"This is an extremely difficult situation. I don't understand what you're experiencing, Corinne, but there are people who want to help you get through it. You're not even forty yet. You've been given a second chance at life. Don't let the things and people you've lost eclipse that."

"I don't think I have much choice in the matter, Carol." Corinne said, shifting uncomfortably in the now restrictive embrace of the chair. "I don't think I have any choice at all but to stay in the dark."

July 13th, 2037

Sparse bushes and short, thin trees dotted the otherwise red-brown Australian landscape. A similarly coloured monolith loomed over the twelve small memory plastic buildings near its base as the sun was slowly blotted out overhead. There were tables filled with local food and beverages plus unusually healthy versions of what Corinne remembered as decidedly unhealthy junk food and carbonated drinks. She sat in yet another impossibly comfortable chair on a large deck as she watched the moon smother the sun over Uluru, the clear plastic roof over her specifically altered to make viewing the celestial event possible without destroying her recently fixed eyesight. A large woman in a loose gray blouse with an animated SX logo moving across it, blue jeans, and black sandals sat down in the chair beside Corinne. A thin,

metallic blue circle about an inch in diameter was attached to her right temple, one of its two green lights blinked every few seconds.

"12C?" the woman asked while taking off her shades and placing them on a small table next to Corinne.

"I'm more XL...but yes," Corinne replied.

"Adamma Sexton. Sorry I'm late. At least I haven't missed it," she said eyeing the dying sun. "Pleased to meet you."

She extended a light brown hand which Corinne then shook.

"How are you enjoying your first Aussie trip, Corinne?"

"I was afraid you were going to always call me 12C, Madam Billionaire."

"Numbers don't lie unless you have a very good accounting staff," Sexton said with a matter-of-factness that made Corinne smile. The bit of sweat this woman who was richer than 2037's equivalent of Bill Gates then wiped from her forehead added to Corinne's amusement.

"The numbers say that I'm used to this heat. Island girl, remember? This is a normal day in the West Indies."

"With the last of the weather modification aerogels released into the atmosphere, I was hoping it would be much cooler for my first Outback summer."

Sexton tapped a panel on a table next to her. The temperature in the temporary building around them dropped by five degrees Celsius.

"Outback winter," Corinne corrected her. "Everything's turned around down under. I like it. Fits my current situation perfectly."

Corinne sipped her rum and coke a bit, inspecting the almost completely blotted out sun.

"Some things still get make me stop and stare," Corinne told Adamma Sexton. "Square toilet bowls with adjustable bidet wands, two hundred storey buildings whose exterior windows are all one huge moving ad for the latest interactive movie or sporting event, the electric cars powered by wireless energy with no exhaust… Those things wouldn't have been too shocking in my time but here in this time they're everywhere, as ubiquitous and commonplace as the internet interfaces on everyone's temples."

Corrine pointed to the device on the other woman's head.

"Well, everyone but me," Corinne continued. "I don't trust those things, plus it'd take serious mental gymnastics for me to use one successfully. Is this how my parents and grandparents felt back in the 80s when they couldn't get the VCR programmed or the microwave clock set? At least they had time to adjust to becoming dinosaurs. I skipped right over that, skipped right through time to become instantly obsolete. Time hasn't adjusted me."

"I know exactly what you mean. I created the A.I.-brain bridging software… then I missed a whole generation learning to use it. Look at it as a challenge, Corinne. The universe is the great teacher."

"I wish we had a second, independent marker for its exams."

"I was told about your dark humour."

"I find that merging laughter and tears works best for me," Corinne explained. "It helps plug the hole in my soul."

"All the tears in the world, all the waters of the ocean won't fill a bucket with a hole in it," Sexton replied.

"Not unless the bucket is at the bottom of the ocean."

"And here you are in the middle of an almost desert."

"I grew up on an island. What better place to be than an almost desert on the literal other side of the planet?"

"Australia's the world's biggest island."

"Or smallest continent," Corinne countered, raising her right index finger. "It's all about perspective."

"Were you this quick before they titivated your genes?"

"Only on paper or in hindsight. My eyesight is better than 20/20…a year I unintentionally skipped."

"You didn't miss anything interesting."

"The nano-cleaning of all the gunk in my lungs, brain, and circulatory system from thirteen lucky years of smoking probably helped, too."

"Probably. I'm surprised you're sober."

"That's me: sober, conscious, and not buried under at least three naked people."

"Lots of jumpers from my plane did just that. Some from your plane, too."

"13C, the woman behind me? She got two new 3D printed kidneys all for the extra low price of losing her marriage and not watching her kids grow up. There's nothing to mourn or to celebrate, Adamma Sexton. Every person I love…loved…is dead. A few of my former supposed friends are only interested in me because of my fourteen minutes and fifty-nine seconds of fame. The rest aren't interested at all. Some guy wants me to document my story on whatever invasive procedure passes for social media these days…these years."

An unusually large fly tried to come from the open air onto the porch, most likely following the aroma of the healthy junk food. There was a flash of light and a small crackle as the invisible anti-bug shield slaughtered it.

"Is that why you're here, Corinne?" Sexton inquired. "Hiding out? Capturing this for posterity and money?"

"Whether for religious or advertising reasons or both, the Anangu specifically invited the 246 jumpers to view the 2037 Great Australian Eclipse here. I'm the only one who took them up on their offer. The others all had things to see, people to do, lives to try and rebuild. I just wanted needed some time. Hhn. Like I need any more time," Corinne scoffed.

"We never got invited anywhere," Sexton said, a bit annoyed that her jumpers had been kept in isolation for weeks while being examined in excruciating physical and psychological detail.

"Here I am now…somehow," Corinne said. "The Aboriginal traditional beliefs revolve around continuity, stories and rituals that connect people and culture across tens of thousands of years. Time jumpers, poor bastards who skipped twenty years of their personal stories, should be the last ones invited here."

"That might be the point, though, Corinne. They might want to show you all... well, you...that the connections haven't been broken, that your stories continue despite the interruption."

"And what connects you to them, Ms. Sexton? How do you get a private view of the sun dying above the former Ayer's Rock?"

"A few hundred billion dollars helps."

"Monetary lubrication, eh?"

"One of my companies built and upkeeps the Uluru-Kata Tjuta National Park's solar generators."

"That's sounds better."

"I think so," Sexton agreed.

"I should also thank you for looking after all my fellow jumpers' whims and fancies."

"I remember what it was like landing in a different time, zoned out, alone. My green initiative investments and A.I. advancements had paid off exponentially in my own temporal absence. You will want for nothing, Corinne."

"I have nothing...and I'm fine with that."

"Really? You'd be the first."

"I'm not mentally ill... anymore. Do you still have those, Ms. Sexton?"

"Less and less."

The darkening of the sky quickened as the eclipse neared totality.

"Hhh. After Flight 246 was confirmed lost, XNX Airlines made sure my parents wanted for nothing. My apparent death provided more for them than my confirmed life ever could. I cried like a baby for days after going to their graves...but I eventually realized that I'm free. No one depends on me. I have no one to limit how I live my life. That space-time anomaly cut this puppet's strings."

"If you could go back and string yourself up again, would you?" Sexton asked.

Corinne took a breath, looking up through the electromagnetically polarized canopy at the day-night sky. It was 11:45 AM and the moon fully engulfed the sun.

"In a heartbeat," Corinne replied.

Totality.

"Beautiful. I was hoping to hear that, Corinne. I've had my people working on time travel into the past since my plane arrived in this future a few years ago. You should be thankful you were flying in a 969. After we came through our rift, our arrival in that old bucket of bolts was a cheap disaster movie complete with dead electronics and an emergency landing off Jamaica."

"And you want me to continue my time travel adventures for you?"

"Live as if you were to die tomorrow. Learn as if you were to live forever," Sexton quoted.

"Gandhi, right? Gandhi hated black people," Corinne countered. "I doubt he'd want me taking his words to heart. We steal, you know."

"Gandhi's early views were problematic but he became wiser...in time," Sexton corrected Corinne while leaning in closer to her. "Wanna help me steal time?"

Corinne looked at her with a mischievous grin that mirrored Sexton's.

"And who exactly does one steal time from, Ms. Sexton?"

"Anyone stupid enough not to keep a close eye on it, Ms. Cohen."

They sat in silence for a few more minutes and watched the black hole sun. Never to be denied for long, the first rays of Sol blasted past the moon as the eclipse's totality ended. Once again, there was light.

July 27th, 2037

Most of the moon overhead was a dull brown, nowhere near the biblical blood red people always foolishly hope to see. The lights of and above San Francisco were even more beautiful in the Earth-muted moonlight.

"Time is a cruel thief to rob us of our former selves," Adamma Sexton quoted as she and Corinne walked into the time ship hangar for the last time. "We lose as much to life as we do to death."

"Elizabeth Forsythe Hailey's 'A Woman of Independent Means'," Corinne replied after touching the device on her own forehead briefly. "You love your quotes, don't you? I hope that isn't on this thing's dedication plaque, Adamma."

"You could soon be a woman independent of time, Corinne."

"Just when I was getting the hang of this neural interface, too," she joked.

Corinne wore a blue flight suit with silver piping while Adamma's black business suit looked appropriate for both boardroom and funeral. The hangar was big enough to hold several commercial airliners. The Cessna-sized blue-gray time ship with its organic shape and flying fish-like wings sat near the huge main doors. Six black spheres with frantic red lines glowing across them lined the hangar walls, each sphere almost half as tall as the building. Near the rear sat Flight 246. Corinne hadn't taken much time to look at the plane when she boarded it at Tokyo Haneda Airport in 2017. She certainly hadn't taken any time to look at it as she disembarked at San Francisco International Airport in 2037, her attention focused on the circular runways surrounding an airport that looked more grown than built. Corinne remembered, however, looking out her window at the massive engine nearest her during take-off from Haneda, wondering what she would do if she saw a gremlin trying to destroy it at 20,000 feet. She dismissed the notion then quickly went to sleep. A week of representing the interests of the West Indies Communication Coalition at an international media conference had left her so drained that any gremlins could wreck both engines for all she cared. She didn't realize that the gremlins would instead tear apart space-time and, by extension, her life. Her two weeks in Japan leading up to her trip into the future hadn't been all work and mental fatigue, though. Corinne managed to take in the beauty of the city and the end of the Sanno Festival with a wagashi confection and tea ceremony on the grounds of the Hie Shrine in Chiyoda. There were no grand parades and processions for 2017 but she would have missed them thanks to the conference, anyhow. Time, missed events, fatigue? Yes, the universe was the great teacher but one must be ready for and receptive to its lessons or else they're ignored as background noise.

"He takes men out of time and makes them feel eternity," Sexton said.

"Emerson."

"You didn't need the interface for that one. If the time ship had a dedication plaque, Corinne, that would be on it."

"In this case, 'she' takes 'women' out of time."

"Quite right. I think the time ship definitely needs a dedication plaque now," Sexton joked.

"A bit late but, barring paradoxes, I should be able to fix that."

Sexton and Corinne stopped next to the time ship.

"I wish it could be me going back," Sexton revealed with sadness in her voice. "There's so much I would change...but there's already one me climbing the corporate ladder in 2017. No need to add another layer of possible complication to this."

"How much longer will the vacuole exist?" Corinne asked.

"Our continuum mapping says less than a day. We would love more...time to run more tests but there's nothing else we can do apart from just doing the damned thing," Sexton replied, pointing back to the black spheres. "Three gravity distortion generators will reopen this end of the vacuole, then the other three will go through ahead of you to open the 2017 end from the inside."

"Sure I won't arrive before I've departed?" Corinne asked.

"Highly unlikely. Both ends are moving through space-time plus our manipulation will cause some minor fluctuations."

"Minor?"

"Well within safety parameters," Sexton explained.

"It's funny to talk about safety parameters when the laws of causality might not even let this happen, Adamma."

"My people already won Y-Prizes for generating both artificial gravity and anti-gravity. They'll win another one for retro-time travel, just you wait and see."

"Why wait?"

Adamma tapped her neural interface. Corinne did likewise.

<Stable link, good. Now we can talk privately,> Adamma said to her fellow time traveller via technotelepathy. <Once the time ship A.I. pilots it through, you know what to do.>

<Quite well,> Corinne thought back. <Use your secret override to bring the three gravity spheres into 2017 then shut them down, closing my end of the vacuole.>

<With only three left here, there's no way anyone can go after you. Many people on this project wouldn't want any changes made to the timeline. They think this is just a test using a willing subject with no past self in the target time period. The few who do know want things to change, and we couldn't have done this without them. That time ship is loaded with the past twenty years of history, knowledge, and technology>

<And I'll find you to make sure you fly through your own vacuole that brings you into the future,> Corinne continued.

<Another paradox to be avoided. My plane jumped after yours did but we arrived sooner. Since I know how stubborn I am, the message I've left for my past self is explicit in tone and language. I'll fly into the future even if I have to learn to fly a plane myself.>

<I'd suggest the time ship but it'll be stripped apart for its secrets by then, Adamma.>

<Sexton Industries will help start the Green Age sooner than expected.>

<While making billions,> Corinne point-ed out.

<And saving billions of lives,> Adamma added, tapping off the neural connection as several temporal mechanics came to do one last check of Corinne's flight suit and the time ship. Once finished, they gave the all clear.

"After years dreaming of running away..." Corinne began.

Adamma embraced Corinne. After the briefest pause, Corrine hugged her back.

"World enough and time, Corinne Cohen," Sexton quoted with a smile.

"Adamma Sexton," Corinne replied in kind, "we will make him run."

August 21st, 2017

If the laws of causality and every imaginable and unimaginable paradox were merciful, if the experiment succeeded, the time ship would emerge over the Caribbean Sea during the 2017 Great American Eclipse, less than two months after Flight 246 disappeared. The eclipse would only be partial when viewed from the Lesser Antilles but that was fine. There were technologies and discoveries and cures to be delivered; there was hope. Corinne hoped to watch as the engineered coral-steel pylons grew to support the Maglev trains connecting the US mainland to each Caribbean island down to Guyana in South America. She hoped to see Barbados' dying sugar cane industry switch to biofuel production. She prayed that millions of lives would be saved in the 2018 influenza pandemic, and that research into human biological immortality would be successful. Beyond all that and far more importantly, she had friendships to make or reinforce, family to hold tighter out of love instead of obligation, perhaps even a companion to find instead of living in fear of how society would react. The world, her world wouldn't be saved by chance or luck; it would be saved by choice, her choice.

Corinne would make her own totality.

TRIPLET CROSS

by Patrick S. Baker

Big, strange trouble comes with four great gams and two beautiful faces.

The identical twins, Judi and Trudi Freyasdottir, were in their mid-twenties. They were tall, approaching my own six-feet, with long, shapely legs. Their porcelain skin glowed with health. Their white-blonde hair was cut in identical bobs. Their sea-foam blue eyes shined. In deference to the hot summer, both wore identical white linen skirt-suits with white blouses. Neither wore the slightest touch of make-up, nor did they need any to enhance their flawless, Nordic loveliness.

After introductions, they sat in my two clients' chairs, Judi on the right and Trudi on the left, and crossed their magnificent legs showing a pleasing amount of thigh as they did so. They both spoke with slight accents I couldn't place. I sat behind my desk and waited.

"Mr. Lancelot MacLeod," Judi started, very formally.

"We need you to find our sister, Audri," Trudi finished.

"She went out last night with a man," Judi went on.

"And she did not return at the agreed hour," Trudi added

"Nor did she return by this morning." Judi finished.

"She's only been gone a few hours," I said. "Maybe she is simply shacking up with her man friend."

"Shacking up?" Judi asked.

"We are not familiar with that," Trudi stated.

I shook my head. *Babes in the woods.*

"Maybe she decided to spend the night with the guy," I said.

"No, she would not," Judi said.

"That would not be protocol," Trudi added.

"Protocol?" I asked.

The two sat silent for a moment, looking at each other, than Trudi said: "*Die Kinderhort?*"

"We have just escaped of the crèche," Judi said.

"Crèche?"

"We have just left of a convent." Judi clarified.

"So we have much to learn of this land," Trudi said.

"We have protocols."

"Returning to our residence at a specific time is required."

"For safety," Judi finished.

Listening to the girls talk was like watching tennis. My neck started to hurt.

"I'll take the case," I said, mostly to save myself from whiplash, and because I had nothing better to do. "My fee is twenty dollars a day, plus expenses. I'll need a double sawbuck up front."

"A double sawbuck?" Judi asked.

"Twenty dollars," I said, before Trudi could pipe-in.

They both reached into their identical white purses and each gave me a ten dollar bill.

Audri had, the twins explained, met her man-friend at the central library. His name was Waldo Kilgore and he was a librarian. The two girls did not have his address, or phone number. They gave me their address and phone number.

"Do you have a picture of Audri?" I asked.

"A picture?" Judi asked.

"No picture," Trudi said. "We are looking alike, we are triplets."

"I see," I said. "But I still need a picture to show around."

"Yes," Judi said. "But we still have no pictures."

"I'll call you when I learn anything, or if I have more questions for you," I ushered them out of my office. I watched their two magnificent bottoms as they walk down the hallway to the stairs.

I tucked Lady Gwen, my M-1911 .45 automatic, into a shoulder holster and Laird Clay, my Fairbairn knife into my outside jacket pocket. I locked my office door and walked out.

I parked Bitsie, my 1946 Pontiac Streamline Coupe, under the only shade tree in my office-building's parking-lot. I'd spent too much on the car, over 2000 smackers, when I'd mustered out of the Corps, that I was not going to let the sun fade the interior. I passed the parking-lot attendant. Ricky was a nice kid just back from the army, I passed him an extra dollar a week to make sure I could park in the one shady spot. Because of the heat, both windows were down, although that made the interior just bearable. I started Bitsie up and backed out. As I turned around, Ricky put a reserved-parking sign in the now empty space. A dollar a week well spent.

I drove the few blocks to the library, slowly and carefully. Kids, out of school for summer, played on the sidewalk and in the street. Some enterprising soul opened a hydrant and water sprayed everywhere. Open windows tried to catch the slightest breeze and competing record-players blared Sinatra, Perry Como and Jo Stafford. I caught a movement of Prokofiev's Symphony Number 6 as I stopped at red light and made a slow turn. A brand new, black Series 62 hardtop Cadillac followed me.

The library was a gray granite building, five stories tall that took up a whole city block. I drove by the full parking lot, down the street to an open, metered space.

I dropped a nickel in the parking-meter for an hour. My first expense on this case. The black Caddy went by the spot and parked up the street. After a run-in with some mobsters last year, I was very sensitive to being trailed, so I marked the car in my mind. I didn't need some mook making his bones on me.

When I went into the private investigation business, I quickly found that a properly dressed man gets more answers than one that looks like a bum. So, I slipped on my blue and chalk pinstriped suit jacket, concealing Lady Gwen. I put on my wide-brimmed fedora, and pulled it low over my eyes to keep the sun from blinding me. I pulled up my blue necktie and straighten my collar.

I found the library's calm, well-lit interior full of people taking advantage of the fancy, new, air-cooling system. I walked up to the circulation desk and flashed my buzzer at the girl behind the counter.

"I need to speak to Waldo Kilgore," I said.

"May I see that badge again?"

I showed her my reserve police officer button again.

"Be right back," she fairly squeaked and stepped into a back room.

I cooled my heels for a few minutes and watched as some mothers and their children checked out books. I felt a tug on my sleeve and a brunette girl about five looked up at me.

"Are you my daddy?" she asked, her brown eyes wide with hope.

"No darling, I'm sure I'm not," I replied, gently removing her tiny hand from my coat.

A women about my age, call it late twenties, with the same color hair and same wide, brown eyes as the tot's, clearly the girl's mother, quickly approached and took her daughter's hand.

"I'm sorry," the mother said. "She thinks any man alone is her father."

"You said daddy would come home soon, you said!" the girl protested.

"I know what I said, Emily," the mother

replied.

I looked down at her hands. A diamond engagement ring and wedding band on her right ring-finger; a war widow.

"Well, little Emily here did no harm, ma'am," I said.

Then Emily's mother notice my Marine Corps honorable discharge pin. I saw her mouth tighten and that look in her eye. That look I'd seen in a dozen women's eyes, a look that said; *how come you made it back and my man didn't?*

"Roger was a Marine, too. He died on Peleliu," she said.

"I was at Tarawa and Iwo Jima," I said, by way of an excuse. *I was nowhere around when your husband bought it*, I thought.

Then the young librarian returned with an older, pinched face woman dressed in gray, with gray hair in a tight bun.

"I'm Mrs. McGrath, the head librarian," the older lady announce as Emily and her mother walked away. "How may I help you?"

"I'm looking for Waldo Kilgore."

"May I see your badge?" Librarian Mc-Grath rasped.

I showed her my buzzer with a Photostat of my PI license in the flap.

"Lancelot?"

"My mother was a fan of Malory's *Le Morte d'Arthur.* I got off lucky, my brother's named Gawain," I smiled.

"Why are you looking for Mister Kilgore?"

"He went out with a young lady last night," I responded. "That young lady did not come home, so her sisters asked me to look for her."

She nodded.

"Miss Wilbur," the head librarian said to the younger woman. "Please get Mr. MacLeod, Mr. Kilgore's home address and phone number."

Miss Wilbur scurried away.

"Mr. Kilgore works here. He is an assistant librarian in the reference section, where a man is sometimes required, for moving large volumes and that sort of thing. I'm afraid he has a bad reputation for, uh, I think the young people say, trying to 'make time' with our younger female staff and many of our lady patrons." She paused and then added. "I don't know why I told you that."

"'I was unjustly accused of being a politician,'" I quoted.

"'Because I was privy to the secret griefs of wild, unknown men,'" Mrs. McGrath gave a small smile as she finished the quote. "I am far from a wild and unknown man."

Just then Miss Wilbur returned with Kilgore's information neatly written on a note card. Taking the card, I smiled broadly, thanked the ladies for their help and exited the cool confines of the library into the brutal sunshine.

* * * *

As I pulled away from the curb, the black Cadillac pulled out as well and followed me. Either these guys didn't care that I saw them, or they were terrible at staying unnoticed. Either way, I wasn't going to let them, whomever they were, continue to shadow me.

I accelerated, forcing them to speed up as well. Halfway down the block I jammed on my brakes and slewed Bitsie sideways, blocking my side of the street, driver's door toward my pursuers. The Caddy panic-stopped, screeching to a halt. I hopped out with Lady Gwen in my hand.

Racing to the Caddy driver's side, I yanked the door open and clubbed the driver on top of the head medium hard with Lady Gwen's barrel. This dazed him and he rocked back in his seat. The passenger reached for something under his jacket.

"Hey, don't be stupid," I said, aiming my pistol at him.

They were identical twin brothers with dark blonde hair, muddy blue eyes, high cheek bones and strong, cleft chins. Both had thick necks and broad shoulders. They wore identical brown suits, white shirts and brown ties. *A set of triplets and now a set of twins in one day was truly odd.*

"Who you jokers working for?" I asked.

They both just stared balefully at me. The driver holding his right hand to the top of his head. A small trickle of blood ran from his hairline, down between his eyes and off the tip of his nose forming a red stain on his shirt.

A line of cars was building up behind us, all honking loudly.

"Ok, don't tell me," I said. "I don't like being followed and if I see you two bastards behind me again. I'll shoot you both."

With that I smacked the driver again, this time on his right hand. I backed up, still covering them both with Lady Gwen. I drew Laird Clay out of my jacket pocket and stabbed the left front tire. I moved quickly to the passenger side and did the same thing to the right front tire. Still covering them, I hopped back in Bitsie and drove away. I looked in the rearview, the Caddy didn't move.

Kilgore lived in a neighborhood of tiny bungalows in the factory district. They had been built to house defense-workers and were now occupied by young families and single people without a lot of money. In the common parking lot, I pulled up next to a pre-war Buick held together with bailing wire and rust.

I marched up and down the dirt paths and dead, dry lawns until I found Kilgore's place. I knocked loudly. A man swung the door open.

"Mr. Kilgore, can I come in?" I said in a rush and brushed passed him, while flashing my badge. "I'm MacLeod and I'm looking for Audri Freyasdottir."

Kilgore was a good looking kid, about twenty, with soft, delicate, almost womanly features. He had lustrous brown eyes, blonde, unruly hair and even, white teeth. He was about five-six and looked like he might of weighted 150 dripping wet. He was wearing brown pants held up with suspenders over a white undershirt and no shoes or socks.

He shut the door behind me and slowly turned. He looked like he been up all night.

"I'm sorry, who are you looking for?" he said.

"Audri Freyasdottir," I prompted him. "You were supposed to take her out last night."

"Yeah, I did."

"She didn't get home. Her sisters are worried."

"Sisters?" he perked up at that. "Do they look like Audri?"

"Yes, they are identical triplets."

He was wide-eyed at the thought of the lovely sisters.

"Kid!" I said. "Tell me what happened last night with Audri."

He sank into an overstuffed chair with a torn slip cover.

"I met her at the library after closing. We walked up to Gerry O'Toole's on Fifth and Board. It's a nice place, good food, good beer and not too expensive. I can't afford much." He said and waved his hands around.

"Go on."

"Audri, man, she is one weird frail. All she could talk about was this place she had gotten away from, sounded like a cross between a prison work farm and a place where nuns live."

"A convent?"

"Yeah, a convent." He nodded. "Anyway, she is one gorgeous dame, so I didn't give a damn if she spoke Chinese, know what I mean?"

"Sure."

"I'd planned to walk her back to my car and drive her here, see if she was hot to trot, you know? But we'd barely got out the door of O'Toole's when two bruisers came out of nowhere. One slugged me and knocked me down, while the other grabbed Audri and hustled her into a car."

"What did these bruisers look like?"

"Like Nazi Stormtroopers; big, blonde, and mean and punched like a freight-train," Kilgore pulled up his shirt. His ribs were black and blue, "this why I called in sick today."

"Why didn't you call the cops?" I asked.

"The one that whipped up on me, said that his brother was Audri's husband and she'd run-off and he was taking her back home. I didn't want to get in the middle of a family thing."

"Still, you should have called the cops," I declared.

"The one that beat me took my driver's license and said if I called the police, he'd find me and beat on me some more."

I nodded. At least Kilgore had enough balls to tell me the story, if not call the cops. If this story was true, and I had no reason to disbelieve him. One thing was sure, he'd been beaten and seemed pretty scared.

I tossed him a business card and told him to call me if he thought of anything else, or if the bully-boys showed back up. I left him sitting on his torn chair.

The sun cast long shadows as I drove to the Freyasdottir sisters' apartment building. Their building was a five-story art-deco dream and had a doorman dressed like a Turkish admiral. I parked across the street and jaywalked to the door.

"May I help you, sir?" The doorman asked.

"I would like to see the Freyasdottir sisters," I said and handed him my card.

The admiral stepped into a glass booth and spoke on an R/T intercom.

"I'll buzz you in, sir. First door on the right just up the stairs."

I thanked him, passed him a dime and entered the building. The lobby was a mere foyer with stairways leading up and down. I went up and knocked on the first and only door on the right.

One of the girls opened the door, I couldn't tell which one. She was still dressed all in white.

"Welcome, Mr. MacLeod," Judi said. "Come in, Trudi is here."

I went in. The girls' apartment occupied half the floor. The door entered into a sitting room with expensive looking rugs and pricey new furniture. To the right was a short hallway with three doors off it, presumably bedrooms. To the left was a kitchen and a dining area. Beyond the dining room, through a French door was a veranda. Even from the entryway, in the fast fading sunlight, I could see a splash of greenery through the door. The building had a well-watered yard or garden in back. The place was classy.

How could three runaway nuns afford such a place? I wondered.

"Please be sitting and tell us the news," Trudi said as I sat in an overstuffed chair facing the door. Judi switched on the lights. Then both girls sat on a Davenport facing me.

"Well…" I started.

The lights snapped off. The front door exploded inward and the bully boys from the Cadillac, only there were four of them this time, rushed in. All carried actual ray-gun looking weapons. They dodged in through the wreaked door; two to the left and two to the right. I dived to the floor, drawing Lady Gwen as I did. A searing pain cut my right shoulder and my jacket burst into flames. The chair behind me also caught fire. Both the women dropped to the floor as well. I fired blindly over the back of the Davenport as I rolled right, trying to put my jacket out. As I rolled and shot, Trudi and Judi scuttled like crabs to the left. The ceiling caught fire and plaster started to fall. I reached out to drag at least one of the sisters to the right with me, but a large piece of flaming debris fell and drove me further away from my clients.

I fired blindly twice more and Lady Gwen's slide locked back. As I switched magazines, one blonde bastard jumped over the back of the sofa and landed inches from me. I fired up without really aiming and nailed him. He gave a loud *oof*, jerked back and fell over. I low-jumped through the door into the dining-room and felt another searing pain in my left calf. Now my pants were on fire. The doorjamb smoked.

I levered myself up on my right leg and

tried to run. I made one step as my left leg collapsed like an overdone noodle. I sprawled face down. A line of flame sketched across the wallpaper behind me as I scrambled away. I crossed my arms over my head and jumped again, crashing through the French door window, a gout of flame following me. I pulled myself up and tumbled over the veranda rail. I fell flat on my back on a pile of woodchips and grass cutting and rolled away.

I lay on my back staring at the sky, panting; my coat and pants still smoking. I thought I was a dead man as another big blonde man hulked over me.

"Is he still alive, Baldur?" an unseen woman asked.

"Yes, Freya, surprisingly he is," the man, Baldur, said.

"He is tough. Good. Pick him up and let's go."

The man hefted me over his shoulder like a sack of potatoes and I finally passed out.

My eyes popped open and looking down at me was a very nice looking, older, blonde woman. Her hair was pulled back and had just a touch of grey. She had the same blue eyes and the same excellent bones structure as the Freyasdottir girls.

Bright summer sunshine poured through an open window and I heard chickens clucking and a single cow lowing. I was in the country. I was nude and in a very comfortable bed

"I'm Freya," she said. "How are you feeling, Lancelot MacLeod?"

I did a quick inventory. My right shoulder, left calf and back were sore, but not unbearably painful. My shoulder was covered in a white salve. I flexed my arms, legs and sat up; everything seemed to be working.

"Pretty good," I said. "For the ass kicking I took last night. I was shot, twice, and my clothes were on fire at one point?"

"Yes, that is true. My husband, Baldur, and I have some advanced medicines we used on you. By tomorrow you'll be com-

pletely healed, without even a scar."

"A mere 'thank you' somehow seems inadequate," I said. "For pulling me out of the fire, almost literally, and then giving me this remarkable medical treatment. Did the sisters get out?"

"It was not all altruism." She smiled, ignoring my question. "We have a job for you and an explanation, if you want them."

"Is the explanation contingent on taking the job?"

"Oh, yes, indeed it is."

I scowled a bit.

"Would it help you decide if I told you that Trudi, Judi and Audri are, well, call them our daughters and we are concerned for their safety? The job is directly related to insuring their safety."

"Freya," I said. "First are the girls alright? And all this is way over my head. A set of identical triplets was attacked by a set of identical quadruplets with real Buck Rogers' ray-guns."

I paused, hoping she would respond. She did not.

"The only thing we should do," I continued. "Is call the cops and maybe the FBI and that is what I'm going to do."

"The situation is more complex than you can currently know," Freya frowned. "But you should know the girls are in no immediate danger, but we cannot afford to wait too long to retrieve them."

"That is good to know, finally. But I also know what I saw. This is more than I can take on. Are you going to let me go to the law?"

"Of course, we will not hold you against your will," she said. "Your clothes were ruined so Baldur will give you some."

She left the room. Baldur came with a set of well worn, but clean, work clothes. He looked like an older version of the thugs that had attacked me and the girls. All the clothes were about a size too big all the way around, but tightening my belt kept the pants up. I wore my own shoes and Baldur also gave me back Lady Gwen, Laird Clay and my holster.

The pistol was not loaded, but a magazine was in it. He also gave me back all my other personal effects as well. Baldur hulked silently as I dressed.

Freya returned and gave me a slip of paper with a telephone number.

"If you change your mind about the job, please call this number to contact us."

I put it in a pocket.

"For our security," Baldur finally spoke as he led me outside. "I'm going to blindfold you for the drive."

I didn't like the idea, but if these two had wanted to hurt me, they could have done so at any time. Also, I felt weak as a kitten, so I doubted I could have resisted much.

He sat me in a prewar Ford pickup truck and placed a brown burlap bag over my head and we drove away.

We drove for some time and then without any warning, Baldur pulled the bag off my head. I blinked in the bright sunshine. He pulled over to the curb.

"Your vehicle is that way," he pointed down the street. I got out and he drove away without another word.

The fire had left the apartment building scorched. The fire department was still hauling things out and dosing them in water to prevent a flare-up. Two bored uniforms watched the firemen do their work. Bitsie was still parked where I had left her. I dug a spare magazine out of my glovebox, slipped it into Lady Gwen and tucker her back in her holster. I then drove to the central police office on 12th and Broad.

Police Central was a Gothic stone tomb of a building, all grey granite and black iron decorations. Fortunately, the architect had skipped the gargoyles. I parked in the visitors' lots and walked in. Patrol Sergeant Steven Murphy was working the front desk.

For about five minutes between graduating college and Pearl Harbor, I worked as an investigator for the District Attorney's office. That job required me to go through the police academy and be sworn as an officer of the law, but I worked directly for the DA, not the police. The job had me sometimes work with the cops. Because of my previous employment and now that I was private, my relationship with the police department was tinged with a vague dislike shading to outright hostility. My personal connection with any given police officer on the force depended on the cop. Murphy and I were on a first name basis, and I thought of him as a friendly neutral.

"Hey, Murph," I said as I approached the high desk.

"Hey, Lancer," he said and indicated my clothing with a wave. "Down on your luck?"

"No," I responded. "Just incognito."

"What can I do you for?"

"What's the word on that apartment building fire over on Greene?"

"You mixed up in that?" he asked suddenly suspicious.

"Nope," I lied. "But might have some information about it, or at least some information about the occupants of the place."

"What the reports say," he leaned forward and said quietly. "Is the two girls living in the place burned it down trying to cover-up the murder of a boyfriend. One or both shot him in the dick and then lit the place up and lammed it. Found only one body, a big man's, in the place."

"Who's working the case?" I asked. "I could have some news for him."

"Guy name Steiner, Peter Steiner," Murphy straightened up. "You know him?"

I shook my head.

"New kid. Transferred from somewhere back east. College boy, like you. I'll get him for you." Murphy signaled a young patrolman with a cast on his arm to man the desk while he disappeared into the bowels of the building. I paced around a bit and was suddenly ravenously hungry.

My last turn around the waiting room took me near to the exit. As I turned, I saw Murphy come into the waiting area with Detective Steiner. I turned again and walked out the exit and sprinted to my car. I drove away as fast as I could. Steiner was one of *them*. One of the blonde bastards that had followed me and had attacked my clients. Twins, triplets, quadruplets, now, maybe quintuplets. This was just getting, as Alice said "curiouser and cusiouser", and much more dangerous.

Whoever they were, they knew me. I couldn't go home or to my office, so instead I drove to my bolt-hole. On Flores, near the hospital, I rented a small studio apartment in the basement of a building mostly occupied by medical students, nurses and interns. Nothing was in my real name. I paid cash for everything. I stocked it with emergency supplies. Once a month always at night, I restocked the place with food, cleaned it up and left the rent and utilities payment.

I parked Bitsie so she couldn't be seen from the street and went in the back. I took a shower and put on some of my own clean clothes. I made a fried egg sandwich with ham and cheese and ate some peaches straight from the can, all while standing. My mother would not have been happy with the way I dined. After I ate, I was suddenly exhausted, so I lay on the divan and went to sleep.

I woke up feeling great. Completely healed and well rested. I also had about half a plan to start figuring out what was going on and maybe take the fight to the bad guys.

I left my hideaway as the sun went down. I walked over two blocks and rented a new black Caddy from a local car-rental place. I drove it back to my bolt-hole and loaded it up with some sandwiches and a thermos of coffee. I dressed in navy-blue dungarees and work-shirt, with tough, well-worn work boots and, of course, Lady Gwen. I put Laird Clay into an ankle sheath.

By the time I got to Police Central, it was fully dark. I parked across from the employee's parking lot. I walked over to a phone booth and dialed the police switchboard number from memory.

"Police Department," came the switchboard operator's nasally female voice. "How may I direct your call?"

"Detective Peter Steiner, please."

"One moment, please."

There was a series of metallic clicks and a short buzzing.

"Detective Steiner," a deep male voice said. I heard the noise and babble of a policeman's bullpen in the background

"Detective Steiner, I know who and what you are." I said and hung up.

I went back to my rental and settled in to watch and wait.

Surprisingly, I didn't have to wait more than fifteen minutes. Steiner walked out of Police Central and without even looking around he got into another black Series 62 Cadillac. I pulled on a Washington Senators baseball cap and a pair of horn-rimmed glass with plain glass lens. *Lancelot MacLeod, master of disguise.*

As Steiner drove off, traffic was moderate, so I slipped into the flow three cars behind him. He didn't take any precautions against being followed. He didn't make any U-turns, nor did he unexpectedly speed up or slow down, or make any sudden turns. He probably didn't even look in the rearview mirror. I trailed him straight through downtown, out along the river to the industrial district, south of town.

Warehouses and factories lined both sides of the cleverly named Industrial Parkway. Workers on the nightshifts were travelling to work. Steiner and I traveled along like any other commuters on our way to the daily grind. Then Steiner made a quick turn right into a short drive way. I tooled by a moment later, slowed a little and looked over, in what I hoped was a not too obvious way. The driveway lead to a guarded gate. The guard was a grey-haired man with a huge belly, he wore a cop's blue uniform with no badge. The place was surrounded by a ten-foot high, chain-linked fence with barbed-wire on top. The building was an otherwise unremarkable factory or warehouse. Plain cinderblock walls with green glass windows at the top and a couple of small doors in the front.

I took the next right, which twisted up a bluff. Then another right on a gravel road that ran along the top of the ridge. At the base of the slope was a creek, across the waterway were the backsides of the buildings on the west of Industrial Parkway. I marked the place that Steiner had entered. It was the only building with a barbed-wire topped fence. I drove on long enough to discover the gravel road looped to the left and then joined Highway 19 that would take me back into the city.

With my escape route scouted, I turned around and drove back and pulled over, directly behind my target. Getting out my Bureau of Ship 6 X 30 binoculars (reported as lost in combat in 1945), I low-crawled to the edge of the bluff and scrutinized the structure below.

I watched for an hour. The fenced area was well lit by street lights and the full moon. A two-man foot patrol walked the perimeter every fifteen minutes or so. While I watched, workers, dressed in identical gray coveralls and hardhats loaded two trucks with some large crates. I couldn't make out much detail about the guards, or the workers, other than they were big men. There was no obvious place for me to enter unseen.

The building to the right of my target was empty and surrounded with a collapsing hurricane fence. I decided to move. I put my binoculars away, painted my face with some flat black shoe polish and pulled a black knit cap over my hair. I checked that Lady Gwen and Laird Clay were securely in place.

The hillside rose about twenty-five feet from the creek and was steep but not impossibly so. I waited until the patrol turned the corner away from my position. Then I moved right about a hundred yards and slipped over the edge, feet first, facing out, and made a semi-controlled slide down to the creek. Just three feet from the bottom, my right foot caught a root and I flipped forward splashing face first into the filthy water. I came

up spitting and crawled my way to the opposite bank where I hunkered down, panting. I waited ten minutes for a response to the loud splash and my flailing, but nothing happened.

I crept to the top of the creek bank and looked. The two guards had their backs to me heading away. Once the guards were out of sight, staying bent over, I just hopped over the collapsed hurricane fence and took a position at the corner of the abandoned building, well hidden in the shadows.

I scanned the chain-linked fence and quickly spotted a section where the wires holding the fence to the poles were broken and the lower part of the fence bent up from the ground toward me. The gap looked big enough that I could slip through. The guards passed the spot without noticing the damaged section. Keeping low, I scurried over and got a closer look. I could fit through. Pushing the fence up, I wiggled through the opening. Once through, I turned and dashed across the access road and slipped among some broken crates. I crawled forward and pushed myself up against the wall. The guards walked by again without noticing anything.

I snaked along the ground for about ten yards to a hole in the wall, waist high that let a group of pipes into the building. I peeked through the opening and got an excellent view of the loading area. Some kind of meeting was going on. It looked like a military formation. There were about thirty men standing in neat lines while an older man spoke. Every guy in the group looked like Steiner. Even the group leader looked like Steiner, only older. The six dames in the gathering were dead ringers for the triplets. I had no idea what was going on. I had a vague feeling of having read about or seen something like this before. Whatever it was I didn't like it.

The leader picked a ray-gun rifle off a table. He spoke German and then aimed the gun at a sheet of metal across the room. A flaming hole appeared in the target. The older Steiner took a deep breath, said something else and swept the weapon left and right, cutting shallow, flaming lines in the target. The group applauded. The leader called them to attention with a loud *"achtung!"* and then dismissed them.

I had seen enough to know I didn't have any idea what the hell was going on. But I did know who might be able to tell me. Discretion being the better part of valor and all that. I crawled back to my entry point. Someone had discovered the breach in the fence and the guards were watching a worker repaired the gap. No one appeared overly alarmed, so likely they didn't know that I had slipped in. But now I needed to find another way out. A truck rumbled down the road between the fence and my hiding place. The guards waved to the driver and he waved back.

The worker finished his repairs on the fence and the guards nodded their satisfaction at the job. They left.

From my earlier observations, the workers took about ten minutes to load a truck. Seven minutes after the guards and repairman left, I pushed a crate into the road. A moment later the truck turned the corner and rattled toward my position. The driver stopped and got out, cursing in English, as he pushed the box out of his way. I took a step, hit the bumper and pulled myself into the bed. I snugged up close to the tailgate. For some reason the driver walked around to the back of the truck. I pulled Laird Clay; ready to kill the driver if I had to. He turned and went back to the cab. I heard the driver's door slam and then the truck started rolling again. The truck paused at the gate as the driver and the guard exchanged a few short words and then it was out of the factory compound and on the road.

On impulse, I pried up the lid of one of the crates. It was filled with ray-gun pistols neatly stacked on wooden slates. The weapons were the same size as a .45 pistol, but smooth and rounded. The barrel ended in a glass concave disk; no opening. The weapons had identifiable grips, triggers, and a red

button that I presume was a safety. Next to each gun were two items that looked like pistol magazines and like they would fit into the pistol's grip. I took one ray-gun and two of the magazines and shoved them in my pockets. Then I resealed the crate as best I could.

The truck stopped and I jumped out, careful to not let the truck driver see me. Quickly walking away. I was at the corner of Industrial Parkway and Clarke, about two miles from my car. Smelling like raw sewage and looking like I'd bathed in a septic tank. I walked back to my car, careful to keep my head down and look like a just another night-shift worker making his way home. No one gave me a second glance. While I walked, I thought about my next move.

I reached my rental car and drove back to my hide-out apartment. I quickly showered and tossed my ruined and stinking clothes into the incinerator. Exhausted from the night's activities, but with no time to waste, I called Freya's number. She answered. We set a meeting in two hours at a truck-stop dinner on the edge of town. Following the old soldiers' rule of never passing up a chance to, piss, eat, or sleep, because you never knew when you might get another opportunity; I made and eat another egg sandwich and sacked out for an hour.

* * * *

Trucker's Rest was one of those combination diner, gas-station and motels that had sprung up all over the place after the war. I arrived thirty-minutes early for the meeting, parked out of sight of the road and scouted the place out thoroughly. No one appeared to be setting an ambush for me.

Freya and Baldur arrived ten minutes early and took a booth in the back. I walked in exactly on time and sat opposite them.

"Decided to take the job?" Freya asked without preamble.

I nodded and told them what I had done and learned since Baldur had dropped me off.

"...What is going on?" I asked when I finished my story.

"Did you ever read a novel titled *Brave New World* by an Englishman named Huxley?" she asked me.

I nodded and then it all snapped into place; why that group of identical people had seemed so familiar.

"Bokan-something groups? Masses of identical people stamped out like machine parts at factory?" I felt dizzy and slightly ill at the thought. "That is sickening."

"Huxley called it the Bokanovsky's Process," Freya nodded. "He didn't get the science right, but his concept was sound. We call them clone groups."

"Clone?"

"An American named Webber coined the word in 1903. It comes from the Greek and literally means a part of a plant that's broken off for the purposes of propagation. To us it means an exact copy of a person. Like identical twins are natural clones of each other."

"What—How—?" I stuttered, stunned.

"A German biologist named Rudolf Steiner developed a technique for cloning humans in the late 1920s. Of course, the German government kept it a secret and when the Nazis took over they started to try and use it on an industrial scale."

"Like Mengele?" I asked.

"Mengele was a butcher, a sadist that liked to pull the wings off flies. His so-called experiments were worthless," she answered, flatly. "When Steiner and his colleagues saw that the war was lost. They smuggled their people and equipment into other countries, with idea of establishing fifth column organizations and eventually taking over the world and imposing their idea of order. A genetic hierarchy with Steiner and his closest followers at the top, served and worshipped by armies of clones."

"What about you two?" I asked. "How'd you fit in to this?"

"Baldur and I were the prefect models for Steiner's plan. Strong, intelligent, and for some reason, our germ-plasma was perfect for the cloning technique. Steiner kidnapped us when we were in our late teens and held us for years against our will. Taking cell samples from our stomachs every time he needed more servants or soldiers. We were treated barely better than breeding livestock. One day while moving us from one place to another we got into a car accident. Baldur killed the driver and a guard and we escaped. Since then we have been building an organization, helping our younger clones, our sons and daughters, if you will, escape and trying to bring down Steiner's scheme."

"Wait a minute," I held up my hand. "You say this all started in the Twenties. That would make the oldest, what-you-call-it, clones, only about twenty or thirty years old."

"A disciple of Steiner named Mueller invented a way to force grow human. Using the Mueller Process, the clones grow to maturity in about a year. As they are force-grown they are conditioned and trained by direct brain stimulation. So they emerge from the maturation tubes fully grown and functioning."

"Yet some still escape?" I asked.

"Sometimes clones are sent out into the world for more education, or to perform specific tasks. Like your Detective Steiner and others that have infiltrated the government and business. We try and get them to defect, like we did with Judi, Trudi and Audri. The organization's loyalty condition doesn't always take, even now. The organization will try and re-train them, re-condition them, first. Since clones are expensive to make and grow."

I sat for a moment and considered. I already trusted Freya and Baldur, or I wouldn't have called them. Also, they had already had many chances to bump me off, if this were some kind of double-cross. Lastly, Freya's explanation fit all the facts as I knew them.

"I'm in," I declared. "What now?"

"We are going to rescue our girls, collect evidence of the conspiracy and get it to someone we can trust."

"What do I need to do?" I asked.

They both smiled wolfishly.

* * * *

Two nights later Baldur and I huddled close to the cab in the back of an army surplus deuce-and-half still painted flat green. Jason Rennie was at the tailgate. Jason was a small guy, maybe 150 pounds, barely five-foot six. He was missing two fingers off his left hand; the gift of a Jap sniper. He'd been my weapons' squad leader on Iwo. Despite his small size, he could handle a .30-06 Browning Automatic Rifle like most people handled a .22 rifle.

Rollo Podalak, my former platoon sergeant, drove the truck. Rollo was huge, over six feet tall and fast approaching 300 pounds of "hard fat", he was a maestro with a tommy-gun, his bulk and brute strength helped him hold the .45 caliber sub-machine gun steady.

"Hey, buddy," Rollo said as he drove up to the gate of the clone factory. "Suppose to pick-up some stuff."

"Yeah," the guard said. "Let's see some paper work."

Roland handed the guard a set of papers that Freya had ginned up. I heard the guard shuffling them and then hand them back.

"Go around to the left of the building, someone will meet you at the loading dock."

"Thanks, pal."

Rollo ground the gears as he drove the truck away.

Baldur and I moved to the tailgate. I reminded Jason not to fire unless fired on and hopefully we would get away without getting in a gun fight. He just nodded.

Nobody was at the loading dock, as we had anticipated, since it was Wednesday and shipments only went out on Tuesdays and Thursdays. Rollo u-turned the truck so it faced out. Baldur and I hopped out. We were dressed in workers' gray cover-all. A quick dye-job turned my brown hair blonde and my own baby blues were close enough in color to a clone's. I pulled a surgical mask over my lower face. Baldur assured me that many of the clones wore such masks while working in parts of the factory. A set of heavy boots gave me a bit more height. At a distance, I could pass for one of the worker bees.

We both had canvas bags about half the size of a sea-bag. Baldur's had time-bombs and the ray-gun I had stolen. Mine held Lady Gwen, Laird Clay and Miss Daisy, my M3A1 .45 Grease-Gun.

"Signal Lorrie," I told Rollo. He flashed the truck's lights twice. On the high bluff about the creek two flashes responded. Our sniper, Lorenzo Guzman, was in place and knew we were going in. I pictured Guzman, tall and lean, cradling his M-1903 Springfield, one startling green eye pressed to the scope, hardly even blinking and never wavering.

We went to a side door and simply walked in like we belonged. Out of the corner of my eye I saw a couple of workers moving boxes around the loading dock. They paid us no attention.

Baldur and I had studied a map of the place provided by a defector. He took the lead. We went down a flight of stairs and through a heavy metal door which opened onto a huge under-ground room. The factory was like an iceberg, only ten percent showed above the surface. In one part of the huge room, ray-guns, both rifles and pistol, were being crated for shipment. In another area, the weapons were tested. The room was hot, dusty and noisy.

We passed through a sound-proof door into a short, carpeted hallway.

"We split up here," Baldur said.

Baldur took out the ray-gun and held it down to his side, his canvas bag hung from the same shoulder, partly obscuring the weapon. I took out Lady Gwen and held her in the same manner. He went back into the noisy factory. I went to the first door on the right, the records room.

The records room was unoccupied and full of filing cabins. Freya had coached me on what to look for, so I took out Lady Daisy and Laird Clay and put them down by the door and starting pushing files into my bag. Files marked *"Planen-48-49"*, *"Freundschaftsspiele"*, and *"Der Vorbote"* were particularly valuable. When my bag was full of files, I put it down by my weapons.

Now came the hard part. Putting Lady Gwen in my pocket, I took Laird Clay in my right hand and went back into the hall. I went to the door marked "*Überholung*" and opened it. A Steiner clone in a grey uniform, with a holstered ray-gun sidearm, was at the far end of a small anteroom. He raised his hand in a "halt" gesture, said something in German and advanced on me. I tried to look confused, like I was just in the wrong place. When the guard was within arms' reach, clearly planning to physically eject me, I struck. I clapped my left hand over his mouth, pushed him back hard against the wall and rammed my knife through his left eye into his brain. For an instant his feet drummed the floor, a small trickle of blood rolled down his check, then he slumped against me.

I gently lowered the body to the floor, took his pistol, trucked it in my pocket and took out Lady Gwen. I didn't have to be quiet for the next part. I went through the other door into a larger room. On my right were my triplets, stripped nude and shaved bald. They were shackled cruciform to three tables. Clear liquid dripped through a needle into their arms, weird dark glass masks covered their faces, they wore earphones and electrical wires were attached to their skulls.

An older female clone and male clone manned a control console on my left. The male strode around the console and approached me. I shot him in the chest. He fell back. The female reached for something, I didn't know for what. I shot her in the face and she dropped back, too.

Freya had told me what to do. I raced over to the drug cabinet on the wall opposite me. I broke the glass with Lady Gwen and got out three doses labeled *Anlage Antagonisten*, whatever that meant.

I pulled out the needles and tore off the wires and other things off the girls and then gave them each a shot of the *Anlage Antagonisten*. Almost immediately after the injections, their eyes fluttered open and they

started to ask questions, in German.

"No time for that now," I said. "We have to get out of here."

I went back into the antechamber and dragged the dead guard into the *Überholung* room, stripped him and put on his uniform, while the girls put on the coveralls they got from me and the two older clones. There were blood stains on all of them, but some strategic wrinkling made them less obvious.

With me in the lead, we hustled back to the records room and found Baldur waiting. Each triplets gave the older man a quick hug. I picked up my bag full of papers and slung Miss Daisy over my shouler. With Balbur in front and me at the back, all five of us went back the way we came. Again, no one paid us any mind as we trooped through the factory.

We were just about to the stairs when the alarm went off.

"GO!" I shouted and we ran.

One of the weapons-testers spotted us and fired. I felt the heat of the ray-gun singe my dyed hair. A short burst from Daisy sent all the clones running or diving for cover. I shoved the heavy door behind me and dead-bolted it.

Baldur and the girls huddled on the stairs. I heard the distinct reports of a BAR and a tommy-gun. Rollo and Jason were in a gun fight. I slinked to the top of the stairs and peaked over the top. A handful of clones were firing ray-guns through the open loading dock door. Heavy caliber bullets came back at the clones, tearing up boxes and splintering the wood. No one seemed to know we were there.

"Let's go," I said and started to rise up.

Baldur grabbed me and pulled me back under cover as a heat-ray scorched the wall behind were my head would have been. We were well and truly trapped. Spots on door at the bottom of the stairs were red-hot and the paint was smoking as the clones locked in the factory tried to burn their way through the heavy metal.

Baldur looked at his watch and he smiled

broadly. I heard our truck roar to life and then it shot backward though the open loading-dock door. A baseball-sized object flew from the back of the truck and exploded; a hand-grenade. Then another and another. Clones were killed, flung around, or driven back from this sudden onslaught.

A noise so loud that I felt it more than heard struck. A gout of fire shot from the stairway behind the surviving clones and one burst into flames, he screamed and writhed on the floor. The door in our stairway bulged toward us, but held.

"NOW WE GO!" Baldur shouted loud enough for my damaged ears to hear and took off running the ten feet to the outside door.

The triplets were right on his heels. I came last. A heat-beam creased my right thigh as I ran. I half-turned and rattled a long burst at my attacker. At least three .45 caliber rounds hit his chest and he was thrown back behind a crate.

I burst through the doorway to the outside. Our truck pulled forward. Baldur and the triplets were already in the back. I jumped, caught the tailgate and vaulted in. My thigh hurt like hell. I landed face down on the girls.

"GO! GO!" I shouted.

Rollo downshifted and the trucked roared away

I rolled onto my back and looked at Jason.

"You didn't tell me you had grenades," I said.

"Didn't ask," he responded.

"True."

As we pulled forward, Rollo shouted: "Son-of-a-bitch."

The canvas cover caught fire in three places. I heard the report of a 03 Springfield. Rollo shifted gears and continued to drive straight.

"Enemy in the way," Rollo yelled over his shoulder, put his tommy-gun between the truck-door and his left arm and started hammering. The hot brass falling on the steering-wheel and his legs.

Now the wooden staves holding the truck's canvas cover were on fire.

Rollo drove the truck straight into the chain-link fence, that gave way and we kept going. Jason popped up and emptied a magazine at the clones as we drove on. One of the triplets grabbed a fire extinguisher to douse the flames.

I heard two more shots from Lorrie Guzman. He was discouraging any pursuit.

Rollo drove over the fallen hurricane fence into the lot of the next building over. We turned left and then right as we pulled out on to Industrial Parkway.

Five miles later, with no sign of anyone following us, Rollo pulled over into a vacant lot screened from the road by an overgrown hedge; our rallying point. Freya was waiting for us. We all unloaded from the truck. I threw my arms around my huge former sergeant. He and I supported each other as we went through the shakes. We always got them after combat. A headshrinker once called it a "stress reaction." I don't know about that. All I know is most guys did what I did. We trembled and sweated. I relived every frightening thing that had just happened. Jason Rennie just looked on with a cold eye. He never had a "stress reaction." My leg really started to hurt. I noticed Rollo had taken a nasty burn on his left forearm. The triplets were hugging each other as well and talking in rapid German with Baldur.

Freya sat me and Rollo down on the truck's bumper and treated our wounds with her miracle salve. Lorrie Guzman rolled up in his candy-apple red, pre-war Studebaker Champion.

"*Madre de Dios*, that was some excitement!" the sharpshooter declared as he stepped out of his ride. Lorrie never had a "stress reaction" either. Jason eyed the sniper and shook his head in disbelief.

Freya went to her truck and from the passenger-seat took three bundles of one-hundred—and-fifty $20 dollar bills. She handed each man a bundle; three thousand smackers each for Jason, Rollo and Lorrie.

"You have received your pay in full now," Baldur declared.

"*Si*, we are good," Lorrie said as he riffled the stack of bills

Rollo and Jason just nodded as they did the same.

"We are," I said. "If I need more help, I'll give you a call."

"*Que vaya con Dios, Jefe*," Lorrie said as he hugged me and then hopped in his car.

Jason merely nodded to me and got in the passenger side of the red Studebaker and they drove away.

"Can I come along with you, Skipper?" Rollo asked me.

"Sure," I said.

We all loaded back into the two-and-half ton truck, this time Baldur drove. Freya followed in the farm truck. As we rode along, Rollo looked long and hard at the triplets.

"Those are some good looking dames, even with no hair," he commented.

I nodded in agreement.

"Think one of them would like to go out with me?" He asked.

"I don't know," I said, rather grumpily. "You could ask one of them?"

"How can I pick?" he said. "They look exactly the same."

I shrugged and closed my eyes to get some rest.

* * * *

Two days later I sat with Baldur, Freya and the triplets in the office of US Senator Michael "Mickey" Stone, while Rollo was in the parking lot with his tommy-gun, guarding our vehicles. The then Lieutenant-Colonel Stone had been my battalion commander on Iwo and we had kept in touch after the war. I could trust him with a problem as big as this one.

Stone sat back after two solid hours of reading the stolen papers and listening to Freya's explanation.

"Lancer," the senator finally said. "It just seems too incredible."

"Need more proof?" I asked and pulled

out the stolen ray-gun. "Got something you don't mind seeing burn?"

Stone shrugged and pulled a lurid pulp sci-fi magazine out of his desk and stood it up on a side board. I crossed the room and fired. The magazine burst into flames and the wall was scorched. The senator jumped up and wordlessly emptied a water carafe on the flames.

There was a yelp from Stone's outer office. The door flew off its hinges and crashed into the middle of the room. Three Steiner clones rushed in waving ray-gun pistols.

Stone had not lost a step from the war. He hurled the empty water-flask into the face of the clone on the left and dove behind his desk. The glass container shattered and blood flowed freely from the clone's lacerated face. He fell back against the wall and slumped down.

I stepped sideways and shot. The heat-ray burned through the right-hand Steiner's head and he dropped without a sound to the carpet. The middle clone fired and burned Baldur through the right shoulder down to the elbow. Freya leaped to cover her husband as Judi, Trudi and Audri stood as one and rushed their enemy. One jumped and body-checked the last standing Steiner low, causing him to fall forward. The second girl grabbed his gun-hand in her two hands and pulled as he fell. His thumb and trigger finger broke with loud pops and he dropped the weapon. The last triplet jumped high, swung her legs over the enemy's shoulders and pivoted until she was behind him breaking his neck with an audible crack.

Stone sprang up from behind his desk, .45 auto in his fist. Rollo burst in brandishing his Thompson, but the fight was over. Stone's secretary poked he head around the door. Stone looked around, wide-eyed at the carnage in his finely appointed office. He picked up the phone and dialed from memory.

"Hello, this is Senator Stone, may I speak to the president please? Yes, it is very urgent."

SEA BOUND-1

by Eddie D. Moore

"**O**rbital-1, this is Sea Bound-1. Do you copy?"

"Orbital-1 copies, Sea Bound-1."

"We have a successful splash down five miles off shore. Anchors are down and we're secure."

"Copy, Sea Bound-1 is secure. Your location is confirmed. Splash down was dead center of your target area. It appears that John owes you a bottle."

"You tell him I'll be expecting payment when the mission is over. I told him that I could plummet through the atmosphere with the best of them."

"Ha! I wish you could see his expression, Major. He was looking forward to drinking that. If he tried to walk right now I think he would step on his own bottom lip, and don't worry, I'll hold your winnings for you."

"I don't care who holds it as long as it is still sealed when I get back."

"No worries. Do me a favor and wish our eager biologists good luck on their multibillion dollar fishing trip."

Major Fields grinned as she saw the temperature change on Dr. EJ Hinks' face. She

was currently using the inferred feed her ocular implants offered. Seeing EJ's face heat up made picking on the, easily aggravated, biologist extremely amusing. His face always flushed no matter how hard he tried to hide it, and she was always goading him just to see the reaction.

"Will do, Orbital-1. Let the fishing begin. Sea Bound-1, out."

Dr. Hinks scratched the stubble on his chin and shook his head. "This is an historic trip, Major, and those transmissions will doubtlessly one day be of historical significance. Dr. Gillerson and I have high hopes of making discoveries here worthy of remembrance, and we'd like to be remembered for

more than a glorified fishing trip on another planet. Please keep that in mind."

Major Fields shrugged. "I wasn't the one who called it a fishing trip over the comlink."

"You've been calling it a fishing trip since we left Sol System, Major."

"Call me Patients, Doc, and don't worry. We've all made the history books just by surviving splash down. You're welcome by the way."

Dr. Hinks sighed, unlatched his safety harness, and looked at Dr. Gillerson. "Well Avery, shall we begin gathering samples?"

Dr. Gillerson flashed a quick know-ing smile at Patients as Dr. Hinks walked away. He turned to follow as he said, "But of course, EJ. I'll grab a kit, and we'll get to work."

Patients spoke up as the biologists walked out the door. "We only have a couple hours before dark so make it quick, and let me know if you catch a big one."

Patients heard Dr. Hinks grumbled some-thing unintelligible, and she chuckled to herself. Dr. Gillerson removed a sample kit from a storage bin and then turned to face her. "You do realize that none of the probes we sent here found anything living larger than your thumb? This wouldn't be a very good fishing spot."

Patients changed the view on her im-plants back to normal with a thought and a blink. She returned Dr. Gillerson's smile. "Of course, I've read the reports. We're here to find out why there's nothing larger living in these waters. I just pick on him because it doesn't take much to get under his skin." She winked. "And it's rather entertaining."

Dr. Gillerson nodded once. "Ah, that's what I thought... Well, let's go see what this new world has to offer. Shall we?"

Patients followed Dr. Gillerson to the deck, closed her eyes, and took a deep breath of the salty air. She held the breath for a long moment and then sighed with pleasure as she released it. She winced at the bright sun-light when she opened her eyes and blinked until the implants applied the proper filters.

The biologists were already running tests on water samples, and they were engaged in an animated discussion. Dr. Hinks waved his hands wildly as he spoke while Dr. Gillerson seemed to keep one eye on the test tubes and one wary eye on Dr. Hinks' hands to avoid getting smacked by accident.

Patients removed a small tablet from here pocket and keyed in a few commands. A compartment at the waterline unsealed and slid open to reveal three WPCs, Water jet Propelled Craft. Her heart picked up its pace as the bottom door dropped and water rushed in and around the sleek water craft.

She turned to the biologists and said ex-citedly, "Oh, these WPC's look fast and fun! Are you sure you guys wouldn't rather go play for a few minutes? Or umm... Look around?"

Dr. Hinks looked up, shook his head, and then went back studying the vial he was holding. Dr. Gillerson held a thumb up be-hind Dr. Hinks' back while they continued their discussion. Patients sighed and walked each WPC through a safety inspection. There may not be anything bigger than her thumb in these waters, but security was her job on this mission, and she took her job se-riously. For all she knew, the bottom of the floating science station could be cracked and sinking. The WPCs could be essential to their survival.

After finishing the inspections, Patients eyed the horizon for a moment. She sighed and said to herself. "You had to think about sinking." She shrugged her shoulders. "I guess I'll use one of the remote submersibles and inspect the bottom, just to be sure."

Three hours later darkness surrounded them, and the sky filled with twinkling stars. Patients studied the sky for a few moments and then singled out a small light that was slowly arcing across the sky.

"If you look just below those three bright stars, you can see Orbital-1 from here."

Dr. Gillerson glanced up and a moment later said, "We're done here. Are you ready to get something to eat?"

"Are you kidding me? I'm starving, but since you guys didn't catch anything, we'll have to use our rations."

Dr. Hinks shot an annoyed glance Patients' direction, and said, "You two go ahead, I just need a moment to myself."

Dr. Gillerson nodded once and followed Patients back inside. She removed three food packets from a storage compartment and tossed them onto the table. She opened another door and asked, "Do you want the cheese cake or peach cobbler?"

Dr. Gillerson raised an eyebrow and said suspiciously, "It's pudding; isn't it?"

Patients grinned. "I knew you were the smart one. Chocolate or vanilla?"

"I'll pass thank you. I do wish they would have planned a more robust menu for this mission. I was sick of that pudding by the time we reach midpoint."

Patients raised an eyebrow and pulled out a chocolate packet. "It's probably cheaper to order it in bulk. What do you expect? This mission is government funded."

Dr Gillerson grunted. "Ugh... I've been on privately funded missions as well. They're just as bad about skimping on meal variety. They both cut corners where ever and whenever possible."

After finishing his meal, Dr. Gillerson g JOURNAL lanced at the third meal packet and shook his head. "I'm going to check on Dr. Hinks. He has got to be hungry."

Patients held up a forestalling hand. "Let me go get him. I should probably stop picking at him so much, and try to be a little friendlier... Umm... Wish mc luck with that. Would ya?"

"I have at least two decades experience on you, and it still takes a great effort on my part to maintain a working professional relationship with the old grouch, so I wish you good luck."

Patients walked out of the room, but less than a minute later, she came running back. "Dr. Hinks is gone!" She dashed to a work station and typed furiously on the keyboard. A video appeared on the screen as Dr. Gill-

erson positioned himself to watch over Patients' shoulder.

Dr. Hinks sat on the edge of the deck watching the rolling waves when the water began to roil and glow blue beside him. Clearly surprised and intrigued he leaned closer to see what was happening. A small jellyfish looking blob leapt from the surface of the water and landed on his left hand. He held his arm out and smiled at the glowing blob. Another blob landed on his leg, and as he looked at it, six landed on his other arm and several more joined the first one on his right arm. He opened his mouth to shout as hundreds leapt out of the water covering his face and body. The animals appeared to stick together as the touched each other. In a matter of seconds one large blob covered Dr. Hinks from head to toe. They saw him struggle for a few seconds then the blob shifted, and slid silently out of sight beneath the waves.

Paitents slammed her hand down on a panic button. "Orbital-1, this is Sea Bound-1. Do you copy?"

While Paitents waited for Orbital-1 to reply, Dr. Gillerson took the work station beside her and activated a submersible. He gasped when the unit turned to display the underside of Sea Bound-1. Millions of the little animals formed a large blob and now hung from the hull. Tens of thousands more were adding their mass to the pile on by the second. The view from the submersible became nothing but a blue blur as the creatures latched onto it. The floor shifted under them as the weight of the creatures began to pull Sea Bound-1 down.

The speakers beeped once. "Orbital-1 copies, Sea Bound-1."

Patients spoke frantically, "Sea Bound-1 declaring and emergency. We have lost Dr. Hinks. Review our transmitted video feeds for current status." Patients glanced at Dr. Gillerson and continued. "We are abandoning Sea Bound-1 and will contact you from the shore for extraction."

"Copy, Sea Bound-1."

The slope of the floor continued to climb and gain speed as they ran for the exit. They scrambled up the rising deck to the WPCs and found that they had been completely lifted from the water.

Patients unlocked the WPCs from their docks as the open door was pulled under the surface and water began to fill Sea Bound-1 "Hold on tight, Doc. When we hit water again, open the throttle to full and run as fast as you can that way!" She pointed toward the distant shoreline.

The water around them glowed a haunting soft blue as Sea Bound-1 sunk faster and faster. They held tight to the grips on the WPCs as the water began to fill in around them, and as soon as they began to float again, they started the engines and arced toward shore.

Patients glanced behind her as Sea Bound-1 dropped below the surface of the water leaving a single WPC bobbing in the waves. A moment later, the WPC was covered by glowing blobs and pulled under.

Dr. Gillerson pulled his water craft closer to Patients and shouted, "Don't slow down! They are chasing us!"

Patients tried every filter and type of vision her implants offered, but she couldn't see anything other than the increasing luminosity under the water as the creatures gave chase. A small blob leapt out of the water and landed next to her foot. She stomped her foot down on it, felt a satisfying squish, and tightened her grip on the throttle while hundreds of glowing blobs dived in and out of the water behind her. She glanced at Dr. Gillerson and fought back panic.

Dr. Gillerson's back was covered by the glowing creatures and Patients shouted,

"Don't give up, Doc! We're almost there!"

They hit the beach without slowing and slid across the sand several feet before coming to a stop. Many of the creatures followed them to the bank, and they began to accumulate in a pile behind the WPCs. Dr. Gillerson stripped off his shirt and pants to rid himself of the creatures as the growing blob reached out blindly still searching for its prey.

Patients unlatched the seat on her WPC and unpacked the emergency flare gun. She fired a flare into the creatures amassing on the beach, and they quickly pulled away from the flame. Smiling, she reloaded and fired three more times.

The creatures slowly pulled themselves back into the water, broke apart, and disappeared as they swam to deeper water. A few seconds later, the glow in the water diminished leaving Patients and Dr. Gillerson to watch the waves roll onto the beach.

Patients sighed and ran her fingers through her hair. "Well Doc, I guess we know now why there is nothing large living in these waters."

Dr. Gillerson nodded slowly. "I suggest we drop Sea Bound 2 in waters teeming with a verity of life."

"That idea has my full support." She shook her head sadly. "I'll be sure to pack my fishing pole in Dr. Hinks memory."

Dr. Gillerson found a rain coat under the WPC's seat and pulled it on with a shiver. "And I will make sure he gets full credit for the discovery of this species."

Patients reached for the radio on her WPC. "It's definitely a discovery for the history books, and that is what he wanted."

DEFIANT, DEVIANT, DEVOID OF SOUL

by Russell Hemmell

The hall was sombre, humid and with ubiquitous shelves coiling up to the high ceilings in daring, gravity-defying architectures. Hanging bridges crossed over at different levels, only partially visible from the entrance but equally intimidating. Wooden flowers, graphene-grade dragonflies and mushroom-like shelving units crowded the marble surface of the humongous library immersed in a dim light. Heloim walked in and approached, staring at the object in the boy's hands. He was sitting on the floor, alone, engrossed in his activity.

"Hello, Treuwan," she said, with a smile. "They told me you were here."

He didn't acknowledge her words.

"I live in the Etemenanki Palaces next door, and I've never noticed this place. I mean, I did, of course—it's huge—but I thought it was a military complex—" She stopped. "Treuwan?"

After a long moment, he raised his head. "Good evening, Heloim."

"May I sit down?" she asked, dropping on her knees before he could reply. "You always bring strange stuff to class, as if you needed extra-attention by our educators. Take this one," she added, extending her finger. "What's that? They're everywhere." She turned her head around, pointing at the shelves, where compact objects of many dimensions and sizes piled up with no apparent logic.

"They're books."

"What are they for? They look so primitive."

"They're not primitive, they're old," he replied, with a serious stare that made him look older than thirteen. "They contain knowledge—stories, sometimes memories. They entertain you; at times, they make you cry. And they always affect your mind."

"Like games, then."

"Nothing of the sort." Treuwan showed her the one in his hands. "With books, it's your brain that builds the scenarios and plays the stories. You're not played by them."

"I don't see the difference."

"You'll have to find it out by yourself," he replied with a shrug. "You've learnt how to read."

Heloim nodded. "Couldn't avoid it. Father was adamant, even though I found it a waste of time. What do you need it for?"

He pointed at the shelves. "To unlock what's inside. You can't get it by direct uplink—not now, not ever. Certain kind of knowledge resides only in books."

"Why?"

"Control, I suppose."

"You can still restrict access to repositories."

"You can hack whatever is restricted, Heloim, but you can't access something you don't know it exists."

Heloim observed the hall around them. A subtle aroma of incense was mixed to the smell of old artefacts and shelves' moisture. How strange, she thought. Why to perfume a place where nobody ever goes? But she found that scent eerily appealing, almost inebriating.

"They have poetry too, I suppose."

She located one volume with miniature-decorated sonnets and began reading.

* * * *

"Which books have you found so far?" Heloim asked when they were walking back home a couple of hours later. "The one I read this afternoon was about sonnets of fire and death. So nicely written. And yours… it was poetry, too, wasn't it?"

"Yes. A beautiful one, from Merope Five."

"I don't know this city."

"It's not a city; it's a planet."

She blinked. "Is this why you never hang out with us…to go and read poetry alone in the library?"

"It's not poetry what I go there for, even though I enjoy a book or two once in a while," Treuwan said. "It's for this." He took a book out of his backpack.

"What's that?"

"The history of humanity. Our history. Since the moment we left Old Earth until we settled down here in Ashtarot."

"I like history," she said. "And now that you talk about it…I'm sure what they've told us in class are all fairy tales. I don't believe for a moment They gave us the technology we used to come here in the first place."

"I'm not interested in aliens, or race issues, only in Old Earth," he replied.

"They're subhumans, how could have they done it?" she continued.

"I said I'm not interested." He stopped, looking at her with a stare so cold that she stepped back instinctively.

"I'm sorry, Treuwan. Given your family, I thought—"

"You thought wrong."

They keep walking in silence, then Heloim pointed at her house. "Do we go back there tomorrow after class? I'd like to join you. No more talk about Them, I promise."

Since that day, Heloim accompanied her classmate in the library every day after school, discovering she loved the place, and not only for its suave, pervasive smell. Reading proved to be a captivating experience, and what was available in a written form was different from anything she could access in the shared holo-repositories everybody was plugged to. She enjoyed poetry and old stories from worlds that didn't exist any longer, and others that were real only in the mind of their creators.

But more than anything Heloim enjoyed history, and with Treuwan they began mapping Old Earth's civilisations, in an effort that took them busy for several weeks.

"Treuwan, I don't understand," she said one day, closing a huge volume. "You said we have here the entire human history from its origins on Old Earth—about 15 thousand years ago—up to the foundation of the city of Ashtarot and the beginning of Modern Era."

"It's correct. So?"

"So, there's something strange. You see," she showed him her notes, "I was able to find details about the start of our civilisation, the star systems we colonised and all the other human entities in space. That is, just us."

"What do you mean—us?"

"If you search for Them, you only have sporadic information, mainly referring to the Solar System's colonisation."

"I told you I'm not—"

"Something is missing, Treuwan. It looks like we have a gap in the Ancient Era's Annals. A huge gap."

"I haven't got there yet with my reading," he frowned. "How huge?"

"Huge enough. If my calculations are correct, about 700 years. There's simply no recorded history—not for Ashtarot, I mean. What we have is related to other systems in the stellar neighbourhood."

Treuwan remained silent for a couple of moments, staring at her diagrams. Before she could add anything else, he stood up and walked toward the staircase. "Wait. Where are you going?"

Heloim followed him across the library up to the office of the Master Librarian, a monk that Heloim found the weirdest possible. In her (limited) experience, all monks were racially Amuryans—therefore dark-haired, small and rather ugly as all humans that had not used genetic enhancing invariably were. Belonging to the Ecclesia was the Amuryan way to live a privileged and rather sheltered life, and they flocked there, becoming monks and working in a wide range of professions. But this one, Heloim noticed, looked like her or Treuwan: handsome, clear eyes and chiselled features. His platinum blond hair was collected in a long braid—another curious detail—that shone like precious metal in the glimmering light of the room. Odd.

"The repository is not complete," Treuwan told him quietly. "Where's the rest?"

The monk shrugged. "You're the first one to mention this detail in a long, long time. Probably because the others that came here before you were old men as I am, who knew better than requesting something that can't be obtained."

This one, an old man? Heloim thought, observing him but trying not to stare, he looks thirty at best. But the oddest of all things was that Treuwan seemed not to notice how strange it sounded.

"Why, has it been destroyed?"

"No. It has never been written. Not here, at least."

Treuwan's eyes narrowed.

What's going on?

"Tell me what I'm not going to find, then. Tell me what's so sensitive that even the central library in Bysanthium is not allowed to hold it on records, no matter if only a few would understand what it means." His voice became low like a whisper, resounding in a hostile note. "Tell me what is not supposed to have ever happened."

"You already know; otherwise, you wouldn't ask," the monk answered. "You only ignore the scale."

Treuwan became pale and bit his lips, and Heloim was sure she had never seen him so tense.

"You're a son of Ashtarot, young man, from a family of Founders," the Librarian continued. "Few know all the details, and none of them will talk to you. Nobody would trust a future Inquisitor, especially not one that has somebody like your sister—so high in the echelons of supreme power—in his family. The others who could, and you might well guess who they are—" a soft smiled appeared on his handsome features, "they won't come near you, not on this planet. Your kind only hurts them. And outside… it's you that would probably get hurt."

"There must be a place, or someone, that holds what I'm searching for," Treuwan said.

"Indeed, there's a place, but you might not come out of there alive," the other replied. "Without mentioning that your family will forbid you to go. Not only it's too dangerous for you to go there; it's inconvenient."

"Let me decide. What's the name?"

"Greenside."

"I didn't know you were here," Heloim said, walking into the library one evening after school. She had not got back there since Treuwan had left, and she was surprised to find him in one of the small chambers. When she glanced at him with more attention, she almost didn't recognise her friend. He was pale as if he hadn't seen the light of the day for a long time, and dark circles contoured his beautiful violet eyes with golden streaks. He looked more slender than the usual, and his expression was gloomy. "When have you come back to Bysanthium?"

He glanced at her with blank eyes and said nothing.

"I haven't seen you in six months." She came nearer and put her hand on his shoulder. "I've asked around. They told me you were sick, and your family sent you away for holidays. Where were you?"

"Don't get involved, Heloim."

"If you're talking about the library, I'm already involved. Tell me what's all this is about, or I'm going to ask your sister the same question."

A dry smile appeared on his face. "That would be a bad idea, and dangerous one."

"I'm not afraid of Kerstin, Inquisition or not," she replied. "I thought you went to Greenside, wherever this place is, not on holiday."

"I was away in the family's estate for a couple of months. I was confused, and I needed to put my priorities in order."

"What does it mean?"

"It means that school is finished for me." He smiled again. "In one-month time, I'm going to join the Order, and undertake my theological training."

Heloim regarded him without hiding her surprise. "But you have never wanted to become an Inquisitor. You always said power corrupts minds and souls, that the Inquisition's power is the worst, and after College you wanted to leave Bysanthium and study medicine elsewhere. Away from your family and all the politics."

"I've changed my mind."

"Treuwan—"

"I'll become as they are: devoid of soul. There's no use for the one I have. Goodbye, Heloim." He collected his books, bowed to her and left the library under her astonished stare.

Heloim didn't talk to Treuwan in the following days, even though she saw him around at school. He didn't behave any different—aloof and reserved as usual—and his schoolmates were already used to treat him with caution, considered which family he belonged to. His only known friend, a boy of a couple of years older than them, had previously left to join the military academy, and Treuwan was now always alone.

Once her disappointment had passed, however, Heloim thought again about the whole story. I was ready to swear he left Ashtarot for that place the monk mentioned. It's not like Treuwan to leave something pending. She had known him her entire life, and one thing she was positive about was that his friend was gentle and brilliant, but as stubborn as a red donkey.

That day, she went back to the library and got straight to see the odd-looking Master Librarian.

"You know what happened to Truewan."

"He found what he should have not searched for in the first place."

"His sister must have punished him. This is why he's joining the Order even if he's still a boy."

His expression gave away nothing. "Knowledge always comes with a price."

"Stop talking riddles, monk," she replied. "I'm not the sibling of an Inquisitor myself, but I promise you troubles anyway if you don't tell me what's going on. I won't let my friend be forced into a life he didn't choose, doing something he abhors."

"Are you sure it was not his decision?"

"No. I know Treuwan. He abhors violence. He's even kind with the subhumans, you see, the aliens. How can he torture anybody?"

The Librarian looked at her with a strange smile, and for the first time she noticed his long robe was emanating the same, delicate scent of incense so pervasive in the building. As if the two were made of a common, subtle essence. He's not a man, he's a sprite or—

He gestured Heloim to follow him. They walked across the huge hall and went down through a lateral, winding staircase, small and steep. They descended several stores, and, once underground, passed through a long, vaulted corridor leading to a system of crypts. Each one of them had wardrobes in steel with padlocks and graphene cladding, with wooden desks here and there. Curved on one of them, she saw Treuwan, surrounded by huge and dusty leather-covered volumes. The Librarian left, and Heloim sat down.

"Annals V of the Millennium War?" She said, opening one volume and looking at the text. It was engraved in an old font, with precious miniatures and silver lining. In one of the minute drawings, a winged, demon-like creature with two-inch nails like blade and a black outfit was defending a wounded, faired-haired man against others of the same kind. Snakes and mantis-like insects were crawling on the ground, biting the victim. But apart from the title, the rest was written in a language she didn't understand. "This is different from the rest of the books."

"Because it doesn't belong to the same collection. It comes from World Number Four."

"What's that?"

"Greenside."

"So you did go."

His eyes blinked. "I found out there what was missing: the volumes you see on this table. And I confronted my sister."

"Kerstin? Why?"

"Because of what's written in them. You were right all along; there were 783 hundred years not included in the records, which relate the only war between us and Them. Our entire civilisation, the one we are so proud of, was built on the systematic annihilation of another intelligent species. We have killed the first resident aliens in our systems, the ones that have lived with us since the beginning of the Space Era and that represented a challenge to our supremacy. Not happy with that, the Inquisition now persecutes anybody suspected of being sympathetic with the enemy, or what remains of it."

"I didn't know anything."

"Why should you? History is the tyranny of the winners, and losers don't have a place. And you know what's even worse? That it's going to happen again—this time, against somebody else. If there's one valuable lesson history has taught us is that when you can't remember the past, you're doomed to repeat the same horrors."

"Your sister...did she know?"

"Kerstin is Inquisition. She's one of the people actively involved in this denial. Yes, she knew alright."

They remained in silence, and Heloim browsed one of the volumes' pages, reading those strange words aloud without making any sense of them.

"How can you read it?"

"This is elleniki, the language we spoke in the Ancient Era and that we shared with Them." His eyes were cold, almost expressionless. "An Inquisitor has to know everything, especially what is forbidden and what is the enemy's precinct. My sister made me learn it when I had no idea what it was in reality. It was only in Greenside I've discovered it."

She breathed heavily, as if the air had become too rich in oxygen.

"It seems incredible," she said, "and awful. Whatever we think about Them, there's never a good reason for extermination. We are evolved enough to find other ways to address diversity. After all, even on Old Earth we had this kind of issues."

Treuwan didn't reply and kept staring at the book.

"How was that place? Greenside, I mean."

"As dangerous as the Librarian told us."

Out of an impulse, she took his hand. It was cold and limp, like the one of a dead man.

"You talked about war … you think we will have another war? Against Them, I mean."

"The war has never ended; it has only changed modalities and become more insidious. As you'd expect, since it's the Inquisition that's in charge of it now. Do you know, Heloim—Them, the ones among us here and now, we can tell They are aliens. We can spot their otherness, and humans fear everything that's different and that can't control." There was a heart-breaking sadness in his voice. "But the ones we killed? They weren't even different. They looked human. They looked just like us."

"So why are you joining the Inquisition?" Heloim said, after a long silence.

"Is it not clear?"

Treuwan gazed at her, and his eyes lightened up in a nasty glint. He's no longer a boy. He's a man now, one that's ready to fight.

"It's dangerous. Not even your sister can protect you if they realise what you're up to."

"She'll strangle me with her own hands if

they do." He smiled. "But when an enemy is too strong to be fought in the open, you need to become him, and gnawing at him from inside out."

Heloim caressed the book's rough leather cover. "You have never been interested in Them, either for harassment or entertainment; you've lived as if They didn't exist. Why are you doing this for Them now?"

"You're mistaken. It's not for Them, it's for us." Treuwan stood up, taking the book from her and holding it as if it wanted to crush it with his bare hands. "Humans are better than the evil deeds of a minority, no matter how powerful; our civilisation is better than that. We need to stand up for what our beliefs are, whatever it takes."

Heloim was the only one in their class to attend Treuwan's admission to the Order. All the others sneered that the weasel had finally shown his true colours and joined the despised but feared Inquisition. When one of her girlfriends took fun of her, saying that she had chosen the wrong one because now he wouldn't be able to marry her, she replied she had never been interested in the first place. It was only half a lie: as much as she liked him, Heloim knew he couldn't be the companion she wanted. He had been remote even before leaving, inhabiting a world where she, or any other girl, had no place.

She silently wished him luck and went to the library.

Sitting among those towering shelving units, she thought for a moment how her world had changed in those months. Once you've seen what is in a room, you can switch off the lights, but you know things will stay there whether you see them or not. Chasing your consciousness, slithering in your thoughts, challenging your peace and creeping into your dreams. You might choose to ignore them; they won't disappear.

"You're back," the Librarian said, observing Heloim with an unreadable look.

"Yes."

"Do you want me to choose some poetry for you? We have old authors from the Heian Period, the original one, translated in our language."

"No." She took out one of the books Treuwan had brought back from Greenside and that had left in her custody. "Teach me how to read this one."

"Maybe I don't know that language."

"I know you do."

"Maybe you don't want to know that either."

"I know too much already, and I've made my choice, monk. I'll stand up for your kind, too. Not because I'm your friend, or I understand you. I ignore everything about your species, including why you came to us in the first place or how it's even possible you look like me. " She extended her hand, brushing with the tip of her fingers the sleeve of his robe. "You appear to me as incorporeal as this cloud of incense that surrounds you. And I still fear what it's alien to me. But it's the right thing to do. I can learn. I can say no."

He hesitated for a moment. Heloim saw him bowing his head, and their fingers touched briefly.

"I'm Sima Qian."

"Heloim."

"It's going to take time, Heloim."

"Let's not waste another moment then."

I'll keep your soul safe with me until I'm ready to join your fight, Treuwan. Heloim smiled and followed the monk. They walked in silence and descended in the vault, in the eerie quietness of the deserted library.

THE BLOOD RED SKY OF MARS
by Adrian Cole

A hundred years have passed since the fall of the Zurjahn Empire, a vast, decadent confederation of planets that had encompassed the entire Solar System, ruled by the Dream Lords, humans with superhuman gifts, mental powers with which they enforced rigid control. They had administered their sprawling empire from the largest of the planets, Zurjah, re-writing history and creating a new destiny for Mankind, based on deceit and untruth, enabling them to maintain peace and order. Galad Sarian, son of a Dream Lord, rebelled and was sent to the prison planet, Ur, which had been the original homeworld, Earth. There, in a bloody and barbarous revolution, he had brought down its tyrannical ruler, Daras Vorta, Warden of Ur, whose own dark ambitions had led him into a blasphemous union with evil powers and the nightmare god, Shaitan.

The fall of the Dream Lords led to the collapse of the Empire, and Man slowly migrated back to Earth, gradually quitting the worlds and technology it had used for so long. Gradually the planets became as they had once been, Man's footprints were erased, and the cities and space centres returned to dust, swept away by the remorseless reinstatement of alien environments.

Now, other than Earth, only one planet yet retains a human colony: Gargan, formerly known as Mars. Closest to Earth, it supports a smaller, shrinking population, split between the ailing space depots, the miners, and a few secretive military training centres.

Here there are little more than traces of the once dark and terrible powers that existed, and a handful of dedicated warriors committed to eradicating them. They are the Witchfinders.

Overhead, the sun was a tiny ball, floating in a crimson glow, the rocks and desert terrain of the planet a fusion of monotonous reds and russets, dusty and rock-strewn, desolate. Out here in the wilderness, the entire planet beckoned, apparently lifeless and empty. There was little to tempt the explorer. As far as Man was concerned, Mars had no more secrets to offer.

Arrul Voruum studied the ridge immediately ahead of him from the sanctuary of an outcrop. He wore the obligatory suit of an armed trainee, which had been expertly designed to give him the gravitational weight equivalent to what it would be had he been on Earth. It was on the homeworld where his talents were ultimately to be deployed, provided he survived his training. Not everyone did. Mars had taken a cruel toll of lives among those aspiring to attain a commission in the elite military service.

Voruum had been singled out when he was ten years old, a quiet, unassuming boy who had mental skills that were becoming less and less common these days, as though, in some perverse way, humanity had veered away from its mental evolution and taken a simpler, more physical path. The Dream Lords had been supreme examples of man at his most powerful mentally, but when their ambitions led to chaos, all that had changed. Such things now were hunted out, seen as aberrations. There were a few exceptions, paradoxical but useful.

In the heat haze, the air shimmered but revealed nothing. The horizons were devoid of movement. It was midday, a time when any life form here would have found even the most basic of activities exhausting. Voruum was very fit and agile. He had applied himself religiously to all tasks set him.

At eighteen, he was one of the youngest of the current batch of recruits, but his agility and quickness of reaction had marked him as having strong potential. It earned him the envy of his fellows and in some cases rivalries that were bordering on dangerous.

He blended in with the rocky landscape, keeping low and moving quickly along a gully that zigzagged towards the ridge. Beyond it would be the large sand bowl that was his rendezvous point. Kaarri would be near at hand, as fused with the rocks as he was. They had been paired up for this exercise, far away from the administrative centre of Melkor, one of the last of the planet's human cities. It was demanding work, and one slip or error of judgement could be fatal, but Voruum considered it routine, a way of life to which he had acclimatised

Dropping to all fours, he wriggled up a narrow declivity and reached a break in the rocks. He was almost at the crest of the ridge. From here he could see the sweeping curve of the sand bowl, several miles across. As promised, the central area was a jumble of rocks and slabs. A more discerning eye perceived them as the long dead ruins of a citadel, the weathered bones of a time long gone. Voruum twisted his head around to look along the ridge. A bright light winked away to his right. Kaarri had parked the ground-hopper somewhere out there. Once they'd achieved their goal, they would fly back in the two-seater aerial machine, their only link with humanity, as this test of their worthiness demanded. It would be a relief to get out of the remorseless sun.

Something tugged his mind, like a distant wave lapping at a sea shore, although there were none here on Mars. He had seen images of such vast expanses of water—they existed on the homeworld, and maybe when he reached his ultimate destination he would get to see them. They always conjured in him a strange desire, luring him to them, appealing to something deep and atavistic in him. Kaarri had admitted the same feelings on the rare occasions she opened up to him.

It was her now, her mind power seeking his. They touched warily, as if too strong a contact would be harmful, or trigger responses they'd not be able to control. Mind power was a double-edged sword. It gave strength and potential, but it could open dark passageways and there were other powers only too eager to slip in. *Always be on your guard*, Voruum's teachers had warned him.

He responded carefully to her, pinpointing her position. Satisfied that there was no immediate danger ahead, the two of them synchronised their movements and slithered through the thick dust down the sloping sand bowl towards the collapsed buildings below. They reached them together, meeting at a leaning stone that could once have been an obelisk. Its cracks and crevices, weathered by the hostile air, gave an impression of an extinct language. The ruins could have been pre-human, relics of the Garganian age long before Man first arrived here.

Kaarri, like Voruum, wore a thin mask over the lower part of her face. It filtered out the choking dust. She was his age, more slender, but no less agile and ambitious. Among the trainees, she had excelled, the only one of them able to compete with Voruum, which was why they'd been paired for this exercise. He was certain she seemed determined to surpass him, never sure whether to be flattered or annoyed. He closed his mind to her, although at times he had to open it up in order to work with her. Times like now.

"You sense anything?" she said. The air was still, sound carrying, so that even a whisper travelled.

He shook his head. "This place is as dead as the desert we came across."

"They want us to think that, of course," she said, with a vaguely dismissive frown. "It'll be a trap."

"Certainly. How many soldiers do you think there will be? A dozen?"

"Possibly less. I think we'll be tested by their best, so they won't stack the odds against us. They have to give us a chance. Even so, they must know if they pit a score or more of their less able soldiers against us, we'll just take them out."

Her expression made him grin. She had absolute faith in her ability, but that was okay—so did he. He drew the sword from its long scabbard, and made a few simple, silent passes. She did the same.

"What about the target?" she said. "Where will it be?"

"On the one hand, it could be in the very centre of the complex. The time-worn, straightforward test. Penetrate their defences, snatch the golden egg, or whatever it is, from the inner sanctum and bolt back into the desert."

"Or?" She waited for his answer with more than a hint of a smile.

"It'll be hidden somewhere else. Not guarded as fully. A little bit of mind probing will probably tell us where. These soldiers will have very limited boosted mental powers. They'll be swordsmen—and good ones. We won't disarm them easily. If they surround us, we'll lose out."

"Okay. So one of us goes for the target and the other creates a diversion," she said.

Voruum could almost taste her eagerness. "You realise they may be anticipating that."

She looked annoyed. No, she hadn't thought of it, he could tell. "I think we should appear to do what they're expecting. Then actually do the opposite. In the confusion, we'll take the prize," he said.

"Fake a diversion?"

"Combine our mental abilities and, yes, deceive them."

She glared at him for a moment as if he'd spoken some kind of heresy, but then grunted assent.

He led the way further into the ruins. Although there had once been streets here, they had become so choked with sand and fallen rubble, some were impassable and the two figures had to weave their way through buildings and across narrow spans where the streets fell away into forbidding darkness far below. The silence swallowed them, shock-

ingly empty, as though they'd lost their auditory senses altogether.

Pressed up against a leaning wall, Voruum concentrated. "Can you feel anything?" There should be something nudging his mind, the suggestion of life that would reveal the presence of the soldiers. Yet the ruins beyond were devoid of any hint of life.

She shook her head. "Unless they've gone deeper underground, there's no one here. This trap is more devious than we thought. Maybe we should go back and do a comprehensive scan around the perimeter—"

He held up his hand for silence and she responded instantly, freezing.

"Someone is here," he whispered. "Humans. Their minds are impenetrable."

Her scowl deepened. This test was threatening to turn ugly.

Voruum moved forward again, silent as the air, and she was behind him, straining to hear anything, physical or mental.

"There's an open area ahead," he said. "It's been cleared of debris, and recently. It could be the central area. It may be under surveillance. Can you feel *anything*?"

Again she shook her ahead. "They're just not here. They've abandoned this place."

Slowly he led them to the edge of the central area, a wide quadrangle that opened up to the bloody sky, far overhead. Towers and blocks of stone loomed over it as though inevitably they'd fall inward and bury this entire place. From the seclusion of one of the great pillars, Voruum studied the open area. Now he saw them.

Bodies. A dozen of them, strewn about the floor, contorted and twisted horribly, leaking great pools of blood. The daylight added to the gruesomeness of the carnage.

Kaarri saw them, too. Her mind shut down at once.

"The soldiers," said Voruum, indicating their uniforms, and the discarded swords. Whatever had killed them had flung them aside like broken dolls, careless of their weapons.

"What could possibly have done this?"

said Kaarri. "Did they fight?"

Voruum scanned the entire perimeter of the area, cautiously using his mind to seek out anything that could give a clue to the slaughter. There was nothing. Whatever had done this had withdrawn. "I need to examine the bodies. Cover me."

Kaarri was too professional to argue. She waited at the edge of the hall, prepared to defend him if the need arose.

Voruum went to the first victim. The man had been torn open from chin to abdomen, and there was a deep cut in his neck—his head lolled at a ghastly angle. His death appeared to be the result of an attack both by a weapon and by claws, or something similar. All of the soldiers had been similarly ripped apart. Voruum's mind told him the killer, or killers, were no longer here. The place had been abandoned.

Kaarri glided over to him, silent as a shadow.

He shook his head.

"I found a trail," she whispered. "Blood, and something else. You'd better come and see."

She led him to a place at the edge of the area to where something had been daubed wetly on a pillar. It was a crude sign, a bloody circular smear, with two lines curving upwards on either side.

"Do you recognise it?" she said, and he could feel her shudder, as if a cold flow of air washed over him.

"Devil worshippers. The Brotherhood. It's believed to be hidden away in remote parts of Earth, but I thought it had been eradicated here on Mars."

"Apparently not."

"Unless that's what we're supposed to think."

"We should report this."

He nodded. "Let's take this way out and see if there's anything else."

Doubly cautious now, they moved between ageing pillars and cracked walls, watching and listening, minds softly probing. It remained a sterile environment. In the dust they saw scuff marks, as though several creatures, possibly men, had passed through here. When they reached the outer walls and the pink radiance of the Martian daylight, they found another sign, similar to the first.

Voruum studied the sands beyond, sloping up to the ridge of serrated rock. A dark line running vertically to the fallen scree suggested an entry into the rock face. He pointed it out.

"You want to investigate?" she said. He could sense her eagerness.

"Is the ground-hopper secure?"

Her eyes fixed him in a stare that clearly said it wasn't necessary to ask, but she nodded.

"Okay, let's take a look. As long as we head back to Melkor before dusk." He led the way across the open sand, watching for any sign of movement, but there were none. There had been no dust storms for several days, and no sign of anything on the far horizons. They wore miniature wrist monitors that would warn them of potential changes in the weather. The calmness around them was eerie. They crossed the dust bowl quickly.

When they reached the tall crack in the rock wall, they could see it was a natural cleft, a product of the heat.

"Guard my back," said Kaarri, stepping into the shadow and snatching the initiative from him. He would have been irritated, but he smiled wryly and waved her into the opening. He took up a position under the jagged arch and switched his attention from desert to dark passageway. Kaarri had opened her mind a fraction to allow him to track her.

She flicked on the tiny flash-light on her shoulder and its beam picked out the details of the natural declivity. The floor was sandy but made for an easy descent, so she went on, her senses attuned to the rocks and any faint echo or reverberation. She caught a hint of sound, water dripping, but nothing else. The stone was unmarked, no more signs. If the killers had come this way, they had not left any indications.

Voruum heard the slight fall of rubble

and eased himself deeper into shadow. Something was moving above him, beyond the jutting rock overhang. More dust and stone trickled down and then a larger chunk dropped. He gripped his sword. A sharp, hissing heralded the appearance of an elongated, flat head and a tongue that flickered from side to side like a whiplash. Voruum had seen drawings of the bloodworms that were supposed to inhabit the far reaches of the Martian deserts. As this one swung down into view he recognised it at once.

Its tongue probed for him and he slashed at it, cutting into the wet flesh and severing the tip. The creature hissed and uncoiled, dropping to the ground in a cloud of dust, twisting insanely in its pain and fury. It must be twenty feet long, Voruum realised, the thickest part of its body equal to the circumference of his own trunk. He dashed into the opening behind him, his movement a signal to the thrashing monster. It was eyeless, a blind thing of darkness and deep stone that must have caught his scent and writhed up here in search of food. Its head swung up over the entrance, circular mouth wide, ring upon ring of countless teeth gleaming in the red sunlight, its own pink flesh blending with the terrain.

Voruum moved quickly down into the deep cleft. Behind him the bloodworm hissed, the stench of its breath appalling, a smell of cadavers and rotten flesh. And it came on, ramming itself into the opening, splitting the first of the rocks. Voruum went as quickly as he dared down the slope and into the inviting darkness, switching on his flash-light. He knew that these bloodworms were capable of moulding themselves to the rock fissures, oozing gelatinously down their own underground lairs. This one would not be held back by rock alone.

Some distance below him, Kaarri had found a wider section of the tunnel. Its roof was invisible and the walls on either side of her loomed upward, creating an impression of a vast building, or at least of a cavern scooped out of the bedrock. There were shelves above her and she could hear movement up there. She used her light to pick out shapes, small, humped things. They were tracking her and she realised it would be foolish to go on. As she turned to retrace her steps, more of the hidden creatures gathered. Abruptly two of them jumped down from the ridge and blocked her path.

They were squamous, with bloated heads, no necks and saucer-like eyes that fixed upon her. As they rose up, they displayed scores of arms, insectoid, wriggling and reaching out. She struck swiftly, driving her sword point straight into the eye of the first of them. It crashed back into the stone wall as if it had been hit by a huge fist. The other hopped forward, about to come down and land on Kaarri's shoulders, but she ducked and swept her blade in an arc that tore into its flesh, opening it up and spilling out its innards.

She realised there were a dozen or more of these horrors coming up the tunnel and she would have no hope of fighting them off. Instead she fled back the way she had come, conscious of more of the creatures on the ledges. She saw a wavering light ahead and in a moment Voruum had joined her. He saw their predicament at once.

"Can't go back up," he said. "Bloodworm."

"It's a trap," she snarled angrily. "The lower tunnel is filling with these oversized fleas. We're just going to have to carve our way out."

Her fury made him smile in spite of their situation, but there was no time for further discussion—they set to defending themselves, hacking and slashing at the gathering things from the dark. They caused havoc, reducing countless assailants to squirming, pulpy ruin, but it became evident they were going to be overwhelmed, if not by this horde then by the bloodworm from above. Fending off despair as well as the press of insectoid horrors, they were pushed back against the tunnel wall.

Abruptly a section of it gave way to reveal another, lower tunnel. A single figure stood within it, calling to them.

"It's a Garganian," said Kaarri. "It's okay. It wants to help."

There was no time to discuss it and Voruum followed Kaarri into the tunnel. As he did so, a metal grille slammed shut behind him, cutting off the press of insectoid bodies. A section of stone slid across the opening beyond the grille, crushing several as it did so, shutting out the remainder.

Kaarri followed the small figure. It was two thirds her height, of slender build, though with a broad chest. Its eyes gleamed in a natural light from the stone walls, eyes that were wider than human eyes, regarding them with an expression that suggested shock.

"Not a trap this time," Kaarri whispered back to Voruum. "Be careful—their minds are much more fragile than ours. If you exercise your mental powers too strongly, you could kill it."

Although Voruum had never been close to a native Garganian before, he knew this, but chose not to say so.

"There's a community down here," said Kaarri after they had wormed their way further into the lower areas of what could now be seen as a honeycombed system of tunnels and caves. Voruum knew the exact numbers of the small race were unknown, although it was believed by the scientists of Melkor they were shrinking, in danger of extinction. Their relationship with Man was uneasy, especially in the difficult aftermath of the fall of Daras Vorta and his acolytes, who had used the Garganians cruelly.

Although their guide did not seem to speak the human tongue, it was able to make itself understood easily enough with gestures and expressions. Voruum sensed its fear, but an underlying desire to help them. Something else had disturbed it far more, and he wondered about the killings up in the dust bowl citadel. It led them through a very tall chamber, the sides of which were overgrown with bulging saprophytes, cultivated banks of mushrooms that Voruum knew were the staple diet of the Garganians.

They were met by a trio of the creatures, all of whom were armed, and after a brief consultation were taken beyond through another tunnel to a hallway that appeared to be the antechamber to a building, and the first of a small city. There was simple stone seating here and they were clearly asked to sit and wait. As they did so, Voruum studied the hall. It merged perfectly with the stone from which it had been cut, and its soft lighting was diffused from a particular strata. In the centre of the hall a small fountain of water bubbled, the light coruscating like jewels. There were various pictographs etched into the flatter walls, and a few statues, carved into tall pillars. Overall, there was an impression of the ages, the voice of lost aeons.

After a while, they were joined by another Garganian. This one was robed in soft grey materials, and wore a simple hat, which appeared to be his badge of office. He spoke clearly, obviously understanding the words of Men. "I am Ephral, what you would call a councillor. I spent many years studying in your city of Melkor."

Voruum and Kaarri bowed to him. "We're grateful to you for having us rescued," said Kaarri. "Were it not for your guide, we'd likely have perished."

"How well do you understand the dangers around us?" said Ephral.

Voruum answered. "I thought the bloodworms were only to be found much further out in the desert wastes. We are a long way from Melkor, but even so, I was taken aback."

"I know why you came here," said Ephral. "You followed a trail. You suspected a trap. Well, you were right to do so. Do you realise who set it?"

The other Garganians had drawn back respectfully, but their deep unease at Ephral's words was not lost on either of the two humans. Ephral studied them evenly. "There is a Brotherhood. We do not speak its name, nor that of the master who once controlled it. He who was destroyed on your homeworld."

"It is here?" said Voruum, his voice ill disguising his concern.

"Yes. Its remnants gone to ground, where they have festered for a century since the Fall. They grow in numbers and in daring."

"Daring?" said Voruum. "You suggest they plan a revival?"

"They do," said Ephral. "Beyond this citadel, out in the desert, under its burning sands, they prepare. They have a long reach and have tainted more of your people than you would believe. Once they were scattered across Gargan, defeated and shrinking, bound for extinction. Now the vestiges of their hellish cult have come together for a final attempt to wrest back power."

"Then Melkor must be warned," said Kaarri.

Ephral nodded. "The danger is deeper. There are men in Melkor and other citadels of Man who are themselves servants of the Brotherhood. It is like a corruption, a disease. If you were to return to Melkor now in a bid to alert its government, these traitors would deflect your accusations easily."

"We saw the dead, the handiwork of the Brotherhood," said Voruum. "And the sign they left."

"By now nothing will remain. There will be no proof. Already your enemies have moved ahead of you. They brought you here to destroy you. They have your flying machine. Their plan was to kill you and plant you in the machine in a false accident."

Kaarri's anger flared. "They won't keep us from getting back."

"How do you know these things?" said Voruum.

"Through the work of the *phorud*. It is a secret enclave of Garganians, centuries old. Indeed, Galad Sarian, the renegade Dream Lord who brought down the Empire, once used it here on Gargan. The Brotherhood has spread, but the *phorud* draws on the experiences of millennia. It is everywhere, here, out in the deeper deserts, and in cities such as Melkor."

"You spoke of a plot by the Brotherhood," said Voruum.

"Yes. An attack, a strike that will reduce the community of Annakor to ruin and turn it into a base for their eventual bolder strike on Melkor. What do you know of Annakor?"

Kaarri and Voruum exchanged glances. "Neither of us has been there," said Kaarri. "It is a small, remote city, run by scientists who study geology and to some extent agrarian pursuits. It was once more prominent, but since the decline of Man on your world, it has become an isolated backwater, some would say superfluous."

"Quite so," agreed Ephral. "There are those in Melkor who would have it abandoned. The Brotherhood plans to take it. When the attack is unleashed, it will be over quickly, long before Melkor can respond. Indeed, there will be those in Melkor who will dismiss the loss as unimportant. Not worth a counter-attack. The Brotherhood, of course, will not be implicated. Gargan, with its storms, its deep desert creatures, such as the bloodworms, and general environmental disadvantages, will be seen to have reclaimed its own. The Council in Melkor will easily be persuaded to let it go. Most of its members, corrupt or otherwise, wish to return to the homeworld. The last days of Man on Gargan are at hand."

"We cannot allow this to happen," said Kaarri.

Voruum studied Ephral, careful not to exert mental pressure on him. "What would you suggest?"

"The Council at Melkor must be made to understand the danger of the Brotherhood. Your masters, those who train you, know this well enough. Yet they are a minority in the game of power both in Melkor and in Karkesh, the principal city of the homeworld. If you can expose this evil plot, Melkor will have to take note and send reinforcements. It must conduct a full purge. You must help the *phorud* defend Annakor, and with your powers the balance of that conflict would stand a chance of shifting in our favour. We could thwart the Brotherhood."

"This is a dangerous game you propose," said Voruum. "Kaarri and I are bound to our masters. Their authority is not yet invested in us. We are merely trainees. What you are asking us to do would be considered by some, if not all, of our superiors, as insubordination."

"I understand that," said Ephral calmly. "Of course, we can defend Annakor without you. It's just that the odds against us would be so much greater. Meanwhile the night is drawing on. You should eat and rest. I will prepare rooms for you. It will give you time to consider my proposal. Should you wish to return to Melkor, I will see that you have help in doing so."

Voruum and Kaarri ate a meal consisting of sliced mushrooms, cooked in a delicious gravy and complemented with Garganian vegetables which the cook had somehow contrived to make extraordinarily palatable.

Kaarri grinned. "Why can't our cooks give us this kind of quality?"

Voruum took a draft of the ice cold water and felt his body reacting to it as if he had swallowed a powerful drug. "These are the true Garganians. This is their world. We never truly belonged here."

"You think of the homeworld? You long for it?"

"I'm not unhappy on Gargan. I am curious, though. Somehow I sense my destiny lies on earth. And you?"

"Yes. It has been my dream."

"What do you think of Ephral's words?"

She sat back, stretching, her gaze briefly far away. "We can't just leave them to fight the Brotherhood. Yet it seems if we attempt to summon our masters, we'll be dismissed. We're rookies, aren't we?"

"If I thought we could truly influence this conflict, then I would do it. Perhaps the answer is a compromise. One stays and fights, the other goes back."

She sat up, scowling. "And I suppose you want *me* to go back?"

He watched her for a moment, feeling her annoyance like a warm radiance. He laughed softly. "Of course not. I'd be a fool to suggest it."

"So you'll go back?"

He laughed again. "No. I think we need to work as one. And I think we should visit this citadel. If it can be defended, then perhaps we have our answer."

She stopped bristling and sat back, sipping her own water. "Yes. We should visit Annakor."

They went to the small rooms that Ephral had provided for them. Voruum washed and stretched out on the simple bed, his guarded thoughts going over the bizarre events of the day. If he and Kaarri could help the *phorud* to defeat the Brotherhood, surely that would win them much kudos with their masters and be a major step to attaining their promotion. It would be a gamble, but Voruum knew that all of life in these times was skewed that way.

Much later, a few hours before the dawn, he woke from a light sleep and knew someone was close at hand. He sensed no threat, and a brief mental scan told him Kaarri had entered the room. For a moment an unbidden thought stirred him in a manner that caught him unawares. Quickly he blanketed his emotions. Behind the girl stood Ephral.

"What is it?" he said, rising.

"The Brotherhood," whispered Kaarri. "Already it is moulding its plans. Many of it s members gather in their secret place."

"The *phorud* can take you there," said Ephral. "You may learn something through observation."

Quickly they followed the Garganian and were met by a small group of others. They bowed stiffly. Each of them was armed with a short, stabbing sword.

"Go with them," said Ephral. "They will show you."

Voruum gestured for them to lead on. At once they were taken through numerous twisting passageways, some barely large enough to accommodate them, weaving downwards and then upwards in a long climb which their guides told them led to the surface. They must have travelled a few miles,

Voruum calculated, before they clambered up a final flue, the Garganians like spiders, nimble and silent. Beyond the opening the night sky arced overhead like a brilliantly lit dome, its stars dazzling in their profusion. One of the twin moons blazed like the eye of a god, igniting the terrain.

They could hear a repetitive chanting, a monotonous dirge that rose and fell, the swelling of many unified voices. One of the guides, Rumel, pointed to the small crater spread out below, a natural hollow, its rocks and shelves picked out vividly by the lunar light. Voruum and Kaarri were high up, well hidden from the events occurring on the flat central area of the crater. They realised at once that the gathering of some hundred figures below could only be the Brotherhood of the Goat. Each of them wore a cowl, their faces well hidden. Voruum wondered if there were humans there, men from Melkor. He dare not mind probe them and whispered as much to Kaarri, who nodded.

At one end of the crater, a set of slabs rose like steps to a flattened top, where twin braziers glowed, sending showers of sparks upward. Between these stood a solitary figure, its thick grey robes blurring its shape, although its own features were visible. Neither Voruum nor Kaarri recognised the man, although it was not a Garganian. The head was large, seemingly without a neck, the face daubed with markings, the eyes bulging, gleaming in the firelight. The man wore a headdress, a bone-coloured helm with twin, curling horns, those of a great goat.

Rumel leaned close to Voruum. "He is Rannas Kavannian, their high priest. It is said he has inherited Dream Lord powers."

The high priest lifted his arms and the chanting ceased immediately. The night fell utterly silent, an airless void. "The day of retribution will soon be upon us, children of Shaitan," he said. His voice was powerful, disturbingly so. Voruum felt it strike him like a wave, as if it would flow into him and flush out his secrets. He felt Kaarri flinch beside him, similarly stunned. Below them the

gathered minions raised their own voices in a unified reply.

"As Shaitan commands us, so shall we obey."

"Those who defy Shaitan will be purged. Soon we shall smite them."

Again came the reply, ringing out eerily around the rocks and stone parapets of the crater. Voruum felt something in that sound, an undercurrent, something evil and vast, beyond the confines of this place. A cruel, avaricious power was bending over them, its talons reaching out. It was an effort to close his mind to it. He found himself gripping Kaarri's hand, but she made no objection, her own eyes narrowing as she shielded herself.

"Brothers, you have your commands," said the priest. "Tomorrow you will make your final preparations. When the dawn of the next day breaks, we will take Annakor. Spare no one! Blood for the Great Goat. He will drink deep. He will increase your powers! All the children will rise and Gargan will fall to us." He pointed at the heavens, to the bright star that was Earth. "There!" he shouted.

Below him the figures lifted their arms in supplication, as though the star represented their god. The sound of their voices rose to a roar, a snarl of hunger for blood.

"Our homeworld calls us," said the priest. "Our brothers who dwell there are gathering as we are. When we meet, the spawn of Galad Sarian will be smitten for the last time. Shaitan will again hold sway." And again the sonorous chanting began.

Voruum pulled Kaarri away. "We've seen enough. This has to be stopped. There's no time to go back and warn Melkor. You heard that monster. The day after tomorrow. We must go to Annakor and warn the men there."

"And defend it," she replied.

"We are agreed?"

She nodded. "We have the element of surprise. And—our powers."

"Yes." However, Voruum shielded his

thoughts on this. Rannas Kavannian would have strong mental powers himself. To go up against him could be foolhardy. And yet there was no other way. Here in this remote desert, they were isolated, with no means of contacting Melkor. Ironically Melkor had sent them here and made it so, as part of their test.

Shortly after dawn, Voruum and Kaarri spoke again with Ephral.

"Where were those men from?" Voruum asked him. "There were so many."

"Some were from Annakor itself. Did you see the high priest, Rannas Kavannian? He is the deputy to Hors Tannis, Governor of Annakor. You see now how you have been isolated. Since you have agreed to help us, I will get you into Annakor. The *phorud* is active there, already preparing to defend the citadel."

They wasted no time and Ephral took them by another system of passageways up to the surface, where the cloudless skies were already filled with the crimsons and pinks of day. The *phorud* provided a number of zmereen, the short-legged Garganian version of horses. Although they were little more than skin and bone, they were hardy beasts and bore Voruum and Kaarri well enough. They set out with a handful of the Garganians, led by Ephral, and crossed the featureless wastes, blending with them, almost invisible. Voruum exercised a little mental power to shield them, though he knew there would be danger in over-using it, and possibly drawing unwanted attention.

It was evening by the time they topped a broken ridge that gave them a clear view of the long slope beyond, where Annakor nestled amongst the crags of a lone outcrop, surrounded by an ocean of red Garganian sand. Its buildings were stark, with long walls dropping to the dust bowl floor. There was no visible sign of potential ingress, and the towers and high buildings presented the aspect of a fortress.

Ephral had the party dismount, and the zmereen were led away to cover. Once again, the remaining party took to the passageways under the ground, sliding deep into the cool embrace of the dark stone, the light fading.

"Rannas Kavannian uses his powers to watch the desert," said Ephral. "He believes the only threat to his plans would come from Melkor, should the city send a force here before he has taken Annakor. He knows it would be unlikely, but nevertheless, he watches."

"Does he know of the *phorud*?" said Kaarri.

"A little. He is dismissive. For many years, Man has thought of the Garganians as a dying race, incapable of defiance. If a few rebels crawl around under the streets, muttering their discord, what does it matter?" Ephral smiled grimly. "We are far stronger than he realises. You will see."

When they reached the lower tunnels of the citadel, Ephral led Voruum and Kaarri to the basement of a storehouse, a vast place, filled with a variety of minerals that had been mined by the people of Annakor, some for use in the laboratories above, others for export to Melkor. The place was tended by Garganians, servants deemed to be simple beings, pack horses for the drudgery of the work in this place. They greeted Ephral eagerly.

"I have had word sent to Komis Ladrac," he said. "He is an administrator, a man we can trust. He will coordinate the men who will oppose Rannas Kavannian's plot. I have told him about you."

Voruum and Kaarri exchanged uneasy glances but nodded. They followed Ephral up a long, winding stairway. Several Garganians had been posted along the way, all of them apparently loyal to Ephral. Voruum began to realise the *phorud's* strength, its slick organization.

High above, they entered another series of rooms, these well furnished, almost opulent, and Voruum could see they were the apartments of officialdom. There were men here, busily going through documents, and none of them appeared to be armed. Some of them were too preoccupied to look up. Others gave Ephral and his human companions no more than cursory glances. He was evidently known to them.

In another room, a lone figure sat behind a huge desk, waiting. He stood and offered his hand to Ephral and then Voruum and Kaarri. About forty years of age, he had a military stiffness, his uniform spotless. He did wear a small sword at his side. "Be welcome in Annakor," he said. "I am Komis Ladrac. Ephral has sent word to me in advance. We are more than glad to have you with us, though our forces are small."

"You know of the dawn assault?" Voruum asked him.

Ladrac nodded. "Rannas Kavannian will want to wipe out all my colleagues that have not come under his sway, and when he does that, his supporters will be ready to kill anyone who protests. It will be a blood bath. Fortunately my colleagues have been forewarned. When the Brotherhood strikes, we will defend ourselves. Rannas Kavannian will not be expecting that. The whole affair will be in the balance. Tell me, what level have you two attained?"

Voruum could sense the underlying fears of the administrator. He lacked confidence, knowing the power of his enemies. "We are training to be Witchfinders. We came out into the desert to undertake our final tests."

"You mean—you are novices?" Ladrac could not keep the disappointment out of his voice.

Voruum would have replied, but the door opened and one of the men came in, closing it quickly and facing Ladrac, his face lined with anxiety.

"Sir, you are to be visited. Rannas Kavannian is almost here."

Ladrac swore softly. "Very well. Ephral—take your companions and get behind that arras." He indicated the rich tapestry that covered one of the walls. "Can you shield yourselves?" he asked Voruum. "Do your powers extend to that? If not, and Rannas Kavannian discovers you, you'll be taking no further part in our defence of Annakor."

Voruum nodded. He, Ephral and Kaarri did as bidden. There was an alcove behind the arras, barely large enough to accommodate them. No sooner had they secreted themselves before they heard the door open again. They felt the presence of a newcomer. Rannas Kavannian had entered the room, accompanied, Voruum sensed, by two other men, likely bodyguards.

"My dear Komis, you must pardon this late intrusion," came Rannas Kavannian's rich base tones. "I'm sure you're a busy man."

"Never too busy to speak to a colleague. All is well with you?"

"Indeed," said the visitor and Voruum could almost picture that huge head, those bulging eyes. And more—he could feel the mind probe. Rannas Kavannian was a cautious man, his mental cloak spread around him. No doubt it would always be.

"I'm sure this will be inconvenient, Komis, but it occurred to me we have not had an inspection and all the requisite drills for some time."

"That's so, Rannas. However, all's quiet here. We've a lot to do—"

"Invariably. However, I've spoken to Hors Tannis and he has approved my recommendation. I want everyone turned out an hour after dawn. That's the entire population, not just the guards."

Ladrac murmured accession.

Rannas walked across to the tapestry, which was a slightly faded panorama of an old Garganian battle. He stood before it, his eyes widening as he studied it and ran his fingers across it. "Some of these old Garganian works are very impressive. What battle was this?"

Ladrac had not moved, masking his fears for the two novices and Garganian hidden behind the tapestry. "Oh—it was fought close to Melkor. Galad Sarian striking at the acolytes of the forces who once sought to overthrow the capital. He is the central figure. The Garganians still regard him as a kind of messiah."

Rannas Kavannian scowled. He touched the massed ranks of the shapes rising from the forest, swarming in the air, and the thick black clouds above the entire scene, where they boiled in the shape of a horned head. Sarian's gleaming weapon, a brilliantly lit star lance, that could cast molten fire, formed the centre of the drama. "The Garganian weavers amaze me, with their predilection for sensationalism. I suspect the battle has been grossly exaggerated. If I recall my history correctly, Sarian was taken in chains to Earth shortly after this incident."

Behind the arras, Voruum could sense the murky probing of Rannas Kavannian's mind. Voruum reached out and grasped Kaarri's hand. Their fingers interlocked as they silently formed their defence. Voruum took the initiative and raised a physical wall in front of them, something to deflect the workings of the Deputy Governor, so close to them. Voruum's body trembled slightly as he applied himself, drawing energy from deep within him, daring to stretch himself beyond the barriers he had previously set himself. He could feel Kaarri shuddering beside him.

Ladrac had no mental powers other than those attributed to a normal man, and it took all his self control to cloak his relief when Rannas Kavannian turned away from the tapestry.

"An hour after dawn," said the Deputy Governor. "Have everyone prepared." He left abruptly, the door closing behind him.

Ladrac waited until he could be sure the man was not coming back. He locked the door and went to the arras. "It's safe to come out."

Voruum, Kaarri and Ephral emerged, all looking a little shaken.

"I thought he would expose you," said Ladrac. "You were lucky the tapestry deflected his attention. Perhaps that had something to do with Galad Sarian. Even now his powers sometimes touch us."

Voruum nodded, deciding to say nothing about the strength of the shield he had erected.

Kaarri remained equally silent, regarding him oddly, as though in sharing and aiding his powers she had been bruised, or at least shaken by their intensity.

"I am certain that Rannas Kavannian will want to observe as much of central Annakor as he can during the coming conflict. There is a tower, the tallest in the city. From its parapets he will be able to study, and no doubt conduct, events below. As the high priest of the cult, he will draw upon the darkness he is wedded to. I fear for our people."

"Are there other towers?" said Voruum. "Somewhere where he can be watched?"

Ladrac nodded. "If you go there, you would be be in grave danger of exposure, highly vulnerable."

"We'll have to take that chance. Kaarri?"

She nodded, for a moment wrapped up in her thoughts.

"I will go and see to the *phorud's* last preparations," said Ephral, leaving them.

"This mock inspection," said Voruum. "What will it entail?"

"If everyone in Annakor is brought out into the daylight, they will be easier targets for Rannas Kavannian's killers. There are just over three hundred of us. Our ranks, however, will be swelled by the *phorud*. We may have the balance in numbers, but only a few of us are trained fighters. If the battle hangs in the balance, much will depend on the dark forces that Rannas Kavannian unleashes. As for you—"

"We will oppose him directly," said Voruum.

Kaarri threw him a glance and he felt its intensity, its undercurrent of fear. This would be dangerous new ground for them. They were untested. She looked at the tapestry and the boiling darkness it depicted. Were those horrors again to be summoned up from the pits of night?

* * * *

Dawn was spreading a rich red glow over the horizon as the twin Garganian moons slid together below the rocks and crags of the outer desert. A deep crimson flowed across the heavens, drinking the last of the night sky stars, a crimson that warned of blood and carnage and all the horrors that a war would bring. Everything was still. From the tower where Voruum and Kaarri crouched, they watched the daylight, fast as a tide, limning the sand and its fangs of rock, highlighting the taller buildings of Annakor and in particular the tower beyond them. This was the highest point of the city, where Rannas Kavannian must be readying his ultimate betrayal.

"You seem certain of yourself," Kaarri whispered to Voruum. "I felt something within you, a strength beyond anything I have known myself. What have you inherited?"

He shook his head. "I am afraid of it, Kaarri. I have sensed it before, but wondered if it might be a darker part of me. Yet if we are to confound Rannas Kavannian and the forces he will bring, perhaps it is right to tap into it. All battle, conflict is ugly. It cannot be suppressed, however much merit there may be in the use of power. To kill and destroy, even evil things, is necessarily unpleasant."

"Yet you are committed?"

"This is no time to falter. What comes must be driven back, at all costs."

Beyond them, up on the high tower, Rannas Kavannian appeared, wearing his goat's head helm and bearing a carved staff, which he held aloft, both his arms outspread. His voice carried as he invoked something invisible in the bloody heavens. From the tip of his staff, power speared upwards and a sudden rush of clouds curdled overhead, a massing of shapes, whirling and twisting. Faces leered, demonic, hateful, and lightning crackled around Annakor. A sudden boom of thunder rocked the city's very stones.

Down in the streets, voices came up to Voruum and Kaarri, shrieks and cries, the sounds of torment and chaos. Voruum crawled to the parapet and looked down. In spite of the dawn, darkness coiled around the streets like an immense serpent, but the shapes within it clashed and fought, the ringing of steel clear. It was impossible to determine how the battle was unfolding.

Voruum turned his attention upon the high priest, who was now bathed in the crimson glow of the heavens, as if in blood, his head flung back, his words of power stirring the massed clouds that were lowering. If those terrible entities, creatures of the ultimate darkness, were allowed to spew forth upon the struggling masses below, Annakor would be lost, snared by Shaitan's servants. Voruum slowly stood, his hand reaching out for Kaarri's. For a moment she stared up at him, her terror evident, but them she drew herself upright, her face a mask of determination, her expression the one Voruum knew best.

Their hands locked and they stood on the parapet, facing the monstrous Rannas Kavannian. The high priest was so immersed in his convocation of the legions of hell he didn't at first notice them. Beside him, a trio of guards did see the two figures on the lower tower. At once they unleashed a dozen arrows, but as they hummed through the air, Voruum's mental shield scattered them.

"Let me be the focus," Voruum said to Kaarri. "Lend me your own powers. Blended with mine, they may yet provide a diversion for Rannas Kavannian."

He felt her body shudder, but she drew on whatever resources she could and allowed the power to flow through her arm and hand into him. With a supreme effort he flung a bolt of energy upwards. He felt it strike the high priest, who staggered, his concentration crippled. His connection with the nightmare hordes overhead momentarily snapped and the lowering of those screaming clouds paused. Rannas Kavannian screamed in outrage and swung round to look down at the interlopers.

He directed energy from his staff at them, a bolt of pure hatred. Voruum's defence caught it like a shield, bending and buckling under the awful pressure, his mind reeling, teetering on the brink of madness. He gripped Kaarri's hand more tightly and redoubled his efforts. Above him, Rannas Kavannian screamed his rage. He was forced to turn and face the things in the skies, the swirling whirlpool of fiends he had conjured. Without his control, they threatened to tear themselves apart, or sink into the city and wreak unchecked havoc, totally beyond control.

Voruum sensed that the high priest could not risk such loss of command. His nefarious plans depended on control of the demonic forces. As he again raised his staff and pointed it upwards, Voruum flung a bolt of energy up at him and saw it smack like a wave into him, the high priest shuddering, almost losing his balance on the parapet. Again his control of the sky beings wavered and as he righted himself, a fist of crimson cloud swung downwards and smashed aside the other men on the tower, their bodies swatted like flies, sent tumbling over the edge and down to their doom far below.

Voruum could feel Kaarri reaching the end of her strength. It had drained from her and she sagged, her fingers loosing their grip on his. He stood over her, snarling his rage, hurling yet another bolt of mental energy upwards. He felt it smack up against Rannas Kavannian, who, torn between defending himself and a desperate bid to control the overhead powers, lurched sideways and lost his footing. Thunder detonated overhead and a sudden collapse of the clouds smothered the high tower in a bloody shroud.

Below him, Voruum also fell to his knees, his own powers seeping away like fluid down a drain. He felt the darkness closing in, all sound diminishing. The last thing he heard before he passed out was something clawing its way across the stone towards him, a fanged horror, eager to swallow his life.

When he came to, Kaarri was again holding his hand. Behind her, the stones of the tower's floor were smeared with oozing muck, as if something living had burst.

Voruum tried to speak, but the girl put her free hand on his head, soothing him.

"Rest," she said. "You stood on the brink of death's precipice."

"You...brought me back?"

She smiled grimly. "I almost joined you and that final plummet into oblivion. What energy I had left I used to destroy that abomination." She indicated the remains of whatever had died on the stones.

Voruum studied the sky. The sunlight had shredded the last of the clouds and the crimson bowl of the heavens curved overhead, shimmering with the rising heat of day. Below the tower, the city had fallen silent, apart from a few shouts. The noise of battle had been displaced with something far more tranquil. Someone came up on to the tower with them, and through the haze, Voruum recognised Ephral.

"Is it over?" Voruum asked him, rising unsteadily to his feet.

Ephral helped Kaarri get Voruum to his feet. "Yes," he said. "We have been up on to the tower where Rannas Kavannian attempted his coup. The dark powers he tried to control turned on him and tore him apart. And you? You are able to walk?"

Voruum nodded and Ephral led the two of them down into the tower and along silent corridors to the building where Komis Ladrac had his offices.

"I should warn you," said Ephral. "Ladrac suffered in the conflict." He opened a door and the three of them went inside. Two guards stood on either side of the Deputy Governor, who was slumped in a chair, his face drained, his eyes unusually wide, gazing into the distance.

Voruum could feel the damage done to the man, his ruined mind. It had been charred, as though whatever energies fuelled it had failed it. Ladrac seemed to be gazing on something deeply disturbing, if unfocused.

"He remembers nothing," said Ephral. "You will be no more than passing shadows to him now."

* * * *

The Governor of Annakor, Hors Tannis, was a short, stocky man of middling age, who looked more of an administrator than a fighter, Voruum thought. Tannis rose from his seat as Voruum and Kaarri were escorted into his presence, and he regarded them nervously.

"I understand from my staff that you are neophytes from Melkor," he said in a soft, anxious voice. "I also understand that you were recently involved in an incident out in the desert where a number of soldiers were killed."

"We believe," said Voruum, "that it was the work of Rannas Kavannian's Brotherhood. We were fortunate to escape."

"I gather Ephral and his Garganians protected you."

"Indeed, sir."

"Just as well. Your training would have come to a sticky end had you not kept yourselves out of the affray. Blooding yourselves against a monster like Rannas Kavannian would have been disastrous."

Voruum read something in Ephral's mind, a hint of amusement.

"That madman over-reached himself. I am glad to say that his servants fell apart and surrendered to us once their high priest died. I'm sure some got away. Perhaps your masters in Melkor will set you and others like you after them. I don't hold with these mind powers myself. They can only bring pain and suffering, and if Man persists in toying with them, he will regret it in the end. My advice to you is to go back to Melkor and concentrate on your physical attributes. Be soldiers by all means, but do not seek to become Witchfinders."

Voruum and Kaarri bowed. "We understand, sir."

Later, outside the gates of Annakor, Voruum and Kaarri sat with Ephral and a number of the *phorud,* all mounted on zmereen. Ephral's warriors had located the ground-hopper where it had been hidden in the desert, and led the way across the sweeping sands to the place of its concealment.

Voruum edged his mount close to Kaarri's. "What will you say in your report?" he asked her.

Her eyes avoided his. "I know what I should say. I should tell the truth. That you have powers beyond those of a normal man. More, that is, than those of us who are selected to train to be Witchfinders. The kind of powers that could be shaped and developed into something forbidden. Dream Lord power, perhaps."

"You exaggerate—"

"Do I?" She flashed him a reprimanding look. "I felt something when we touched and stood against the high priest, a power that separates us. It drew me, I admit. But I fear it, as you should. My own mental powers are small compared to yours, a frightened bird compared to an eagle."

"You will report this?"

She turned away. "No. I will not betray you, Arrul Voruum. You must learn to deal with this for yourself."

"And our partnership?"

Still she faced away from him, looking up at the crimson skies, where nothing stirred in the blazing heat. "Once our training is over, we will go our separate ways. Earth is a wide planet, with room enough to distance us."

Voruum said nothing more. He knew what was inside her: he'd felt it during the wild moments of union, when she could not mask her emotions any more than he could. It was closed to him now. Perhaps, he thought, that would change, before their destinies parted them, beyond Melkor.

⚛

HORIZON

by John Gregory Betancourt

In one of my earliest complete memories, my twin brother Jacob and I are lying comfortably in a nograv field some five or six kilometers above the ground. This is our birthday; we are five years old. Like me, Jake is tall and thin for his age, with wavy brown hair, eyes the color of molten gold, strong, high cheekbones, and a scattering of light freckles on his face. When we laughed together, as often we did in those days, our voices held music.

That particular night ten billion stars lit the heavens. The air tasted cold and crisp and thin, but this high up we felt no breeze and had no real sense of movement. We simply lay on the air as though on a mattress, floating high above the planet. I searched among the stars for signs of the Freedom Brigade's ships closing in on Horizon, but of course they were impossible to find, too small and insignificant amid the greater cosmic vastness.

"Teddy," my brother said.

I looked over at him. I could see a fierce determination in his eyes. He was scared, but did not want to show it. He could put up with anything this night, when epic wonders had been promised. He always wanted so desperately to be brave like me.

"There's nothing to be afraid of," I said softly. I held out my hand and he took it. Together we waited.

Suddenly the sky lit up with lancets of white fire. Pulse cannons from the Brigade's ships split the darkness overhead with brilliant pyrotechnic effect again and again. I felt Jake cringe a little beside me, and I squeezed his hand, trying to be brave for both of us. The weapons were in space, so of course we heard and felt nothing, and yet I imagined a far-off rumble like distant thunder.

At last the cannons stopped. Bright spots swam before my eyes. I blinked rapidly until they went away. Then, slowly, like a mist descending, white and pink and yellow streaks of light began to paint the heavens above and around us: not weapons this time, but debris cascading down in a gentle rain of color. The Brigade had blasted several dozen asteroids to rubble, creating a spectacular cosmic fireworks display such as few worlds had ever seen.

They had done this just to amuse my brother and me. It was, after all, our birthday. That's how important they considered the twin sons of Faraday Meriman III, the only direct heirs to the Meriman Empire.

That was my first important memory. My second is this:

When we were twelve, our father took us with him on an inspection tour of fifty Outer Rim planets. Officially we saw him only a handful of times in the two month trip, always when he had important speeches to deliver and we were required to stand beside him in silence as he made them. Then he wore his deep red Emperor's uniform, with twin rows of gold buttons on the front of his blouse and gold piping on the sleeves, shoulders, and chest. On his right breast he bore the Meriman family crest stitched in platinum thread: a pair of Mother Earth lions facing each other, holding a crown and a planet in their paws. He seemed a different man in his uniform: serious, unsmiling, somehow cold and aloof, a force to be reckoned with. I felt uneasy in his presence.

Unofficially we dined with him almost every evening aboard the *Pegasus*, flagship of his hundred-thousand-ship fleet. Then, when we were alone, he made a special effort to return to his old self, talking to us like equals, telling stories from our family history, making jokes, the thin lines crinkling up around his eyes with laughter.

But those few stolen minutes each day seemed fleeting, scarcely enough. Mostly we spent our days aboard the *Pegasus* as we spent them at home, in studies, strenuous physical exercise, and other training designed to prepare us for the day we took on more responsibility in running the Meriman Empire. Already we had begun receiving the deep mental stims that would allow us to govern effectively. My mind turned constantly like a well oiled wheel, analyzing, calculating, computing.

When we reached the thirty-fifth stop on the tour, an undistinguished planet called Dulap's World, Father agreed to personally address an assembly of local politicians, since that was their custom. We all rode down in the *Hydra*, one of our planet-hoppers, but of course his advisors clumped around him in the main salon like predatory birds, rehearsing his speech. He had no time for us now.

Sighing, I crossed to the huge oval portal set in the starboard side of the hull. Jake already stood there, arms behind his back, gazing out. As always when we accompanied Father for a speech, we wore red uniforms that matched his in style and cut, complete with red caps with black brims, shiny

leather boots, and short capes with red silk linings. I hardly recognized Jake in his uniform: he looked older, more dignified, more important.

As I joined him, he continued to stare out the portal, not smiling. I cleared my throat.

"Fifteen more worlds," I told him.

"I hate it here," he said.

I put my hand on his shoulder. "Me, too. It's a horrible little planet."

"Not Dulap's World. *All* of it. Space. I want to go home."

"I know," I murmured. I felt the same way. After seeing the splendors of Horizon, who could possibly want to go anywhere else?

Leaning forward, I gazed down at the soft, cloud-wisped grayish sphere below us. A single continent covered most of the planet. From orbit, the mottled browns and grays of the land seemed singularly uninviting. The few small, splotchy seas seemed almost out of place. *Dulap's World.* Planets should have more color, I thought: green trees, brilliant blue-green oceans, dazzling white polar ice caps. What drab, colorless people must live here.

"We won't stay long," Jake said.

"How do you know?"

"I called up Father's speech while you were dressing. It's sharp and to the point. The people here petitioned for sovereignty,

but of course that's ridiculous, and they must be put in their place. He doesn't even plan on granting audiences afterward."

"Ah." It sounded like we'd be back aboard the *Pegasus* by dinner time.

Our planet-hopper entered the atmosphere with the faintest of bumps. We descended rapidly, soaring over barren, almost desertlike expanses, and soon a small spaceport came into view: several square kilometers of reinforced gray duracrete and a handful of squat brown administration and maintenance buildings.

As we landed gently, the artificial gravity shut off and my stomach gave a brief lurch. Dulap's World had slightly less mass than Horizon. Then our ship equalized atmospheric pressure with the outside world and broke the environment seals. My ears popped.

Field attendants floated out to meet us on broad nograv sleds. They all seemed to be wearing gray uniforms with our family's crest in black over their hearts.

"At least they're punctual," I muttered.

Several dozen Argents, elite members of the Freedom Brigade who served as our family's personal guards, poured forth and began to scan everything and everyone with their detection equipment. So far, they had uncovered two assassination attempts against Father this year—both by the Borgialis, our main rivals among the human Families—so I didn't mind the delay. They commandeered a nograv sled from the welcoming committee and flew off toward the arena where Father would speak. They would secure it before we arrived.

"Jacob. Theodore," a high old-man's voice said behind us. "You know your duties here, of course."

"Yes, sir," we both said without turning. It was Timon Crote, our father's chief advisor and second in authority over the Meriman Empire.

"It is polite to look at someone when he addresses you."

"Very well." I turned, frowning. "I had not meant to be rude."

"Of course not."

Mr. Crote's deeply set brown eyes searched my own. He had pinched cheeks and a narrow, almost hatchet face. His graying black hair, cut short with more practicality than style, accentuated the thinness of his features. He wore black and gold, with the Meriman family crest over his heart.

"What did you want to tell us?" Jake asked.

"It is very important," he said, "that you appear quiet and dignified at all times in public here. The Dulapers prize that in children."

"We know," Jake said.

"You have already told us twice today," I added coolly. Crote had grown up without mental stims, I reminded myself. He had no real knowledge of how they changed and matured you. "We have always done our duty, Mr. Crote. Father may depend on that. As may you."

He nodded. "But you are both still children. It *is* easy to forget."

"Not for us." As if our stims would let us forget anything. I nodded toward the hatch. "It's time for us to go, I believe."

He glanced out the hatch, saw that the Argents had secured the spaceport, and nodded. Father, still surrounded by his advisors, was already descending through the airlock and onto the main sled's platform.

"Hurry, then. We don't want to be left behind."

Jake and I followed our father out, then came Mr. Crote, then more advisors and Argents. A static shield crackled over us as we stepped aboard the nograv sled; it would protect us from dust and wind as we traveled. Jake and I found benches to the rear and sat, putting our feet up, watching the bustle of preparations. Crote headed forward, probably to check on our father. He might be our shepherd, but Father remained his chief concern.

"What did they feed you today?" Jake asked me suddenly.

He didn't mean food, but stims. We tended to be a day or two apart on them. At the moment, I was ahead.

"The history of the N'gao Family." I made a face. Political stims were always the worst, since you couldn't see any immediate applications for the knowledge. "Did you know that six hundred and forty-three years ago, Constance N'gao lost Earth in a minor war with our seventeen-times great grandfather, Hubert Díaz Meriman?"

"Did I care?"

"Probably not." I certainly didn't. It wasn't like Earth held a position of strategic or political importance even before our great-grandfather[17] Hubert had removed the entire human population and turned it into a natural game preserve. Nor did I care that Fyodor N'gao had vowed to obliterate our family ten generations ago, or that Fyodor's grandson, Edward, had made an honorable peace with us that lasted to this day. The N'gaos were a minor Family now, controlling only a few hundred planets. Why should they concern me?

When everyone had boarded safely, the sled rose, raising a thick cloud of dust which did not penetrate the static shield. Engine whining faintly, we turned and headed east.

The rising sun, large and pale orange, did nothing to color the land. We glided over kilometer after kilometer of arid near-desert, broken only by clusters of lumpy yellow vegetation. Finally irrigated farmlands appeared, orderly fields of golden wheat and rye and oats, broken here and there by small clusters of human-style buildings. Dulap's world exported a dozen different grains to the rest of the Meriman Empire, I knew; much of the work was done by autons or menial aliens like shais or jibbs. Barely two hundred thousand humans lived here. All led spartan existences, devoting themselves to religion and eschewing material goods.

Ten minutes later a small city appeared. Stims told me its name: Secula. It sprawled more than towered, with plain duracrete and steel buildings no taller than four or five stories. I had little time to examine it. Our sled veered sharply to the left before we got close, heading toward what looked like an open-air stadium. As we passed over it, my mind ran unbidden through calculations: two thousand three hundred and ten seats, though only three hundred and sixty-one Dulapers had yet arrived. All were men and women with dark brown or black hair, and all dressed in shades of gray. We had arrived early. More Dulapers would undoubtedly show up while Father prepared to address them.

The sled landed on the far side of the arena, and the Argents waiting on the ground signaled that everything had been secured: no energy weapons, bombs, or usual power sources had been detected. One of our liaison officers—a tall red-headed man with the Meriman Family crest blazed in silver on his right breast—hurried aboard the sled and knelt before Father. Jake and I were too far away to hear their words, but his report apparently met with approval, since Father rose and allowed himself to be escorted inside the stadium. The rest of his advisors and attendants began to file out. Jake and I came last.

"The Dulapers like blood sports," Jake told me in a low voice. "Every town and city has an arena like this one, where men and women fight and slay wild animals."

"That isn't in the planetary report," I said, giving him a puzzled look. "How did you find out?"

"I overheard some of the Argents talking about it," he said, "before you reached the planet-hopper."

"What weapons do the Dulapers use?"

"As primitive as possible. Sometimes knives and swords. Sometimes nothing but bare hands."

"Interesting." It made sense, now that I thought about it. "They live such repressed lives, this must be how they vent their emotions."

"That was my conclusion, too."

Mr. Crote had been waiting for us at the foot of the ramp. He ushered us inside to a small nearly unfurnished gray room. Hard benches lined the walls. I wondered briefly if the Dulapers had ever heard of cushions.

"Perhaps they're punishing us for owning their planet," Jake said with a grin, as if he'd been reading my thoughts.

"If so, they're punishing themselves, too. The arena didn't have any cushions, either."

We sat anyway. I could hear Father's booming voice from next door as he spoke with various local dignitaries. They were discussing trade and climate control, dull stuff all, and my attention wandered to the fabric of my uniform. There were one thousand, six hundred and thirteen individual threads in my pants, and when those threads were stretched out, they would extend roughly oh-point-two-six-five kilometers from end to end. A useless fact. I began to pick at the threads, wondering briefly how they were made. Stims heightened mental computational abilities, or provided raw facts when you needed them, but only within their narrow areas of expertise. Clearly no one thought I would ever want to know the manufacturing process of textiles.

"Stop that, Theodore," Timon Crote said from the doorway.

I looked up guiltily, letting my hand drop to my side. There were twenty-two thousand and four threads in Crote's black uniform. Thirty-six gold buttons. Three-point-six-three meters of gold piping. *Useless facts.* It was hard to shut down your brain when you were bored.

Crote knelt before Jake and me. Mentally I rolled my eyes: another of his little lectures. When would he learn we no longer needed them?

"The speech and ceremony won't last more than an hour," he told us, straightening my collar. I searched his old brown eyes for any trace of sympathy, but found none. "This has been a troublesome world," he went on, "and your father needs you beside him to show the value he places on family. The Dulapers appreciate that. Do you understand?"

"Yes, sir," Jake and I both said together. It was the same on every world. The sooner we

agreed, the sooner we could move on.

"Good." He nodded solemnly. "I'll make sure you get a surprise tonight after dinner if you hold up your end of the bargain."

"You don't need to bribe us to behave," I told him.

"Then you won't have to do any work to earn a reward, will you, Theodore?"

"Perhaps . . . chocolate?" Jake asked.

I sighed and glanced at him sideways. "You're not helping," I told him. He pretended not to notice. He had always had a weakness for Mother Earth delicacies, especially chocolate. I preferred Horizon's own confections, particularly the delicately layered pastries which our cooks prepared on high holidays.

Crote said, "It would not be a surprise if I told you, would it, Jacob?"

"No, sir."

Crote stood, brushing imaginary dust from his black-and-gold sleeves. "We will be going outside in a minute. Come with me now. You will follow right after your father."

"Yes, sir," we both said again. No sense in arguing: he would shepherd us whether we needed it our not.

He led us into the larger and much more crowded room next door. Twenty Argents had changed into red and black dress uniforms and now lined the walls, but as always, Father was the center of attention. A dozen solemn Dulapers in their traditional loose-fitting gray shirts and pants surrounded him, listening raptly as he spoke. Several held datapads and expertly transcribed his every word. Father noticed us and winked in the middle of his conversation, and I grinned back. He had a way of making you feel like you belonged beside him no matter what the time or situation. No stim could do it. That was why he was Emperor.

The red-headed liaison officer entered the room again. "The entire Greater Dulap Assembly has convened, sir," he told Father. "Whenever you are ready."

"Very well," Father said. He motioned the Dulapers away. "We will finish this interview from orbit," he told them. "Our liaison office will arrange it."

Bowing, they backed away, then filed out through the side door. The liaison officer was now deep in talks with Mr. Crote and another advisor. They had to be discussing security. Crote had argued against this tour of the Outer Rim planets, but since Father had insisted, everyone was taking great pains to keep us safe.

Old fashioned trumpets sounded outside. Everyone in the room shifted anxiously, and two Argents pushed open huge double doors leading into the center of the stadium. I craned to see and glimpsed tiers of seats packed with men and women dressed in various shades of gray.

Twenty more Argents in red and gold dress uniforms had been waiting against the far wall. They paraded out first; they were acting as honor guard and would surround Father while he spoke. Next came Father himself—not walking, but floating half a meter above the ground on a personal nograv sled. Like a returning hero, he raised one hand in salute as he passed through the portal. Jake and I followed on foot. Next came Timon Crote and the liaison officer, then finally another twenty Argents, these men and women dressed in full battle gear: black body armor, boots with gravity plates in the toes and heels, and helmets with the protective visors down. They all carried heavy energy pulse rifles.

Outside, without the protection of a static shield, the air felt cool but dry. Strangely aromatic pollens spiced the air, giving it a curious scent somewhere between sesame and caraway. Above, orange cumulous clouds glided across a yellowish sky.

A replica of Father's gold-and-ivory throne on Horizon, though smaller and a little less magnificent, sat in the center of the stadium on a low dais. It seemed to shine with an inner light.

Father stepped from his nograv sled onto the dais, then seated himself. All the time he gazed off into the distance as though deep in thought. His body language spoke of strength, confidence, and power. As Jake and I took our places at his right hand, Mr. Crote and the red-haired liaison officer moved to his left. Trumpets sounded once more, but as yet nobody spoke.

I kept my head still, moving my eyes only a little to take in the crowds. Empty seats filled the upper sections of the arena. Exactly eight hundred and fifty-three men and women had assembled here to listen to Father's speech, I calculated. There was a strange stillness to them which I could not quite read, and they all looked grim, as though they come already determined to find fault with whatever Father said.

Trumpets sounded again. The honor guard snapped to attention and gave three short cheers. As they finished, Father rose and noticed, seemingly for the first time, those gathered before him.

"We are one people in a hostile universe," he said, as we had heard him say on so many worlds before this one, the words thundering out so all could hear. "We are one people, and we must continue to work as one or we will surely perish."

He spoke for exactly an hour, telling stories of the wonders of the universe . . . and the terrors. He told of the alien Pollox, who had tried to enslave three human worlds before the Freedom Brigade drove them off. His anger and outrage hung thick in the air, and I shivered as he described the torturous concentration camps in which humans had been forced to live and work and breed like animals. Next he told of the Garwan Empire, so close to our own, where aliens forced captured humans to fight each other to the death for their amusement. I shared in his anger and disgust as he painted an image of a homeworld so brutal, so savage and inhumane, that the Freedom Brigade had no choice but to destroy it. And lastly he told of the Irenz, whose ships raided our commerce lanes because they considered human flesh a delicacy. I felt horror and rage run through me like an electric current as he described their killing rooms, where humans were dismembered and eaten, often while still alive. Hunting down the last of their pirate fleet had been a worthy crusade, benefiting all humanity.

It was a variation on his standard speech, nearly the same as he had given on the thirty-four Outer Rim worlds we had already visited. His carefully modulated voice and artfully choreographed hand and head movements brought depth and emotion to his stories. The first time I had heard this speech, I cried from the sheer emotional impact.

Now, only half listening, I stared out across the faces in the crowd and wondered what these people were really like. Did they have children? Did they play games and dance and sing? Their expressions remained fixed, dour men and women with sallow complexions, long noses, and pinched cheeks.

"All these dangers and more await mankind," Father said somberly, starting to wrap things up. "It is only through strength and careful planning that we will maintain our place at the top of the galactic order. *Peace. Brotherhood. Strength.* These must remain our watch-words. There are other human Families who protect human worlds, but none have been as successful as the Merimans have been. With your strength and your loyalty, we will share the bounties of the universe together!"

He sat to light applause. I saw him frown and instantly I understood. On every planet before this one, the people had cheered for five or ten minutes whenever he spoke. I glanced at Jake and found that he, too, now watched the crowd with an uneasy expression.

"They don't like Father," he whispered to me, barely moving his lips. "Could they be shielded from the power of his voice?"

"I don't know. They fear him, at least."

"But how much?"

I had no answer. Our philosophy stims taught that love guaranteed loyalty, and after love the most powerful binding force was

fear. That's why those who didn't love Father feared him.

A man with a short graying beard came forward from the front row of Dulapers. He wore long, sweeping gray robes, and around his neck he carried the signet of the planet's governor. From his stance, I saw that he had undergone some minor stim training to boost his authority, but it was nowhere near as extensive as what Jake and I had already gone through, and before our father's towering presence, he seemed little more than a mewling snowdrab.

He dropped to one knee and proffered a rolled-up paper scroll. Timon Crote retrieved it and carried it to Father.

"Sir," the man said in a strong deep voice that I found too self-consciously controlled for my tastes. Like all such career politicians, he had been protected against the little betrayals which trained senses such as mine could read in raw humanity. I could fathom no emotion in him, neither truth nor lie, neither love nor hate for Father, nor anything in between. "We of Dulap's World have served you loyally since you brought our planet under your protective arm twenty-eight years ago. Our tithes have always been timely, our children have joined your Freedom Brigade willingly, and our hearts have rejoiced for you in your multitude of triumphs. Truly you have ushered in an age of peace for all the worlds under your rule. However, our forebears came to Dulap's World to live apart from galactic events. We have no interest in outside politics or the influence of the great Families such as yours. Indeed, we have patiently borne the loss of the cream of our youth to your Freedom Brigade and the plundering of our planetary resources. Now, though, our warehouses lie empty. Our children have gone, and there remains nothing more for you to take. Therefore we beseech you to grant us our independence. Let us live our quiet lives in our secluded corner of the galaxy, alone and at peace by ourselves."

Father still did not glance at the scroll, but I saw his hand tighten around it until his knuckles turned white. I began to tremble. Seldom had I seen him lose his perfect calm. I knew, then, that his anger was beyond all control.

Slowly, he stood. When he spoke, the words struck like the blows of a giant:

"It is the Meriman Family's destiny to unite humanity, to link the myriad human worlds and human Families, to bring forth a new Golden Age of Mankind. For the first time in generations we stand beneath the stars and know *our place is safe*. We—all of us humans, on the greatest of our worlds to the least—have forged an empire of equals the like of which has never existed before. Today all voices can be heard and all citizens can rise to the height and breadth of their ability." His voice dropped from thunder to a roar, and notes of reassurance and strength crept in. "Do not view the Freedom Brigade as a drain on your planet's resources. Step from the provincial to the galactic point of view. Those who leave Dulap's World to join the Brigade are free to return here at the end of their five years of service. If some do not return, it is because they have found new homes amidst a greater community. Be happy for them, for they have risen beyond that which can be attained here."

Suddenly he ripped the petition in half and cast it aside like a worthless bit of scrap. "Your petition is denied. Any further actions along these lines will be viewed as high treason—treason not only against the Meriman Empire, but against all humanity. For only in unity do we find safety."

The man had grown very still and very pale. He bowed his head, and I saw tears on his cheeks.

"Then we have no choice," he whispered. When he looked up, a rage equal to Father's had filled his eyes. "Death to tyrants!" he screamed. Pulling what looked like a small bone knife from one of his pockets, he leaped at us.

Father's honor guard shot him before he made it two steps. Crimson beams from twenty energy weapons danced across his body, quickly incinerating him beyond recognition. As he crumpled into himself, little more than a smoldering lump of charred meat, I smelled the sickly-sweet reek of burnt clothes and flesh, and I half gagged. Bits of gray bone showed here and there through sloughed-off skin and blackened muscle.

The governor's suicide attack had only been a diversion, I realized an instant later, as I looked up and found that all the Dulapers in the front row of seats had pulled out small hand-sized weapons of some kind. But how could this have happened? Hadn't the Argents run checks for odd energy sources?

Father was on his feet, shouting. But before he could finish, the Dulapers opened fire.

I gaped dumbly. Soft popping noises filled the stadium. What sounded like insects zipped past me on all sides. Projectile weapons? So primitive, the Argents didn't detect them. Then something hit my arm with the force of a club, half spinning me around, and I found myself staring at a raw red wound just above my right wrist. I felt nothing—no pain, no anger, no fear—and that too surprised me. Blood began to gush.

Only a heartbeat had passed since the attack began. Then someone tackled me from behind, knocking me off my feet. It was Timon Crote, I realized after a moment's struggle.

He pressed his mouth to my ear. "Keep your head down!" he said fiercely. I went limp beneath him. "Don't look up! You'll be less of a target!"

He covered me with as much of his body as he could. A few seconds later I felt him twitch and give a muffled groan. He must have been hit. His breath grew raspy. At least it told me he still lived. I bit my lip and tried to press myself down into the ground.

The popping noises lessened. Turning my head, I found I could see out a little between Crote's arm and shoulder. As far as I could tell, Father's entire honor guard had fallen. Some of the battle-ready Argents still seemed to be standing, though. They raked energy beams across the arena's seats, burning down everyone there, whether they held weapons or not. Distantly, as though far away, I could hear screams and cries of pain. A haze of acrid smoke began to descend around us, filling the stadium. Still the Argents fired and kept on firing.

The loud thrumming of a starship's engines abruptly smothered all sound. A sleek black ship, a hundred meters long, with graceful decorative fins at the tail and sides, landed between the dais and the seats. It was the *Hydra*, I saw with relief. I squirmed, trying to get out from under Crote, but he didn't move to help. He had become dead weight. Unconscious? I thought so. How badly he had been hurt? And what of Father and Jake?

The shuttle's side hatch popped open and twenty more members of the Freedom Brigade in full battle gear poured out. They dashed forward, trying to secure the area, and I heard the high-pitched whine of more energy weapons being fired. Next from the shuttle came a half dozen lammachs in white medical robes. The aliens, huge and ungainly, with unblinking black eyes, smooth featureless heads, and leathery skins of mottled green and brown, scurried toward us with hand-held stretchers.

Only now did Timon Crote try to rise. With little ceremony, two of the lammachs pulled him away, lifted me gently onto a stretcher, and carried me toward the shuttle. When I raised my head, I could see a crimson starburst on Crote's shoulder and a smear of blood on his left cheek. His eyes were glassy with shock.

"Take Mr. Crote first," I said. "He is hurt far worse than I."

"You are more important, young master," one of them said.

I lay back. It would do no good to argue with a lammachs. Besides, Crote would have agreed with them.

Aboard the shuttle, they carried me straight to the medical bay. Three more lammachs lifted me gingerly from the stretcher, carried me into a small cubicle, and set me on an examination table. I sat up and held out my arm as Dr. Sanjarin, my personal lammachs physician, activated the privacy screens. A featureless gray wall flickered into existence over the doorway and a hushed artificial silence settled over the room. Suddenly I could hear my heart thundering in my ears and my breathing felt too rapid and shallow. With a shudder, I forced my body to relax, lowering my pulse to seventy beats per minute, then sixty, then fifty-five. I had to be calm and in control, I told myself.

"Just the arm, young master, yes?" Dr. Sanjarin asked me. His large unblinking black eyes looked me over carefully. I recognized grave concern from the way the dark green skin around his throat had deepened in color.

"Yes," I said. "It's a minor wound."

"No wound is minor when it is a Meriman's. Inhale, yes?" He sprayed a fine pink mist at my head from a little canister, and I leaned into it, breathing deeply. A spicy-sweet scent like claffin flowers filled my nose and throat. Then the drug within the mist began to act on my brain, blocking pain receptors, and in half a second the tips of my fingers and toes tingled pleasantly.

Dr. Sanjarin touched the wall and a tray of medical equipment pushed out toward him. He selected a pair of surgical sheers, cut my sleeve, peeled it away, and examined my arm. It appeared to be a clean wound, I thought, drawing on my anatomy stims and trying to be objective. The projectile had passed through soft tissue, missing the bone.

"Some muscle damage here and here, yes?" he said, pointing with one of his clawed fingers. "The projectile is not embedded. You will heal well, young master, yes?"

"I hope so," I said.

"Shall I leave the scar?"

"No."

He foamed away the blood, then dabbed on a pungent green healing gel. After that he sprayed the whole area with plasts of artificial skin. I tried not to squirm as the synthetics, feeling like a thousand crawling insects, meshed with my body tissue. As my new skin slowly tightened, my arm began to throb, but it wasn't really painful, more like an unexpected pressure. After a few seconds the wound had completely disappeared.

"Inhale," he said, spraying a yellow mist before my nose. I took a deep breath, caught a faint whiff of wildflowers, and my physical senses began returning to normal. When I flexed my right arm, a dull deep ache rose inside it.

"No strenuous exercises for two days, yes?" Dr. Sanjarin cautioned.

"I'll try to be careful," I said. I slipped to the floor. My sleeve hung in tatters, so I shrugged off my uniform's cape, then the blouse, and threw them both in the corner disposal bin. I felt more comfortable in just the red undershirt. "What about my father?"

"He is already aboard. We shall see about him now, yes."

Dr. Sanjarin adjusted the room's controls. The privacy screen vanished, and I found myself gazing out into noise and commotion. Lammachs scurried this way and that with medical equipment, chattering frantically to each other half in English, half in their own tongue. I felt an undercurrent of tension in the air, and a coldness touched my heart.

He's dead, I thought numbly. *Father is dead.*

I looked around, but couldn't find my brother. I hadn't seen him since Timon Crote had tackled me. Had the Dulapers killed Jake as well? Was I the sole surviving Meriman?

Dr. Sanjarin stopped one of the apprentice lammachs medics, chittered to him, then nodded to me. "This way, yes, young master," he said softly, steering me toward a larger cubicle at the end of the medical bay. "Your parent—"

I didn't want to hear it from him. I darted ahead and pushed through the privacy screen, already dreading what I'd find.

Inside, Father lay on a medical table surrounded by half a dozen desperately working lammachs. Insectlike clusters of pulsing, beeping, chirping medical machines hunched over his body. Tubes carrying various red and white and yellow liquids pierced his arms and went down what remained of his nose and throat.

I almost broke down and cried. He had been hit by projectiles too many times in his face and chest. I could see shattered teeth through the hole where his left cheek had been. His left hand dangled over the side of the table, and blood dripped steadily from it, forming a puddle on the floor.

"He has stopped breathing again, yes," I heard Dr. Espoja, the senior lammachs physical aboard, saying to another of his people. "Get him back on the respirator, yes?"

"*Necha zo daq.* I have a pulse, yes . . ."

"Teddy—"

I glanced over. My brother stood in the corner to my right. His face was as pale as cream, and dirt or ash smudged his nose and cheek. Though filthy, his red uniform looked intact. Apparently he had not been hit. One of us had been spared, at least.

Our eyes met, and in that second I knew I'd been mistaken. He had been injured as much as me—perhaps more. Only none of his wounds were physical. He had seen everything that happened to our father. Not even his stims and body control training could hide that fact from me. It had shaken him and changed him in ways I could not quite identify as yet.

Softly he touched the new patch of skin on my bare arm. "Teddy . . ."

"I know, Jake," I whispered. "It was bad."

"He will be all right." His voice held an almost desperate note of conviction.

"He *will* be all right," I echoed. I only hoped it was true.

A dull vibration ran through the deck underfoot when the shuttle's engines powered up. I felt a moment of vertigo as we lifted, then artificial gravity cut in and smoothed the transition to space. We would not be completely safe until we reached orbit. The Dulapers had limited space-based weaponry at their disposal, I knew from the planetary

report—a few old atomics, a few extraplan-
etary missiles—and depending on how far
this conspiracy ran, surviving assassins
might try to use them against us. Our flagship, the *Pegasus*, would be able to handle
anything they had, of course. But first we
had to make it there.

Timon Crote pushed through the privacy
screen and stared at Father for a second. He,
too, had been patched up, with fresh synthetic pink skin on his left cheek. Someone
had found him a new shirt several sizes too
big which made him look even smaller and
thinner than he really was.

"Jacob, Theodore," he said softly, his
stim-augmented voice calm and persuasive
in the midst of confusion, "let the lammachs
do their work. I need you to come with me
now."

He held out his hands, and Jake and I
joined him. He led us out through the medical bay to the deserted corridor. There he
knelt and hugged us, and we hugged him
back. Then he held us at arm's length and
looked into our eyes.

"Children," he said, and then he swallowed. His eyes had become bright with un-
shed tears that no amount of control could
hide. "Ted, Jake, this is important. The lammachs will heal your father—do not worry
about that. They got to him in time. It will
take days, maybe weeks for him to fully recover, and until then we have to be strong
for him. That's what he would want. Do you
understand?"

Gravely, we both nodded.

"The entire Sixteenth Fleet has been
summoned. They will be here in a few hours.
As soon as they arrive, you must both speak
to their commander. She must see you two
together, alive and well, for in you lies the
clear line of succession to the throne. You
must try to take your father's place until he
is better. Can you do that?"

"Of course, sir," I said. There was a huge
lump in my throat. I didn't think it was possible for anyone to take our father's place,
not Jake, not me, not Timon Crote, not any-

body. But we would do our best.

"Good," he said. "We will blockade the
planet for now, until the plot can be rooted
out at its source. We will take care of that
when the fleet arrives. I will stay with your
father until he is transferred to the *Pegasus*.
As soon as we dock, go to your cabins and
get cleaned up. Put on fresh dress uniforms.
I will come for you as soon as I can, and then
we will talk more about what must be done.
Go on now."

Crote stood. Jake and I regarded him for
a moment, then turned and ran toward the
shuttle's front hatch. I could already hear
the telltale clangs of the *Pegasus*'s docking
clamps locking on. The huge metal arms
would be pulling us into our flagship's belly,
next to the five other shuttles she carried.

Atmospheric pressures had already
been matched and the airlocks flung
upon when we reached the *Hydra*'s forward compartment. Argents, now stripped
of their heavy combat gear, trudged down
the ramp with their packs and weapons over
their shoulders. Tired as they looked, they
still snapped to attention and saluted as we
reached them. Returning their salutes, Jake
and I dashed past and into the shuttle bay,
a huge echoing chamber about twice the
size of the arena in which we had been am-
bushed. Maintenance crews already scurried over the outside of the Hydra, searching for damage, and I saw another team of
lammachs surgeons hurrying toward us with
a nograv gurney in tow. That had to be for
Father.

"Dignity and authority first," Jake said
softly, slowing to a leisurely walk. He took
a deep breath and drew on his stim training.
I saw his shoulders straighten, his awkward
gallop of a run change to a confident stride,
his expression self-assured.

I mirrored his control and matched his
pace. He was right, of course. We could not
be seen running madly down the ship's corridors since it might panic the crew. We had
to remain calm and in control of ourselves,

the masters of any situation. Mr. Crote expected it of us. Father would have demanded it.

As if we had all the time in the world, we strolled up the ship's central corridor. It was as broad as a highway and as long as the *Pegasus*. Nograv sleds piloted by silvery, man-shaped autons hummed up and down its center at a rapid pace, shunting supplies from one end of our five-kilometer-long ship to the other. The air here had a sterile, recycled smell, touched with odors of machine oils and plastics.

Smaller corridors split off every twenty-five meters, leading to storage compartments. This whole level was used primarily for cargo and supplies, since it had such easy access to the shuttles. We saw few people about, mostly human overseers with work crews of squat, hairy shais or jibbs, but we nodded politely to everyone we passed. Several people stared openly at the fresh patch of pink skin on my arm, but they said nothing. Rumors would be sweeping the ship soon enough, I thought, and it was good for them to notice Jake and me so calm and unconcerned.

We passed from the red section to the blue section, and then from the blue to the gold: each color designated a different one-klick stretch of the *Pegasus*. Our family's personal quarters occupied the fifteenth deck of the gold section. We boarded a gold lift, asked for our level, and waited half a heartbeat while the computer scanned our DNA before complying.

When the blast-proof durasteel doors opened, it was like entering a different world. We might easily have been home on Horizon. I felt a deep melancholy as I stepped out onto rich, deep, sound-absorbing carpet. Delicate scents filled the air, roses and strawberries and pine needles. Soft Mother Earth music of violins and muted horns replaced the omnipresent hum of machinery.

Simulated windows lined the walls, looking out upon scenes from Horizon's two southern continents. To the left we gazed out upon a Troian savanna full of grazing roebeasts, their long serpentlike yellow necks curving over the brilliant orange grass. To the right I found winter in the mountains of Bélan. We might have been at one of our family's many secluded lodges on Horizon rather than fifty thousand lightyears away in space, I thought.

Jake and I shared a suite several doors down from father's. We had nothing fancy, just five rooms, the bare necessity for travel. As we entered the salon, we found an auton straightening up. It was a man-shaped machine, all silver, with four hands and two legs. Graceful as a ballet dancer, it started to fold itself up to roll under the sofa, but I stopped it with a curt wave.

"We need replacement uniforms," I told it, "just like the one my brother is wearing, but black and silver. Find them."

It bowed as it unfolded itself. While it glided into the closets and began selecting appropriate garments, Jake shrugged off his cape and went into his washroom. I heard splashing as he scrubbed the dirt from his face. When he came out again, he looked clean, but different. Older, somehow. There were tiny lines around his eyes that hadn't been there before, and he didn't smile like his usual happy self. He was still worried about Father, I supposed.

When the auton emerged with our clothing, Jake accepted his new uniform silently and went into his bedroom. To my surprise, his privacy shield flickered on. He probably didn't want me to see him cry, I thought. He had always been more emotional than me.

Sighing, I took my own uniform from the auton. Crote should have dived on Jake rather than me, I thought. I could have handled Father's wounds better. At least, I wanted to think so. Jake would adapt and recover, though. He just needed time.

Following my brother's example, I washed up and changed. When I returned to the salon ten minutes later, Jake was waiting, a blank, almost unreadable expression on his face. He might have just returned from a stim-course on nospace mathematics theory. If he had been crying, he hid it well.

Pulling my trim black uniform straight, I studied my reflection in one of the mirrors. I, too, looked different now . . . more somber, more grown up. I frowned. The change disturbed me. If this was what growing up meant, I would rather have done without it for the present.

I glanced at Jake. "It hurts, doesn't it?" I said.

"I'm not going to let it hurt," he said softly. His voice held a passion, a determination, I had never heard before. "Father's all right. You're all right. We're all going to live and be happy again, just like always." He turned to me, and his golden eyes had taken on a hard sheen. "We are going to be happy again, Teddy."

"Yes," I said, sounding more certain than I felt. "Yes, of course we're going to be happy."

Half an hour later, Timon Crote summoned us to one of the small salons off the main dining room. Here the walls showed lush jungle growth teaming with animal life, and the excited chatter of Mother Earth monkeys surrounded us. Every now and then I glimpsed a sleek black maduna rummaging through the undergrowth on six pods, eyestalks extended as it searched for grubs. This scene came from Troi, Horizon's smallest continent.

Crote sat on the other side of the dining table. Several small white handguns lay before him. One had been completely dismantled.

"These are their weapons," Crote said. "Examine them."

I picked one up. The grip felt cool but not cold and had an odd, almost greasy texture.

"It's not metal," I said. "Is it organic?"

"Yes, human bone reinforced with some kind of high-tensile resin. It fires using compressed air."

"Where was it made?" Jake asked, turning one over in his hands.

"We don't know yet. Not on Dulap's World, certainly."

"It's from the Borgialis," I said. They had never forgiven us for taking a third of their empire in a border war sixty-two years ago. Most assassination plots could eventually be traced to their satellite worlds.

"What proof do you have?" Crote leaned forward.

I hesitated. I couldn't quite put my finger on it, but somehow I knew. The Borgialis specialized in this sort of organic technology. And they had a history of assassination attempts against our family. But actual proof?

"None," I had to admit.

"Tell me when you're certain. Until then, we have agents working on it." He sat back, studying us. "Every security measure has a loophole," he said. "Never forget that. Never think you are safe, not even in your beds in Meriman City on Horizon. Never."

I nodded. Father had made that mistake, I thought. And yet you couldn't lock yourself away from the universe. You couldn't make your home world a prison.

Solemnly I returned the handgun to the table. I knew it had come from the Borgialis. Time would prove it. We should have moved against them long ago.

"You both need food." Crote rose, crossed to the far wall—it faded from jungle to a gray at his approach—and the autochef console folded out. He told it what he wanted, accepted the large tray it produced, and carried everything to our table. His hands trembled faintly, I noted, probably from stress. Slowly he set bowls of thick vegetable stew, heaps of crackers, and large glasses of fruit juice before us.

He hadn't bothered to count calories or analyze nutrients to properly balance our meal, I realized. He had just called up a hot, hearty dinner. Normally I treasured excursions from our carefully planned diets, but for once I found I didn't care. I poked at my stew with a spoon for a minute, then nibbled a few crackers and swallowed a few gulps of juice. I had no appetite, nor apparently did Timon Crote, since he left most of his untouched as well. Only Jake wolfed down his meal. When he finished, he traded bowls with me. I watched him finish my stew with a measure of puzzlement. He seemed to be taking great pleasure in the animal act of eating, I thought. Perhaps it helped prove he was still alive.

When Jake finished, tipping back in his chair and wiping his mouth on a napkin, Crote said, "We should wait in the command center. The Sixteenth Fleet will be here any minute now."

Jake stood. "Right," he said firmly. "Let's go."

I rose silently. Jake was up to something, I thought, and unbidden my mind began to turn through the possibilities. I did not like many of them. Overcompensating for his shock and pain seemed most likely.

We followed Crote up two more decks to the command center, a large room filled with monitoring equipment and staffed by several dozen men and women in black and silver uniforms. Mostly the monitors showed financial reports from Father's empire, with data streaming through so fast that you could never have followed it without stims, but with the present situation on Dulap's World, one wall had been given over entirely to tracking the Freedom Brigade's movements.

The duty officer, a young lieutenant named Schmidt, snapped to attention and saluted. Jake and I returned the gesture.

"Report," Mr. Crote said. Crote might not hold any official rank, but I'd noticed that everyone accepted his authority without question.

"Rumors are spreading that the Emperor is dead," Schmidt said bluntly. "The Dulapers broadcast that claim, along with a declaration of independence, shortly after the attempted assassination. We blocked it seconds after it began, of course, but it was too late."

"The result?"

"As our simulations indicated, there is panic throughout the empire. Everyone is trying to sell what they own of Meriman Family companies. Our agents say there is growing unrest on Davidia, Paradise, and a dozen other worlds."

"They all expect chaos, collapse, perhaps invasion from our rivals," I murmured, understanding. I had once heard a visitor to father's court phrase it this way: <u>Emperor Faraday casts a long shadow.</u> For the first time, I realized fully what it meant. Our Father's rule affected not just his family or the worlds he ruled directly, it influenced every human who worked in every company he owned, from the greatest of scientists to the least of the maintenance men . . . hundreds of billions if not trillions of people.

"Let them sell," Crote said. "Do nothing to allay their fears."

"But sir—"

Crote held up one hand, silencing him. "We must take an aggressive stance," he said. "There is a clear line of succession and change should not bring panic. Let this serve as a lesson to all. Buy everything available as it hits thirty percent below estimated value. We have the financial reserves to cover the expansion. Use them on my personal authorization."

"And the dissident worlds?"

"Move extra ships to their solar systems so they know we are prepared to move against them swiftly, if necessary."

"Aye, sir," he said, turning back to his station. Quickly he began calling orders. With puzzled, anxious looks, the others in the command center turned to their stations and began carrying out their new instructions.

Mr. Crote knelt to talk to Jake and me. "Don't worry," he said quietly, "your father will emerge better seated. No rival Family will be able to touch him after this, when the scope of his new acquisitions are revealed."

"Then the Dulapers may have done us a favor," Jake said.

"Attempted murder is never a favor," Crote said gravely. "Do not dismiss the pain, suffering, and personal humiliation your father must feel. Or the loss of stability throughout the empire."

"But the ends—" I said.

"In the constant maneuvering for power among the nine great Families, we must turn tragedy to our advantage whenever possible."

"I see," Jake said with a nod. I wasn't quite so certain.

"Sir," Schmidt called. "The Sixteenth Fleet just emerged from nospace. Their commander is hailing us."

"Put her on." To us, he whispered, "Remember our plan."

We took our places before the large viewscreen from which Father normally addressed his troops. Crote took a deep breath, pulled himself to his full height, and placed one hand on each of our shoulders.

The screen suddenly showed a stern-faced woman in a black and silver battle uniform: Admiral Miranda Sherman. Behind her, I saw vague outlines of the command center of the *Nathan Meriman*, the flagship of the Sixteenth Fleet. Although she wore her dark brown hair pulled back in a simple style and her uniform had none of the gold piping Father's had sported on Dulap's World, you could not miss her aura of authority. She did not need the five gold stars at her collar to show her rank. You looked at her and you knew.

"What is your situation, Mr. Crote?" she asked.

"The Emperor has been moderately wounded by rebels on the planet below. As you can see, his children are fine."

"I must speak with His Excellency."

Crote shook his head. "Tomorrow," he replied. "Our medics are still putting a few final cosmetic touches on his wounds."

She nodded and seemed to relax a little. "Do you have instructions from him?"

"Nothing specific as yet. What would you recommend?"

"A full blockade around the planet, to begin."

"Destroy it," Jake said suddenly. He looked up and met the admiral's startled gaze. "Make them pay for what they did to Father. We need swift, decisive action, not a pretty little blockade."

Too shocked to speak, I stared at Jake's hard expression, then up at Mr. Crote. Clearly pained, Crote nodded.

"Do it," he told the admiral.

"It's not—" I began, but Crote's hand tightened painfully on my shoulder. I knew the signal: shut up and let him do the talking.

"Are you certain that's what you want?" Admiral Sherman asked, looking only at Crote now. Her voice had gone utterly flat and emotionless.

I wanted nothing of the kind. I knew I had to stop the wheels Jake had set in motion. Suddenly resolved, I began to turn. But Crote must have sensed my intentions, since he gave my shoulder a second sharp squeeze. I tensed, then forced myself to relax. He knew best what to do. He always did.

Crote said, "We must make an example of this world, Admiral, as Jacob Meriman has said. An attack on the person of the Emperor cannot be allowed to pass without instant and total reprisal. If the Dulapers cannot learn from their mistakes, surely other worlds will."

"As you command," she said in a suddenly husky voice. She swallowed visibly. As her image faded, I thought I saw tears on her cheeks. Financial reports began to flicker across the screen again.

I glared at Jake. "You spoke out of place," I snapped. "That was not your decision to make. Not alone."

He glared back. "They deserve it."

"But—" I broke off. Most of the command staff had paused to stare at us. Crote looked pained. Clearly this was neither the time nor the place for an argument.

I swallowed my anger. "We will discuss it later," I said calmly. He nodded almost imperceptibly.

"Come with me," Crote said to both of us. He ushered us to the lift, then up one more level to the observation deck. Here, you could look out onto all of space through thick transparent panels. Dulap's World hung to the left and above, a suddenly small and insignificant gray sphere covered by faint wisps of cloud. The Sixteenth Fleet —four hundred long, tapered silver battle-cruisers with heavy armaments—had already broken formation and begun to take up positions around the planet. We watched in silence until they had completed their maneuvers some ten minutes later.

"You have just ordered the murder of two hundred thousand people," Crote said to Jake, "many if not most of whom were innocent of any crime. Look upon what you have wrought, and may you feel their despair."

The bombardment began. Even from space you could see the explosions. The Brigadiers were using a mixture of high-powered pulse energy beams and traditional planet-buster missiles, the analytical part of my mind realized. The emotional part saw only unspeakable horrors.

Ugly red wounds opened on the planet's surface. The land seemed to crawl with yellow-orange flames as huge walls of fire swept across everything in their path. I wanted to cringe away, to avert my gaze, and I had to force myself to take it all in. I could never allow this to happen again, I vowed. Neither Crote nor Jake nor even my father would prevent me from stopping this kind of act. *Two hundred thousand people.*

Still the missiles fell. The atmosphere itself caught fire and burned. Then the planet's crust split like an over-ripe melon, and suddenly the outer mantle disintegrated into bubbling lava. Thirty seconds later a thick gray shroud of smoke and poisonous gasses completely covered the planet; nothing more could be seen. For all intents and purposes, Dulap's World had died. Nothing would live down there for millions, perhaps billions of years.

"Two hundred thousand people," Crote said again in a heavy voice, "are dead because you didn't think through the conse-

quences of your command, Jacob."

Stricken, I tried to picture that many faces and couldn't come close. But I could still see the faces of every single man and woman who had assembled to hear Father speak. And I could imagine the faces of their husbands, wives, and children.

"I—" Panicked, Jake looked at me, then at Crote. "I—why didn't you stop it?" he cried.

"Because," Crote said, "until your father is well, you and your brother are the rulers of the Meriman Empire. No one may be seen to criticize you in public. The Family must come first, and I will never do anything to undermine your authority, young masters, no matter who or what suffers, even unto my own death."

"What—consequences—" I had to struggle through sudden tongue-tiedness—"will this act have?" That's exactly how Father would have put it, I thought. He always worried about the consequences of his actions, event following event in long causal chains.

"For one thing," Crote said, returning to his businesslike self, "it will cost us Admiral Sherman. She came from Dulap's World. Her whole family just died there. She killed them for you. That's how great her loyalty was. Despite her stims, we will no longer be able to guarantee your safety around her. I expect she will resign, and if she doesn't, she must be dismissed."

I heard Jake swallow. He was gazing out at what was left of the planet. Then his expression hardened as he forced himself forward. You could not undo what was done, as our father always said.

When Jake turned to Crote again, he showed not the slightest bit of emotion. No remorse, no regret. Just my brother, letting the stims take over and guide his actions, analyzing, computing, calculating like an auton. I had never felt so far removed from him.

"Then," he said coolly, "we shall have to replace her, Mr. Crote. See to it at once."

"Jake—" I began.

He looked at me. Nobody else could have seen it. I only did because I knew him as I knew myself. Deep inside I saw the day's fear and anger still coiled up and waiting to explode. He was just a boy, like me, despite how we tried to deny it, despite all our stims and training, despite all our drills and exercises and years of instructions. He was just a boy, and he had taken his first real step into a larger adult universe before he was ready. He didn't like it. But there was nothing he could do now. He could never go back. I knew it . . . and I saw that he knew it, too, and that hurt him most of all.

He turned away so I couldn't see his expression. I reached out to touch his shoulder, then paused. *Not here. Not now. Not in front of Crote.* I dropped my arm to my side heavily.

"Find her replacement, Mr. Crote," Jake said, and I heard the stim-given crack of authority in his even tones. "Now."

Timon Crote bowed his head. "As you command," he whispered, "young master." He backed away. I glimpsed terror in his eyes and knew he must be wondering what kind of monsters he had loosed upon the galaxy.

At that moment I realized Crote did not expect Father to live. Panic flooded through me. If so, then Jake and I would be the sole rulers of the Meriman Family and the Empire. No wonder he had not wanted to contradict Jake publicly. I forced my thundering heartbeat down again. Calm. I had to remain calm.

When the lift doors closed, Jake said, "Don't. I know it was a mistake, but now it's done and we must swing it around to our advantage."

"All right," I said. There didn't seem to be anything to add. We all made mistakes. Hopefully we would both learn from this one. If only the cost had not been so high.

Silently we watched the Sixteenth Fleet's withdrawal. One by one the silver ships turned, graceful as swans on a lake of stars, and assumed new positions around the Pega-sus. Only those seething black clouds now covering Dulap's World, with their ugly dead look, marred the perfection of the image.

My mind continued to play through cause and effects, the results of Jake's actions spreading outward in ever-expanding rings. The immediate threat had ended: the traitors and would-be assassins on Dulap's World would trouble us no more. But what of their off-world friends and families? Besides losing a valuable human resource in Admiral Sherman, we would have to dismiss all the other Dulapers in the Brigade. How many? Unbidden, stims gave the number to me: One thousand forty-two. A tiny number, when you considered the nearly thirty million Brigadiers who served us. But one of them had been Admiral Sherman. And sixteen others held officer rank.

And we had not eliminated the true threat, whoever had been behind the assassination attempt. *The Borgialis*, a soft voice whispered in the back of my mind. *It has to be the Borgialis.*

Any pluses? One, perhaps: Jacob's punishment would be remembered. Nobody would forget the destruction of a whole planet for treason. And if Father did die, well, that would be justification enough to most of the galaxy. Life would continue elsewhere without pause. On the nearly forty thousand planets our family owned, few people would care if one obscure world vanished forever. And yet it would show that Jake and I had sharp teeth behind our young faces. Yes, I thought, perhaps he and I would both emerge better seated. Those who did not love us would fear us.

Firing their maneuvering thrusters, the last of the Sixteenth Fleet's ships broke away from the burning planet and took up a protective formation around the Pegasus. I watched until they reached their stationary positions. The show had ended.

A chime sounded, then a life-sized holographic projection appeared before Jake and me: Timon Crote. Behind him, half formed, I saw vague outlines of the command center.

He bowed.

"Young masters," he said. I noticed for the first time that he had stopped calling us 'children' now. "Admiral Sherman has transmitted her resignation, and I have accepted it. I have taken the liberty of naming Captain Julian De Marco as commander of the Sixteenth Fleet. Your father will make it official when we return to Horizon."

"An excellent choice," I said. I did not add, *Should our father live that long.* De Marco had an exemplary service record, my stims told me. "Keep us informed of new developments."

"As you wish, young masters." He bowed again and the holo faded away.

I looked at Jake.

"Valuable lessons for everyone," he said. He tilted his head and regarded what remained of Dulap's World. I could see he had run through the same logic chains.

I gave a nod. "Except for the cost," I added.

"Cost?"

"The people who died down there. Remember them?"

He shrugged. "They were inconsequential."

"No human life is inconsequential."

"We are Merimans," he said, drawing himself up to his full height and facing me. "Nothing matters but us. You, me, and most of all Father. That's it. And when Father's gone, it's just going to be us."

"Morals—ethics—" I began, nearly at a loss for words the second time that day. I couldn't believe what he'd just said.

"Grow up, Teddy. You know we don't have time for abstract concepts now."

I took a step back, shocked. His statement went against everything we had ever been taught. Rulers had to serve and protect their people. Rulers had to govern and guide and most of all care. He seemed to have forgotten that. I found myself gazing into his eyes of a stranger.

"It's only the stress you're under," I told him after a heartbeat. That had to be the answer. "You don't really feel this way."

"I do. And so will you, if you think about it."

Slowly I shook my head. "Never."

But what if he's right? some inner part of me demanded. Timon Crote and practically everyone else we had ever known treated us as though we mattered more than anything else in the universe. *Then why would they give us stims that stressed ethics and morality if those concepts don't apply?*

"Well?" he prodded.

"I want to be alone," I told him. My mind was a confused jumble. Dulap's World . . . our father's injuries . . . and now this. "I have to think."

"Good." He nodded once, turned, and strode to the lift as though he owned the universe. It opened, and I heard him ask for the fifteenth level.

Turning, I stared out at Dulap's World, the Sixteenth Fleet, and the stars, wondering.

When I awoke the next morning, I found myself soaked with sweat. Bad dreams full of lammachs physicians, medical machines, and burning planets had plagued me. Shivering a bit, I pushed them to the far corners of my mind.

I had gone to bed determined to let my subconscious resolve the problem Jake had thrust upon me. Now, in the clear morning hours, I realized that I still believed in the morals and ethics which bound my life. They defined me. They made me who and what I was . . . who I had always been. Born to high rank, but no better than anyone else. Only my special training and stims set me apart. If anything, I felt more tied to that code of behavior than ever before. Jake and I should be leading by example, I thought, and setting the standard for those below us. I still did not quite understand how Jake had reached the opposite conclusion.

Taking a deep breath, I nodded, my decision final. Jake had clearly been wrong. Father would tell him—

Father.

Sitting up, I called for light. The room brightened. While I slept, autons had taken away my old uniform and laid out new clothes for me. I saw shorts and a sleeveless gray shirt with the family crest no larger than a handbreadth in the exact center, my usual workout clothes for my morning's exercise in the gym. It seemed our routine had been restored. What did that mean?

"Computer on," I said. "What is Emperor Meriman's status?"

"Emperor Meriman is in excellent spirits, following light cosmetic surgery," a soft sexless voice told me. *"In consideration of recent tragic events involving Dulap's World, he has decreed a day of mourning throughout the Empire in sympathy for the lost souls who tried so ruthlessly to assassinate him—"*

I snorted. That was a bland statement for the crew, not what I wanted or needed right now. I should have known better than to ask the computer.

At least he wasn't dead. That was good news, at least.

"—According to the Emperor's ministers, he will reschedule the rest of his Outer Rim tour for later this year. Meriman Family holdings have increased in value by 8.29 percent, following a sharp fluctuation in—"

"Stop!" I told it. I didn't need the overnight financial summary this early. I would go over it in detail with Crote and Jake this afternoon. "What's my itinerary today?"

"One hour of exercise, commencing in fourteen minutes, followed by breakfast of—"

"Stop!" I said. "When will I see my father?"

"In two hours and forty-four minutes."

I leaned back. Our lammachs physicians had worked their usual wonders, it seemed. Father not only lived, despite Timon Crote's fears, but had recovered enough to see us. Excellent news. He would know whether my brother had made the right assessment of our situation and the moral issues involved.

A weight had been lifted from me. Feeling almost giddy, I washed up, changed clothes, and headed for the gym. On the way, I spotted Jake in the corridor ahead and jogged to catch up. He turned as I approached.

"You've heard about Father," he said.

"Of course."

He nodded. "The Empire is safe from our rule a while longer, it seems."

"Idiot!" Laughing, I gave him a shove, then danced away from a half-hearted punch. "No one will *ever* be safe from a menace like you!"

He gave chase. For a second he snagged my shirt, but I wrenched away and dashed up the corridor. He followed.

Cornering me by the lift, he grabbed my arm, twisted, and managed a sudden flip that sent me skidding down the corridor on my back. He had been practicing; I hadn't seen that move before. I would have to find a counter.

"Yield!" he said, looming over me, face tight with mock severity.

"You're dreaming!" I rolled into his legs, knocking him off balance, then sprang to my feet. This time he fled up the corridor, laughing so hard tears rolled down his cheeks, and I followed. Simple horseplay, but it felt good: we could be young a while longer. Catharsis. Father restored, our world made whole, the universe in balance again. Free.

Panting, we both reached the gym at the same time and drew to a halt. Inside, through the open double-doors, we could see strangers: two lean, dark-skinned men in their middle thirties, with broad noses, thin red lips, and long, narrow, closely shaved heads. They wore white shorts and shirts with our crest stitched in red over their hearts. Swallowing, I calmed my rough breathing. New instructors? It had to be. I traded a glance with my brother, then stepped forward. We might as well get it over with.

Both men had noticed us. "You are late," the one on the right said, frowning. He stalked forward. From his accent he came from Coven, a low-gravity world some forty-seven lightyears from Horizon. Other than that, I could tell little about him.

"Only a few seconds," I said.

"Seven, to be precise," Jake added.

"Mmm." He set his hands on his hips and circled us like a Mother Earth wolf studying its prey, dark hungry eyes taking in our bodies. His gaze transfixed me. He made no attempt to hide his displeasure and made a clucking noise deep in his throat.

"What do you think Sameel?" he finally said, turning to his companion.

"Pitiful," Sameel said in a rough, gravely voice. He drew out the word. "Pi-tee-ful."

My brother bristled. I put my hand on his shoulder, and Jake shut his mouth with a snap.

"Mr. Crote's work," I muttered. Jake gave an almost imperceptible nod. We had not reacted swiftly enough to save ourselves the day before, I thought, so now we would have new instructors. Our old regimen of weight lifting, wind sprints, and calisthenics would be replaced by—what? Martial arts? I could only guess.

"Where are Uri and Silas?" Jake asked in a voice so calm and relaxed it made you want to yawn. I recognized his full stim training in every syllable.

"Your old trainers? Gone. Pfft!" The Covener waved toward the ceiling. "I am Boris Visha," he said with a flourish and a slight bow, as if his name would mean something to us, "and your training has been given over to me. My assistant is Sameel."

Sameel nodded slightly. I considered their names with growing uneasiness. None of the men listed aboard the Pegasus or any of the ships of the Sixteenth Fleet had the surname "Visha". Where had these two come from?

"As you must already know," I said, matching Jake's calm, leisurely voice and manner, "I am Theodore Meriman, and this is my brother Jacob."

"Of course we know who you are," Visha said with a sneer. "The pampered whelps of a helpless old man. Twin bullies who kill hundreds of thousands from the safety of orbit."

Now it was my turn to bristle. Jake did that, not me, an inner voice cried. Did people truly view us this way? Ask Admiral Sherman, I told myself almost bitterly. Ask anyone whose family lived on Dulap's World.

But I was still the Emperor's son. Nobody talked to us this way . . . at least, not without good motive. My eyes narrowed. Plots always turned within plots around us, and nothing unusual happened without good cause. I suspected some hidden purpose in Visha's abuse. What better way to provoke an angry, unthinking response?

"You forget your place," I finally said. If he wanted a confrontation, that was the last thing I would give him. I could play these games, too. I had been raised for them. Pointedly, I looked to the far side of the room, trying to appear bored and disinterested.

My strategy seemed to work. After a heartbeat, Visha snapped, "Five minutes of stretching, then join me in the nograv chamber to begin your training."

He stalked to the far end of the gym. A small round door appeared in the wall at his command, and he ducked through.

"Interesting fellow," Jake muttered.

"He does not like to be kept waiting," Sameel said.

I forced a smile. "Neither do we."

Sameel tugged on his lower lip with thumb and forefinger, but did not reply. I couldn't quite figure out what to make of him or his master. Coveners were not known for their physical strength or stamina; coming from a low gravity world, they were slight of build and lightly muscled. I would never have selected one as my trainer. And yet some instinct warned that Visha wouldn't have been placed in charge of us if he didn't have something to back up his arrogance.

Shrugging, I began to limber up, hugging my right knee then my left knee to my chest and going into slow lunges. My arm felt well today, so I decided I wouldn't worry about the wound I'd suffered. Dr. Sanjarin always took more care than necessary. Right now I had more important things to think about, like Boris Visha. I had to find out more about him. No matter where he came from, there had to be records about him in one of our databases. We had files on every one of the seventy trillion-odd sentients in the Meriman Empire, after all.

The muscles in my calves and thighs began to stretch and loosen. I touched my toes, pressed my palms flat on the deck, stood up, began to twist left and right. Beside me, Jake did the same. I tried a handstand, then a quick back-flip. My muscles didn't object. So much for Dr. Sanjarin, and so much for Visha and Sameel. I could have run rings around all of them.

All the while my mental clock ticked. Fifteen seconds before Visha's five minutes were up, Jake and I paused simultaneously and exchanged a quick glance. Without a word we headed for the nograv chamber. In my mind I could hear Sameel's voice saying, "Pi-tee-ful" again, and I felt a flush of anger spreading down my cheeks and neck. I would show him the first chance I got. The sons of Faraday Meriman were anything but pitiful.

The nograv chamber extended some twenty meters in every direction, a huge empty cube with padded walls and soft handgrips on every surface. As I ducked through, my head swam with sudden vertigo. Gravity had been turned down, but not off—ten or twelve percent of Horizon normal, I estimated. We had practiced freefall gymnastics since we were old enough to walk, so I knew I'd be fine once my inner ear adjusted.

Visha balanced lightly on his toes by the far wall. He wasn't smiling now.

"Computer, lock the chamber!" he called.

The privacy screen materialized over the doorway behind us. I heard three low bleeps as the computer engaged locks.

"Why—" Jake began.

"Computer, do not monitor this chamber," Visha said, ignoring my brother. "Shut down all recorders and monitoring devices."

"You shouldn't do that," I told him. "We'll be trapped in here."

The computer confirmed my words. "Warning: you will be unable to open this room—" it began.

"Acknowledged," Visha barked. "Do it!"

"Override that order!" I shouted. But it was already too late; the computer had shut off its eyes and ears. We were trapped.

Visha pulled up his shirt in one swift movement. Two long, flat sheaths adhered to his stomach. A sudden chill swept through me. He should not have been able to get within a hundred meters of us carrying weapons, not aboard the *Pegasus*. Someone must have helped him—someone very high up.

He killed our old instructors, I thought. *He killed them, and now he's going to kill us!*

"This is for Admiral Sherman!" he snarled, drawing both knives and throwing them. Then with a battle cry he kicked off against the wall and launched himself at us.

A sudden bubble of calmness surrounded me. Everything seemed to be slowing down. My eyes narrowed to slits as my attention fixed on the knives. I did not panic.

—moving five meters per second—

I had learned my lesson well on Dulap's world. Do not hesitate. Find the threat. Avoid it.

—two point two seconds until impact—

I could duck, dart to the side, or kick off against the floor and jump over them. It would be easy in this low gravity.

—one and a half rotations before they strike—

Something clicked. I blinked as my stims confirmed the calculations. The hilts would strike our chests, not the blades. This attack was nothing more than an act. I found myself starting to relax, then forced myself to stop. Everything had been carefully choreographed to throw us off balance, to convince us that our lives really were in jeopardy. Clearly this was an important test, one we could not afford to fail. Next time, with someone else, the knives might be real.

Everything moved in real time again. Stretching out my left hand, I plucked the first knife out of the air before it hit Jake.

With my right hand, I caught the one aimed at me. Their hilts, still warm from Visha's body heat, yielded faintly. Rubber. Of course.

A startled expression on his face, Visha tried to stop his charge, but couldn't in the reduced gravity. Off balance, arms windmilling, he pitched forward. With his foot, he finally snagged one of the handholds set in the floor and drew to a stop half a meter in front of us.

"Tag." I pricked him under the chin with the tip of one rubber blade. It wasn't sharp enough to draw blood.

His eyes grew wider still. "How—" he began.

Then Jake clobbered him with a double punch to the side of the head, followed by a kick to the stomach. Glassy eyed, gasping for air, Visha sagged to the floor and half curled into a fetal position. I could see one huge dark eye peering up at us. Terrified. Was he wondering if we would kill him as easily as we had stopped his attack?

"Well done," I told my brother.

"And you." Jake seemed to notice Visha on the floor for the first time. "Oh, I'm sorry," he said almost sweetly, crouching. "You did want me to defend myself, right? Your attack was quite good. Except for that last part, where you fell down."

"I saw room for improvement," I told Jake. I tossed the rubber knives to the floor. They bounced and went spinning to the sides in the low gravity. "His battle cry..."

"It could have been more chilling." Jake cocked his head slightly and asked Visha, "Would you care to try again? At a lower pitch this time. And maybe a little louder."

"Definitely louder," I said.

Shuddering, Visha forced himself up. He took a series of deep breaths. After shaking his head to clear it, he smiled. Then he grinned. Then he threw back his head and laughed like it was the funniest thing he had ever heard.

"All right," he finally said. "That's enough, you two. Well done. Very well done. Best responses I've ever gotten from raw recruits." He rubbed the side of his head almost ruefully.

"You aren't angry?" I said. I had half expected him to crawl out, too humiliated to return. If he could get the door open, that is.

"Far from it." He stood and bowed to us. "Pardon, young masters, but I needed an honest gauge of your responses in a crisis situation. It was necessary."

"Who are you really?" I said. "There's no one named Boris Visha assigned to the *Pegasus*—or anywhere in the whole Sixteenth Fleet, for that matter."

"No," he admitted. "It's Havis, actually."

Havis. The name leaped out at me this time. Lieutenant Adam Havis, chief security officer from the *Nathan Meriman*. 'Visha' was a slight rearrangement of the letters of his name. I should have seen it before.

Lieutenant Havis had spent ten years training Argents on Janus before accepting a promotion and new assignment aboard the *Nathan Meriman*, my stims informed me. He had personally trained more than fifteen thousand Brigadiers, and he had an impressive service record stretching back twenty-two years. Father had twice commended him for exceptional service, once personally.

"My assignment," Havis said somberly, "is to prepare you both to act and react properly under combat situations. You must learn to protect yourself at all times."

"Like today."

"Yes." He gave me a puzzled look. "I have never seen anyone snatch knives out of the air like that. Not by the handles, not so fast. How did you learn to do it?"

I shrugged. "Simple math. Speed and rotation are easy to calculate. I knew where the handles would be, so I put my hands there first and caught them."

"Ah." He shook his head. Clearly it was beyond him. But then, Jake and I had more deep stims than almost anyone he would have encountered in the military. "All right, back to work." He kicked off the floor, bounded to the right side wall in the low gravity, and caught a handhold halfway up, clinging there like a tree osslox from Bélan. "New scenario," he called. "This ship has been hit by enemy fire. Gravity is nearly off. The Irenz are boarding. Jacob, you are unarmed. Theodore, you are a pirate attacker. Get past his guard."

"All right." War play might well prove an interesting change, I thought.

One rubber knife had landed two meters away. I dove for it, scooped it up, tucked into a roll, and bounced off the far wall with a sharp kick. When I came at Jake, I gave a battle cry like Havis's.

Jake fell over laughing, so I poked him in the chest with the rubber knife. The blade bent all the way back. Pausing, I looked helplessly at our new instructor.

Havis sighed. "Pi-tee-*ful*," he said in a fair approximation of Sameel's voice. "You are dead, Jacob. That will cost you fifty pushups when we're through in here."

"Hey—" Jake began.

"Make it a seventy-five," Havis snapped, all business now.

Jake gulped, but shut up.

"And quit your gloating, Theodore," Havis said. "That will cost you twenty-five."

"Gloating? Me?" I put on my most innocent expression.

He wasn't having any of it, though. "Make it fifty," he said. "Now try it again, this time like you mean it!"

Jake and I spent the next forty minutes tumbling, fighting, and floating this way and that. My muscles began to ache from unexpected pulls and twists. My arm burned where I had been shot, but Dr. Sanjarin's patches held. I would have to do more stretching exercises to loosen up tomorrow, I thought, if Havis planned this kind of routine every day.

Finally Havis called a stop. Out of breath, dripping with sweat, I came to a halt. My arms trembled with fatigue. My back and legs ached. I had never felt so tired in all my life.

The low gravity slowly pulled me down to the floor.

"That's enough for today," he said. "We will pick up tomorrow where we left off."

As if on cue, the round door appeared behind us and Sameel poked his head through. "Still alive?" he asked. I wasn't sure if he meant Havis or us.

"Barely," Havis called. "These two cubs took me out in three seconds, Sam."

"Oh?" Sameel's eyes widened in surprise. I took it as a sign that Havis routinely attacked new recruits and wasn't used to losing. Well, chalk up one mark in our favor.

"Still think we're pitiful?" I asked him.

He shrugged. "All recruits are pitiful. It is a state of being which only time and experience will change."

Recruits, that's how they viewed us. It explained a lot.

Jake turned to Havis. "Then your assignment here is permanent."

He inclined his head. "Yes, Jacob. Until you and your brother master all I have to teach."

I nodded. That sounded like Timon Crote's decision, all right. Despite how I had cut short Havis's attack, I knew we could learn a lot from him. Stims gave Jake and me an edge, but they only went so far. In real combat, nothing would compare to actual training. Crote had made the right decision.

"*Now*," Havis said, and I had a sinking feeling inside, "let's not forget those pushups."

Twenty minutes later, my brother and I limped into the dining room together. Jake groaned and held his back like Timon Crote, and I couldn't help but laugh. Even that hurt. I had never been so exhausted after a workout. My whole body felt abused. Despite a hot shower under massaging needle sprays, I could feel muscles tightening up all over. Today would be bad, but tomorrow . . . far worse. And we had another workout with Havis scheduled first thing after we woke. Painful, but ultimately worth it.

"What do you think of him?" Jake asked

as he slid gingerly into his seat on the far side of the table.

"He seemed all right." I took a deep breath and sat.

"Ah—"

Two alien domestics had been standing patiently in the corners. They were shais, anthropoids but shorter than humans, with sloped brows, thick yellowish knobs protruding like blunt horns or tusks from each side of their jowls, and two small black eyes. The sleek fur on their thick arms, legs, and faces shimmered with a faint iridescence. Both wore round white caps blazed with red and short white tunics with our family crest in gold on the fronts. I recognized the one called Beej by the pattern of dapples across on the bridge of his wide, flat nose.

"Serve us," Jake told them.

"Please," I added.

In silence, they retrieved our scheduled breakfasts from the autochef and carried them over. Beej moved gingerly, setting first my plate, then my glass, then my utensils neatly in place. I studied the food; back to routine indeed. Lightly toasted wheat wafers, six large sections of meaty green glava-fruit, and a small Earth peach, pitted and peeled . . . a low-calorie and all too sensible meal, exactly what the dieticians always wanted us to eat. At least the tartness of the peach would make a nice contrast to the sticky sweetness of the glava.

"Thanks," I told Beej.

"Yes, Master Jacob," he said, bowing. "Beej serve good."

"I'm Theodore," I told him. Shais were useful, but not very bright. "Theodore, remember?"

He squinted at me. "Not Jacob?"

"Not Jacob," I said heavily. Theodore." I motioned him away, and he shuffled back to the corner to watch us eat.

Jake was smirking as he pretended not to notice. Then abruptly he became serious.

"How did you do it?" he said softly.

"What?" I looked up, meeting his eyes. His gaze was intent.

"How did you catch those knives?"

I shrugged uneasily. "I don't know. I just did. If I can do it, you can, too."

"You moved as fast as he did. Faster, maybe."

"Would you rather be hit with a knife?"

He began to poke at the food on his plate. "I froze," he finally said. "All I could see was him charging straight at me. Those knives were blurs, stims or not. He threw them hard."

"Not *that* hard," I said. "It seemed faster than it really was."

"I guess."

"I went through the same thing on Dulap's World," I told him reassuringly. "When we were in the arena with Father, I just stood there staring. I couldn't believe what was happening. If Crote hadn't knocked me down . . ."

"What was different for you today?"

I hesitated, trying to put into words what had happened. How could I explain it? I couldn't say time slowed down. That sounded stupid, even to me, and I had been there.

"It was almost instinctive," I finally said. "When he attacked, my stims seemed to take over. The second he let go of the first knife, I knew everything. The velocity, the rotation, everything. That's when I knew it wasn't a real attack. I saw that the hilts would hit us."

"That's it?" he said skeptically.

"Sure. You could've done it."

"Right." But as he frowned and studied his plate, I knew he had doubts.

"Finish up," I told him, starting in on my food. "We see Father next."

At the appointed hour, Jake and I made our way to the fifth level of the Pegasus, which also housed the ship's medical complex. We had fifteen thousand forty-two humans aboard, plus several thousand menials, and my stims told me an average of thirty-three people could be found in sickbay at any one time. Reasons varied, of course. Illnesses, broken bones, muscle sprains and strains—the lammachs treated all infirmities with equal adeptness.

For privacy as well as security, Father had a suite with an entrance from a gold-section lift. The doors slid open when the computer verified our DNA, revealing a large, comfortable waiting room with couches against the walls and a burbling holographic fountain in the middle, where water sprayed from the mouths of giant stone lions. As we stepped inside, I heard the soft tinkling music of wind chimes announce our arrival.

Timon Crote strode from a side room half a second later. That must to be where they had Father, I thought. My pulse quickened as I thought back to the day before, when I had seen Father shot to pieces and the lammachs working frantically to keep him alive.

"Good news, young masters," Crote said, smiling broadly. "Your father is eager to see you both."

"Is he really conscious?" Jake said.

"Dr. Espoja kept the Emperor sedated most of the night, but he came out of it half an hour ago. He just asked about you both, in fact." Turning, he led us toward Father's room, still chatting happily. I shared his relief.

Inside, Father lay in his bed, propped up by half a dozen square red pillows. Not only were his eyes open, but he was studying financial statements playing out in the air before him. His face had huge red splotches from synthetic skin plasts, but those would fade in a week or two. Beneath them, his nose and cheeks and chin looked as strong as ever. The lammachs had done a perfect job of reconstructing his features.

When he noticed us, Father made a quick hand gesture and the computer display vanished. He pulled himself higher in bed, wincing a little. Clearly his strength had not yet returned completely.

"Boys," he said. I noticed that his voice had changed, no longer as smooth and polished as an obsidian blade, but deeper and slightly raspy.

Jake went to his left side and I went to his right. I grinned madly. It felt good to see

him. Two weeks, I thought, and the plasts would fade. He would be his old self again. By then we would be home on Horizon.

"Boys," he said again, staring at me now. His right eye jumped with a nervous tick.

"I will leave you alone now," Timon Crote said. "Call me if you need anything, Excellency." He activated the privacy shield as he went, and the doorway vanished behind a new gray wall.

"Father," I said softly, "how are you feeling?"

He stared up into my face. "Better, no thanks to you."

No thanks to me? Puzzled, I glanced at Jake, who suddenly had an uneasy expression.

"Max," he whispered, gazing through me. "Why did you do it, Max?"

"Who's Max?" I said. I didn't know anyone by that name. Three people in Meriman House were called Maxwell, stims told me, and one of the Argents on board the *Pegasus*. None of them came into direct contact with Father.

I stepped closer, bending to look into his eyes. Could his injuries have affected his vision?

"It's me," I said, "your son, Theodore."

"You should have known," Father went on, still gazing through me, starting to ramble, "that you wouldn't get away with it, Max."

"Father, you're confused," I began.

He raised his right hand as if to touch my face, but instead he lunged forward with desperate, unexpected speed. His powerful fingers closed around my throat.

"Murderer!" he screamed. His face contorted. "Assassin!"

I clutched at his arm, trying to pry it away. He had caught me completely off guard. I couldn't move, couldn't breathe. I felt my face starting to purple.

"Father!" Jake said.

"Shut up, Marcus!"

I made a gurgling sound, trying to wrench away. He was crushing my windpipe. Cartilage ground against cartilage deep in my throat. I felt my eyes bulging. My lungs began to burn.

Jake cried, "Father, let him go!"

"Die!" he snarled at me. His right eye twitched again and again. "Die, you abomination!"

Jake threw himself across the bed, pinning Father's left arm with his body while pulling at the hand around my neck with both hands.

Father's grip loosened. I pried away his thumb, then bent it back until it broke with a dry snapping sound.

Shrieking, Father released me. "Assassins!" he shouted. "Murderers! Help me, Timon!"

I reeled to the wall and slid to the floor, coughing and choking. My vision dimmed. I still couldn't breathe. My head pounded and my lungs ached. I thought I was going to die.

"Let *go*!" Jake was bellowing, just as loud as Father. "Let go of me!"

I fell to my knees, head down, almost on the floor. Finally I managed to suck in a lungful of air. It hurt worse than not breathing. I began to cough and choke. Bile rose in my throat.

Something wet spattered me from the bed. I touched my cheek. Blood. I forced my head up to see.

Father's left cheek had split open along the seam of a plast. Blood poured out. As he flailed at my brother, pounding with his arms, trying to kick with his feet, his face started to peel back like a mask coming off, revealing bone and corded muscle and so much blood underneath.

"Stop it!" Jake pleaded, almost hysterical. "*Father*!"

I wanted to curl into myself, but that wouldn't help any of us. I forced my mind back and let stims take over. *Stay calm. React with purpose.* We needed help. *Help is outside.*

"Privacy—screens—off!" I croaked. Crote or the lammachs physicians would be waiting out there.

The gray wall flickered away. Timon Crote strolled in.

"What in all the worlds—" he began, gaping at the struggle.

"Assassins!" Father bellowed. A flap of loose skin folded back across his twitching eye. "*Murderers! Assassins—*"

I felt a sick shock running through me. "He's—gone—crazy!" I gasped out. "Tried—to kill—me!"

"Father, let go!" Jake was still shouting. Finally he broke from Father's grasp and reeled to the wall across from me. He had a bloody nose and raw scratches around his left eye.

"What did you do to him?" Crote demanded of us, a horrified look on his face.

"Nothing!" Jake said. "He attacked Ted!"

"It was Max!" Father cried, levering himself up with his elbows. "Max tried to kill me! *Assassins! Murderers!*"

Crote blanched. "Get out, you two!" he said to us in a terrifyingly quiet voice. "Computer—this is a medical emergency. Summon Dr. Espoja to the Emperor's room."

"*Assassins!*" Father screamed, rocking violently from side to side. He threw back his head and howled the word. "*Assassins!*"

Almost in tears, Jake fled to my side and pulled me to my feet. We made our way into the outer room, leaning on each other. I collapsed on the couch by the door, wheezing and massaging my throat. Jake stood beside me, staring at the door to Father's room. He pressed the tail of his shirt against his nose to staunch the flow of blood. Now and then I saw him dab at his injured eye, which had begun to swell shut.

I couldn't believe what had happened. I stared into the fountain, watching the lions spew water. Far off, Father continued to scream.

Then soft wind chimes played as half a dozen lammachs physicians, including Dr. Espoja, pounded past us. Medical devices filled their arms. From Father's room, I heard the hiss of a sedative. Father's cries of "Assassins!" faded away. Then came a low murmur of talk as Mr. Crote explained what had happened.

I hugged myself, rocking back and forth. The weight of the Empire pressed on my shoulders again. *We must be strong.* I heard Father's voice echoing in my mind. *We must always be united in times of crisis.* When I looked up at my brother, though, I remembered him ordering the destruction of Dulap's World, and I remembered our argument. He seemed as much a stranger as a part of me.

I pressed my eyes shut. Father had called me "Max" and Jacob "Marcus." We had only one Marcus in Meriman House, an elderly gardener who specialized in Davidian spice-flowers. It couldn't be him.

"Jacob—Theodore—" Crote began. I looked up and found him suddenly before us, twisting his hands together. "The lammachs had to sedate your father. They are examining him now."

"He's insane," I said, voice weak. I swallowed several times. My throat felt like pins had been driven through it.

"I think—" Crote began.

"Don't shield us," Jake said sharply. He dropped his shirt and I saw smears of blood all over his face and hands. "We aren't blind. We can see that he has severe brain damage."

Crote shuddered. "He seemed normal just a minute ago! What did you say to him? What did you do?"

"Nothing," Jake said. "We didn't have time."

"The lammachs missed something," I said, thoughts racing through a thousand volumes of human biology. "Or perhaps he had a stroke, or—"

"No." Crote seemed to sag into himself. "Dr. Espoja warned me yesterday that there might be lasting side effects. He said your father's wounds might affect his memory and his emotions. Might. I did not want to believe him."

"What does Dr. Espoja recommend?" I demanded. "What treatments exist?"

"Only time. And a complete cure is still not guaranteed. Dr. Espoja had to reconstruct quite a few neural clusters when he removed all the bullets and fragments of bone from your father's skull."

Jake said, "But what can be done now?"

"Constant mental stimulation—that's why His Excellency was reading the overnight financials—"

"We cannot wait," I said, rising and beginning to pace. "Father must be seen publicly."

"We can be on Horizon in a week—"

"That's too long, as you know." My thoughts had already begun turning through the possibilities. "He must be seen today. Tomorrow at the latest."

Crote shook his head. "We cannot risk an outburst like that in public. It could undermine the stability of the whole Empire!"

"Perhaps it's not an insurmountable problem," I said softly. "If we can maintain the illusion of normality, all else will fall into place."

"What do you mean?"

"Father appeared perfectly well when we first entered his room," I said. "Seeing us triggered some kind of faulty mental logic chain. If we avoid whatever stimulus set him off—I assume it was seeing Jake and me—he should be able to make a public appearance."

Crote hesitated. "It's dangerous."

"It's an acceptable risk, if all precautions are taken." I ticked them off on my fingers. "First, he must be kept lightly sedated to keep his emotions level. Second, Dr. Espoja must trim back his peripheral vision to keep his attention focused. Third, you must be there to distract him if something begins to set him off."

I could see Crote working through the ideas in his own mind. "Perhaps a review of the Sixteenth Fleet," he finally said. "They're still here, after all."

"An excellent idea," I told him. "With Admiral Sherman gone, he needn't spend much time with Captain de Marco. Just long enough for a handshake and a pat on the back. You'll be at his side the whole time. You can steer him through it."

"People will notice if both of you are absent."

"A hint that we are temporarily out of the favor should suffice," Jake said flatly. "I ordered Dulap's World destroyed without permission, remember. No one will question it if we are snubbed tomorrow."

Crote finally nodded. "We also have a few Argents who deserve commendation for their work on Dulap's World. A brief ceremony for them might be in order, too."

Jake snorted. "Medals? For almost getting us killed?"

"It wasn't their fault," I said. "They followed standard security procedures."

"A lot of good it did us."

Crote said, "I am most concerned with an Argent named Ethan Pierre, who saved your father's life. He shielded the Emperor from the worst of the weapons' fire with his own body. He will receive the Gold Star Cluster, posthumously."

"Did he have a family?" I asked.

"A wife and three sons."

"Add an annual stipend to cover his family's expenses." That's what Father would have done, I knew. "Thus are heroes rewarded."

"Yes, young master." Crote seemed a little more self-assured, I thought, since we had settled on a plan. "I will make the arrangements," he said. "We can broadcast it throughout the Empire—on time delay, of course, in case anything goes wrong."

"Play it up as a great event," Jake added. "Father, fully recovered, reviewing his triumphant troops."

"And then," I said softly, the full scope of my plan coming into view, "you will announce the continuation of his inspection tour of the Outer Rim worlds."

"What!" Crote stared at me, aghast. "Impossible!"

I smiled slowly. "I knew you would say that. But this is the perfect time to continue."

"Yes," Jake said after a second's thought,

eyes distant, analyzing the situation. "The illusion of Father's recovery will be complete. Everyone will think he must be well. Why else would he go on?"

Crote stared from me to Jake and back again. "No," he said. "It's foolhardy."

"The three of us will manage Father's schedule, not Father," I said, letting stims add persuasive undertones to my voice. "We will visit three more planets—Tripper's World, Erewhon, and Blessing." That would take us to three different sectors of the Empire and add a full two weeks to our schedule.

"But that's not a very convenient itinerary," he began.

"No, it's not," I said. "Deliberately so."

"It will delay our return to Horizon," Jake said, "long enough for Dr. Espoja to continue his work toward Father's full recovery."

"Perhaps we could allow the governor of each planet a brief audience," Crote whispered. "Ten minutes each, no more."

I nodded. "Then we are agreed," I said. "Please see to it."

"Of course, young master." Crote bowed, then headed for the lift, his gaze already far away. He would soon have the details well in hand, I knew.

"Wait," I said as the lift doors slid open for him. We still had one lingering piece of business to take care of.

When Crote turned to face me, I demanded in my most authoritative voice, "Who are Max and Marcus?"

He blinked. "They do not concern you."

"Let us decide that!"

He hesitated, then finally said, "Computer, cease monitoring this area for five minutes."

"Warning—" the computer began.

"Yes, yes," he snapped, "Just do it!"

Jake stared silently at Crote. I felt a nervous prickling along the back of my neck. This was important, some instinct told me. Perhaps as important as anything Crote had ever told us before.

"They're real, aren't they?" I said.

"Yes," he said, "they were real. But it is

forbidden to mention their names. It is forbidden to even think of them."

"Forbidden by whom?" Jake demanded.

"By the Emperor."

"Father brought it up," I said.

"He is not himself." Crote swallowed. "If I tell you, you must both promise never to mention them again. It might prove very dangerous. Do you understand?"

"Yes," Jake and I both said.

He licked his lips. "Maxim and Marcus Meriman were your father's first two sons. He executed them for treason thirteen years ago, when they—" His voice broke. He swallowed air. "When they tried to assassinate him and seize the Empire."

Turning, Crote fled to the back of the lift.

"Wait!" Jake cried.

"Let him go," I said. I realized Maxim and Marcus still meant something to him.

Crote's fingers stabbed blindly at the manual controls. Finally he hit the right buttons and the lift closed. Perhaps Crote had cared for Maxim and Marcus as much as he now cared for us, I thought. Perhaps he had raised them and nurtured them and given them all he had, only to be betrayed as Father had been betrayed. And then to have them executed for treason and virtually erased from existence —it had to hurt.

"You shouldn't have stopped me," Jake said, looking at me with his one good eye. "I wanted to ask about our mother."

"He wouldn't have said anything more." I didn't think that particular mystery would be solved anytime soon: we had been told not to ask about her ever since we were old enough to realize we didn't seem to have a mother anywhere in Meriman House.

"Perhaps not." Turning, he stared at the lift. "But at least we know we weren't alone. We did have other family besides Father."

"Yes."

Brothers. Strangely enough, it did not really surprise me. Although their names, their lives, their very existence had been stricken from every record I had at my mental call, knowing about them made pieces of a larger

puzzle fall into place. Odd looks and misspoken phrases, especially when we were very young, suddenly made sense. As did the great emphasis on morals, ethics, and responsibility we received through our stims . . . the morality which Jake had rejected only last night . . . the morality which Maxim and Marcus Meriman also must have rejected.

I swallowed. Could Jake be right? Could our morality be an artificial construct designed solely to control us? The idea merited further consideration, I thought. But not here, and not now.

"We must resemble them very closely," Jake went on. I heard awe in his voice. "They could not have been much older than us when they tried to seize the Empire."

Assuming they were born after Father assumed the throne, they could have been sixteen at the most, I realized. More likely fifteen, or even younger. Perhaps our age.

"The key word is tried," I said. "Father had them executed, remember. They were traitors. We aren't. So don't get any ideas." I held his gaze. "Your nose is bleeding again."

He dabbed at the blood with his shirt. "So you'll wait for Father to order our executions for crimes we didn't commit?"

"No." I paused, realizing I didn't have a plan. My head began to throb. I rubbed my temples. "I—I don't know."

"Father is not fit to rule," he said quietly. "Not in his current condition."

"Give him time."

"You know how unlikely it is that he will have a full recovery." I heard his stim training in every word, his voice calm and persuasive, carrying me along with him. "Father poses a threat not only to himself, but to us. To the continuation of his bloodline. To the existence of the Empire."

I felt my heart jump. "That's treason." Was this how Max and Marcus began their conspiracy? Had we inadvertently set our feet on that same path?

"No," he said quietly, "it's necessary."

As I stared at him, my thoughts automatically began to turn through the implications of his proposal. Removing Father from power would create an ever-expanding ring of reactions, many of them bad in my opinion. Father did not hesitate to execute his first two sons, I reminded myself, when they plotted to seize the Empire.

Jake sat next to me, folding his hands in his lap. "Do you want to die?" he asked. I heard the stims augmenting his voice, playing off of my already turbulent emotions. "Think about his hands on your neck, Ted. Think about his fingers choking the life from your body."

"No!"

"You know I'm right."

I stood and paced violently away from him. "I agree that Father is not fit to rule in his present condition," I said in a deliberately soft, "but he must be given time to recover. He deserves every chance—"

"That's what I meant!" He leaped to his feet and followed me. "Of course he must be given every chance to recover. But he must be removed first to ensure our safety."

At least he wasn't advocating murder, as I'd first suspected. Or had he changed his plans to fit my reaction? I studied him, hesitant to commit myself to anything he might propose. Father had to come first.

I finally said, "We can both name a dozen people who would plot to restore Father to the throne, sane or not, the moment he was deposed. Do you know how many people in Meriman House alone have personal loyalty stims to him? Those won't expire until his death. And there are undoubtedly many others we don't know about. He would become a magnet for intrigue."

"All new rulers have purges. We can tighten security."

"Our family has enough enemies already without adding more through purges. Besides, would you really want to start our rule with a bloodbath? Especially after Dulap's World?"

He frowned. "Go on."

"If Father did recover enough to take the throne again, suppose we stepped aside for him. What then?"

He paused, eyes distant, analyzing the scenario as I had already done.

"Civil war," he finally said. I heard disappointment in his voice. I knew he saw rioting on the Outer Rim planets, the entire Freedom Brigade mobilized to quell revolts, and possibly even invasions from the other Human Families. "A long and violent struggle to hold territory and regain control."

"That's right," I said. "A hundred planets with borderline loyalties would declare their independence the moment Father returned to the throne. It's exactly what the Borgialis have always prayed for. You know they would exploit the situation."

"So we're left with only two choices. Either we take decisive action now, or we wait. You vote to wait."

Decisive action had to mean killing Father. I swallowed, feeling sick at the thought. Then I remembered his hands on my throat, choking my life away.

That wasn't Father, I told myself. That was someone else, someone different, inside his body. We still had time to wait. Father would recover. Things would return to normal. They had to.

"How do you vote?" I asked.

He met my gaze. I saw fear in his eyes.

"One slip by Father and we're dead."

"I know." I remembered the crazed gleam in Father's eyes, the shouts of "Assassins!" and "Murderer!" But I also remembered the quiet man who made us laugh, who told us crazy stories of our family history at dinner, who had loved and cared for us all our lives. I could not turn my back on him, not while he had a chance to recover.

Softly, Jake said, "I'll wait, too."

I let my breath out. He had made the right decision, I thought. Hopefully time would fix everything. Time and Dr. Espoja.

"Notice," the computer said, "this area is now being monitored for security."

I said, "Discussion over."

"For now." He gave me a pointed nod. This isn't done yet, I thought. He isn't satisfied.

The lift doors opened for him, and as he stepped inside, he called for the main medical bay. Probably going to see his own physician about that eye, I thought. It had to hurt.

I sank down on a couch. For now, Father would be safe. That was the most important thing. I knew Jake wouldn't take any action without my support. We worked best as a team, counterbalancing one another. He had forgotten that yesterday, and the price had been high. I wouldn't let it happen again.

"Computer on," I said after a few more moments of introspection. "Where is Dr. Sanjarin?"

"Dr. Sanjarin is in Medical Bay 3."

"Summon him. I need medical assistance."

After a heartbeat, it said, "Dr. Sanjarin is on his way."

My thoughts returned to Maxim and Marcus Meriman, my older brothers, whom I could never meet. I wondered whether they truly looked like us, what they had thought, what they had dreamed. Treason . . . it seemed impossible. And yet Jake had just proposed the same thing.

How like Maxim and Marcus we must be. I wanted desperately to know more about them. We promised Crote we would forget what he told us, I reminded myself. Somehow, I knew it wouldn't be possible.

#

It only took Dr. Sanjarin a few minutes to stop the swelling and fix the bruised tissue in my throat. He made faint shuffing sounds of sympathy as I told him what had happened with Father, though he probably knew the whole story. Our physicians kept no secrets between them, since they always consulted with one another. Doubtless Dr. Sanjarin knew more of Father's condition than even Mr. Crote.

"Tell me truthfully," I said when he began tucking his instruments away. "What are my father's chances of a full recovery?"

"It is difficult to say, young master." The green scales around his neck deepened in color. He knew something, I realized, that he hadn't volunteered. "There are so many variables, yes?"

"You must have some idea," I said.

"Young master, your father is a strong man. He will rule for many more years, yes."

"Yes." I sighed. I hadn't really expected answers from him, but this had been a day of surprises and I could always hope.

"Now, young master, there is something else, yes?"

"No. Thank you."

He bowed and headed back toward the main medical bay.

I called the lift and rode one deck down. Since my schedule had generously allotted a full hour for visiting Father, I hadn't missed my morning stim session. In fact, I was a few minutes early. Might as well get it over with, I thought.

I got out at the Education Center. Its name always conjured visions of traditional schools in my mind, the kind with desks and teachers and happy students lined up for a chance to learn. Unfortunately, Jake and I never had the luxury of time. To help rule the Meriman Empire, we needed more skills and information than could ever be learned by rote, and that meant stim implants.

As the doors slid open, I stepped into a large round chamber. A cluster of six stim pods, shiny and black, sat on a raised platform in the exact middle. They looked like eggs sliced open lengthwise and leaned up against one another. Soft black cushions and upholstery hid the machinery within them. Jake already reclined in his pod, eyes closed, threads of silver running into his ears and nose. I glanced at the bio readouts projected over his head. They showed a slightly elevated body temperature, sluggish blood pressure, and low heart rate. The only spikes came from his highly charged brainwaves: normal for stim training.

To the right, at the monitoring station, stood two lammachs in pale yellow robes. They held lower social rank than Dr. Sanjarin or Dr. Espoja, and they averted their gazes as they bowed to me.

"What are you feeding me today?" I asked.

"History, young master, yes," said the one on the right, Dr. Evlara. He tapped the controls before him with one claw and a pod rotated soundlessly to face me.

History again. I made a face, but slid inside the pod to the left of Jake, settling my head between the cushions.

Soft motors hummed as the seat shifted slightly, accommodating my position and touching sensors to my skin. Dr. Evlara activated the equipment. Small vents opened over my face, releasing a mist of rose-scented psylocaine. I breathed and dizziness swept through me. My head seemed to be expanding. All at once I could see everything in the room simultaneously, down to the tiniest detail on the smallest mote of dust. Pressing my eyes closed, I still sensed every movement in the room, from the soft rush of air in the vents to rustle of the lammachs' robes to the faint rasp of Jake's breathing to my left.

I felt cool threads of silver crawling like insects across my neck and into my ears, then along my jaw and into my nostrils. I stiffened, uncomfortable, as their tiny probes connected to the stim receptors in my brain.

The unpleasant sensation ceased, and abruptly the universe exploded in lights and sounds and smells and textures, all moving too fast to follow. I felt myself rising on a tide of data, higher, rushing—

Until everything went black.

When I awoke, the insides of my head ached. I blinked as images flashed before me and stray bits of data bubbled up.

—a white-haired old man in archaic eyeglasses—

—a beautiful, haughty woman in silver and lace—

More and more faces and biographies of people long-dead flashed before me. I groaned and levered myself up with my elbows, blinking through crusted eyes. The stim had worked perfectly, as always. I sud-denly knew more about the Gates Family than I cared to, from their megalomaniacal ancestors on Earth to their early bids to take over the galaxy through overly elaborate computer systems which, of course, only their engineers could properly control and maintain. The advent of artificial intelligences capable of running themselves and managing human needs better than human programmers had been the Gates Family's ultimate downfall.

They had coasted through two centuries, until Philo Gates accidentally ceded half their empire to my great-grandfather[12], Albert Constantine Meriman, through a six-hundred-page trade agreement which Gates and his advisors didn't quite understand, until they discovered great-grandfather[12] Albert's people had taken over the governments of nearly five hundred Gates worlds overnight. I also knew how great-grandfather[10] Patrice Meriman had reneged on that same trade agreement two generations later, annexing most of the rest of the Gates Empire. Today their Family controlled one hundred and seventy-two star systems and barely half a hundred civilized worlds.

Dr. Evlara loomed over me suddenly, offering a glass of *cieana* juice. "Drink, young master, yes?"

"Thanks." I drained the sweet pulpy mix in three gulps. The electrolytes would help my body recover.

Stretching, I pulled myself up. Already my headache had begun to fade. In a few minutes, I would be completely recovered.

Jake had already gone. I had been under for a little over two hours, I noted as my mental clock ticked away the seconds. Lunch came next on our schedule.

\#

Head filled with a hundred thousand new images, I wandered into the dining room. Today the walls showed a twilight desert scene from Horizon, complete with giant tortoises and half a dozen brightly winged sawbucks sailing overhead. Jake, already seated, acknowledged my presence with a nod. He had new skin plasts around his left eye, I noticed. The swelling had vanished.

"Is Mr. Crote joining us?" I asked, sliding into my chair.

"No, it's just you and me."

Crote had probably gone back to stay with Father, I thought, after the lammachs finished with him. That's what I would have done in his place . . . not only to observe his actions, but to protect us from him. Or him from us.

"You may serve," Jake told the shais on duty.

They brought us cold salad plates, followed by warm Arcturan gelfish in roe, then finally a broad blade of dark chocolate with the family crest drawn in white crystal sugar. Our promised treat from yesterday, I supposed.

As we finished, the ship's computer sounded three soft tones. That meant a time warning for Jake and me.

"Are we late for something?" I glanced at my brother. According to the morning's schedule, we weren't due to go over the financials with Crote for another sixteen minutes.

"Computer on," Jake said, "Explain the last alert you sounded."

"*Timon Crote has cancelled your afternoon sessions*," it said in its soft, sexless voice. "*You are to report immediately to Lieutenant Adam Havis in room 1410, Blue Section.*"

"Why?" I demanded. The blue section housed the Brigadiers, not the gym. "Hasn't he seen enough of us today?"

"That information is not available."

I sighed. *Wasn't talking to you.*

"We'd better get going." Jake pushed his chair back. The shais hurried to collect his dishes. "I don't want another fifty pushups for being tardy."

I joined him, and we headed for the lift. Mentally, I called up our ship's schematics. Blue Section's Room 1410 was a small conference room used primarily for briefing Argents: hardly the place for training. Or did

our new instructor have something else in mind?

"You're late," Lieutenant Havis said as we stepped in from the almost frenetic bustle of the blue section's 14th level. A steady stream of Argents in gray and white fatigues, passing in the corridor outside, kept glancing in curiously. They all saluted when they saw us.

"Sorry," Jake said to Havis and Sameel. "We came—"

"Never apologize!" Havis snapped. "You are the Emperor's son! That will cost you ten push-ups." He motioned to Sameel, who raised a privacy screen across the doorway.

"Yes, sir." Jake said. "Now?"

"When we're done. Come inside." Turning, he stalked toward the broad table across from us.

Things were not starting off very well, I thought, following him. The conference room had eight long, curved benches facing the table. Near the far wall, the computer projected images of Argents in red and gold dress uniforms. Each image rotated slowly, like store models displaying the latest fashions. I stared at gold helmets with red visors, padded red shirts and pants with our family crest in gold over the heart, and shiny black boots with gravity plates in the toes and heels. Rather than heavy pulse rifles, these Argents carried compact energy pistols and long double-edged knives.

Havis nodded to Sameel, who produced two medium sized packages from behind the conference table. Sameel tossed one to Jake and one to me.

I fingered the thin, crinkly wrapping material. It felt like cloth and metal inside, I thought. Clothing? My gaze returned to the models behind Havis and Sameel. Uniforms? It had to be.

"Go ahead," Havis told us. "Put them on."

I ripped my package open, spilling red cloth with gold trim. Part of our family crest appeared. What I'd taken for metal turned out to be a helmet with visor and boots. Yes, definitely the dress uniform of an Argent.

I spread out the boots, helmet, and bulky feeling jumpsuit on one of the benches. It seemed strait-forward enough. Quickly I stripped, folding my clothes neatly, then slipped on the jumpsuit. When the protective cup fitted over my genitals, a catheter wormed its way into place, creating a brief moment of discomfort. I tabbed the seals from my crotch to my chin. Hissing faintly, the uniform expelled trapped air and formed a skintight bond. It fit me perfectly, of course. I picked up the boots and sat on the bench.

"You're both too short," Havis told us bluntly, "but I think you can pass."

"We are only twelve," I said, holding up my head. "Our full growth is still a few years away."

"No excuses. That will cost you fifteen push-ups when we're done."

I carefully blanked my expression. "Yes, sir."

"I take it," Jake said, tabbing his suit closed at the neck, "that we are to join Father's honor guard tomorrow."

"Crote thought it best," Havis said. "He wants you both involved, though behind the scenes for the moment. Fortunately all eyes will be on the Emperor tomorrow, not his honor guard. That's your only saving grace."

Did Havis know about Father's injuries? "May I ask," I began, staring up at him, wondering how to phrase such a delicate question, "your grasp of the present situation?"

"My grasp is that I have been fully briefed about the Emperor's condition, if that's what you're softfooting around. Sameel and I will complete the Emperor's honor guard tomorrow. It will be a dry run for the rest of His Majesty's tour of the Outer Rim planets."

"Thank you."

I noticed Jake struggling to get his feet into his boots. He began pounding the heels on the floor.

"Is there a problem?" Sameel asked.

"They're too small."

I looked down. My boots looked big enough. But then, so had Jake's.

"There is a trick." Sameel crouched next to my brother, pointing. I leaned over to watch. "Place one hand at the heel—yes, there—and press while you push your toes against the floor."

Jake did as instructed, and it worked. I followed his lead, applying pressure at the correct spots, and my boots slid on easily, too. They fit so snugly, they might have been part of my body. As I watched, they meshed with the fabric of my uniform, forming another airtight seal.

Standing, I tried to imagine how I looked. With my shoulders thrust back and my head up, I must cut a rather striking figure, I decided with satisfaction.

I pulled on my helmet and lowered the visor, sealing myself inside the uniform. Instantly computer displays flickered to life: several images of the conference room, layered over one another. I found I could toggle through them by nudging my chin forward: first heat and energy sources, then magnetic fields, then radiation levels, and then light well into the infra-red end of the spectrum. As I breathed deeply, I felt clean air pumping steadily from the small gills under my arms, through the purifiers in my shoulderpads, and to my face. Pausing, I listened to soft purr of my equipment as it adapted itself to the rhythms of my body like a second skin. I had never tried on an Argent's uniform before, but it was similar to half a dozen other environmental suits I'd worn. You could live for days in one. I found it more than satisfactory.

"How does it feel?" Havis asked. His voice sounded a little flat, but perfectly clear.

"Good," I said. Jake echoed my sentiments.

"You have a full communication system inside your helmet. Focus your attention to the far left for the switch."

I did so, and four options appeared:

ENVIRONMENT	NOISE REDUCTION
UNIT	BRIGADE

I focused my eyes on each in turn. EN-VIRONMENT provided me with normal hearing. NOISE REDUCTION did the same, but subtly muted. It probably flattened loud noises like explosions to a tolerable level, I thought. UNIT let me hear Jake breathing, and BRIGADE suddenly opened me to chatter from every open channel aboard the ship.

I found I could activate two comm options at once and selected ENVIRONMENT and UNIT.

Havis said, "Walk for me."

I blinked, not sure I'd heard correctly. "Did you say walk?"

"Yes. Across the room and back."

I had learned my earlier lessons well. I did not question or argue. I simply walked to the door, turned, and came back.

Sameel shook his head and made a laughing sound deep in his throat. "Pitiful."

"What?" I demanded, hands on my hips. My voice sounded abnormally loud inside the helmet.

"You swagger like you own the ship," Havis said. He put one hand to his chin thoughtfully. "Anyone with eyes can see you're not a Brigadier. Now, watch Sam and learn how a real combat veteran walks. Sam?"

Sameel walked to the door and back. His steps were precise, even, and very carefully controlled. His arms swung a little, but no more than necessary for balance. He kept his every movement economical, and when he stopped I had the impression of a dancer poised to leap. All Brigadiers walked that way, I realized now that I thought about it. I glanced at my brother. It seemed we had a lot of work ahead if we were going to pass as Argents tomorrow.

"Now," Havis said, "you try it, Jacob."

Jacob took a deep breath and marched to the door and back. He did better than me, but not by much. His movements were too self-conscious, I realized as I heard the gravity plates in the toes and heels of his boots tapping against the floor. Brigadiers in general and Argents most specifically moved silently and with an almost liquid grace. They didn't

need to think about it, I realized. That walk had become part of them.

Havis frowned, but did not criticize. "Watch Sam again," he said to both of us, "and this time, note the placement of his feet. Sam?"

They drilled us for six hours straight on how to walk, then how to stand at attention, then how to salute properly, then every other detail of an Argent's deportment. From the largest motion to the slightest gesture, Havis left nothing out. Patiently, Sameel demonstrated over and over again how to do things the Brigade's way. I had never realized how much work went into being a member of the Freedom Brigade.

Finally, as my stomach began to growl with hunger, Havis called a halt. "Change back into your civvies," he said. "That is enough for today. You are not going to improve more before tomorrow."

"So you're satisfied with us," Jake said, pulling off his helmet.

"Each member of the Freedom Brigade goes through a three-month indoctrination process," Sameel said. "Argents undergo an additional six months of training. Such instruction cannot be crammed into a few hours. But," Havis added almost grudgingly, "you might pass muster if you stay behind Sam and me. Let anyone who looks at the Emperor's honor guard watch us. Keep your movements to a minimum. Do nothing to attract attention to yourselves, young masters."

"We won't," I said, sitting and tugging at my boots. They came off with little sucking sounds. "That's the last thing we want."

He nodded. "Good."

As soon as I had changed back into my old clothes, I did the twenty-five push-ups he had charged me with. Jake had gotten off more lightly this time with only twenty. Then we climbed to our feet and looked at our uniforms, now folded neatly on one of the benches. How would we get them back to our quarters? We had both shredded the pouches they came in. With the constant traffic outside this room, dozens of people would spot the uniforms if we carried them out. From that information, a clever person might well deduce the identities of the two short Argents accompanying the Emperor on his inspection of the Sixteenth Fleet tomorrow. Our success depended on complete secrecy.

"Computer," I said, "are any autons assigned to this room?"

"*There are no autons assigned to this room. A cleaning detail of six shais is dispatched after every conference.*"

Sameel raised one hand. "Leave them," he said. "I will get them cleaned and delivered to your room before tomorrow."

Probably a wise move, I decided.

"When will we—" Jake began.

Havis said, "The computer will post your instructions tomorrow. Dismissed, young masters."

When we returning to our suite, we found autons laying out a light supper in the salon: cold sandwiches, chilled soup, and diced fruit. It seemed we weren't going to go over the daily financials with Crote after all. Nor were there any updates from him about Father's condition, except in the most roundabout way: when I asked for our father's schedule, the computer informed us that the inspection of the Sixteenth Fleet would take place at 08:00.

After a leisurely meal, I showered again, changed into night clothes, and slid into bed, determined to get a long night's sleep.

"Computer on," I said, lying back. "Play sleeping hypnotics." I didn't want any more bad dreams. The last few days had been more demanding than any I could remember, and with Father's condition so uncertain, I could not depend on our schedule getting easier. As if Crote would ever let me take things easy, I thought, already drifting toward sleep. Or Havis, either, for that matter.

The computer began to cycle through ocean sounds from Horizon. Soft hypnotics underlying the lap of waves and the distant calls of Mother Earth gulls exhorted me to relax, sleep, dream pleasant dreams.

I had just begun to doze when a soft computer tone sounded. I awakened instantly, sitting up. A visitor—Jake?

"Who is it?" I asked the computer.

"*Timon Crote wishes to see you,*" it informed me.

"Let him in." Rubbing my eyes, I called for lights, and a pleasant glow filled the room. I had been in bed only eleven minutes. It was still early.

The privacy screen over the door vanished. Without preamble, Crote entered and sat beside me. "Ted," he said, not meeting my gaze, "I have always tried to let you and Jacob have as much of a free hand in your lives as possible. At times it has been difficult, considering your positions as heirs to the Meriman Empire. But I have always tried to give you enough room to think and act on your own. As I did—" His voice choked. "As I did with the other two we discussed."

"Yes." My mouth went dry. With Crote, such statements usually came before punishments. What had I done? *He knows we discussed Father,* I thought suddenly. *He knows Jake wanted to kill him.*

But that wasn't impossible. Crote himself had turned off the computer monitors in Father's suite. I had heard him do it, and the computer had confirmed it.

"Neither you nor Jacob," Crote went on, still not looking at me, "has ever given me pause to wonder about your futures . . . until now. I knew, as I know your characters, that you would always do exactly what was expected of you. Your duty."

"Yes." I barely breathed. *'Until now.' He said 'until now.'*

"Computer," he said, "cease monitoring this room for ten minutes."

"Warning—"

"Do it."

He opened his right hand, revealing a small silver datadisk. He clicked it, and a miniature replica of the waiting area outside Father's room appeared, completely with burbling lion fountain, soft couches, and Jake and me. Jake bled from his nose. I hugged myself and rocked back and forth, wheezing faintly, clearly in pain.

As I watched, Crote emerged from Father's room, told us the news, and together we worked through a plan of action. The whole scene played through exactly as I remembered it.

Then Crote ordered the computer to stop monitoring the area. It complied . . . and the recording continued through the parts he had instructed the computer to ignore. As I stared, my sense of horror growing, Jake and I began talking about how to best protect ourselves from Father.

"Father is not fit to rule," the recording of Jake said quietly. "Not in his current condition."

"Give him time."

"You know how unlikely it is that he will have a full recovery. Father poses a threat not only to himself, but to us. To the continuation of his bloodline. To the existence of the Empire."

"That's treason," I said.

Crote clicked off the disk.

I met his gaze. His eyes, so bleak, sent a chill through me. *He knows everything.* I swallowed. *It's treason, just like Maxim and Marcus.*

"Sir—" My voice cracked. I didn't know what else to say.

"How could you two even think it?" he finally whispered. "How could you? Dulap's World was bad enough, but *this*—"

"Are we foolish to take precautions?" I asked after a heartbeat.

Crote opened his mouth, but no words came out. We had hurt him, I realized, as Maxim and Marcus must have hurt him so many years ago. Only Jake and I had decided not to act. We had decided to work toward Father's recovery. Didn't that prove our loyalty?

"Not foolish," he finally said. "*Stupid.* There is a difference."

I swallowed. "What do you want us to do?"

"What you are told. Nothing more. These difficulties with your father will resolve themselves in time. For now, you must hide your concerns and keep your thoughts private. Wait, learn, and most of all trust no one—not even your brother. You yourself called Jacob's suggestion treason. This recording is enough to get him killed, and needlessly. If it fell into the wrong hands . . ."

"How is it possible," I finally said, hoping to steer us toward a safer subject, "that this recording exists?"

"Requests for privacy shut off official monitors. But they also activate more sensitive ones which both the Emperor and I may access at will."

Panic surged through me again. "Then Father—"

"The Emperor is sedated. Dr. Sanjarin added a second web of minor blood vessels to the frontal portion of his brain, increasing blood flow. There is a chance it will help."

I nodded. "And this recording?"

Crote rose. "The Emperor will never see it, unless you show it to him." He tossed the disk onto my bed. "Guard yourself well, Ted. Do not repeat the mistakes of those who came before you. Or of your brother."

I swallowed. "And Jake?" I whispered. Would Crote write him off? Would he turn my brother in for treason?

He hesitated, searching my eyes. "You must never again speak of this matter unless you are truly alone. I will erase this conversation from the database, as I erased the one I just gave you. Jacob will undergo additional loyalty stims when we return to Horizon. And Theodore . . . in life, you seldom get a second chance. Keep your brother safe."

He left, and as the door shut behind him, I picked up the disk and fingered it absently, my thoughts far away. I had been kept ignorant of a number of important factors, it seemed. My elder brothers. My illusion of privacy. How much else?

"Dim the lights," I said. "Resume sleep mode." Darkness crept in around me. Ten seconds later, ocean sounds began.

I switched the disk to "record" mode, letting it take in the waves and rushing water, drowning out the words of Jake's treasonous proposal for all time.

Let it end here. I set the disk down on the pillow beside me. I would have to warn Jake tomorrow, somehow. And I would have to watch him from now on, even as I watched myself.

The next morning, I awoke slowly. The hypnotics had done their job well and I felt much refreshed. I hadn't dreamed of Crote or Jake or conspiracies against Father. I had a slight stiffness in my muscles, mostly in my wounded arm, but that would pass in time.

In the dimness of my room, I sensed autons scurrying as they prepared for the coming day. Time to get up.

"Lights on," I said.

At the foot of my bed, a silver auton finished laying out an Argent's red and gold dress uniform. Bowing, it folded up both sets of arms and rolled out of sight.

"Computer," I said, "are there any messages for me?"

"You have one message from Lieutenant Adam Havis."

"Go."

A holograph flickered in front of me. "Young masters," Havis said, bowing slightly, "all arrangements are complete. Report to the *Gatsby* at 07:30. We need to be in position before the Emperor arrives. Do not forget your walk, and do not forget to keep your visors down in the public corridors. Havis out."

The *Gatsby*, smallest of the shuttles aboard the Pegasus, only had three passenger compartments above an engineering deck, I saw as I called the schematics up in my mind. It also had an observation bubble on top. Doubtless Father would ride up there as he looked over the Sixteenth Fleet. And we would be behind him.

I slid from the sheets. We had a little more than an hour to get to the *Gatsby*. Plenty of time. Shrugging off my night clothes, I began to dress.

Twenty minutes later, I wandered into the dining room. Jake was just finishing his meal. Like me, he wore his black Argent's uniform.

"Business is good," he said. He had been studying the night's financials over breakfast. Now he waved off the computer display, tilting back in his chair as the hologram faded.

"Of course it is." I slid into my seat, stifling a yawn, and set my helmet on the table. Two shais began serving me: jellied klioberries in sauce, melon balls warmed to blood temperature, and six crisped wheat wafers. "Father's continuation of his inspection tour must have stabilized everything by now."

"That should make Mr. Crote happy," he said.

"Not to mention Father."

I ate quickly, and when I finished my last wafer, I motioned for the shais to clear my dishes. They began to do so slowly and with meticulous care.

"I trust we didn't make a mistake yesterday," he said, staring across the table at me.

I shook my head slightly. "Not here," I mouthed.

He gave me a puzzled look, but grew silent.

We still had fifteen minutes before our time to report to the *Gatsby*. Together, we strolled to the lift and *Gatsby* down to the ship's main corridor. Just before the doors opened, I put on my helmet and lowered the visor. Jake followed suit. I switched to UNIT and heard Jake's breathing in my ears.

"You there?"

"Yes," he said.

We stepped out into bustling crowds. Argents and technicians and autons and alien menials all packed the main corridor, hurrying on various pressing tasks. Nograv sleds whizzed down a narrow aisle in the center, transporting supplies to the far ends of the ship. Nobody yielded to us, and after a second's hesitation I jumped into traffic and found myself matching pace with a group of technicians heading toward the shuttle bay. I let my legs fall into the easy gliding rhythm of a seasoned veteran. Quickly we passed from the gold section of the ship to the blue.

My brother caught up. "What did you mean at breakfast?" he asked.

"I'm not sure this is private enough," I told him.

"It's an encrypted channel. Just us."

"Havis and Sameel are on it, too."

"If they're listening."

"Sam?" I asked. "Lieutenant Havis?"

Neither of them replied.

"See?" Jake said.

Still I hesitated. Would Crote and Father be able to monitor securely encrypted Argents' channels for suit-to-suit chatter? *Probably*, something inside me said. *It's better to be safe.* Perhaps I could couch my words so only Jake would understand.

I said. "I can only say this: never assume you are alone, brother, even when the computer monitors are turned off."

"Why?" he demanded. "Did something—"

"Yes."

"Yesterday?"

"With Crote."

I heard him swallow. "Am I in danger?" he finally asked.

"No. I took care of it."

After another minute, he said, "I trust you, Teddy. You know that, don't you?"

"Yes. But you shouldn't."

"Don't you trust me?"

"I have been warned not to trust anyone," I said. "Not anymore. Not even you."

"By whom?"

"I . . . can't say."

He turned his head to look at me for a second, but I couldn't see his eyes through the shiny black visor. We walked in silence. It was just as well, I thought. The less we said, even here, the better off we would be.

We passed from the blue section to the red, coming to the vast shuttle bay. Pausing, I gazed past our two planet-hoppers in their cradles, the *Hydra* and its exact counterpart, the *Medusa*. Beyond them sat two smaller shuttles, the *Garnet* and the *Jersey*, and beyond them the *Tolstoy* and the *Gatsby*. Nograv sleds piloted by silver autons glided across the cavernous room. Technicians seemed to be everywhere, calling orders, carrying small diagnostic machines, and running equipment checks. No one paid us the slightest bit of attention.

I led the way toward the *Gatsby*. My mental clock told me we were a full two minutes early. That should make Havis happy, I thought.

The lieutenant met us by the shuttle's open hatch. The *Gatsby* was an elongated little vessel, scarcely thirty meters from end to end, with graceful decorative fins at its sides and tail. Technicians in red and silver crawled across its hull, checking every inch of its surface.

"You're late," Havis said. He wore a dress uniform identical to ours, but with the visor pushed up.

"Yes, sir," Jake and I both said simultaneously. Never mind that we were actually two minutes early.

He grinned suddenly. "You're learning. Follow me."

He led us up the ramp and into the Gatsby's belly—the engineering level. Half a dozen technicians, along with our pilots, busied themselves with systems checks. We might have been invisible, for all the attention they paid to us. Then Havis led us up a set of rungs to the passenger level. Here, in the main salon, I found Timon Crote, Dr. Espoja, and several other lammachs physicians. They had our father on a nograv gurney; he seemed to be sleeping soundly.

I started toward Father, but Havis caught my arm. "On to the observation deck," he said. "That's where the honor guard belongs."

Nodding, I followed him to a tiny lift. The three of us rode up to a round dome eight meters high and twice as broad. A replica of Father's gold throne on Horizon already sat there, in the exact center, facing toward the front of the *Gatsby*.

Pushing up my visor, I walked once around the chamber, finding little of interest. No chairs, no refreshments, nothing but the throne. Blast shields covered the dome, so we couldn't even see outside.

"Where is Sameel?" I asked.

Havis said, "He will accompany the Emperor up in the lift."

A soft warning tone sounded.

"That's the signal," Havis said, lowering his visor. "Get ready."

Jake and I lowered our visors, too. I switched the comm system to UNIT and abruptly heard three other sets of lungs breathing softly.

"We are getting into the lift now," Sameel's voice said. "His Excellency is fully awake."

"How is he?" Jake demanded.

"No irrelevant chatter," Havis snapped. "That will cost you ten pushups when we're done." He took his position to the right and slightly behind the throne. "Ted, you stand two paces behind me, like we rehearsed. Jake, mirror his position on the other side."

Jake shut up and followed instructions. We had just gotten into place when the lift doors opened.

"Attention!" Havis barked.

We snapped rigidly upright, arms at our sides, heads back. I gazed out the corner of my eyes toward the lift doors. Father—moving slowly, with Timon Crote and Dr. Espoja bracing his arms—walked to the throne and sat heavily. He had dark circles under his eyes and his cheeks sagged. It struck me how much older he looked today.

"Parade rest!" Havis barked.

I set my feet shoulder width apart and folded my arms behind my back, chest thrust out. I didn't move, didn't speak, hardly dared breathe. I tagged the STANDARD comm setting, too, to hear what everyone else was saying to Father.

"—will be all," Father said, waving Dr. Espoja away.

Crote nodded once to the lammachs, who led his team back into the lift. As the doors closed, I felt the deep rumble of heavy machinery through the deck at my feet: the ramps had begun to retract into the ship.

Timon Crote took his place at Father's right hand. "It's time, Excellency."

Father sat up a little straighter. "Launch us," he commanded.

I felt the slightest flutter of vertigo as the docking cradle began to lower us. I knew we were descending slowly from an open hatch in the docking bay's floor. I had seen it so often, I could picture it exactly in my mind: the huge bay doors swinging open below the *Gatsby*, the shuttle floating down and out in a shimmer of light as forcefields and static screens kept the ship's atmosphere safely in place.

As we cleared the *Pegasus*, the blast shields covering the dome overhead slowly peeled back, giving us a splendid view of the heavens. Four hundred silver starships hung in the darkness. Directly above, the *Pegasus* lay bathed in full sunlight. The hatch in her central section began to close. All along the starboard side, I could see tiny faces pressed up against all the viewports, cheering.

Father raised his right hand, giving a triumphant wave.

"Now," he said, voice a little slurred, "forward to the *Nathan Meriman*." The pilots below heard and followed his instructions, accelerating gently toward the flagship of the Sixteenth Fleet.

As we neared, a life-sized hologram of Captain Julian De Marco appeared before the throne. He wore a black dress uniform with twin rows of silver buttons and four silver stars at his collar. He knelt, bowing his head.

"Highness," he breathed.

"Rise," Father said, voice growing louder and stronger. "We thank you for your years of service, Captain De Marco. We are pleased to offer you command of the Six-

teenth Fleet."

"Thank you, Highness."

Father began to drone on about the duties of a good officer, how the Freedom Brigade served not just the Meriman Empire but all humanity. It was much the same speech he always gave on such occasions. Doubtless he had it well memorized. Even so, his hand gestures—so firm and decisive on Dulap's World—now seemed fluttery and weak to my trained eyes.

My attention began to wander. I gazed out at Dulap's World, counting the dozens of roiling storms that now swept through the upper atmosphere at hundreds of kilometers per hour, then the one-thousand-sixty-eight visible viewports on the *Nathan Meriman*, then the four-thousand-two-hundred-four faces (human and lammachs, shai and jibb) visible at all those viewports.

A faint shimmer in the space next to Dulap's World drew my attention. It started like the faintest of rainbows, but rippling outward like rings in a pond. I blinked and squinted, trying to make it out. An optical illusion? A trick of the sun? A hydrogen cloud?

Or . . . a ship emerging from nospace?

The ripples expanded, glowing brightly. Definitely a ship, I thought, intrigued. Probably some tramp freighter that hadn't heard of the planet's destruction, making a routine stop. Still, it was best to make certain.

I nudged my comm system to UNIT. "Lieutenant Havis," I began quietly.

"Later," he snapped. "Brigadiers never speak while their Emperor is talking. That will cost you twenty-five pushups when we're done."

Another nospace ring appeared beside the first, then a second, then dozens more, all in the space of a heartbeat.

"Listen to me," I said urgently, "we have incoming ships, a lot of them, just beyond Dulap's World!"

"Eh? Where?" He pivoted to see.

An instant later an emergency alert sounded inside my helmet, a piercing tone followed by a communications officer's cries of, "Battle stations! All Brigadiers to battle stations!" over every channel.

Father droned on, oblivious, praising the Freedom Brigade for their especially fine efforts in hunting down the Irenz pirates six months before. De Marco's hologram flickered and vanished as the captain sprinted away from the projectors.

I tore off my helmet, not caring for the moment whether Father saw me. Something was very, very wrong, I knew. I gazed up through the observation dome as yet more nospace distortion rings appeared, fifty, then a hundred, then more than even my stims could count. Jake pulled off his own helmet and gazed at them, too.

The whole Sixteenth Fleet began to shift, maneuvering thrusters firing.

"Pilot! Bring us around!" Havis called, striding forward decisively. "Put us behind the *Nathan Meriman*! Fastest speed!"

"Who are they?" Jake asked softly. "Ted?"

Dozens of huge rectangular battle cruisers slid into normal space simultaneously, and more followed right on their tails. Each was nearly as large as the *Pegasus*. I had never seen their design before.

"Identify them!" Crote was shouting. "Bring the fleet around! Prepare to fire! De Marco! *De Marco*!"

"The Borgialis," I breathed. We had stayed here too long. They had mounted a surprise assault, designed to finish the botched assassination attempt.

Ripples of light began flashing along the ships' sides—missiles being launched. They had fired on us. What had they targeted? How long till impact?

My thoughts ran through the possible trajectories, and I pinpointed more than one thousand distinct lines of fire streaking across space and closing fast with our fleet.

"Protect the Emperor!" Havis bellowed. "Sameel—"

"It's too late!" I cried.

And then the first missile hit.

Brilliant light flooded the observation dome, so bright the automatic filters couldn't compensate for it. I shaded my eyes a fraction too late and wished I'd kept on my helmet.

Three seconds later it faded. Blinking through afterimages, I gaped out at the Pegasus. A line of flames stretched from her bow to her stern, huge gouts of fire and plasma fed by escaping oxygen and ruptured power conduits. Then came a quick series of flashes, like fireworks only several magnitudes brighter, as atomic warheads detonated inside her . . . planet busters, fired directly into the ship. I winced. The Borgialis weren't taking chances. If the attack didn't kill us outright, they wanted radiation to finish us off.

"By all the gods," Sameel said softly. He and Lieutenant Havis had pulled off their helmets, too. I heard Sameel muttering the Brigadier's Prayer for those comrades now lost.

I blinked and fell back on military tactics stims. Every single missile had targeted the *Pegasus*, I saw now. Had the Borgialis fired at open targets, the *Gatsby* would almost certainly have been destroyed; we had no battle armor or heavy shielding to protect us. Not that they would have done much good against such firepower. I felt a sick dread rising up to overwhelm me.

I turned my attention back to the *Pegasus*. She rolled end-over-end now, out of control, beyond any possible help. The battle took on the inevitable, inexorable pace of a computer simulation, and I deliberately studied those long, rectangular enemy ships, trying to take in every detail. Any information I gathered might prove vital later. Each stretched about five kilometers long, with two hundred evenly spaced weapon batteries on each side and shuttle bay doors on the bottom and aft. How many ships? More than thirteen hundred so far, my stims told me, and more kept appearing.

"—if you please, Excellency," Crote was saying insistently.

I took a moment to glance at the throne. Havis and Crote had Father by the arms, trying to lever him up.

"Why, Timon?" Father asked with child-like simplicity.

"This way, Excellency," Crote said soothingly. "We must get you below, where it's safe."

"That's right," Havis said. "The battle—"

"Never leave until a battle is won!" Father sat back stubbornly, shrugging off Crote's hand. "Call my commanders! Where is Admiral Sherman?"

"Sir—!" Crote cried, wringing his hands.

I stepped forward. Clearly Father was in no condition to command anything right now.

"The lammachs must sedate him again," I said. "Fetch Dr. Espoja."

"Max," Father breathed, focusing on me.

"Do it!" I snapped to Crote. "Now!"

With a frightened glance at Father, Timon Crote fled to the lift. Havis gave me a half nod of approval. Sameel's eyes were all the way open for, I think, the first time since we had met him, though his gaze still fixed the *Pegasus* and his lips still moved with prayers.

"Guard the Emperor," I told them. "Make sure he's kept safely in his throne."

They took positions to either side of Father, ready to act if necessary. We didn't have time for arguments. *Havis will guard our backs*, I thought. *He will keep Father's hands from around my throat.* It would be up to Dr. Espoja to get Father sedated and bundled off below.

I turned my attention back to the battle. Why hadn't our ships begun to fire? Only twenty-eight seconds had passed since the alarm went up. It seemed an eternity. Battle-ready status had to be attained within 30 seconds in simulated battle drills, according to the Freedom Brigade's regulations.

"Assassins," Father whispered. "Assassins."

"Not now, Father." I pointed at the *Pegasus*. "We saved you from that ship. Without us, you would be dead now. Think about that before you accuse us of treason."

Father grew silent. So much for our plans. We would have to bring him back to Horizon immediately. Assuming we got away from here alive.

Everything swung dizzily as our pilot maneuvered the *Gatsby* around the *Nathan Meriman* on full thrusters. As I focused on the Borgialis' fleet again, they fired a second volley . . . five hundred twenty-two missiles this time, my stims counted. Once again every single shot targeted the *Pegasus*. If they had fired all available weapons in their first volley, they still had at least twice that many missiles loaded and ready to launch . . . probably held in reserve for the rest of the Sixteenth Fleet, which now included us.

Something pinged on the hull, then twice more on the observation dome. I jumped, startled, and suddenly it sounded like a hailstorm.

"Debris!" Jake said.

It had to be small pieces of the *Pegasus*. Nothing like that could penetrate the *Gatsby* tough outer hull, but I saw no sense in taking chances. We had to protect ourselves in case anything bigger followed.

"Computer," I said. My voice sounded flat and utterly emotionless. "Close the blast shields."

As the protective durasteel skin crawled over the observation dome, that second volley of missiles hit the *Pegasus*. This time she broke apart like an eggshell when the atomics detonated, and long coils of plasma snaked through the wreckage, igniting more fires. I hadn't realized how much a starship could burn, even in the vacuum of space.

"Did you see any lifepods?" I said, glancing at Havis.

He shook his head. I swallowed. Even before I'd asked, I had known that no lifepods could have escaped. It had happened too fast, too violently. The crew, Dr. Sanjarin and the other lammachs, and even our own Argents had all died within seconds.

My hands tightened into fists. The Bor-

gialis would pay for this, I vowed. We would see their empire broken, their Family scattered, their homeworld destroyed like Dulap's World.

"I swear it," I whispered aloud.

Then a dark shape eclipsed the plasma fires where the *Pegasus* had been. Our pilot had brought us safely behind the *Nathan Meriman*. We were out of the line of fire for the moment.

The blast shields locked together overhead. I took a deep, calming breath. We had more important things to worry about, like getting Father—and the rest of us—to safety.

The lift doors opened and the lammachs trotted out with a nograv gurney, heading toward Father. Crote lingered between the open doors.

Before Father could speak, Dr. Espoja sprayed a blue mist over his face. Father slumped, snoring softly.

"What do we do now?" I asked Havis.

"Run," he said. "Shall I give the orders, young master?"

I looked at Jake, who nodded. We agreed on one thing, at least.

"Yes," I told Havis.

"Pilot," he said, "prepare for a nospace jump, fastest speed. Set course for the nearest Freedom Brigade baseworld." I knew we would be safe there, surrounded by thousands of ships and hundreds of thousands of Brigadiers.

"Aye, sir," came a distant response over the intercom.

Even working frantically, it would take him a few moments to set it up, I knew.

I turned to the lammachs, who were now maneuvering Father's gurney into the lift. There wasn't room for us; we would have to follow in a minute.

"Tactical," Havis called, and the computer displayed an abstract of the space around us. The *Nathan Meriman* appeared in mid air, then one by one the other ships in the fleet followed. The computer had tapped into the Sixteenth Fleet's tactical feed, but data came sluggishly. We weren't a combat ship, so we received low priority; other ships in the fleet needed Tactical's resources to stay alive and fighting, I knew. But it was frustrating nevertheless.

At last all the ships came up, and pinprick sparks began leaping from one side of the display to the other, as everyone exchanged fire and jockeyed for position. Two of the Borgialis' huge ships vanished, destroyed or knocked out, then six of ours.

"What will De Marco do?" I asked Havis.

He hesitated. "I don't know exactly," he finally said. "It is never wise to second-guess a superior officer."

The slightest quaver in his voice, the sweat on his forehead, and his defensive body language betrayed his lie to my stims. He knew, just as I knew, that De Marco would buy us time to escape with his life. The battle was clearly lost. The Sixteenth Fleet was outnumbered and outgunned. The most they could hope for was to go down valiantly, taking out as many of the enemy as they could while we got away to continue the battle from home.

"Our ships are firing again," he said.

I watched sparks leap from our ships to theirs on the display. Another one of their ships vanished, and five of ours. More sparks flew. Three of our ships winked out.

"We're being cut to pieces!" Jake said.

"Statistics?" I asked the computer.

"1523 enemy ships remaining," it told us. "382 Freedom Brigade ships remaining." I swallowed. Things did not look good.

The lift doors opened. "Time to get below," Havis said. He and Sameel ushered us inside, and we rode down to the passenger compartment in silence.

As we stepped into the main cabin, everything seemed strangely hushed. Dr. Espoja and four other lammachs clustered around Father, talking softly. The human technicians had vanished, probably to duty stations or their quarters. Timon Crote stood in the doorway to the pilot's compartment, watching everyone work. Yet despite the seeming calm, an hot wire of tension ran

through everyone and everything. I had never felt anything like it before. It made me jumpy and nervous.

"How long until we can make a nospace slip?" I asked Crote.

"A few more minutes," he called.

"Computer, transfer the Tactical feed here," Havis said.

The projection appeared before us. I spotted the *Nathan Meriman* and the *Gatsby* at once. Forty-five enemy missiles were converging on our position . . . rather, the *Nathan Meriman*'s position. Clearly they had made the flagship a high priority target. I gulped. We had hidden in the wrong place.

"Brace yourselves!" Havis shouted. He grabbed a rung set into the wall. "We are too close—"

I reached for a handhold, but before I had it, the sparks converged on their target and everything slammed sideways at high speed. The lights went out and an alarm klaxon began to ring. I found myself mashed against the bulkhead under someone who seemed to weigh several tons. Jake?

Green emergency lights came on. Jake stared into my face, pale and terrified. Artificial gravity quit. We began to float.

"Teddy—"

"Get off me," I said. "I can't breathe."

"Sorry." He kicked off the bulkhead and grabbed a ceiling rung.

I glanced around. The green light gave everything an unreal look. Small dark spheres that could only be blood filled the air at the far end of the cabin. The lammachs darted everywhere, medical instruments out, jabbering frantically in their own language. Dr. Espoja seemed to be doing something with Father. Sameel hung motionless, dead or unconscious. I couldn't see Crote anymore.

Havis headed hand-over-hand toward the pilot's compartment. Forcing the hatch open manually, he crawled over Crote, who seemed dazed, and vanished inside the pilot's compartment. Abruptly the alarm klaxon switched off.

Something hissed distantly. Escaping air.

We had been hit. Panic swept through me.

"Havis?" I shouted.

"Put your helmets on!" he called back. "We have a hull breach!"

"I know!"

The hiss lessened; were automatic safeties sealing the hole?

"Computer?" I demanded. "What happened? Computer!"

It didn't reply. Offline?

Jake had located and retrieved our helmets, which had been knocked to the far end of the cabin. Bouncing off the far wall, he hooked a rung next to me with his left foot.

"Here," he said. With his free hand, he pulled his own helmet over his head.

I did the same. Terse battle orders filled the open BRIGADE channel. I listened intently. Command seemed to have fallen on Captain Wang aboard the *Jersey*, who wasted no time in marshalling the remaining ships for an all-out assault. He probably didn't know we were still alive, I thought. At least he wasn't surrendering or running yet; we still had time.

I clicked to UNIT in time to hear Havis saying, "—feeds are down. Our pilot is dead and the copilot badly wounded. Send the lammachs back here fastest or we aren't going to live through this."

"Dr. Espoja is still looking after Father," I said.

"We will all be dead, including the Emperor, if we don't get our copilot conscious long enough to make a nospace jump!"

"Acknowledged."

"I'll do it," Jake said. He pulled off his helmet and kicked his way aft.

"What about the hull breach?" I asked Havis.

"Can you locate it? Is it getting worse?"

I pulled off my own helmet and strained to hear.

The hiss continued, but not as loudly as before. Either that, or the background noises drowned it out pretty effectively. Where was it coming from? The observation dome? The lower deck? I turned, straining to hear,

but couldn't quite locate it. Then abruptly it ceased: the safeties must have sealed it off.

Then Dr. Espoja and most of his lammachs hurtled past me and entered the forward compartment faster than I'd ever seen a lammachs move before.

I reported the as leak sealed to Havis.

"Good news for once," he said tersely. A few seconds later, he added: "Dr. Espoja has awakened the copilot. Backup systems are coming online. Calculations are complete in the computer. Get everyone prepared for a nospace slip in twenty seconds."

"Aye, sir." I pulled off my helmet. "Prepare for nospace!" I called. "Fifteen seconds from . . . mark!"

The two remaining lammachs lashed down Father's gurney, then snagged Sameel and hooked him into a safety harness. Jake and I pulled harness restraints from the wall bins and slid our arms through them.

And suddenly we slipped.

Nospace travel is different in small ships than large ships. When you travel in a vessel as huge as the *Pegasus*, you take such a large bubble of normality with you that the sensations are subtle.

In a small ship like the Panic swept through me. , though, it's like a sudden, unexpected plunge into a pool of icy water.

Colors blurred. Sounds became mute. My head swam dizzily.

A small bubble of normal space surrounded us, I knew, but beyond that was something else, something strange and unfathomable to untrained minds. It reached out like tendrils of fog, penetrating my mind. I couldn't think straight, couldn't tell up from down or left from right.

It was enough that our ships' computers, aided by our pilots, could find shortcuts through that strangeness. I pressed my eyes shut. Hopefully it wouldn't be more than an hour or two till we reached the nearest Freedom Brigade base.

I blinked suddenly, and normality returned. "What—" I gasped. The jump had been too short. We couldn't have gone more than a handful of light-years.

"What happened?" Jake demanded of Havis over the UNIT circuit.

Havis said, "The co-pilot collapsed. Dead . . . no, just unconscious. But he got us away from the battle."

I nodded. "Good. We're safe for the moment, then. Where, exactly, are we?"

"I am not sure . . . wait." A few seconds dragged out. "twenty-six light-years from the battle, orbiting a yellow-white star catalogued as BR2571-Y."

Only a catalog name. That meant no human settlements. My stims could not provide me with more details about this system. Clearly it was inconsequential, of no real value or interest. And the Freedom Brigade certainly didn't have a base here.

Artificial gravity came on suddenly, about a quarter normal, and slowly it began to increase toward Horizon normal. My perspective did flip-flops as the wall behind me became the floor. I shrugged off my safety harness. Jake and the two remaining lammachs did the same.

"Repairs are continuing," Havis said in my ears. "Dr. Espoja says the co-pilot won't be able to try another nospace slip for at least a day."

"How are repairs coming?"

"Navigation systems are coming back online. The computer estimates another two hours for full restoration of power. That should speed up repairs."

"How is Mr. Crote?" I asked.

"Dr. Espoja is working on him now. Battered, not fried."

I blinked.

"That's a Brigadier joke, son," he said.

"Ah." I nodded, comprehending. Things were under control for the moment; he could break the tension.

Behind me, Father stirred and moaned. *Almost under control.* At the observation dome, he had called me "Max" again. Father had to recover, must be forced to recognize us. That, or . . . or Jake's proposal would be the only viable course of action.

I licked my lips. Two lammachs technicians stood over Father. Havis, Crote, Dr. Espoja, and most of the lammachs were still in the forward compartment. Sameel was unconscious.

"Father?" Jake asked.

"Go forward," I told him, hardening my voice. "Make sure none of the others comes back here until I call."

He nodded. He understood exactly what I had in mind . . . what I might have to do.

I peeled off my helmet and walked back toward Father. The two lammachs bowed to me.

"Wake him," I said. "Then see to Sameel."

They chittered at each other, clearly uneasy. But while Dr. Espoja or Dr. Sanjarin might have had the strength to stand up to me, clearly these two did not. The one on the right sprayed a pale yellow mist over Father's head, then retreated toward Sameel.

Father's eyes fluttered open. He stared into my face.

"Do you recognize me?" I asked.

"Max . . ." he breathed.

"No, Father," I said, voice hard. "Look at me. Look at my face. I'm your son, Theodore. Teddy. Remember?"

"Teddy?" he said. His mouth twisted. He looked like he wanted to cry. "Yes, Teddy . . . yes. My boy."

"Do you know me?" I demanded. "Do you really know me this time?"

"Of course I know you." He tried to lever himself up, but couldn't because of the restraints. His face twisted again, and it seemed to me that parts of his old intellect began slip back into place once more.

"A battle . . ." he said. "I remember . . ."

"We escaped. We're safe. Jake and I saved your life."

"Where is Jake?" he said. "Where are we?"

I could breathe again. I felt myself sweating all over, and my heart began to pound with nervous relief. I loosened his restraints and let him sit up.

"Jake is in the front, with Mr. Crote."

"Good. We have to . . . have to . . ."

"Get back to Horizon?" I suggested.

"Yes. That's it." He leaned on my shoulder, looking around in confusion. "Where—"

"This way." I took his full weight, and together we made our way to the forward compartment.

Crote lay on the floor, surrounded by lammachs. I could hear his breathing, and it sounded like a faint bubbling wheeze. My medical stims told me that broken ribs had punctured a lung. Fortunately, the lammachs seemed to have things under control. Lieutenant Havis and Jake were busy at one of the control panels, probably trying to get the computer back online.

Father sagged into the pilot's seat. Dr. Espoja hurried over, making clucking sounds deep in his throat.

"Sir!" Havis said, snapping to attention and saluting.

"Get us home," Father said. He sounded old and tired, but enough of his old strength carried through to reassure Lieutenant Havis, who saluted again and returned to the tasks at hand with renewed energy.

Then Father waved Espoja away. "See to Mr. Crote," he said. "He needs you far more than I do."

I grinned. I had said those same words only a couple of days before, on Dulap's World, but it seemed a lifetime.

"Why are you so happy?" Father demanded of me. "Do you like having ships shot out from under you?"

"No. But I'm glad you're back with us."

"We're all glad, Father," Jake said.

Father regarded first me, then Jake. "It was the Borgialis," he said after a heartbeat. "You know that."

"Of course," Jake and I said together.

"We are going to have to do something about them. We have let their get away with too much for too long."

"Will there be war?" Jake said gravely. "Will you destroy their homeworld?"

Father snorted. "War? With the Borgia-

lis? Certainly not. This is but a minor scuffle among the Great Houses. They will pay, and pay handsomely, to avoid all-out war with us." He studied Crote almost absently. "We shall demand half their empire in compensation. That seems fair"

Even I gasped at the boldness of such a move.

"Yes," Father went on, nodding. "We shall send Timon to work out the details. He will have a personal interest in wringing the maximum of justice from their pocketbooks. And then they will never trouble us again."

"Excellency," said Havis. "May I speak?"

"What is it, Lieutenant?" Father said.

Havis swallowed. "The whole of the Sixteenth Fleet is lost. Two hundred thousand people are dead because—"

"You do not question the Emperor's decisions," I said sharply, and I took a place by Father's right hand. Our family's ranks always closed against outsiders. It had always been our greatest strength. Raising my head, I looked Havis in the eye. "We may have lost people here, but it is a small measure against the billions or trillions of our people who would die in a real war."

Father looked at me and smiled proudly. "You begin to understand, Max."

I gulped mentally, but said nothing. Jake shot me a pained look. *You should have done it when you had the chance,* his eyes seemed to say.

I shook my head faintly. No. I couldn't. Perhaps I was weak. But perhaps, just perhaps, I was stronger than we both realized. Our family had come through this crisis, and something told me we would be the stronger for it.

"Of course," Havis said, blushing. "I only wanted His Excellency to know the full scope of His loss today."

"We know it," Father said heavily. "And it weighs on us all. Now, about this ship . . ."

And Havis began to fill him in on the technical problems we faced.

That is my second important memory. As I look back on the events of those long-ago days and consider the frantic hours of work it took to get the *Gatsby* repaired for the long voyage home, it all seems so inconsequential now. What matters is that we tested the bonds of our family and forged them anew, stronger than ever. Twice more Father called me "Max," but four times he also called me "Teddy." It was as though both Max's and my lives had somehow blended together in his mind. He certainly seemed to have lost interest in having me executed.

It's enough, I thought. *With Father alive, the Meriman Empire will stand firm. And that's what counts in the end.*

Of course, the Borgialis threat still had to be dealt with, and of course nothing went quite as planned; but everything worked out in the end, as it always does.

And now, as I reflect on those long-ago days, as I sit on the emerald throne and watch my own twin sons—so like Jake and me, an heir and a spare—I realize the end of the story is not blood and pain and sacrifice, but love and trust and faith. More than power, more than fear, it is the bonds of family that hold us together. These are the ties that will sustain us, and our children, and our children's children through all the ages yet to come.

❋

STARTLING STORIES™

WILL RETURN

in

FEBRUARY, 2022.

Watch for it!

THREE FOR A QUARTER
by Robert Silverberg

I had to wait 65 years to see a story of mine on the contents page of *Startling Stories*. The magazine was a great favorite of mine when I was a young science-fiction reader, but it went out of business in 1955, just as my writing career was getting under way.

Here we are in far-future 2021, though, and *Startling* is back among us after that 65-year gap, and, finally, here I am too.

I bought my first copy of *Startling Stories* around Christmas of 1948 at Jackson's Bookstore, a seedy second-hand emporium in a dreary part of Brooklyn, where old pulp magazines were sold at a price of three for a quarter. I didn't have much of a discretionary budget, back then when I was just entering my teens, but whenever I had a spare quarter I made the pilgrimage to Jackson's and picked up a little bunch of s-f mags, having discovered science fiction earlier that year via a couple of extraordinary hardcover anthologies.

I was an uppity sort of kid, then, the sort who had signed up to study Latin in what would now be called middle school, and the magazine I preferred was John Campbell's sober, dignified *Astounding Science Fiction*, which published work by the writers I already knew were the best in the field, though a lot of them went over my head.

But this December day I found myself staring at the July, 1948 *Startling Stories*, and, despite some hesitation, I pondered buying it, since there were no new issues of *Astounding* available that day.

I was hesitating because it didn't really look like my sort of thing, as I understood my thing in those days. It was printed on cheap pulp paper with untrimmed ragged edges, and the cover painting was a trashy one showing a terrified blonde woman in a tattered red gown against a murky background, and I didn't much like the garish logotype, *Startling Stories* in big red lettering with yellow outlines. But I looked inside and found that it offered three stories by writers I had come to value—Henry Kuttner, Jack Vance, Edmond Hamilton—and so, overcoming my adolescent elitism, I bought the gaudy thing, along with two other similar pulps. Three for a quarter—hours of lively reading.

I thought it was a terrific magazine. I loved every story. I bought a couple of other back issues, and then, four or five months later, I plunged an entire quarter at the newsstand for the newly released July, 1949 issue, which had stories by Kuttner again, Arthur C. Clarke, and Ray Bradbury. I never missed an issue after that. I even began to write fan letters to its editor, who was anonymous in the magazine but whose name, which I knew from having met him about that time at a local s-f fan group, was Sam Merwin, Jr. (The first of those letters is in the May, 1950 issue, commenting on the one dated January, on which I lavished all of my teenage wisdom.) I began to send in stories, too, for I thought it would be an extraordinarily wonderful thing to have a story of mine published in *Startling*, where all of science-fiction fandom, and maybe even some of my classmates (I was in high school, now) would see it and gaze upon it in awe and envy.

Everything I submitted came back, of course. At fourteen I wasn't ready for prime time. The first ones came back with little printed rejection forms attached, but then I began getting encouraging notes from the editors, and Merwin even addressed me as "Dear Bob," because he remembered having met me at that fan group. That wasn't as good as getting a check, really, but it still gave me a moment of great pleasure.

I began collecting *Startling*s, too, and in a surprisingly short time I had a complete file, going back to the first issue, January, 1939. (It wasn't hard to find old magazines in the second-hand shops then, and at surprisingly low prices.) *Startling*'s special concept was that it ran a 40,000-word "novel," complete in each issue, something no other s-f magazine was doing. The very first issue featured Stanley G. Weinbaum's splendid "The Black Flame," and later issues brought such excellent fare as Manly Wade Wellman's "Twice in Time," Henry Kuttner's "When New York Vanished," Fredric Brown's "What Mad Universe," and Arthur C. Clarke's "Against the Fall of Night."

As I grew up, *Startling* grew up with me. Throughout its early years much of the fiction had been fast-paced action stuff aimed at teenage boys, but by 1951 it was offering much more soph isticated fare—Leigh Brackett's "The Starmen of Llyrdis," Philip

Jose Farmer's "The Lovers," Jack Vance's "Big Planet," and many another substantial work. The ragged pulp format gave way to a smaller size page with neatly trimmed edges, and the garish logotype that I had actually come to love was replaced with a less flashy one. Sales had increased to such an extent that the magazine, published six times a year since its inception, switched to monthly publication with the January, 1952 issue. Editor Merwin, who had brought the magazine up to a level of quality that was reasonably competitive with that of Campbell's *Astounding*, resigned in 1951 to pursue a free-lance career and was replaced by his assistant, Sam Mines, who if anything improved the magazine still further.

And I was on the brink of a professional writing career. I made a few modest sales of fiction in 1954, when I was still in college, and then, in 1955, my breakthrough year, I suddenly began selling stories as fast as I could write them, to just about every magazine in the field—*Amazing Stories*, *Fantastic*, *Future*, *Fantastic Universe*, even Campbell's awesome *Astounding*. But one remained beyond my reach—dear old *Startling*. Somehow I could not manage to get anything more than friendly rejection slips from Sam Mines.

An older writer named Randall Garrett had taught me, that year, that a New York-based writer like me would benefit from visiting editorial offices and developing personal relationships with the editors. That worked very well indeed for me, and I began delivering my stories in person, which resulted in quick and frequent sales. Some time in the late summer of 1955 I decided to pay a call at the office of *Startling Stories*, in midtown Manhattan.

Editor Mines had moved along by then, and his replacement, a youngish man named Herbert Kastle, came out to greet me. (He didn't seem all that young to me: I was 20, he was 32, and that was a big gap for me then.) He greeted me pleasantly, even admitted that

cont'd on page 252.

SUNRISE ON MERCURY
by Robert Silverberg

Nine million miles to the sunward of Mercury, with the *Leverrier* swinging into the series of spirals that would bring it down on the solar system's smallest world, Second Astrogator Lon Curtis decided to end his life.

Curtis had been lounging in a webfoam cradle waiting for the landing to be effected; his job in the operation was over, at least until the *Leverrier*'s landing jacks touched Mercury's blistered surface. The ship's efficient sodium-coolant system negated the efforts of the swollen sun visible through the rear screen. For Curtis and his seven shipmates, no problems presented themselves; they had only to wait while the autopilot brought the ship down for man's second landing on Mercury.

Flight Commander Harry Ross was sitting near Curtis when he noticed the sudden momentary stiffening of the astrogator's jaws. Curtis abruptly reached for the control nozzle. From the spinnerets that had spun the webfoam came a quick green burst of dissolving fluorochrene; the cradle vanished. Curtis stood up.

"Going somewhere?" Ross asked.

Curtis's voice was harsh. "Just—just taking a walk."

Ross returned his attention to his microbook for a moment as Curtis walked away. There was the ratchety sound of a bulkhead dog being manipulated, and Ross felt a momentary chill as the cooler air of the super-refrigerated reactor compartment drifted in.

He punched a stud, turning the page. Then—

What the hell is he doing in the reactor compartment?

The autopilot would be controlling the fuel flow, handling it down to the milligram, in a way no human system could. The reactor was primed for the landing, the fuel was stoked, the compartment was dogged shut. No one—least of all a second astrogator—had any business going back there.

Ross had the foam cradle dissolved in an instant, and was on his feet a moment later. He dashed down the companionway and through the open bulkhead door into the coolness of the reactor compartment.

Curtis was standing by the converter door, toying with the release-tripper. As Ross approached, he saw the astrogator get the door open and put one foot to the chute that led downship to the nuclear pile.

"Curtis, you idiot! Get away from there! You'll kill us all!"

The astrogator turned, looked blankly at Ross for an instant, and drew up his other foot. Ross leaped.

He caught Curtis' booted foot in his hands, and despite a barrage of kicks from the astrogator's free boot, managed to drag Curtis off the chute. The astrogator tugged and pulled, attempting to break free. Ross saw the man's pale cheeks quivering. Curtis had cracked, but thoroughly.

Grunting, Ross yanked Curtis away from the yawning reactor chute and slammed the door shut. He dragged him out into the main section again and slapped him, hard.

"Why'd you want to do that? Don't you know what your mass would do to the ship if it got into the converter? You know the fuel intake's been calibrated already; 180 extra pounds and we'd arc right into the sun. What's wrong with you, Curtis?"

The astrogator fixed unshaking, unexpressive eyes on Ross. "I want to die," he said simply. "Why couldn't you let me die?"

He wanted to die. Ross shrugged, feeling

a cold tremor run down his back. There was no guarding against this disease.

Just as aqualungers beneath the sea's surface suffered from *l'ivresse des grandes profondeurs*—rapture of the deeps—and knew no cure for the strange, depth-induced drunkenness that caused them to remove their breathing tubes fifty fathoms below, so did spacemen run the risk of this nameless malady, this inexplicable urge to self-destruction.

It struck anywhere. A repairman wielding a torch on a recalcitrant strut of an orbiting wheel might abruptly rip open his facemask and drink vacuum; a radioman rigging an antenna on the skin of his ship might suddenly cut his line, fire his directional pistol, and send himself drifting away. Or a second astrogator might decide to climb into the converter.

Psych Officer Spangler appeared, an expression of concern fixed on his smooth pink face. "Trouble?"

Ross nodded. "Curtis. Tried to jump into the fuel chute. He's got it, Doc."

Spangler rubbed his cheek and said: "They always pick the best times, dammit. It's swell having a psycho on a Mercury run."

"That's the way it is," Ross said wearily. "Better put him in stasis till we get home. I'd hate to have him running loose, looking for different ways of doing himself in."

"Why can't you let me die?" Curtis asked. His face was bleak. "Why'd you have to stop me?"

"Because, you lunatic, you'd have killed all the rest of us by your fool dive into the converter. Go walk out the airlock if you want to die—but don't take us with you."

Spangler glared warningly at him. "Harry—"

"Okay," Ross said. "Take him away."

The psychman led Curtis within. The astrogator would be given a tranquillizing injection and locked in an insoluble webfoam jacket for the rest of the journey. There was a chance he could be restored to sanity once they returned to Earth, but Ross knew that the astrogator would go straight for the nearest method of suicide the moment he was released aboard the ship.

Scowling, Ross turned away. A man spends his boyhood dreaming about space, he thought, spends four years at the Academy, and two more making dummy runs. Then he finally gets out where it counts and he cracks up. Curtis was an astrogation machine, not a normal human being; and he had just disqualified himself permanently from the only job he knew how to do.

Ross shivered, feeling chill despite the bloated bulk of the sun filling the rear screen. It could happen to anyone…even him. He thought of Curtis lying in a foam cradle somewhere in the back of the ship, blackly thinking over and over again, *I want to die*, while Doc Spangler muttered soothing things at him. A human being was really a frail form of life.

Death seemed to hang over the ship; the gloomy aura of Curtis's suicide-wish polluted the atmosphere.

Ross shook his head and punched down savagely on the signal to prepare for deceleration. Mercury's sharp globe bobbed up ahead. He spotted it through the front screen.

* * * *

They were approaching the tiny planet middle-on. He could see the neat division now: the brightness of Sunside, that unapproachable inferno where zinc ran in rivers, and the icy blackness of Darkside, dull with its unlit plains of frozen CO_2.

Down the heart of the planet ran the Twilight Belt, that narrow area of not-cold and not-heat where Sunside and Darkside met to provide a thin band of barely tolerable territory, a ring nine thousand miles in circumference and ten or twenty miles wide.

The Leverrier plunged planetward. Ross allowed his jangled nerves to grow calm. The ship was in the hands of the autopilot; the orbit, of course, was precomputed, and the analogue banks in the drive were serenely following the taped program, bringing

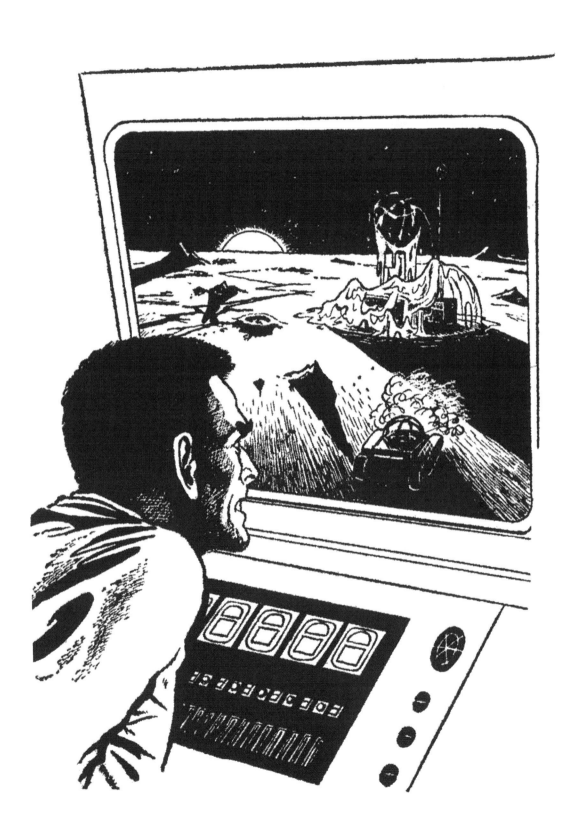

the ship towards its destination smack in the middle of—*My God!*

Ross went cold from head to toe. The pre-computed tape had been fed to the analogue banks—had been prepared by—had been entirely the work of—

Curtis.

A suicidal madman had worked out the *Leverrier*'s landing program.

Ross began to shake. How easy it would have been, he thought, for death-bent Curtis to work out an orbit that would plant the *Leverrier* in a smoking river of molten lead—or in the mortuary chill of Darkside.

His false security vanished. There was no trusting the automatic pilot; they'd have to risk a manual landing.

Ross jabbed down on the communicator button. "I want Brainerd," he said hoarsely.

The first astrogator appeared a few seconds later, peering in curiously. "What goes, Captain?"

"We've just carted your assistant Curtis off to the pokey. He tried to jump into the converter."

"He—?"

Ross nodded. "Attempted suicide. I got to him in time. But in view of the circumstances, I think we'd better discard the tape you had him prepare and bring the ship down manually, yes?"

The first astrogator moistened his lips. "That sounds like a good idea."

"Damn right it is," Ross said, glowering.

* * * *

As the ship touched down Ross thought, *Mercury is two hells in one.*

It was the cold, ice-bound kingdom of Dante's deepest pit—and it was also the brimstone empire of another conception. The two met, fire and frost, each hemisphere its own kind of hell.

He lifted his head and flicked a quick glance at the instrument panel above his deceleration cradle. The dials all checked: weight placement was proper, stability 100 per cent, external temperature a manage-able 108°F, indicating they had made their descent a little to the sunward of the Twilight Belt's exact middle. It had been a sound landing.

He snapped on the communicator. "Brainerd?"

"All okay, Captain."

"Manual landing?"

"I had to," the astrogator said. "I ran a quick check on Curtis' tape, and it was all cockeyed. The way he had us coming in, we'd have grazed Mercury's orbit by a whisker and kept on going straight into the sun. Nice?"

"Very sweet," Ross said. "But don't be too hard on the kid. He didn't want to go psycho. Good landing, anyway. We seem to be pretty close to the center of the Twilight Belt, and that's where I feel most comfortable."

He broke the contact and unwebbed himself. Over the shipwide circuit he called all hands fore, double pronto.

The men got there quickly enough—Brainerd first, then Doc Spangler, followed by Accumulator Tech Krinsky and the three other crewmen. Ross waited until the entire group had assembled.

They were looking around curiously for Curtis. Crisply, Ross told them, "Astrogator Curtis is going to miss this meeting. He's aft in the psycho bin. Luckily, we can shift without him on this tour."

He waited until the implications of that statement had sunk in. The men seemed to adjust to it well enough, he thought: momentary expressions of dismay, shock, even horror quickly faded from their faces.

"All right," he said. "Schedule calls for us to put in some thirty-two hours of extravehicular activity on Mercury. Brainerd, how does that check with our location?"

The astrogator frowned and made some mental calculations. "Current position is a trifle to the sunward edge of the Twilight Belt; but as I figure it, the sun won't be high enough to put the Fahrenheit much above 120 for at least a week. Our suits can handle that temperature with ease."

"Good. Llewellyn, you and Falbridge break out the radar inflaters and get the tower set up as far to the east as you can go without getting roasted. Take the crawler, but be sure to keep an eye on the thermometer. We've only got one heatsuit, and that's for Krinsky."

Llewellyn, a thin, sunken-eyed spaceman, shifted uneasily. "How far to the east do you suggest, sir?"

"The Twilight Belt covers about a quarter of Mercury's surface," Ross said. "You've got a strip forty-seven degrees wide to move around in—but I don't suggest you go much more than twenty-five miles or so. It starts getting hot after that. And keeps going up."

Ross turned to Krinsky. In many ways the accumulator tech was the expedition's key man: it was his job to check the readings on the pair of solar accumulators that had been left here by the first expedition. He was to measure the amount of stress created by solar energies here, so close to the source of radiation, study force-lines operating in the strange magnetic field of the little world, and reprime the accumulators for further testing by the next expedition.

Krinsky was a tall, powerfully built man, the sort of man who could stand up to the crushing weight of a heatsuit almost cheerfully. The heatsuit was necessary for prolonged work in the Sunside zone, where the accumulators were mounted—and even a giant like Krinsky could stand the strain for only a few hours at a time.

"When Llewellyn and Falbridge have the radar tower set up, Krinsky, get into your heatsuit and be ready to move. As soon as we've got the accumulator station located, Dominic will drive you as far east as possible and drop you off. The rest is up to you. Watch your step. We'll be telemetering your readings, but we'd like to have you back alive."

"Yes, sir."

"That's about it," Ross said. "Let's get rolling."

* * * *

Ross's own job was purely administrative—and as the men of his crew moved busily about their allotted tasks, he realized unhappily that he himself was condemned to temporary idleness. His function was that of overseer; like the conductor of a symphony orchestra, he played no instrument himself and was on hand mostly to keep the group moving in harmony towards the finish.

Everyone was in motion. Now he had only to wait.

Llewellyn and Falbridge departed, riding the segmented, thermo-resistant crawler that had traveled to Mercury in the belly of the Leverrier. Their job was simple: they were to erect the inflatable plastic radar tower out towards the sunward sector. The tower that the first expedition had left had long since librated into a Sunside zone and been liquefied; the plastic base and parabola, covered with a light reflective surface of aluminum, could hardly withstand the searing heat of Sunside.

Out there, it got up to 700° when the sun was at its closest. The eccentricities of Mercury's orbit accounted for considerable temperature variations on Sunside, but the thermometer never showed lower than 300° out there, even during aphelion. On Darkside, there was less of a temperature range; mostly the temperature hovered not far from absolute zero, and frozen drifts of heavy gases covered the surface of the land.

From where he stood, Ross could see neither Sunside nor Darkside. The Twilight Belt was nearly a thousand miles broad, and as the little planet dipped in its orbit the sun would first slide above the horizon, then slip back. For a twenty-mile strip through the heart of the Belt, the heat of Sunside and the cold of Darkside canceled out into a fairly stable, temperate climate; for five hundred miles on either side, the Twilight Belt gradually trickled towards the areas of extreme cold and raging heat.

It was a strange and forbidding planet.

Humans could endure it for only a short time; it was worse than Mars, worse than the Moon. The sort of life capable of living permanently on Mercury was beyond Ross's powers of imagination. Standing outside the *Leverrier* in his spacesuit, he nudged the chin control that lowered a sheet of optical glass. He peered first towards Darkside, where he thought he saw a thin line of encroaching black—only illusion, he knew—and then towards Sunside.

In the distance, Llewellyn and Falbridge were erecting the spidery parabola that was the radar tower. He could see the clumsy shape outlined against the sky now—and behind it? A faint line of brightness rimming the bordering peaks? Illusion also, he knew. Brainerd had calculated that the sun's radiance would not be visible here for a week. And in a week's time they'd be back on Earth.

He turned to Krinsky. "The tower's nearly up. They'll be coming in with the crawler any minute. You'd better get ready to make your trip."

As the accumulator tech swung up the handholds and into the ship, Ross's thoughts turned to Curtis. The young astrogator had talked excitedly of seeing Mercury all the way out—and now that they were actually here, Curtis lay in a web of foam deep within the ship, moodily demanding the right to die.

Krinsky returned, now wearing the insulating bulk of the heatsuit over his standard rebreathing outfit. He looked more like a small tank than a man. "Is the crawler approaching, sir?"

"I'll check."

Ross adjusted the lensplate in his mask and narrowed his eyes. It seemed to him that the temperature had risen a little. Another illusion? He squinted into the distance. His eyes picked out the radar tower far off towards Sunside. He gasped.

"Something the matter?" Krinsky asked.

"I'll say!" Ross squeezed his eyes tight shut and looked again. And—yes—the newly erected radar tower was drooping soggily and beginning to melt. He saw two tiny figures racing madly over the flat, pumice-covered ground to the silvery oblong that was the crawler. And—impossibly—the first glow of an unmistakable brightness was beginning to shimmer on the mountains behind the tower.

The sun was rising—a week ahead of schedule!

Ross ran back into the ship, followed by the lumbering figure of Krinsky. In the airlock, obliging mechanical hands descended to ease him out of his spacesuit; signaling to Krinsky to keep the heatsuit on, he dashed through into the main cabin.

"Brainerd? Brainerd! Where in hell are you?"

The senior astrogator appeared, looking puzzled. "What's up, Captain?"

"Look out the screen," Ross said in a strangled voice. "Look at the radar tower!"

"It's *melting*," Brainerd said, astonished. "But that's—that's—"

"I know. It's impossible." Ross glanced at the instrument panel. External temperature had risen to 112°—a jump of four degrees. And as he watched it glided up to 114°.

It would take a heat of at least 500° to melt the radar tower that way. Ross squinted at the screen and saw the crawler come swinging dizzily towards them: Llewellyn and Falbridge were still alive, then—though they probably had had a good cooking out there. The temperature outside the ship was up to 116°. It would probably be near 200° by the time the two men returned.

Angrily, Ross whirled to face the astrogator. "I thought you were bringing us down in the safety strip," he snapped. "Check your figures again and find out where the hell we *really* are. Then work out a blasting orbit, fast: That's the sun coming up over those hills."

* * * *

The temperature had reached 120°. The ship's cooling system would be able to keep things under control and comfortable until about 250°; beyond that, there was danger of an overload. The crawler continued to draw near. It was probably hellish inside the little land car, Ross thought.

His mind weighed alternatives. If the external temperature went much over 250°, he would run the risk of wrecking the ship's cooling system by waiting for the two in the crawler to arrive. There was some play in the system, but not much. He decided he'd give them until it hit 275° to get back. If they didn't make it by then, he'd have to take off without them. It was foolish to try to save two lives at the risk of six. External temperature had hit 130°. Its rate of increase was jumping rapidly.

The ship's crew knew what was going on now. Without the need of direct orders from Ross, they were readying the *Leverrier* for an emergency blastoff.

The crawler inched forward. The two men weren't much more than ten miles away now; and at an average speed of forty miles an hour they'd be back within fifteen minutes. Outside the temperature was 133°. Long fingers of shimmering sunlight stretched towards them from the horizon.

Brainerd looked up from his calculation. "I can't work it. The damned figures don't come out."

"Huh?"

"I'm trying to compute our location—and I can't do the arithmetic. My head's all foggy."

What the hell. This was where a captain earned his pay, Ross thought. "Get out of the way," he said brusquely. "Let me do it."

He sat down at the desk and started figuring. He saw Brainerd's hasty notations scratched out everywhere. It was as if the astrogator had totally forgotten how to do his job.

Let's see, now. If we're—

He tapped out figures on the little calculator. But as he worked he saw that what he was doing made no sense. His mind felt bleary and strange; he couldn't seem to handle the elementary computations at all.

Looking up, he said, "Tell Krinsky to get down there and make himself ready to help those men out of the crawler when they show up. They're probably half cooked."

Temperature 146°. He looked down at the calculator. Damn: it shouldn't be that hard to do simple trigonometry, should it?

Doc Spangler appeared. "I cut Curtis free," he announced. "He isn't safe during takeoff in that cradle."

From within came a steady mutter. "Just let me die...just let me die..."

"Tell him he's likely to get his wish," Ross murmured. "If I can't manage to work out a blastoff orbit we're all going to fry right here."

"How come you're doing it? What's the matter with Brainerd?"

"Choked up. Couldn't make sense of his own figures. And come to think of it, I'm not doing so well myself."

Fingers of fog seemed to wrap around his mind. He glanced at the dial. Temperature 152° outside. That gave the boys in the crawler 123° to get back here...or was it 321°? He was confused, utterly bewildered.

Doc Spangler looked peculiar too. The psych officer wore an odd frown. "I feel very lethargic suddenly," Spangler declared. "I know I really should get back to Curtis, but—"

The madman was keeping up a steady babble inside. The part of Ross's mind that still could think clearly realized that if left unattended Curtis was capable of doing almost anything.

Temperature 158°. The crawler seemed to be getting nearer. On the horizon the radar tower was melting into a crazy shambles.

There was a shriek. "Curtis!" Ross yelled, his mind hurriedly returning to awareness. He ran aft, with Spangler close behind.

Too late.

Curtis lay on the floor in a bloody puddle. He had found a pair of shears somewhere.

Spangler bent. "He's dead."

"Dead. Of course." Ross's brain felt totally clear now. At the moment of Curtis'

death the fog had lifted. Leaving Spangler
to attend to the body, he returned to the astrogation desk and glanced through the cal-
cula-tions he had been doing. Worthless. An
idiotic mess.

With icy clarity he started again, and this
time succeeded in determining their location. They had come down better than three
hundred miles sunward of where they had
thought they were landing. The instruments
hadn't lied—but someone's eyes had. The
orbit that Brainerd had so solemnly assured
him was a "safe" one was actually almost as
deadly as the one Curtis had computed.

He looked outside. The crawler had almost reached the ship. Temperature 167° out
there. There was plenty of time. They would
make it with a few minutes to spare, thanks
to the warning they had received from the
melting radar tower.

But why had it happened? There was no
answer to that.

* * * *

Gigantic in his heatsuit, Krinsky brought
Llewellyn and Falbridge aboard. They
peeled out of their spacesuits and wobbled
around un-steadily for a moment before
they collapsed. They were as red as newly
boiled lobsters.

"Heat prostration," Ross said. "Krinsky,
get them into takeoff cradles. Dominic, you
in your suit yet?"

The spaceman appeared at the airlock entrance and nodded.

"Good. Get down there and drive the
crawler into the hold. We can't afford to
leave it here. Double-quick, and then we're
blasting off. Brainerd, that new orbit ready?"

"Yes, sir."

The thermometer grazed 200. The cooling system was beginning to suffer—but it
would not have to endure much more agony.
Within minutes the *Leverrier* was lifting
from Mercury's surface—minutes ahead of
the relentless advance of the sun. The ship
swung into a parking orbit not far above the
planet's surface.

As they hung there, catching their
breaths, just one thing occupied Ross's mind:
why? Why had Brainerd's orbit brought
them down in a danger zone instead of the
safety strip? Why had both he and Brainerd
been unable to compute a blasting pattern,
the simplest of elementary astrogation tech-
niques? And why had Spangler's wits utterly
failed him—just long enough to let the unhappy Curtis kill himself?

Ross could see the same question reflected on everyone's face: why?

He felt an itchy feeling at the base of his
skull. And suddenly an image forced its way
across his mind and he had the answer.

He saw a great pool of molten zinc, lying shimmering between two jagged crests
somewhere on Sunside. It had been there
thousands of years; it would be there thousands, perhaps millions, of years from now.

Its surface quivered. The sun's brightness upon the pool was intolerable even to
the mind's eye.

Radiation beat down on the pool of
zinc—the sun's radiation, hard and unending. And then a new radiation, an electromagnetic emanation in a different part of the
spectrum, carrying a meaningful message:

I want to die.

The pool of zinc stirred fretfully with
sudden impulses of helpfulness.

The vision passed as quickly as it came.
Stunned, Ross looked up. The expressions
on the six faces surrounding him confirmed
what he could guess.

"You all felt it too," he said.

Spangler nodded, then Krinsky and the
rest of them.

"Yes," Krinsky said. "What the devil was
it?"

Brainerd turned to Spangler. "Are we all
nuts, Doc?"

The psych officer shrugged. "Mass hallucination...collective hypnosis..."

"No, Doc." Ross leaned forward. "You
know it as well as I do. That thing was real.
It's down there, out on Sunside."

"What do you mean?"

"I mean that wasn't any hallucination we had. That's something alive down there—or as close to alive as anything on Mercury can be." Ross's hands were shaking. He forced them to subside. "We've stumbled over something very big," he said.

Spangler stirred uneasily. "Harry—"

"No, I'm not out of my head! Don't you see—that thing down there, whatever it is, is sensitive to our thoughts! It picked up Curtis' godawful caterwauling the way a radar set grabs electromagnetic waves. His were the strongest thoughts coming through; so it acted on them and did its damnedest to help Curtis get what he wanted."

"You mean by fogging our minds and deluding us into thinking we were in safe territory, when actually we were right near sunrise territory?"

"But why would it go to all that trouble?" Krinsky objected. "If it wanted to help poor Curtis kill himself, why didn't it just fix things so we came down right *in* Sunside. We'd cook a lot quicker that way."

"Originally it did," Ross said. "It helped Curtis set up a landing orbit that would have dumped us into the sun. But then it realized that the rest of us *didn't* want to die. It picked up the conflicting mental emanations of Curtis and the rest of us, and arranged things so that he'd die and we wouldn't." He shivered. "Once Curtis was out of the way, it acted to help the surviving crew members reach safety. If you'll remember, we were all thinking and moving a lot quicker the instant Curtis was dead."

"Damned if that's not so," Spangler said. "But—"

"What I want to know is, do we go back down?" Krinsky asked. "If that thing is what you say it is, I'm not so sure I want to go within reach of it again. Who knows what it might make us do this time?"

"It wants to help us," Ross said stubbornly. "It's not hostile. You aren't afraid of it, are you, Krinsky? I was counting on you to go out in the heatsuit and try to find it."

"Not me!"

Ross scowled. "But this is the first intelligent life-form man has ever found in the solar system. We can't just run away and hide." To Brainerd he said, "Set up an orbit that'll take us back down again—and this time put us down where we won't melt."

"I can't do it, sir," Brainerd said flatly.

"Can't?"

"Won't. I think the safest thing is for us to return to Earth at once."

"I'm ordering you."

"I'm sorry, sir."

Ross looked at Spangler. Llewellyn. Falbridge. Right around the circle. Fear was evident on every face. He knew what each of the men was thinking.

I don't want to go back to Mercury.

Six of them. One of him. And the helpful thing below.

They had outnumbered Curtis seven to one—but Curtis' mind had radiated an unmixed death-wish. Ross knew he could never generate enough strength of thought to counteract the fear-driven thoughts of the other six.

Mutiny.

Somehow he did not care to speak the word aloud. Sometimes there were cases where a superior officer might legitimately be removed from command for the common good, and this might be one of them, he knew. But yet—

The thought of fleeing without even pausing to examine the creature below was intolerable to him. But there was only one ship, and either he or the six others would have to be denied.

Yet the pool had contrived to satisfy both the man who wished to die and those who wished to stay alive. Now, six wanted to return—but must the voice of the seventh be ignored?

You're not being fair to me, Ross thought, directing his angry outburst towards the planet below. *I want to see you. I want to study you. Don't let them drag me back to Earth so soon.*

* * * *

When the *Leverrier* returned to Earth a week later, the six survivors of the Second Mercury Expedition all were able to describe in detail how a fierce death-wish had overtaken Second Astrogator Curtis and driven him to suicide. But not one of them could recall what had happened to Flight Commander Ross, or why the heatsuit had been left behind on Mercury.   ❈

cont'd from page 252.

he knew of my work, seemed aware that I had precociously sold a good many stories. But then came the bombshell: there was no point in my offering stories to *Startling*, because the magazine, which had been doing poorly, like most fiction magazines, in recent months, and had already dropped abruptly from monthly publication to quarterly the year before, had been canceled by the publisher that very day. So I slunk gloomily home, sadly contemplating the fact that I would never have a story published in *Startling Stories.*

But here we are 65 years later, and *Startling* is back, and here am I. "Sunrise on Mercury" is a story that I wrote in 1956, to be published in the May, 1957 issue of the long-forgotten *Science Fiction Stories*, edited by Robert W. Lowndes. *Startling* had been gone for a couple of years by then, of course. But the story still seems a pretty good one to me, a credit to its 21-year-old author, and I like to think that if the course of publishing had traveled a somewhat different path back in that remote era, I might have seen it in dear old *Startling*. Which was not to be, 65 years ago. But—of all improbable things—here it is now.   ❈